Lesbian
Love Stories

Lesbian Love Stories

EDITED BY
IRENE ZAHAVA

THE CROSSING PRESS
Freedom, California 95019

Grateful acknowledgment is made for permission to use the following previously published material:

"In The Life," copyright © 1987 by Becky Birtha. Reprinted from *Lovers' Choice* by Becky Birtha, by permission of the author and The Seal Press.

"Humming," copyright © 1986 by Sandy Boucher. Reprinted from *Erotic Interludes* by Lonnie Barbach, by permission of the Rhoda Weyr Agency, Chapel Hill, N.C.

"Care In The Holding," copyright © 1987 by Maureen Brady. Reprinted from *The Question She Put To Herself* by Maureen Brady, by permission of the author and The Crossing Press.

"An American In Paris," copyright © 1986 by Kim Chernin. Reprinted from *Erotic Interludes* by Lonnie Barbach, by permission of the Rhoda Weyr Agency, Chapel Hill, N.C.

"Tommy," copyright © 1986 by Elsa Gidlow. An excerpt reprinted from *ELSA: I Come With My Songs* by Elsa Gidlow, by permission of Booklegger Press.

"Don't Explain," copyright © 1988 by Jewelle L. Gomez. Reprinted from *Love, Struggle and Change* by Irene Zahava, by permission of the author.

"My Subway Lover," copyright © 1987 by Wanda Honn. An excerpt reprinted from *Rapture* by Wanda Honn, by permission of the author.

"Tell Me Where The Road Turns," copyright © 1987 by Carol Orlock. Reprinted from *Crossing The Mainstream* by Ann E. Larson and Carol A. Carr, by permission of the author and Silverleaf Press.

"A Perfectly Nice Man," copyright © 1981 by Jane Rule. Reprinted from *Outlander* by Jane Rule, by permission of the author and The Naiad Press.

"A Special Evening," copyright © 1980, 1987 by Ann Allen Shockley. Reprinted from *The Black and White of It* by Ann Allen Shockley, by permission of the author and The Naiad Press.

"Why The Milky Way Is Milky," copyright © 1982 by Kitty Tsui. Originally appeared in *Common Lives/Lesbian Lives* number 4, summer 1982. Reprinted by permission of the author.

"Two Willow Chairs," copyright © 1987 by Jess Wells. Reprinted from *Two Willow Chairs* by Jess Wells, by permission of the author.

The lyrics to "Don't Explain" are by B. Holiday and A. Herzog, Jr. Northern Music Co. (ASCAP).

Cover photograph by Barbara Adams
Cover design by Betsy Bayley
Book design by Martha J. Waters
   text (11/13) and titles in Clearface

Printed in the U.S.A.

Library of Congress Cataloging-in-Publication Data

Lesbian love stories / edited by Irene Zahava
       p. cm.
    ISBN 0-89594-341-7
    1. Lesbianism—Fiction.   2. Love stories, American.   3. Lesbians'
writings, American.   I. Zahava, Irene.
PS648.L47L44   1989
813'.085'08353—dc 19

88-36426
CIP

Contents

Preface / Irene Zahava

1 Life Line / Gloria E. Anzaldúa

5 The Skill Crane Item / Antoinette Azolakov

13 In The Life / Becky Birtha

27 Humming / Sandy Boucher

43 Care In The Holding / Maureen Brady

55 An American In Paris / Kim Chernin

67 Spring Blossoms / Tee A. Corinne

71 The Confrontation / Judy Freespirit

89 Flossie's Flashes / Sally Miller Gearhart

95 Tommy / Elsa Gidlow

105 Don't Explain / Jewelle L. Gomez

117 My Subway Lover / Wanda Honn

121 Vacation Pictures / Melanie Kaye/Kantrowitz

129 New Year's Eve At A Bar / Lee Lynch

139 Out Of The Frying Pan / Harriet Malinowitz

161 Trespassing / Valerie Miner

179 Silver / Merril Mushroom

189 My Woman Poppa / Joan Nestle

193 The Dating Game / Lesléa Newman

229 Tell Me Where The Road Turns / Carol Orlock

237 Safe At Home / Shelly Rafferty

245 Slumber Party / Louise Rafkin

251 A Perfectly Nice Man / Jane Rule

261 Sapphire / Canyon Sam

269 A Special Evening / Ann Allen Shockley

279 Mixing Business With Pleasure / Judith Stein

285 Why The Milky Way Is Milky / Kitty Tsui

299 Two Willow Chairs / Jess Wells

307 We Didn't See It / Barbara Wilson

325 Contributors Notes

Preface

What does it mean to call this a book of lesbian love stories? Woman meets woman and they live happily ever after? Not exactly!

There are romances in this collection—good old-fashioned love stories about trust, fidelity, security and fulfillment. There are stories about the sweet torment that accompanies a crush; the butterflies-in-the-stomach anticipation of a first date; the confident and passionate sexuality between lovers that comes after years of familiarity with each other's bodies.

But this is also a collection that defies any traditional definition of the term "love stories." It includes tales of betrayal, loneliness and fear; accounts of pain and loss, of fights and break-ups.

The women in these stories are of different ages, colors, sizes and backgrounds. Many of them are out and proud, some are deeply in the closet and others are just beginning to emerge from it. They call themselves lesbians, dykes, feminists, butches, femmes, or, simply, women who are "in the life."

They're the old couple next door, sitting in their overgrown garden; the two young women who play on the high school softball team; the military nurses in their starched uniforms; the woman who loves *herself* enough to confront her father about his abuse of her; the baby butch propping up the corner of the neighborhood lesbian bar; the young girl who experiences her first feelings of excitement for another girl; the dentist and the carpenter and the teacher; the stranger standing across from you in the crowded subway car; the battered lesbian; the recovering alcoholic; the woman who greets her hot flashes with enthusiasm and abandon.

The characters in this book seem familiar because they *are* familiar; they represent some of the many different ways a lesbian can be in this world. These stories prove, once again, the truth in that old saying "We Are Everywhere"—and they show that stories about lesbian lives are truly lesbian love stories.

Irene Zahava, December 1988

Life Line

GLORIA E. ANZALDÚA

LA PRIETA MET SUEL at the university during the summer session. They were both in graduate programs full of whites in a school full of whites. Both were floundering in the sea of white faces and they gravitated to each other as to life preservers. For hours they would sit in the air-conditioned commons buoying each other with iced drinks and talks about their courses, their families, movies, books, everything and anything. They would walk across the spacious lawns of the U.T. campus and then wind their way down a ravine to the creek where they would sit close together on the rocks and listen to the gurgle of the trickling water, fanning each other's hot faces with large green leaves while their feet, submerged in the water, cooled.

Suel never wore make-up. She was 12 years older than la Prieta

la Prieta is a term of endearment for women; it means "the dark one."

1

and she wore her hair pulled back in a bun. When la Prieta asked her to wear it down, Suel said, "Don't be silly, it's too hot to wear down." As Suel looked at la Prieta, a brightness washed over her eyes and something in the depths of her eyes that seemed both naked and curtained refused to hold la Prieta's gaze. La Prieta had seen a similar look in children who were hungry and were ashamed of their hunger, children who knew that food was something they would never have enough of.

One day when the summer session was six days away from ending, they were lying on Suel's bed. They had been up all night working on papers and their heads were hollow from too much coffee and lack of sleep. In a few days they would return to the Valley to their respective hometowns. Their pueblos were sixty-nine miles apart. The more Prieta thought about the sixty-nine miles, the further apart their towns seemed. She wondered if their families would think it strange if one drove to visit the other. It *would* look suspicious. It was peculiar, the closeness that had developed between them was different from the closeness she had with her sister or with her other girl friends.

As they lay with arms and thighs touching, la Prieta wanted to say something about the recognition she'd first glimpsed in Suel's eyes when they had first met, and that she had since then seen every time they looked at each other. She wanted to talk about the dense air that seemed to hang about them when they sat close to each other, the air that became progressively harder to breathe. The room was unbearably hot. 'Do you want to talk about *it*?" la Prieta asked, touching the soft skin at the inside of Suel's elbow.

"Talk about what?" Suel responded in a low voice.

"I think we should figure out what to do about it."

"Do about what?" Suel's voice seemed sharper.

"*Tu sabes?* The feelings between us."

"What feelings?"

"You know, the lesbian feelings." Suel turned her head and stared at her. Slowly, she started backing away. Then, averting her face, she sat up, got up and walked out.

La Prieta waited for two hours. Not wanting to fall asleep on Suel's bed in case Suel returned still angry at her, she returned to her place. The next day and the next and the next, la Prieta went to all their usual hangouts. She stopped and asked everyone who knew them, but no one had seen Suel. As a last resort, she went to the Dean's office. She was told that Suel had had a family emergency and had left without finishing her course work.

A month later, when la Prieta had gotten her courage up, she called Suel's house. Suel's sister answered and yelled out to Suel to come to the phone. At the other end la Prieta heard Suel's voice say, "Tell her I'm not home, tell her I moved away and you don't know where I am."

Again la Prieta waited a few months before calling her again. The mother answered this time. She told la Prieta that Suel didn't live there anymore and hung up before la Prieta could say a word.

A year later at a conference Prieta saw Suel sitting in the middle of the almost empty auditorium. Standing at the mouth of the auditorium she felt like she was falling and that Suel was the only life net that could catch her and break her fall. Smiling and with the lightest step she'd had in over a year, she made straight for the row where Suel sat. She saw Suel's thin neck under the familiar bun and felt something soften inside her. Then she saw Suel's head turn, saw her eyes register shock, saw her get up and, head bent, hurry down the row to the other side and circle back to the entrance. As she watched Suel leave, la Prieta felt the life line slipping through her finger.

From a forthcoming book titled *Entreguerras entremundos*/Civil Wars Among The Worlds (Spinsters/Aunt Lute)

The Skill Crane Item

ANTOINETTE AZOLAKOV

SUSAN SAYS IF BABIES aren't touched enough, they die. She hugs everybody at the bar and the softball games and the Lambda meetings. Not me, boy. I don't need it. I'm no baby. Haven't been for thirty-six years, anyway. I don't need any of that stuff.

When Susan left me after six years, I cried some, but that was all. I missed her around the house, missed her cooking, mainly. And she used to come in from work with the silliest damn jokes. I missed that. Still do, I guess. But we were never that great in bed, anyway not since about the first couple of years, so I'd already found out that I didn't need sex.

Oh, we still *had* sex. But not often, and not very. . .well, not very enthusiastically, if you know what I mean. Oh, I was a lover in my day, babe, don't think I wasn't. But the really best thing about being gay, I've come to think, is nothing to do with what you do in bed. The best thing is being free to be my own woman. You know, dress the way I want, real butch, and cut my hair in a real crew cut, not some half-assed, boyish beauty-shop job. Susan used to cut it for me, but when she left, I learned to run the clippers over it myself, even in the back, and shave it right up to the neckline just like a barber. Took a few tries, but I got it right pretty soon and people quit asking me what the hell had happened to the back of my head. Hell, so it was a little lopsided for a month or so. So what? I didn't have to pay no barber, did I? And I didn't have to beg no lover, either. I tell you, I don't need nothing from nobody.

The funny thing is, as soon as Susan was out the door and I got the crying jags under control, I started thinking about fucking. I mean in a big way. I'd see a woman walk down the street and my jockey shorts would get wet. And shit, these dames were not even my type, half the time. And when I went to the bar, whew! All those beautiful, hot dykes just about blew me away. Hell, I wished one of 'em would have offered to blow me away, know what I mean. I'd have gone home with Frankenstein if she was female, and if she would've just held me a little bit, I guess. Let me fuck her, I mean. I really don't need any of that holding stuff.

Or fucked me. I'm no one-way butch. And, hey, I'm not ashamed of it. So, yeah, I like a little attention down there every now and then. Why not? I mean, I've got a cunt, too, right? I mean, I'm a dyke, not a fucking man, no matter what some stupid-asses think I think. How would they know?

It would've been all right with me if Susan wanted to come over sometime and just fool around in bed a little, but she didn't. She still cried every time she saw me. I never let her see me cry. I got pride.

*Any*way. So I was horny, no getting around it. I knew I didn't need sex, that was a fact. *Need* it. Would've *liked* it, sure, you bet. But you know the trouble with coming on to somebody at the bar or someplace? If they're interested at all, damn, they want to marry you. You know? I just wasn't feeling like having somebody attach herself to me like a leech, right then. I don't need somebody around all the time, because I do better taking care of my own business, and anyway they just leave you in the end, don't they? So I just couldn't get it up to come on to any of the women at the bar, and that was really the reason, too, and not that I was afraid they'd turn me down. Hell, I don't give a rat-fuck if they do turn me down. Who cares? It's no skin off my nose.

So I went to the bar one night but I wasn't about to make any move on anybody, for the reasons I said. So they have this game there. It's called Skill Crane, and what it is, it's a big glass box full of different things, stuff like little plush rabbits and fuzzy dice and furry, silly little critters you can't really figure out what they are, but they're bright colors and I guess they're kind of cute, if you like that kind of thing. It's nice, if you have a girl, to put in your quarters and work the little grabber thingie in there till you win one for her. It's got a little deal like a crane or something with three sort of prongs on it, and you push buttons to make it run back and forth across the top of the box and then it drops, and if the prongs catch hold of something tight enough, it'll pick it up and bring it over and drop it where it'll come out the front and you can get it.

So I thought I'd try it, even if I didn't have a girl to give something to, because what the hell, it gets old just sitting there watching the lovebirds dance. Well, I spent a bunch of quarters, because most times the damn prongs just slide off of whatever they land on. Damn thing's a ripoff. Anyway, a few women were standing around watching me, drinking beer and hollering advice about how I ought to be pushing those buttons, and this little cute gal kept telling me, "Get me a teddy bear, Dandy! Get me a teddy bear!" So I thought, what the hell, I'll try for the damn bear, but the damn prongs picked up something else, and I couldn't even tell what it was.

But there was a lot of hooting and laughing going on, and I reached in the little door of the machine and got it out and looked at it. Well, this thing was a sort of satin stuffed-toy fruit of some kind. It was about six inches long and just about an inch thick, curved. I thought it was a banana, but it had a little cap of green leaves or something glued on the top end, which a banana doesn't, and a little loop to hang it up by, like all those Skill Crane items have, because I notice a lot of people have them hanging on their rearview mirrors. I knew right away what it was shaped like, but, really, you don't expect to find something like that in a box with a lot of fluffy stuffed toys, do you? But I was right, though, because I turned it over and saw it had a little red felt heart glued on the other side, and the heart said "I love you" on it. So I figured right then that it really was meant to be what it looked like. I blushed and stuck it in my pocket real fast.

Somebody said, "Dandy, what're you gonna do with that?"

I said, "Give it to you, if you aren't careful." I thought that was pretty good for the spur of the moment, and I don't think anybody could tell I was embarrassed. I hope not, anyway, It's fairly dark in the bar, and the lights are mostly red, so maybe they couldn't see me blush. I went home pretty quick after that. My luck didn't seem to be too good that night, so no use staying and drinking up the rest of my money.

On the way home, I got to thinking about that little gal that wanted the teddy bear. I knew her just a little. She was nice to me, always smiled and said hello when we'd run into each other. Some people think I'm too scary-looking to be friendly to, but she never seemed afraid of me. Leslie, her name was. I've always liked that name. She's a nurse or a nurse's aid, one or the other. Seems kind of young to be a nurse, to me. But, wow, she'd make being in the hospital a little better, I bet. Pretty sexy gal. I was feeling the beer a little, I guess, because I don't think about sex all that much, but driving home in the dark all alone, I got to thinking how, if I'd got that teddy bear and given it to Leslie, we might have got to talking and she might have come home with me. And we could have spent the night together, and we could have held each other, and I could have tucked my head in between her soft, warm breasts and slept like that, with her arms around me.

I mean after we fucked, of course. That's the whole point, right?

So I was feeling pretty hot and bothered by the time I got home.

Then the damn house was so quiet, and even all the neighbors had their lights turned off already, and everything was dark and lonesome. It might've been nice to have Leslie along, it really might.

I took a shower and dried off and put some nice, silky powder on my body so I'd feel good against the sheets, and I got in bed.

I squirmed around some and then I thought, I wonder what it would be like with Leslie, anyway? I got my pillow and held it like it was her, just holding her, petting her a little, and I thought of how she'd snuggle down against me all soft and warm and solid and alive in my arms, and she'd pet me, too, because she was so sweet to me all the time, and I could tell she'd be sweet in bed. And I'd shift her a little to get my arms both around her, and she'd move over and lie on top of me with her hips pressing against mine and her breasts against mine, maybe with her upper body propped up a little on her elbows so our nipples would just touch, just barely, lightly touch as she moved very slightly, swinging her breasts over me. And she'd smile down at me in the dark, real tender and sweet, and I'd move my head up to kiss her. Oh, and then! Her tongue would slip between my lips, just the tip at first, hard and muscular, thrusting very quickly and darting back, teasing me until I couldn't stand it and then, at long last, she'd enter my whole mouth with that live, wriggling tongue and make me so ready I'd be gasping for breath, spreading my knees apart and pushing my hips up to try to get some hot, wet contact, her cunt to mine, oh, Leslie! And my arms would be locked so tight around her, and I'd be breathing so hard and fast, and so would she, and she'd say. . . .

What would she say? We're really just fucking, and just because I think she's so sweet and I want her to hold me and take care of me like a real friend tonight it doesn't really mean I *need* anything from her. It really doesn't.

She says, "Dandy, I love you."

Her voice is so breathy, right against my ear, the words, when she whispers them urgently, blowing hot puffs of air in my ear, sending fire straight into my belly like flames running down a chain of gunpowder, exploding down there and making me buck against her weight like a horse. "I love you, Leslie, I love you!" I hear myself say. And I do, I love her.

And then she raises up, very hot and in a hurry now, and I'm saying, "Yes, please, baby, come on, please, please!" And she says, "Wait, just wait," smiling at me for being so hot and begging for her, but she's feeling everything, too, and she slides her hand across my breasts and then, in one sweeping motion, down over my belly and into the hair at my crotch, soft and silky from the bath I took, and her fingers, oh! her fingers slip between, down, up, down again into the slick, slick wetness, touching for a second, so quickly, the tip of my clit, oh! baby, yes! and sliding, pressing, now, pressing firmly, feeling the folds, the structure, the fiery heat of me, and at last, oh, GOD yes! plunging in, deep, deep, deep, oh, moving writhing twisting with life and power and strength inside, OH, YES! so deep inside of me.

But it's not enough. Oh, god, oh Leslie, I've got to have more, my fingers don't reach well, not long enough, not big enough, I want you to fill me completely, deep, Leslie, deep, all the way as deep as you can, pressing hard, all the way in, as deep as I can hold, oh, think of something! What would do it? Smooth, and firm and long enough, curved, so I could move it all around and feel it—oh, hurry! Something, the handle of a hairbrush? A candle? But where is one? All the way in the kitchen, and not big enough, not enough, but worth a try—Ah!

And I lurch up, holding my crotch, I grab my pants off the back of the chair, I grope frantically in the pocket, and it's there, my fingers close around its long, satin-covered hardness, and I pull it out and leap back onto the bed. The Skill Crane item.

And it won't go in. I can tell its going to be perfect, but the material needs to be smoother, something that won't soak up moisture. I get the Saran Wrap from the kitchen and get back in one desperate dash, wrapping as I go, and in the bed again I spread my legs wide to receive it and Leslie thrusts her long, perfect fingers all the way to my cervix, in and out, thrusting, thrusting, striking into me with her full strength and we're gasping together, our breathing hard and fast as I bear down on her inside of me, lunging violently with my hips to meet her force with my own, and I come with a deep, full cry as the waves of orgasm take me and roll me over and over and finally recede, leaving me spent, shuddering once as a last spasm shakes me and dies, at last, away.

I pull the thing, banana, dildo, whatever, out gently, Leslie covering my cunt warmly with her whole hand, holding me there for a moment, tenderly, lovingly, and then stretching out close beside me, her head nestled against my shoulder and her hand, sticky and smelling wonderfully of me, lying inert over my breast. I turn my head, slowly, the effort almost too much to make, and kiss her cheek, lovingly, tenderly. We'll sleep together now, lovers, friends, relaxed and satisfied and not needing, not afraid any more.

But, heck, everybody masturbates. It don't mean nothing, babe. Just something your body has to have. It doesn't even have to have it, really. I just thought it was funny about that banana, that's all.

In The Life

BECKY BIRTHA

GRACE COME TO ME in my sleep last night. I feel somebody presence, in the room with me, then I catch the scent of Posner's Bergamot Pressing Oil, and that cocoa butter grease she use on her skin. I know she standing at the bedside, right over me, and then she call my name.

"Pearl."

My Christian name Pearl Irene Jenkins, but don't nobody ever call me that no more. I been Jinx to the world for longer than I care to specify. Since my mother passed away, Grace the only one ever use my given name.

"Pearl," she say again. "I'm just gone down to the garden awhile. I be back."

I'm so deep asleep I have to fight my way awake, and when I do be fully woke, Grace is gone. I ease my tired bones up and drag em down the stairs, cross the kitchen in the dark, and out the back

13

screen door onto the porch. I guess I'm half expecting Gracie to be there waiting for me, but there ain't another soul stirring tonight. Not a sound but singing crickets, and nothing staring back at me but that old weather-beaten fence I ought to painted this summer, and still ain't made time for. I lower myself down into the porch swing, where Gracie and I have sat so many still summer nights and watched the moon rising up over Old Mister Thompson's field.

I never had time to paint that fence back then, neither. But it didn't matter none, cause Gracie had it all covered up with her flowers. She used to sit right here on this swing at night, when a little breeze be blowing, and say she could tell all the different flowers apart, just by they smell. The wind pick up a scent, and Gracie say, "Smell that jasmine, Pearl?" Then a breeze come up from another direction, and she turn her head like somebody calling her and say, "Now that's my honeysuckle, now."

It used to tickle me, cause she knowed I couldn't tell all them flowers of hers apart when I was looking square at em in broad daylight. So how I'm gonna do it by smell in the middle of the night? I just laugh and rock the swing a little, and watch her enjoying herself in the soft moonlight.

I could never get enough of watching her. I always did think that Grace Simmons was the prettiest woman north of the Mason-Dixon line. Now I've lived enough years to know it's true. There's been other women in my life besides Grace, and I guess I loved them all, one way or another, but she was something special—Gracie was something else again.

She was a dark brownskin woman—the color of fresh gingerbread hot out the oven. In fact, I used to call her that—my gingerbread girl. She had plenty enough of that pretty brownskin flesh to fill your arms up with something substantial when you hugging her, and to make a nice background for them dimples in her cheeks and other places I won't go into detail about.

Gracie could be one elegant good looker when she set her mind to it. I'll never forget the picture she made, that time the New Year's

Eve party was down at the Star Harbor Ball room. That was the
first year we was in The Club, and we was going to every event they
had. Dressed to kill. Gracie had on that white silk dress that set
off her complexion so perfect, with her hair done up in all them
little curls. A single strand of pearls that could have fooled anybody.
Long gloves. And a little fur stole. We was serious about our party-
ing back then! I didn't look too bad myself, with that black velvet
jacket I used to have, and the pleats in my slacks pressed so sharp
you could cut yourself on em. I weighed quite a bit less than I do
now, too. Right when you come in the door of the ballroom, they
have a great big floor to ceiling gold frame mirror, and if I remember rightly, we didn't get past that for quite some time.

Everybody want to dance with Gracie that night. And that's fine
with me. Along about the middle of the evening, the band is playing
a real hot number, and here come Louie and Max over to me, all
long-face serious, wanting to know how I can let my woman be out
there shaking her behind with any stranger that wander in the door.
Now they know good and well ain't no strangers here. The Cinnamon & Spice Club is a private club, and all events is by invitation only.

Of course, there's some thinks friends is more dangerous than
strangers. But I never could be the jealous, overprotective type. And
the fact is, I just love to watch the woman. I don't care if she out
there shaking it with the Virgin Mary, long as she having a good
time. And that's just what I told Max and Lou. I could lean up against
that bar and watch her for hours.

You wouldn't know, to look at her, she done it all herself. Made
all her own dresses and hats, and even took apart a old ratty fur
coat that used to belong to my great aunt Malinda to make that cute
little stole. She always did her own hair—every week or two. She
used to do mine, too. Always be teasing me about let her make me
some curls this time. I'd get right aggravated. Cause you can't have
a proper argument with somebody when they standing over your
head with a hot comb in they hand. You kinda at they mercy. I'm
sitting fuming and cursing under them towels and stuff, with the

sweat dripping all in my eyes in the steamy kitchen—and she just laughing. "Girl," I'm telling her, "you know won't no curls fit under my uniform cap. Less you want me to stay home this week and you gonna go work my job and your job too."

Both of us had to work, always, and we still ain't had much. Everybody always think Jinx and Grace doing all right, but we was scrimping and saving all along. Making stuff over and making do. Half of what we had to eat grew right here in this garden. Still and all, I guess we *was* doing all right. We had each other.

Now I finally got the damn house paid off, and she ain't even here to appreciate it with me. And Gracie's poor bedraggled garden is just struggling along on its last legs—kinda like me. I ain't the . kind to complain about my lot, but truth to tell, I can't be down crawling around on my hands and knees no more—this body I got put up such a fuss and holler. Can't enjoy the garden at night proper nowadays, nohow. Since Mister Thompson's land was took over by the city and they built them housing projects where the field used to be, you can't even see the moon from here, till it get up past the fourteenth floor. Don't no moonlight come in my yard no more. And I guess I might as well pick my old self up and go on back to bed.

Sometimes I still ain't used to the fact that Grace is passed on. Not even after these thirteen years without her. She the only woman I ever lived with—and I lived with her more than half my life. This house her house, too, and she oughta be here in it with me.

I rise up by six o'clock most every day, same as I done all them years I worked driving for the C.T.C. If the weather ain't too bad, I take me a walk—and if I ain't careful, I'm liable to end up down at the Twelfth Street Depot, waiting to see what trolley they gonna give me this morning. There ain't a soul working in that office still remember me. And they don't even run a trolley on the Broadway line no more. They been running a bus for the past five years.

I forgets a lot of things these days. Last week, I had just took in the clean laundry off the line, and I'm up in the spare room fixing to iron my shirts, when I hear somebody pass through that squeaky side gate and go on around to the back yard. I ain't paid it no mind at all, cause that's the way Gracie most often do when she come home. Go see about her garden fore she even come in the house. I always be teasing her she care more about them collards and string beans than she do about me. I hear her moving around out there while I'm sprinkling the last shirt and plugging in the iron—hear leaves rustling, and a crate scraping along the walk.

While I'm waiting for the iron to heat up, I take a look out the window, and come to see it ain't Gracie at all, but two a them sassy little scoundrels from over the projects—one of em standing on a apple crate and holding up the other one, who is picking my ripe peaches off my tree, just as brazen as you please. Don't even blink a eyelash when I holler out the window. I have to go running down all them stairs and out on the back porch, waving the cord I done jerked out the iron—when Doctor Matthews has told me a hundred times I ain't supposed to be running or getting excited about nothing, with my pressure like it is. And I ain't even supposed to be *walking* up and down no stairs.

When they seen the ironing cord in my hand, them two little sneaks had a reaction all right. The one on the bottom drop the other one right on his padded quarters and lit out for the gate, hollering, "Look out, Timmy! Here come Old Lady Jenkins!"

When I think about it now, it was right funny, but at the time I was so mad it musta took me a whole half hour to cool off. I sat there on that apple crate just boiling.

Eventually, I begun to see how it wasn't even them two kids I was so mad at. I was mad at time. For playing tricks on me the way it done. So I don't even remember that Grace Simmons has been dead now for the past thirteen years. And mad at time just for passing—so fast. If I had my life to live over, I wouldn't trade in none of them years for nothing. I'd just slow em down.

The church sisters around here is always trying to get me to be thinking about dying, myself. They must figure, when you my age, that's the only excitement you got left to look forward to. Gladys Hawkins stopped out front this morning, while I was mending a patch in the top screen of the front door. She was grinning from ear to ear like she just spent the night with Jesus himself.

"Morning, Sister Jenkins. Right pretty day the good Lord seen fit to send us, ain't it?"

I ain't never known how to answer nobody who manages to bring the good Lord into every conversation. If I nod and say yes, she'll think I finally got religion. But if I disagree, she'll think I'm crazy, cause it truly is one pretty August morning. Fortunately, it don't matter to her whether I agree or not, cause she gone right on talking according to her own agenda anyway.

"You know, this Sunday is Women's Day over at Blessed Endurance. Reverend Solomon Moody is gonna be visiting, speaking on 'A Woman's Place In The Church.' Why don't you come and join us for worship? You'd be most welcome."

I'm tempted to tell her exactly what come to my mind—that I ain't never heard of no woman name Solomon. However, I'm polite enough to hold my tongue, which is more than I can say for Gladys.

She ain't waiting for no answer from me, just going right on. "I don't spose you need me to point it out to you, Sister Jenkins, but you know you ain't as young as you used to be." As if both of our ages wasn't common knowledge to each other, seeing as we been knowing one another since we was girls. "You reaching that time of life when you might wanna be giving a little more attention to the spiritual side of things than you been doing. . . ."

She referring, politely as she capable of, to the fact that I ain't been seen inside a church for thirty-five years.

". . . And you know what the good Lord say. 'Watch therefore, for ye know neither the day nor the hour. . .' But, 'He that believeth on the Son hath everlasting life. . .'"

It ain't no use to argue with her kind. The Lord is on they side in every little disagreement, and he don't never give up. So when she finally wind down and ask me again will she see me in church this Sunday, I just say I'll think about it.

Funny thing, I been thinking about it all day. But not the kinda thoughts she want me to think, I'm sure. Last time I went to church was on a Easter Sunday. We decided to go on accounta Gracie's old meddling cousin, who was always nagging us about how we unnatural and sinful and a disgrace to her family. Seem like she seen it as her one mission in life to get us two sinners inside a church. I guess she figure, once she get us in there, God gonna take over the job. So Grace and me finally conspires that the way to get her off our backs is to give her what she think she want.

Course, I ain't had on a skirt since before the war, and I ain't aiming to change my lifelong habits just to please Cousin Hattie. But I did take a lotta pains over my appearance that day. I'd had my best tailor-made suit pressed fresh, and slept in my stocking cap the night before so I'd have every hair in place. Even had one a Gracie's flowers stuck in my buttonhole. And a brand new narrow-brim dove gray Stetson hat. Gracie take one look at me when I'm ready and shake her head. "The good sisters is gonna have a hard time concentrating on the preacher today!"

We arrive at her cousin's church nice and early, but of course it's a big crowd inside already on accounta it being Easter Sunday. The organ music is wailing away, and the congregation is dazzling— decked out in nothing but the finest and doused with enough perfume to outsmell even the flowers up on the altar.

But as soon as we get in the door, this kinda sedate commotion break out—all them good Christian folks whispering and nudging each other and trying to turn around and get a good look. Well, Grace and me, we used to that. We just find us a nice seat in one of the empty pews near the back. But this busy buzzing keep up, even after we seated and more blended in with the crowd. And finally it come out that the point of contention ain't even the bottom half of my suit, but my new dove gray Stetson.

This old gentleman with a grizzled head, wearing glasses about a inch thick is turning around and leaning way over the back of the seat, whispering to Grace in a voice plenty loud enough for me to hear, "You better tell your beau to remove that hat, entering in Jesus' Holy Chapel."

Soon as I get my hat off, some old lady behind me is grumbling. "I declare, some of these children haven't got no respect at all. Oughta know you sposed to keep your head covered, setting in the house of the Lord."

Seem like the congregation just can't make up its mind whether I'm supposed to wear my hat or I ain't.

I couldn't hardly keep a straight face all through the service. Every time I catch Gracie eye, or one or the other of us catch a sight of my hat, we off again. I couldn't wait to get outa that place. But it was worth it. Gracie and me was entertaining the gang with that story for weeks to come. And we ain't had no more problems with Cousin Hattie.

Far as life everlasting is concerned, I imagine I'll cross that bridge when I reach it. I don't see no reason to rush into things. Sure, I know Old Man Death is gonna be coming after me one of these days, same as he come for my mother and dad, and Gracie and, just last year, my old buddy Louie. But I ain't about to start nothing that might make him feel welcome. It might be different for Gladys Hawkins and the rest of them church sisters, but I got a whole lot left to live for. Including a mind fulla good time memories. When you in the life, one thing your days don't never be, and that's dull. Your nights neither. All these years I been in the life, I love it. And you know Jinx ain't about to go off with no Old *Man* without no struggle, nohow.

To tell the truth, though, sometime I do get a funny feeling bout Old Death. Sometime I feel like he here already—been here. Waiting on me and watching me and biding his time. Paying attention when I have to stop on the landing of the stairs to catch my breath. Paying attention if I don't wake up till half past seven some morning, and my back is hurting me so bad it take me another half hour to pull myself together and get out the bed.

The same night after I been talking to Gladys in the morning, it take me a long time to fall asleep. I'm lying up in bed waiting for the aching in my back and my joints to ease off some, and I can swear I hear somebody else in the house. Seem like I hear em downstairs, maybe opening and shutting the icebox door, or switching off a light. Just when I finally manage to doze off, I hear somebody footsteps right here in the bedroom with me. Somebody tippy-toeing real quiet, creaking the floor boards between the bed and the dresser. . .over to the closet. . .back to the dresser again.

I'm almost scared to open my eyes. But it's only Gracie—in her old raggedy bathrobe and a silk handkerchief wrapped up around all them little braids in her head—putting her finger up to her lips to try and shush me so I won't wake up.

I can't help chuckling. "Hey Gingerbread Girl. Where you think you going in your house coat and bandana and it ain't even light out yet. Come on get back in this bed."

"You go on to sleep," she say. "I'm just going out back a spell."

It ain't no use me trying to make my voice sound angry, cause she so contrary when it come to that little piece of ground down there I can't help laughing. "What you think you gonna complish down there in the middle of the night? It ain't even no moon to watch tonight. The sky been filling up with clouds all evening, and the weather forecast say rain tomorrow."

"Just don't pay me no mind and go on back to sleep. It ain't the middle of the night. It's almost daybreak." She grinning like she up to something, and sure enough, she say, "This the best time to pick off them black and yellow beetles been making mildew outa my cucumber vines. So I'm just fixing to turn the tables around a little bit. You gonna read in the papers tomorrow morning bout how the entire black and yellow beetle population of number Twenty-seven Bank Street been wiped off the face of the earth—while you was up here sleeping."

Both of us is laughing like we partners in a crime, and then she off down the hall, calling out, "I be back before you even know

I'm gone."

But the full light of day is coming in the window, and she ain't back yet.

I'm over to the window with a mind to holler down to Grace to get her behind back in this house, when the sight of them housing projects hits me right in the face: stacks of dirt-colored bricks and little caged-in porches, heaped up into the sky blocking out what poor skimpy light this cloudy morning brung.

It's a awful funny feeling start to come over me. I mean to get my housecoat, and go down there anyway, just see what's what. But in the closet I can see it ain't but my own clothes hanging on the pole. All the shoes on the floor is mine. And I know I better go ahead and get washed, cause it's a whole lot I want to get done fore it rain, and that storm is coming in for sure. Better pick the rest of them ripe peaches and tomatoes. Maybe put in some peas for fall picking, if my knees'll allow me to get that close to the ground.

The rain finally catch up around noon time and slow me down a bit. I never could stand to be cooped up in no house in the rain. Always make me itchy. That's one reason I used to like driving a trolley for the C.T.C. Cause you get to be out every day, no matter what kinda weather coming down—get to see people and watch the world go by. And it ain't as if you exactly out in the weather, neither. You get to watch it all from behind that big picture window.

Not that I woulda minded being out in it. I used to want to get me a job with the post office, delivering mail. Black folks could make good money with the post office, even way back then. But they wouldn't out you on no mail route. Always stick em off in a back room someplace, where nobody can't see em and get upset cause some little colored girl making as much money as the white boy working next to her. So I stuck with the C.T.C. all them years, and got my pension to prove it.

The rain still coming down steady along about three o'clock, when Max call me up say do I want to come over to her and Yvonne's for dinner. Say they fried more chicken that they can eat, and any-way Yvonne all involved in some new project she want to talk to me about. And I'm glad for the chance to get out the house. Max and Yvonne got the place all picked up for company. I can smell that fried chicken soon as I get in the door.

Yvonne don't never miss a opportunity to dress up a bit. She got the front of her hair braided up, with beads hanging all in her eyes, and a kinda loose robe-like thing, in colors look like the fruit salad at a Independence Day picnic. Max her same old self in her slacks and loafers. She ain't changed in all the years I known her—cept we both got more wrinkles and gray hairs. Yvonne a whole lot younger than us two, but she hanging in there. Her and Max been together going on three years now.

Right away, Yvonne start to explain about this project she do-ing with her women's club. When I first heard about this club she in, I was kinda interested. But I come to find out it ain't no social club, like the Cinnamon & Spice Club used to be. It's more like a organization. Yvonne call it a collective. They never has no outings or parties or picnics or nothing—just meetings. And projects.

The project they working on right now, they all got tape recorders. And they going around tape-recording people story. Talking to peo-ple who been in the life for years and years, and asking em what it was like, back in the old days. I been in the life since before Yvonne born. But the second she stick that microphone in my face, I can't think of a blessed thing to say.

"Come on, Jinx, you always telling us all them funny old time stories."

Then little wheels is rolling round and round, and all that smooth, shiny brown tape is slipping off one reel and sliding onto the other, and I can't think of not one thing I remember.

"Tell how the Cinnamon & Spice Club got started," she say.

"I already told you about that before."

"Well, tell how it ended, then. You never told me that."

"Ain't nothing to tell. Skip and Peaches broke up." Yvonne waiting, and the reels is rolling, but for the life of me I can't think of another word to say about it. And Max is sitting there grinning, like I'm the only one over thirty in the room and she don't remember a thing.

Yvonne finally give up and turn the thing off, and we go on and stuff ourselves on the chicken they fried and the greens I brung over from the garden. By the time we start in on the sweet potato pie, I have finally got to remembering. Telling Yvonne about when Skip and Peaches had they last big falling out, and they was both determine they was gonna stay in The Club—and couldn't be in the same room with one another for fifteen minutes. Both of em keep waiting on the other one to drop out, and both of em keep showing up, every time the gang get together. And none of the rest of us couldn't be in the same room with the two a them for even as long as they could stand each other. We'd be sneaking around, trying to hold a meeting without them finding out. But Peaches was the president and Skip was the treasurer, so you might say our hands was tied. Wouldn't neither one of em resign. They was both convince The Club couldn't go on without em, and by the time they was finished carrying on, they had done made sure it wouldn't.

Max is chiming in correcting all the details, every other breath come outa my mouth. And then when we all get up to go sit in the parlor again, it come out that Yvonne has sneaked that tape recording machine in here under that African poncho she got on, and has got down every word I said.

When time come to say good night, I'm thankful, for once, that Yvonne insist on driving me home—though it ain't even a whole mile. The rain ain't let up all evening, and is coming down in bucketfuls while we in the car. I'm half soaked just running from the car to the front door.

Yvonne is drove off down the street, and I'm halfway through the front door, when it hit me all of a sudden that the door ain't been locked. Now my mind may be getting a little threadbare in spots, but it ain't wore out yet. I know it's easy for me to slip back into

doing things the way I done em twenty or thirty years ago, but I
could swear I distinctly remember locking this door and hooking
the key ring back on my belt loop, just fore Yvonne drove up in front.
And now here's the door been open all the time.

Not a sign a nobody been here. Everything in its place, just like
I left it. The slipcovers on the couch is smooth and neat. The candy
dishes and ash trays and photographs is sitting just where they belong, on the end tables. Not even so much as a throw rug been moved
a inch. I can feel my heart start to thumping like a blowout tire.
Must be, whoever come in here ain't left yet.

The idea of somebody got a nerve like that make me more mad
than scared, and I know I'm gonna find out who it is broke in my
house, even if it don't turn out to be nobody but them little peach-
thieving rascals from round the block. Which I wouldn't be surprised
if it ain't. I'm scooting from room to room, snatching open closet
doors and whipping back curtains—tiptoeing down the hall and then
flicking on the lights real sudden.

When I been in every room, I go back through everywhere I
been, real slow, looking in all the drawers, and under the old glass
doorstop in the hall, and in the back of the recipe box in the
kitchen—and other places where I keep things. But it ain't nothing
missing. No money—nothing.

In the end, ain't nothing left for me to do but go to bed. But
I'm still feeling real uneasy. I know somebody or something done
got in here while I was gone. And ain't left yet. I lay wake in the
bed a long time, cause I ain't too particular about falling asleep tonight. Anyway, all this rain just make my joints swell up worse, and
the pains in my knees just don't let up.

The next thing I know Gracie waking me up. She lying next
to me and kissing me all over my face. I wake up laughing, and she
say, "I never could see no use in shaking somebody I rather be kissing." I can feel the laughing running all through her body and mine,
holding her up against my chest in the dark—knowing there must
be a reason why she woke me up in the middle of the night, and

pretty sure I can guess what it is. She kissing under my chin now, and starting to undo my buttons.

It seem like so long since we done this. My whole body is all a shimmer with this sweet, sweet craving. My blood is racing, singing, and her fingers is sliding inside my nightshirt. "Take it easy," I say in her ear. Cause I want this to take us a long, long time.

Outside, the sky is still wide open—the storm is throbbing and beating down on the roof over our heads, and pressing its wet self up against the window. I catch ahold of her fingers and bring em to my lips. Then I roll us both over so I can see her face. She smiling up at me through the dark, and her eyes is wide and shiny. And I run my fingers down along her breast, underneath her own nightgown. . . .

I wake up in the bed alone. It's still night. Like a flash I'm across the room, knowing I'm going after her, this time. The carpet treads is nubby and rough, flying past underneath my bare feet, and the kitchen linoleum cold and smooth. The back door standing wide open, and I push through the screen.

The storm is moved on. That fresh air feel good on my skin through the cotton nightshirt. Smell good, too, rising up outa the wet earth, and I can see the water sparkling on the leaves of the collards and kale, twinkling in the vines on the bean poles. The moon is riding high up over Thompson's field, spilling moonlight all over the yard, and setting all them blossoms on the fence to shining pure white.

There ain't a leaf twitching and there ain't a sound. I ain't moving either. I'm just gonna stay right here on this back porch. And hold still. And listen close. Cause I know Gracie somewhere in this garden. And she waiting for me.

Humming

SANDY BOUCHER

HOW GLAD I AM that she doesn't look like any of my three daughters. In the last years especially, in which I have pursued a meditation practice and the study of the great, elegant texts of Buddhism, often I have felt that time does not exist, or that all of it exists in this very moment, or that the space of a lifetime is no bigger than a drop of dew trembling on a petal of a flower, and as evanescent. Given this perspective, what can our relative ages matter?

Still, if Jeanine were to remind me of one of my daughters, I'd be uncomfortable. After all, I do inhabit the time-limited world of conditions. One condition being my aging body, wracked these days with the storms of menopause. Another being the old shingle house in which Ralph and I live. Rotting at its foundation and threatening to slide down the steep lawn in back, still it sits with shabby charm in the Berkeley hills. The house speaks to some people of a gracious, leisurely decade when trees were more numerous than houses

27

up on the hill; as my presence must awake in some people a nostalgia for the late forties, early fifties, when young people were supposedly more innocent and trusting in life than they are today. I am not, myself, interested in that time of my youth, or in the years of mothering that came after.

I am really only interested in this particular moment in the big shadowy bedroom with its view of the distant Golden Gate Bridge red above the shining water. In this quiet afternoon now and then I hear the cooing of the doves who live under the eaves. A soft gray sound, from somewhere far away, it enters my mind as I look at the black curls lying flat, like a baby lamb's, wet with our sweat and a sweeter, thicker juice. Wisps of curl feather down her thighs a few inches, lie softly up against the undercurve of her belly. This bower of dark hair, thin enough that the skin is visible underneath, damp and warm, welcomes me. I lick each curl, moving to where the hair grows more thickly, the odor deepens. Odor of salty wetness that opens caves in my mind, rich odor of deep-sea secrets, of sun-warmed olives, the sunshine transmuted to a thick golden liquid in which I lie suspended. Jeanine's odor.

I stroke the tender skin of the inside of her thighs, my fingers converging at the rosy lips visible under the hair, brushing lightly over them. Her voice comes, a soft ohhhh of anticipation. I lift my head to look up at her, see her brown eyes watching me with that same intent look that takes over her face when she leans to my breast, takes my nipple in her mouth and examines it gently with her tongue, nurtures it with her lips. Such concentration, such passionate attention. My own cunt has begun to throb, my body going hot and seeming to swell, heightening my skin's sensitivity.

While the fingers of my right hand play in her hair, moving lightly over her vulva, with my left I reach to take her small, callused hand. I kiss her fingers, linger in her palm, suck her thumb, moving my tongue around it in slow revolvings. Ahhhh, she says, lifting her pelvis, offering herself. I let my breast lie against the open lips, feeling their wet warmth on my skin, my tightening nipple. Jeanine shudders, says my name, and I lower my face to brush her thigh, move carefully upward until I am kissing her outer lips. She has begun to move her pelvis in smooth, subtle circles, each coming toward me a gesture of desire, each drawing away an invitation to follow her. I do now. Slightly spreading her lips with my fingers, I place my wet mouth between them, greeting her tight bud of a clitoris, slipping my tongue down to probe the opening of her vagina, moving up again to suck. Jeanine makes a low crooning sound that vibrates through her body into my mouth. Slipping my arms under her lifted thighs, I reach up to cup her breasts, tease the hard pink nipples as my mouth answers hungrily each thrusting, seeking movement of her desire.

These same breasts I gently cradle half an hour later as we sit in the deep hot water of the bathtub. When I invited her into the tub she asked, "When is Ralph coming home?" "Not until seven, I think." Her eyebrows knotted. "You *think!*" But she got in with me, lifting short, muscular legs over the side of the tub, lowering her small ass into the water so that she now sits facing me. I soap her breasts, long breasts with nipples pointing down, while she tells me that when she loses weight her breasts hang like empty bags on her chest. I can't imagine it, they are so full now, overflowing my hands with their slippery weight. She touches mine, and murmurs into my hair, "Your breasts comfort me." "Hummmm," I say, small sound of acknowledgment, of satisfaction.

It is only in these stolen afternoons that we are able to be together. I have been married for thirty years, to three different men. Some women find marriage restricting: I find it liberating, even marriage to a man like Ralph, who runs a metaphysical bookstore and cares more about meditating than making money. He does support me. And I like the safety of marriage, the comforting routine, the coziness. My mother encouraged me to develop a practical attitude to life coupled with a vivid appetite for its pleasures. Jeanine cares about Ralph too: she does not want to hurt him. She carries her love for me like a secret treasure, folded and wrapped, close to her heart. Her desire sends flames up through her body, lighting her eyes. Sometimes those eyes catch me unawares, as when, leaning over Ralph to pour his coffee, I glance up to where she sits on the window seat, the newspaper held before her. She is not reading: her eyes are watching my movements with an attention so focused it startles me. She looks into me, and without moving an inch I feel myself falling toward her, plummeting with her down, down, deep inside to the place we visit together, the place where stillness lies, holding us.

Now, in the bathtub, we have leaned our heads into each other's shoulder; the steam rising from the water wets our faces. I don't know whether it's my rampaging hormones or the heat of the bath that causes the sweat to streak my forehead. As my hands move under the water to stroke her sides, cup her buttocks, Jeanine turns her head to nuzzle my neck. I smile, remembering my first sight of her, how impossibe it would have been for me then to imagine this joy that floods through me at the touch of her lips on my throat. She was a thirtyish woman in dirty blue overalls whose black hair hung limp and straight to just below the ears. She was digging with a shovel in our front yard. I liked watching her work, her arms pushing and lifting, her back bent, then straight. Then I noticed her eyes, which are the color of old mahogany, the flash of interest that lit them when she looked at me. I noticed her mouth, with its full, pouting lower lip. On the second day, she had washed her hair to shiny softness and wore clean overalls; she sat on the porch talking to me, smiling an invitation, before she started work. On the third day I began to help her.

Jeanine and I have often giggled, since, about her having been our gardener, remembering *Lady Chatterly's Lover.* Actually we are far from the classic master-servant model of dime-store romances, for she is only taking a break from the media jobs that have supported her very well during the past five years: now she luxuriates in the physical exertion, the relative simplicity of her job as a gardener. If anyone comes from humble beginnings it would be I, daughter of a widowed mother who supported my sister and me by working as a cashier in movie theaters. Marriage was my way out of the crowded, threadbare apartment where we all slept in the same bed because there was only one; it was my ladder up and out of worry and want. I climbed it gladly.

I am feeling the flat, strong muscles of her upper back and shoulders, kneading them, smoothing them as Jeanine murmurs in appreciation, when suddenly she stiffens, sending a little tidal wave of hot water across my belly. Her head snaps back, her eyes widening.

"Was that a car in the drive!?"

I listen, hearing nothing.

Jeanine rises from the tub, her body streaming, and lunges for the window that faces on the driveway.

"Oh, god, it's *Ralph!*"

The flat sound of a car door slamming rises from the driveway. She comes back to stand next to the tub, her body arranged in odd, stiff angles of panic.

"What should I *do!*" she asks, her eyes on me pleadingly.

I sit in the hot water, surrounded by steam, and the nervousness erupts from me in a low giggle.

She is convulsed for a few moments too, and then she asks again, "But what should I *do?*" spreading her hands in a helpless gesture.

"Put on your clothes," I sputter. "Quick!" For I can hear the sound of Ralph's opening the door downstairs, his footsteps in the living room.

She's pulling on little gray socks, they look so ridiculous, then her corduroy pants, her red shirt, over her wet body.

"He's in the kitchen now," I hiss. "Go down and talk to him."

"Oh, shit, my underpants!"

"I'll hide them."

She rubs the steamy mirror to clear it, looks at her red, moist face, her tangled hair.

I am still giggling.

Halfway out the door, Jeanine turns to me, fixing me with a fierce look.

"I *hate* this!"

Then I see only the smooth white-painted wood of the door.

In a few minutes I hear voices in the kitchen, Ralph and Jeanine carrying on a conversation. He has probably offered her a drink of freshly Osterized carrot juice; she has probably asked him about a book, something mildly exotic and hard to find, like *Initiates and Initiations in Tibet,* by Alexandra David-Neel. This bibliographic communication will make a safe cover for Jeanine's suspiciously flushed appearance, for when queried about esoteric volumes Ralph loses all connection with the world about him and goes off into his mind like an ancient labyrinthine library where one title leads him to the next in contented quest for the most worm-eaten, mildew-encrusted tome ever unearthed. He cares little for the content of these books, or for their physical beings; it is the search that brings color to his cheeks.

In my steamy hideaway, I let myself go, slipping down into the still-hot water, giving myself to the shudders of mirth that contort me. Downstairs, the voices go on, or Ralph's voice, that is. I can imagine his rapt face, the excited lift of his chin. And Jeanine looking at him with big, relieved eyes.

I do not see her again until the next Sunday. Ralph and I have come to the chanting session at the Clear Light Institute, of which he is a director. I had almost decided to stay home because I was suffering the weakness and heat that accompany my periods now. I've heard other women describe hot flashes, but this is different, not a flash but a constant deep radiating heat that leaves me sweaty and lethargic. I'd been in bed all afternoon, reading, when Ralph came to ask me if I wanted to go with him. On reflection, I decided the chanting and meditating might be just the thing to cool my raging blood.

"If women had written the Buddhist canon," I told Ralph as we drove across Berkeley, "there would be special meditations for menopause."

Ralph pondered this, and then began to tell me about the *Therigatha*, a volume of poems written by the first Buddhist nuns. "They were contemporaries of the Buddha. They wrote in Pali, the ancient language. It's quite a volume. . .stories of monastic life, songs of their moments of enlightenment. . . ." He went on for the next ten minutes, telling me of the various translations, the whereabouts of the original and how it was found. This recital was so thoughtfully given, with such erudition and sensitivity, that I was filled with my fondness for Ralph, and reached to rub him gently on his arm.

The meditation room of the Clear Light Institute is hung with sumptuous Tibetan paintings on silk scrolls: blue-faced demons dance before spread fans of orange flames, green-skinned goddesses wave multiple arms. The panels of the walls are painted deep red and that clear flat blue that the Tibetans love. Gold leaf climbs the pillars. Perhaps thirty people sit on pillows, eyes closed, mouths open to sing the sacred syllables, these sounds which vibrate in the belly, in the throat, connecting one up to the great sound that is always echoing in the universe. Sometimes I really do feel that merging of sound, when the chant sings me, rather than I sing it, but tonight I'm restless, impatient with the slow droning, enduring my heat and dizziness. Maybe it was a mistake to come. I consider sneaking upstairs to sit in the lobby or on the porch.

Then Jeanine arrives. I *feel* her enter. It's a sensation like a cool hand slid up my back, signal to wake up. Opening my eyes I see that she has just slipped through the door, her embarrassment at being so late obvious in the stiff way she holds her shoulders. She wears a purple, loose top and jeans; her small feet are bare. A slim gold chain encircles one sun-bronzed ankle.

Does she know I'm here? My heart pounds. It takes all my strength not to call to her, not to lift my hand. Then I realize she has settled herself on a pillow to my right, facing me. Her attention falls over me like a cloak. I feel faint with excitement, knowing she has taken that seat to watch me.

The chant stops now, the last long syllable drawn out into the room by a few deep male voices, loud under the steady higher voices of the other men and the women. And then there is silence, a silence in which the chanting still exists, in which it has built a many-layered sensitivity. I can feel my body still vibrating as I settle myself for the half-hour silent meditation that always follows the chanting.

To ease the stiffness in my crossed legs, I shift position slightly, and then I place my right hand on my knee. A simple action, and simple to describe, but the significance of it is staggering. As I begin to move my hand toward my knee, I become aware that all her attention is focused upon it. There are an excruciating few moments of held breath as my arm moves, bringing my palm-down hand closer to the round promontory of my knee. Jeanine's watching with every cell of her body hangs upon me as if I lift her with my arm and move her through space. My arm is heavy, weighted with its mission, as it traverses the distance and pauses, my hand hovering just an inch above my knee. Then, with a sound not uttered, like the fluttering ahhhh of surrender, I let my fingers sink to touch the cloth of my skirt, my palm settles gently over the curve of my kneecap. It is as if the air has thickened to solidity. There is nothing in the room now but that hand resting upon that knee. It is enormous, utterly deserving of the passion Jeanine offers it. It is magically alight, pearly with the glow of its mysterious presence. The gilded pillars, the faces of demons and people, fall back before its mystic power.

I open my eyes slightly, to see from their corners the figure of Jeanine clenched forward, her mouth slack in dazzlement. I feel how tenderly my hand lies upon my knee, like a cloud of morning mist upon the top of a hill, poised there without weight, holding us both in a condition of grace.

After the chanting, we meet in the lobby. Ralph has gone off for a meeting with the directors, having touched me on the elbow and assured me he will not be long. This gentle patting of one another's arms seems to have developed into a rite between us, expressing the affection and shared inertia that bind us to each other.

Jeanine is studiously not looking at me from the other side of the room, where she talks with one of the young male meditation teachers. So it is my turn to watch her. I like how she responds, even to this young man who is being a little too proprietary with the insistent tilt of his body toward her, his gaze intent upon her mouth. Jeanine hums with a steady enthusiasm when she is with people. He may imagine that her looking full into his eyes is designed to encourage his attentions, but it is only how she looks into everyone she meets. Her hair is sleek and glistening tonight, in that little Dutch-boy haircut that I find so humorous sometimes. The purple of her shirt sets off the brown skin of her throat.

Just now her eyes meet mine, and I find myself grinning in sheer pleasure. Jeanine excuses herself from the young man: she is suddenly before me.

Still smiling, I want to give her myself, my difficult day, my weakness.

As she reaches to hug me, I feel how sticky my skin is, how my body trembles inside.

"I'm sorry. I've been sweating so much. I must smell."

Holding me, she has lowered her head to my shoulder, her cheek against the thin damp cotton of my dress. "I *love* how you smell."

The words come to me as if from her arms, her collarbones, her thighs; and something is pushed aside in me.

"Ah, why are you crying?" Jeanine cups my cheek, wipes the tears with her thumb.

"Come with me," she whispers. "I want to hold you."

I hesitate, glancing around at the people in the lobby, who are chanting quietly in small groups, seemingly oblivious of us.

"I know just the place," Jeanine mutters as she leads me toward the stairway to the basement.

We descend narrow, winding steps to a corridor into which several doors open. At the end of the hall, Jeanine pushes aside a heavy curtain to lead me into a tiny dark room like a cave, lit only by small candles on an altar. This is the room set aside for individual meditation. Jeanine pulls the curtain tight at the door and fastens it, then turns to touch my wrist with cool, reassuring fingers. "You know that when the curtain's pulled," she whispers, "no one would dare to come in."

I look around, my eyes slowly adjusting to the dimness of this familiar room. It is perhaps ten feet square, with one meditation pillow placed near the door, the altar opposite. Rugs and tapestries cover its walls, muffling the sound of the prayer wheel that turns in the corner. The wheel is a tall wide cylinder wrapped in green paper, with a flounce of vibrant red. It hums in its turning, a sound steadily insistent in the room, spinning its assembled prayers out into the universe.

Jeanine folds me into its throbbing as she takes me in her arms. She holds me gently for a time, her chest rising as she breathes deeply.

This room is as dark, as enclosed, as a womb. Jeanine begins to sing with the prayer wheel, the tone like the pulsing of blood in our veins. She rocks me, comforting my body, smoothing my burning skin. Her smell merges now with the odor of incense that permeates the room. Slowly she moves her head back to seek my lips, and I taste her smooth moistness, mint, a slight reminder of the tea she drank after the chanting. Her lips move now, seeking me, her tongue asking questions of my mouth, and my answer is a quickness of breathing that shakes my chest. She teases, probes, tantalizes my own tongue to follow her movements; and I feel a tingling in my clitoris. Abruptly I want her closer and closer to me. I want to enfold her completely, draw her inside me.

The prayer wheel sings of sunshine, bright mountain air, a many-windowed monastery clinging to a cliff as Jeanine invites me to lie down on the layered rugs. "Here?!" I whisper. "How *can we?*" Her brown eyes smile at me, brilliant with desire. "No one will come. . . not with the curtain drawn. They'll think we're meditating."

I glance around, uncertain. The Buddha sits with closed eyes on the altar, minding his own business. The silks spread under him are the color of the soft iner tissues of the body; they glow richly red and rose in the candlelight. On large scroll painting hangs on the wall. It depicts a female deity dancing. She is nude except for a rope of jewels that snakes down between her breasts and laces across her thighs. Her body is silvery, her face golden. Her eyebrows sweep up like birds above wrathful eyes. Her headdress depicts a pig carved of gold and encrusted with jewels.

But Jeanine is touching me, coaxing me, drawing me down until I look up to see the dark ceiling covered with paintings so old their colors have muddied. Now we lie breast to breast, and the heat of my body that has been so unwelcome all day intensifies. "Yes," Jeanine murmurs against my throat. "Oh, yes, love. . ." Her hands have lifted my loose dress to move beneath the cloth, cupping my breasts, her thumbs fluttering against my hardening nipples. She kisses me, her tongue moving deep in my mouth, and I feel myself opening to her, giving in to the heat of my body until it becomes a steady surge, powerful as an ocean wave. Jeanine rides the wave, swimming closer and closer to my center. Her hips move against mine, the firm mound of her pubic bone thrusting ever so subtly, tantalizing me with its pressure.

Then she pulls away a little, and I see that she has caught my heat, her cheeks flushed darkly, her eyes wildly shining. "We've got to take off your dress," she murmurs, "or it'll get all wrinkled and damp."

I glance at the curtained door. "But how can we. . .?"

"Yes, it'll be better. . ." To convince me, she lifts her purple shirt. For a moment her arms are held high, her torso lifted, and my body trembles with pleasure at the sight of her breasts, long and full, the nipples pink tight berries. She is stripping off the blue jeans, throwing them to the side. The ankle bracelet is a fragile gold line on her nude body.

"I'll help you." She lifts the dress higher, works it up over my head. And I am nude too, the air touching my skin.

Slowly she lowers herself to lie full length upon me, one leg between my thighs, and her pelvis seems to sink into mine. I am so without resistance. I feel her heart pumping in quick rhythm against my chest.

She begins to kiss my shoulder, and moves down my arm until her mouth finds the inside of my elbow. Her tongue licks the tender skin, her lips kiss wetly. My whole arm vibrates with pleasure, and I can feel my cunt opening under the weight and warmth of her body. She moves to my wrist now, her tongue examining every millimeter of sensitive skin, until she leaves it to kiss my palm, lingering.

Deftly, she lifts herself and moves down to smooth my thighs. She leans to kiss, her cheek brushing my pubic hair, beginning a hot throbbing in my cunt. She moves down to my knee, her mouth encircling my kneecap, tongue tracing its contour. Then she sucks the muscle just below the kneecap, sending flutters of energy up inside my thigh to my vagina. She moves down again, briefly stroking my calves, and arrives at my feet, which she holds in comforting hands. She kisses my instep, and then sucks, as I begin to moan.

I have opened my eyes to find the image of the deity dancing on the wall above me. Her breasts flicker in the dim light. An arm, a foot, are raised. She tilts toward the next step, establishing a rhythm that travels from her silvery body to mine. Moving, I join her in it, my hips circling now, slowly, subtly, my breasts lifting, hands braced against the rug.

Jeanine comes up to lie upon me, her mouth seeking my breast. I close my eyes as she kisses, teases, lifts and cradles, and I see the body of the silver woman moving in her passionate dance. I recognize those breasts, those neat narrow hips, the thickness of dark pubic curls. Opening my eyes, I see her face bent to my breast, the black hair falling forward, her look of intense concentration. Her lips close on my nipple and she sucks, tentatively at first, tenderly. Our movements happen together now, our hips and thighs undulating. Letting my head fall back, I close my eyes, giving in to this dance as Jeanine sucks more hungrily, her teeth closing with tantalizing care upon my hard, straining nipple. I thrust my breast into her mouth and she takes it, sucking in as much as will fill her mouth.

Her hand has moved down between my legs, seeking in my vagina, so wet and open. She slips her fingers into me, moving them inside, and the heel of her hand slowly rubs my tight clitoris. My clitoris is a nipple now, wanting to be sucked.

My hands grip Jeanine's back, kneading her shoulders, pressing her to me. We are slippery with sweat where we touch. My mouth is hungry to taste her.

Jeanine lifts up, turns, leaving my breast to cradle my hips, lifting her leg across me. Just before she lowers herself onto me, I look up into the dark expanse of hair between her thighs, reach to spread the small silkily pink lips of her vagina. On the wall above the moons of her buttocks, leaps the silver-bodied woman in ecstatic movement.

Then she is upon me, her mouth closing over my cunt, her breasts pressing into my belly, the weight of her hips on my shoulders, and, at last, the hot, soft opening of her vagina for my mouth to suck and stroke. Jeanine moans, moves in quick instinctive shudders as she settles on me. I receive the weight and feel of her whole body; it opens me more. My face is lost in her cunt. We have become one being, our movement taking us in an ancient joyous pattern. There is no inside or outside. There is only this movement, yet I know I grip Jeanine's buttocks, stroke her back, press her even closer inside me. Within the storm of desire are the subtle movements of the dance in our bodies, moving deep inside us, taking us to that moment of dissolution.

Jeanine hums into my vagina, the vibrations lifting my body as I hear the pulse of the prayer wheel loud in the room. We are nothing but sound now, carried out beyond the limits of our minds, as our movement becomes an uncontrollable undulation. I know only the pungent hot softness of her cunt, my face plunged into it to suck and suck. Her own sucking sends waves up through me. The urgency peaks, and there is a moment of wanting so intense it feels like pain. I thrust against her and her mouth presses on me, hard now, she'll stay with me, she'll come with me, I suck and suck.

The moment breaks. I turn my head to muffle my cries against the soft flesh of her thigh. Long high ragged sounds are torn from me. I feel her groan of completion vibrating into my cunt, as my hips jerk, my fingers twitch against her back.

And then we are free, floating outside our contours in emptiness. A stillness, a perfect stasis opens beneath us.

Peace.

I let my arms fall from her body as I lie beneath her. She has rested her cheek against my thigh, absolutely still.

Turning my head I open my eyes to see the dancing goddess once again. She has returned into her fixity, one bangled foot eternally raised. But I see that the expression of her open mouth, which I had interpreted as a fierce snarl, is instead a smile of such rending sweetness that it draws from me a long quavering sigh.

"Yes, love," Jeanine answers me. "Oh, yes, my darling," her breath hot against the inside of my thigh.

We hold each other for a long time before we are able to sit up. And then it is a while before she lifts the dress to slip it over my head, stopping to kiss me, our mouths slippery, wet with the heavy odor of our bodies. Then I watch the purple blouse eclipse her breasts, the jeans slip up over her thighs. We stand touching each other gently, hands on each other's waist, and I sink into those dark eyes, so open now, carrying me deep. The sound of the prayer wheel is a steady throb, reminding us of the eternity we have just left. As we lift the curtain to go out, I glance back at the woman whose body flashes in her dance, whose golden face beams at me.

When we stand outside the room, smoothing our clothes, we have entered another reality. A lighted corridor, blue-paneled, stretches away to the stairs. Closed doors flank us. Jeanine and I look at each other with wide open, sated eyes.

We wander off separately, I to find Ralph, who waits for me on the porch.

"You disappeared," he says, without reproach.

"Feeling better?" he asks as he helps me into the car. And as he gets in the other side he fixes me with a concerned gaze. "You look...hmmm...more relaxed..."

I can only nod, mutely gazing at his long serious face.

We drive beneath old trees, heavily black and looming in the dark. High above is the pale crescent of moon. The night seems ancient beyond believing.

Care in the Holding

MAUREEN BRADY

LAURA WAITED NERVOUSLY while the woman filled out the contract for the rental car. "Two seater okay?" she asked.

"Sure," Laura replied, confused about the question which barely touched down in her float of mind. What was she renting—a motorcycle? Minutes later, she found herself checking out the two-seater—indeed a car—a sporty Ford with bucket seats up front and a long hatch in back. Placing her directions on the other seat, she headed for the Bay Bridge, for her rendezvous with Chana, whom she was picking up at cousin Richard's in Berkeley Hills. Her mind printed an image of Chana—brown eyes with a sparkle in them, soft cheeks, sweet smell—and her heart sent a streak of excitement straight down her gut and into her loins. She'd be lucky if she made the right turns, so excited to distraction was she. She'd been sitting on this excitement a whole month now, since the hike they'd taken back east, which had tripped off a great glow in her heart.

She pulled off the road and stopped in the hills when she sensed she was nearly there, and tried to gather herself. Prepare. For what? She *knew* it would be good. She *knew* they liked each other. She *knew* the day on the mountain had been like magic and they were the same two women coming together again. Breathe, she said to herself. She took ten long, deep breaths. On the tenth she realized she hadn't even checked to see if the charge was correct before signing the contract for the car rental. She dug it out and looked and got further confused because they hadn't filled in the charges. But, of course: they were waiting to see if she'd return it on time.

More deep breaths. She felt light-headed, maybe hyperventilation. What will she be like? The streak of adrenalin in her gut again. The feel of energy in her center, intense, like if *she* wasn't going to move that car, her clitoris would be willing to drive. Go on. Jump. The waiting has been long enough already.

She started up the car. The next left was the cousin's street and time speeded up. She was at the door ringing the doorbell. The door was large, opened out. Disorienting. She'd pictured Chana receiving her, inward, with the opening of a door, but now this door. What?

Chana pushed it open, came out herself with the door and gently hugged Laura, who was near to fainting. Chana radiant, wearing red, eyes friendly; her short dark hair started down over her forehead, then curled back. She invited Laura in. Laura smiled yes, speechless, don't ask me to talk. Chana took her to the back porch where cousin Richard and girlfriend were sitting. They showed off a hummingbird, and the flutter of the hummingbird's wings felt like the stir inside her chest. The house was built on the side of a hill, and the porch felt as if it was suspended in air. She glanced at Chana, caught the intensity of her beauty, and felt as if the house was going to slide down the cliff. Said to herself: keep breathing. Said to them: "Exciting to live here. You must feel on the edge all the time."

"I don't notice it at all," said cousin Richard, oblivious to the intensity of her feelings.

Chana took Laura on a tour of the house. In the bathroom,

she kissed her. Laura held Chana's head, held their cheeks pressed together and, heart pounding, began to feel recognition from the last time. She felt the ways they were strangers acutely, and wanted to hold their bodies together until they knew all the connections that were there.

"Let's say goodbye and go," Chana said. Her cousin wrote out a series of turns to the Richmond Bridge. Chana seemed composed, able to follow the directions, while glancing at Laura, flirting with the sparkle in her eyes. Laura went closer to the edge of the porch, looked out over the long view, but still couldn't look down.

They left. They got lost on the first turn but drove on somewhat aimlessly. "What's your take?" Laura asked Chana.

"I think this will get us there."

"I like the way you follow your instincts," Laura said, going on down through Berkeley, feeling both cocky and lost. They were getting to know each other the same way. Laura alternated between having faith in that instinctual plane and feeling a stranger, both to herself and to Chana. What if they were going blocks and blocks in the wrong direction? She wanted to be at the ocean, out of the car. She wanted to be where they could hold each other. Yet she was glad to have the mission of driving. Needed time to establish a sense of Chana in the real flesh, not fantasy, before they made love. For the past month, they had written sweet and tender love letters; encouraging words, sharing of fragments of their lives such as food tastes, favorite books, excitement about the work each was doing at the moment. Laura had been in residence at a West Coast artists' retreat, while Chana had been home in New York preparing to turn over her first book to her publisher.From the moment she'd arrived in her place of retreat, Laura had noticed that the bedroom alcove was more fit for romance than for thinking up stories. The king-sized bed was made enchanting by the two walls of windows, which wrapped around it. Outside, the branches of an oak reached in close to the windows, and the patterns of the leaves, black at night, had a dreamy feeling to them. In the moonlight they lost their distinct edges and became blots placed in some mysterious order. They offered an entirely different impression, green, in the mornings. She had loved sleeping there, dropping into the dream reality of night, then waking into a gentle California green. She woke with a kind of relaxed openness she hadn't experienced for a long time. And it was in that openness she yearned to wake and look upon Chana's sleeping face next to her. She wanted that openness, that wonder she had seen in Chana's eyes as they pulled back from kissing up on the mountain and looked each other full in the face.

They had found and crossed the Richmond Bridge and were headed for the coast when they came into a misty fog. This was Laura's first time seeing it like this. The other times she'd driven up Route One she'd seen that magnificent long view of the rugged shoreline from the headlands. Now the fog closed around them, and even when she knew they were near the ocean, she couldn't make it out. She'd only imagined bringing Chana here to the long view. Taking her by the hand and leading her down to a quiet spot on the hill and watching her take it in. The view awesome as the strong feeling that travled breast to breast as they held each other. Now what? Chana took her hand and kissed it softly, then held it to her own heart. Laura smiled, warm inside. Scared, too. Who was Chana? Who was she? Why were they feeling so much while knowing so little about each other? She darted looks at Chana but the curving road required her attention. Next time she saw a place to pull off, she did. Said let's go down the hill a little and see if we can hear the ocean.

They both got out. Laura stretched, releasing some of the tension. It took a second for her to realize she was standing still, it was the car that was moving. Rolling backwards. She ran for the door and hit the brake. Embarrassed at her driving ineptitude, she turned red. "You're distracted," Chana said, coming around. Laura put the car in Park and pulled hard on the emergency brake, then laughed. "The navigator will have to see that the car is not left in neutral." Chana pulled her out and hugged her and kissed her. "Lucky we weren't on a big hill," she said.

They moved down to a point where they could see the waves crashing in on the rocks below. First they sat huddled close, as they had on the mountain, and kissed, smelled each other's hair, felt the deep magnitude pulling between them. Then they lay down. The fog created a room for them. They couldn't see the road or the sky. Sometimes they could see the ocean, sometimes not, but always they could hear its rhythm. They held each other and rocked together. "How I've longed for this," Laura whispered. "I know. I know," Chana replied. Their lust flushed their faces as they lay side by side, the full length of their bodies pressed close. The fog provided privacy. The room it made for them was impersonal, without decoration. It had no square corners, no flat walls. It moved in close. A gentle kiss grew into deep passion. When they looked again, the fog had thinned and the room expanded.

Laura felt one with her body and with the cliff they lay on. Her hand moved slowly up and down, charting the soft contours of Chana's body, remembering the curve of her back from the last time. She followed the line of Chana's firm thigh and pictured the gracefulness with which she must run.

Chana pressed her pelvis closer and Laura's lust peaked in response, sending charges like lightning, sharp through her body and back to Chana. She was breathless, delirious, joyous. Chana murmured how she loved her smell, rolled on her back, and Laura rolled with her so she was on top. Laura pressed into her, tasted and smelled Chana's neck, and inhaled deeply of the moist ocean air. She felt the hummingbird stir in her chest while her cunt both beamed a radiant heat and received the hot waves of Chana's sexual energy. Suddenly she wanted her naked. She wanted to be inside her, feeling the moisture she knew was there, wanted to have her own self known that way, free of the covering and constriction of clothes, but she knew this, just as it was, a kind of bliss, deserved its full due. Like a rose opening to full bloom, beautiful in all its stages, it had a timing of its own. She arched her head back and saw in Chana's face a desire that matched hers. How expressive that face was, how its movement reminded her of the waves below. Desire charging, cresting, then ebbing back as her closed lips fell into a quiet smile, broadening her face. Time was no more distinct than the boundaries of the room—seemed long if Laura thought of how much she was alive for each one of the minutes, short in the sense that there was no more waiting, waiting was over.

They stopped in a small beach town for coffee before going on to Laura's studio. Chana did most of the talking. Laura had trouble taking in the words or being verbal herself, though she wanted to make herself known this way. She had the precipice feeling again, like she'd had on Richard's porch, just from sitting across the table from Chana. She found her beauty so striking she was surprised the other people in the coffee shop were acting as if it were an ordinary day and not noticing this clear-eyed, extraordinary woman sitting across from her, sipping coffee and radiating joy. She went to the restroom and confirmed in the mirror that, sure enough, it *was* possible to see the radiance that *she* was exuding, as well. Her eyes looked greener, her hair looked a shiny, light brown. Her skin looked soft and clear, ruddy and inviting. The warmth in her pulsed so she felt brought close to her own essence.

When they arrived at the studio, she felt this closeness still, but also the strangeness of the place, hers but not hers, a gift for the month, and the strangeness of their knowing nothing of each other's homes. She led Chana around, pointing out the skylight dome at the peak of the building, the deck, the small kitchen, the charming bath. Still holding her hand, she led her down the two steps into the bedroom alcove. She fell onto the bed and leaned back, gazing out on her familiar and favorite view. "Come." She reached toward Chana, who stood smiling, then came down next to her. "It is paradise," she said, her voice almost husky. "You weren't making that up."

"Especially now with you here, it is," Laura said.

Then they held each other and Laura's breath went away. She gasped for it somewhere under the lust. She felt the firmness of her own body as well as Chana's as they held tight. It was dusk and the light played on Chana's face which was wonderfully variable. Sometimes soft with pleasure, sometimes scared, or suffused with passion—all looks welcomed by Laura as they broached the complexity of her own feelings. If she and Chana truly were strangers, why did their bodies seem already so well acquainted? And more than acquainted, as if they'd been waiting and yearning a long time for this meeting.

They kissed deeply. Laura rolled on top. Chana put her hand at the base of Laura's spine and rocked her back and forth in a gentle rhythm, and Laura felt the sweet warmth growing in her cunt. She ran her fingers through Chana's hair, held her lovely head, and loved the rhythm they both followed then. Chana pulled their shirts up enough so their bare bellies touched and the warmth spread more fully to there. Laura felt their belly skins kissing—soft coverings overlying those guts pitched high with risk. She rose to take her top off and pulled Chana's off as well. Then they lay breast to breast and felt that warmth course through their chests. Laura cupped one of Chana's breasts in her hand and nuzzled down and tongued the nipple and watched it come erect. When she leaned back to look at Chana's face, Chana admired her breasts, saying they were perfect. Laura murmured her response. They rolled so that Chana was on top. Chana built on the same gentle but spunky rhythm. They built but did not come. What Laura needed for orgasm was no greater intensity than what they had already created; it was the building of trust. To feel the care behind Chana's caresses. And to trust that care.

Laura was raw in places, thin skinned in her healing from the break up with her lover of many years. It had been four months since she'd left their home, their bed, many more since they'd been really alive, sexually, with each other. She remembered times when they'd put great effort into making love and she'd stayed for a long time on the brink, almost coming off that edge but not quite, not quite able to. She remembered after her father died, when she came back home from the funeral, how she felt so alone. Bess didn't seem to really be there. She was, but she wasn't. Laura didn't seem able to ask her for what she needed. More holding. More care. More care in the holding. Bess was still depressed herself from having lost her job, and Bess came from a family where death passed in silence, feelings held in. So Laura had gotten on this brink and stayed there, knowing if she came it would be with a burst of tears, that her pleasure was enfolded by her grief. Sharing the pleasure when she was not able to get the care seemed a betrayal of her body. And her body, often truer to her than her mind, balked. "It's okay," she'd told Bess. "We don't have to be so goal oriented." But Bess became reluctant to initiate sex with her, and this at a time when she wanted Bess to do the reaching.

Chana on top of her was close to her own size. Bess had been a good deal heavier, and this position had verged on feeling stifling to her with Bess. She felt a wave of freedom at having made this choice, and the wave brought her back to the glow in her belly, in her loins. At the same time, she felt tears very close to her pleasure. Chana was rocking her again. Comforting. The rhythm was right for her. How did Chana know to make it that way? Laura looked again to take in her face. Sweet, soft, mystery. She also has memory, she thought. Of what? Of whom? Where did this bonding, this movement towards intimacy, take her? Her concentration was strong, she was all there, deeply inside her body. She called Laura's name. She said, you, you, and Laura was wakened further by the call.

They stopped to kick off their pants and then coming together again was like another new meeting. Like when the door opened out and Chana came with it. Like when they first lay on the cliff and held their bodies full length. Their bellies and breasts, their lips and cheeks came back together, familiar, still new but knowledgeable, warmed to each other. Laura put her thigh between Chana's and felt the softness of the skin that pressed her own. She felt the moisture of Chana's cunt and the beam of heat that burned out from her. She held still because the feeling inside her was already so full and she just wanted to feel it. A deep satisfaction with the awakening of all her senses, her cells. She breathed in the sweet odor of

Chana's neck, squeezed her own thighs and felt the heat coming out of herself. She reached to feel Chana's cunt. So nicely risen, soft and full like a bread with good yeast. Her finger slipped on the wetness as she explored. She felt both nervous and exhiliarated, like nearing the peak the first time she climbed a new mountain. Would she be lost? Would she be found? Hearing Chana's response, she knew when her touch was right. She slid into Chana's vagina, a close cave, warm and moist and soft as velvet. A home. A mystery. How perfect that vagina felt and how forceful its being. Like the tide they'd felt while lying in the fog. She wanted to look, and did. Pulled away from Chana and ran her fingers up the path between the lips of her vulva and saw how pink she was. "A beautiful pink garden," she murmured. Her own excitement increased with her words. She had rarely before expressed herself this way. It was a way of being active, of putting the feelings outside, between them, instead of tucked up close to her heart in a bundle the other would have to slowly work to penetrate. A garden was a place to grow in, a place of wonder. These caresses were the seeding of a love which might grow between them.

Chana pulled her back to a long body embrace, breast to breast. She held Laura tight around the hips and Laura felt the energy build heat in her belly. She felt the waves of Chana's energy driving her own higher. She felt her heart so full of feeling. This woman was a stranger, yet she knew her. The whole month following their hike back in the East, she'd felt Chana's presence very close beside her. A loving presence like a guardian angel. She'd felt her spirit in that very bed, and ached with wanting to have her physical presence there.

Chana on top, raised herself up. She was radiant. Her eyes were joyous. Laura ran her fingers through her dark hair, which stood up from her head. Chana kissed Laura's breasts, her belly, as she moved down to Laura's cunt. There she became the explorer, parting Laura's lips and searching the area gently with her fingers, then licking her. Kissing her. Sucking softly. Laura kept her hands in Chana's soft hair to anchor herself as she rocked her pelvis. She felt vulnerable with the absence of Chana's chest against her own,

with the open air embracing her there instead, but she could feel
love in Chana's mouth on her if she allowed herself to feel there
between her legs. It was hard for her to allow full attention concentrated on herself when she was not in the process of actively giving.
But she talked to herself: Said take it. Let her love you. Let her
find her own pleasure in this. Trust. The receiving required more
trust for her than the giving. But when she was able to take in the
giving, she glowed inside and moved her pelvis in a way that welcomed Chana's loving. She felt very full. She was on the verge of
orgasm. She was on the verge of tears. What would it mean to cry
in this woman's arms the first time they'd ever made love? She did
not come. She did not cry. Chana came back to hold her full length,
her lips next to Laura's ear. Spoke in her soft voice, "I want you to
come."

Laura's lust peaked at this spoken desire. "I'm moved by the
way you touch me, the way you kiss me," she said, knowing as she
released these words, they would take her past the tears.

"You can feel that. . .and, still come," Chana said with quiet assurance.

"What about you?" Laura asked.

"I'm easy," Chana replied.

Laura felt the jets of adrenalin shooting from her heart to her
belly. She felt her desire growing deeper, like a powerful undertow.
Growing stronger and hotter as Chana's invitation ran in her mind.
She reached down between them and spread both their lips so her
clitoris pressed directly into Chana's, and moved against it. Chana
whispered sweet words in her ear. Sometimes she couldn't make them
out, but she could feel the care in them, the concentration. This
was Laura and Chana together. Their histories were in them, all of
the love makings of the past, but this now *was them*. Laura whispered
Chana's name. She let her mind go. She was her body. She was the
fire and the spirit that moved inside her. She rode it. She had been
a long time waiting. Then she tripped off the edge and gasped and
felt the glow spread inside her, like a sun coming out strong from

behind a cloud. She moaned her pleasure. She felt the tenderness of Chana's arms around her. Her breath came quieter as she lay with her gratitude for the way this was possible, for the miracle of this woman, Chana.

Chana proved her ease. She moved with a confident connection to her body. She built, then stopped still for a moment, savoring some place she had reached she did not want to pass. Then she moved again. She was calling Laura's name, she was speaking to her cunt. Laura looked at her face—so full, so fine with desire, it fired her. Then Chana's breath turned to cries, each breath was a cry, each cry had an echo. Each echo touched Laura's heart. She held her. She held her. She was so happy to be holding her.

An American in Paris

KIM CHERNIN

I KEEP TELLING MYSELF that I am very calm, lying on the hotel bed, waiting for the phone to ring. But I am not calm. I am remembering things. Some of them from three and a half years ago. Some from today, wandering about through the piles of leaves that have not even bothered to turn yellow before they drop from the tree. Probably this happens in other places too, but I always think of it as distinctly and outrageously Parisian.

It is late fall, everyone is back in Paris. Today I went over to the cafe where I first met her and they refused to let me have a seat by myself near the window. I had spent the morning in the Turkish bath, my first morning in Paris, lying about for hours in the steam rooms before retiring to the outer chamber. If I close my eyes now I can see it all very clearly: fountain at the center of the room, the stained-glass windows; coats, scarves, clothes hanging beneath them; on the covered mattresses, legs curled up, leaning together, lying down, naked, wrapped in towels, drinking mint tea, eating pastries and fruit, the women talk together in a sprawl of purses and colored plastic bags, massage one another, sit with their eyes closed, keep an eye on each other.

Years ago I heard about this place from her, she mentioned it casually but it stayed in my mind. From the first moment she spoke of it, I thought: "Someday I'm going to come back here, it's going to happen and she will go there with me."

Today, waiting for her to get back from Zurich, I have run through everything by myself. The Turkish bath, the long, cold walk through vaguely familiar streets where I used to walk by myself, the deliberate stroll through the Luxembourg Gardens. It occurred to me, as I stood at the gate facing the cafe, the last time I had done this, leaving the garden, scanning the tables across the street, she was no part of my life. Even the idea of her had not yet come into my consciousness, because I was going to that cafe to meet someone else. She just happened to be there. And happened to know the woman I was meeting.

And then I ran across the street, found the friend who was waiting to meet me, was introduced to Anna. We had breakfast together the next day: coffee cooling, forgotten, indifferently sipped when I could manage to take my eyes from her. Both of us jumping up to hail a cab, race back to my hotel to gather my luggage, the cab waiting, so that I would not miss my plane. I thought, absurdly, putting my arms around this stranger to hug her good-bye, "How will I go on living without this woman?"

It has taken me three and a half years to risk seeing her again, to dare this offer of myself as lover. I look ten years older, I am too thin, I have come back with my pride and arrogance as a lover stripped away, I have let myself be broken in heart during these years and now I can't even say I believe in love any more, certainly not in that kind which roars and breaks into flame and feels fated to transform you and ends badly and drags you down into the most carefully hidden secrets of your past and leaves you there, howling in darkness, to work it out on your own.

I run the water for the shower, pretending to be calm, waiting to hear her voice, wondering how she is feeling, on her train back from Zurich. Is she, too, scared of what we are risking? The audacity of it? Dragging this fantasy by the hair from its dark corner to make it face reality? Is she trying not to think too precisely, as I, too, am not thinking? I remember her face, the broad forehead, high cheekbones, wide, expressive mouth, those yellow, almost slanted eyes with their warmth and intelligence and straightforwardness and provocation. She is taller than I am, more broadly built; the first time I saw her, wearing a T-shirt, her neck and back and arms filmed over with that dark tan only blond people seem to get, I thought immediately I would like to dance with her.

The phone rings; I come running from the shower, pouring with water, to grab the receiver, the shower thundering behind me, the bed already sopping as I leap on and crouch down and hold the receiver to say hello to her. Hello, Anna . . .

The taxi drops me expertly at her door. I'm all thumbs now, counting out the unfamiliar money, laughing at myself a bit too shrilly. He turns on the light to look at me, watches me fumbling with the coins in my palm, very slowly counts them out for me, refusing a tip. Standing in front of the building where she lives I can't manage to get the street door open. I push and shake at it, set my shoulder against it, stand back, feeling ridiculous. So easy to make a fool of oneself at this moment. She could so easily not be what I remember, I certainly am not what I have always pretended to be, a self-assured lover.

At the sixth floor I have trouble with the elevator doors. I jiggle the handle, get the strap of my purse caught in my hands, make use of my shoulder again and then stand there waiting, wondering if someone will come to let me out of this little glass cage.

Am I behaving like this in order to remind myself that my proud sense of invincibility was torn away months ago and can't be drawn on again as a protective cloak? I could weep with shame and embarrassment, dressed in tight pants, polished boots, scarf wound three times around my neck, Parisian fashion. I remember her riding up on her bicycle to have breakfast with me. The way she got off the bike fast to come greet me, putting down the bag of croissants on the table. The sense she gave of a vital intelligence, her face so beautiful in its animation, warm, engaged, intensely alive. I was fascinated by a grace of being, gestures you don't forget for years after, the way her smile carries a memory of earlier sadness, something in her larger than herself looking out through her. She has a way of stopping, holding herself very still, looking straight into your eyes and saying nothing; she holds your gaze, her eyes are open, she is not afraid of this silence, she is thinking, considering what you have said, gathering her agreement or disagreement, the yellow eyes hide nothing, finally she speaks.

I am no longer beautiful, I tell myself, getting out of the elevator at last to walk through the darkness of the hall. Why should this woman whose footsteps I hear on the other side of the door find me any more appealing than a hundred others who have stood waiting for her to open this door?

She kisses me on one cheek; we are awkward and embarrassed in this first moment, I have turned my cheek to receive her other kiss and she has already moved away from me. "So," I say, "it really is you, after all." "Are you surprised?" she says, laughing at me. She looks older, her eyes still yellow, she is taller than I remembered, her hair shorter. It is the same face and I feel ready to cry with the relief of it.

We sit down at the small wooden table, across from one another. She offers me a Eucalyptus cigarette, she seems calm, she leans over to light the small, tightly rolled cigarette for me. She sits very straight, she holds her arm close to her chest, hand raised, holding the cigarette to her lips, head tipped to the side, slightly. "It is three and a half years," I say. "I hardly recognize you," she answers, "you have become a different person." Whatever this is, the conversation building itself from the first moment between us, creating this series of tunnels leading to new vistas, from which we turn back into the chambers and rooms of our shared preoccupations, always in step, reaching out to take one another by the hand or arm at exactly the right moment—it is already a way of being lovers.

We have stood up from the table and gone into the little kitchen to make dinner. I wash the lettuce once only, she doesn't approve. "Just be glad I don't send you back to wash it three times," she says. We are eating rice-and-ginger soup, she dresses the salad. We are telling each other about our sisters who have died. Both of us are crying. We do not ask how we have come to be so intimate.

My hands have stopped shaking. I have my elbows on the table, leaning toward her. We have spoken about her writing and mine, women we have loved, a psychic who told her she had lived many lives before and always as a man, we tell each other about our favorite books, her childhood in Germany, mine in the Bronx. By the time she has driven me back to my hotel we have a history together, the kiss on one cheek, the lettuce I washed once only, the way she showed me to tie a scarf when I asked her: patiently, very precisely. In bed with my eyes open I see her growing out over the earlier memories and I ask myself, Will it be only friendship? She has a lover who lives in Germany. What do I bring that could make her want me?

Morning again, I walk back to her across streets with green leaves piled up underfoot. At the small bakery on the corner I buy bread and croissants for breakfast, Normandy butter, small bottles of yogurt. We are at the little table in the dining room again, drinking coffee from white ceramic cups. I look up, push back my plate and it is evening. I am very tired, far from home, I have walked on nails for two thousand years, trying to find this woman. I remember her, a young Polish boy, setting out for the first time for Paris. The way she gathered the traveling cloak around both of us, against the cold. It was not the first time she said good-bye and I never saw her again. I like the way she stands up from the table to take down a bottle of wine from the shelf overhead without interrupting what she is saying. The authority, the unintended grace of it enter me like pieces of glass. I want to lie down in her arms, my head against her breast, from this I feel desire coming, for the first time ever desire is to be taken, taken care of, to give self in exchange for this.

I am so small, so ugly, so infinitely undesirable. Is it because I've lost the fierceness that disguised this secret need to be cared for by another woman? Has that nakedness revealed a nakedness I've never risked before? And so, I tell myself, as the talk draws us out of her flat; and soon we are walking together along dusk-gathering streets, the others going toward home, fast, purposeful; this is the reason to go slowly, one could not, in the beginning of anything, risk showing that need at its fullest, not to a stranger.

Leaving the restaurant, she puts her arm through my arm. I take her hand, draw it toward me, let it go. But now I will it to return, to find my shoulder, to push back the high collar of my sweater, to expose me. It is a rare joy to walk fast in the sudden very great, dry, winter cold. We are wearing ten-league boots, scarves around our necks, long jackets not really adequate against the cold I love, she does not love it. I can't figure out how we will move from this kinship of mind to a comradeship of body. This could so easily be the beginning of friendship. Between women, as always, impossible to tell.

It has become the third day. We move to a warmer table in the back corner of our cafe, drinking cognac and small cups of espresso, our scarves and bags and coats piled up next to us. People stare at us. There is something about her that says, Love me and you will not end your days dozing at the fire. I think of high places when I look at her. Sometimes, when she gazes back at me in silence there is a hot, still land, more austere than southern, but gracious still with its hills and vineyards. *"Kennst du das Land?"* she says, reading my thoughts. And I answer, recognizing Goethe, *"Dahin, möcht' ich mit dir. . ."*

We do not speak of our relationship, will we be lovers, is there a future, do I love her? I tell myself it is too soon to know. Shall we ever figure it out? One day, perhaps, something will happen and we shall find out. Or it will not happen.

Night has come down over Paris. There is fog, and now from her window we see a light moving above Sacré Coeur, selecting this one building out of all others for our enlightenment. Perhaps we have stood like this at home together many times in some other life. In front of the refrigerator she takes my hand; for a moment there is not the slightest awkwardness between us and I do not know why it has ended, perhaps simply it moved on into the making of salad and soup. "No," I tell myself, "It will not happen." And I understand finally that I have taken it all wrong. This ease between us will make us friends for a lifetime, that is what I have come to learn from her. Intimacy, untroubled by eros.

I am saddened by this, listening to Mahler, both of us standing very still, across the room from one another. She says: "I see another person in you again. You are constantly changing. It's hard to keep up with you. But I like it. With you one never knows what to expect. This one," she stops to consider it: "this person I see now is eight years old."

"Eight years old? Really?" My voice sounds surprised but it is only an effort to gain time. I am trying to adjust myself to the quick change in my perception, something very large has been set in motion, it concerns our bodies, the way blood moves through them, tides of desire and retreat which will not ask us if we are willing. Tomorrow perhaps we shall make plans, a month from now I will call her from California. I shall have put up on my wall, across from my bed, near the door, that photograph of her I saw in her study. Each time I walk out into the hall I will touch the curls in her short hair combed straight back from her forehead. And even then we will go on pretending it is up to us. But for now, in this moment, I know. If I step forward, if I put my fingertips against her cheeks, I will have crossed a line that calls into question my entire life.

I feel it in my breath, in the quick heat of my cheeks, something fundamental to be risked here although I don't yet know the name for what it will cost to love this woman and how it will test me if it does not break me. What was it she said, with anger, of a well-known German actress? "To fall into a lesbian bed, that is not the same thing as to be lesbian."

She is standing with one arm against the table, looking at me very seriously. It is a moment of great delicacy. The words we speak can't do it justice, we have to trust to what we hear in the silence between words, the tension our bodies cast into the space between us.

"Perhaps because I'm feeling so shy? That brings out the child in me? I feel completely unnerved by this vulnerability in my body."

I observe the way her head is turned toward me and does not turn away. She holds my gaze, reading me deeply. "You give an entirely different impression," she says, slowly, as if it were very important to get it right. "You seem at ease. . ." She hesitates, looks for the word, finds it in German. *Ja, gelassen.*

"Calm?" I remember the word from a translation of her story we had worked on earlier in the day. "I feel. . . I'll show you." I put my hands in my pockets and push, with the toe of my shoe, lightly against the rug, looking down and to the side, the way an eight-year-old might, feeling embarrassed and awkward.

"No," she says, "I don't believe it. To me you seem completely at peace in your body."

And then we find nothing further to say. I have no more skill now as a lover than I must have had when I was a child, a tough girl playing with older boys at the edge of the woods, playing with knives. I do not dare to look at her. I can feel her breathing, as if she were standing very close to me. But she is still across the room, near the table. It seems to me very dangerous to let this moment pass. If we deny it we will not dare to arrive at its brink again. Love is lost or gained at moments like this.

I want to hold out my hand to her, but I am incapable of physical motion.

"I am at ease in my body," I say, wondering what I am going to say next. "Yes," I repeat, with a sense that my words are going nowhere at all, "with my body I am at ease." And then I realize that the way has been cleared for me. It happens and it is so simple. "The shyness I feel? That exists only because of what I feel for you..."

There is an infinity of silence; more than enough in which to die of shame. Suppose, I say to myself, she feels nothing like this for me? And then I notice she is no longer standing across from me. She has walked across the space between us, matching risk to risk. It is like the time I ran across the street from the Luxembourg to meet her for the first time. Now she has made the crossing to me.

But I need time for the unique desire that is my desire for her, nothing in it borrowed from an impersonal need to possess a woman, to take her, to make her mine. I don't want to make love to her, I can't possibly, I am eight years old.

"Let's stay children," I say, finally. "I am not ready for anything else."

We sit down on the little bed made for me in the dining room. Suddenly, I want to cry, with the immense improbability this could be happening, this woman from the cafe from the Paris summer three and a half years ago, about to become my lover? My body, inhabited still by its shyness, is making small gestures of contact, all I can manage, touching her knee, holding her hand, letting my hand move through that boyish haircut of hers. And now my face is being held, she has put her hands against my temples. She is looking at me with an expression that says, "Foolish one, why did it take you so long to understand?"

Someone has said—it must have been Anna—we would probably be more comfortable in the bedroom. We are taking hands, old comrades walking together the long, terrible distance. We are in that space lovers create that changes the laws of space for one another, proving two objects can be in the same place at the same time. We are sitting as much as lying, I am moving toward her, it is she who is below me, her face lifted, it surprises me, I would have imagined it otherwise if I'd dared to imagine, I giving myself, she the receiver.

I hear myself speaking. "I don't want to make love to you," I say. "Not now, not tonight. I'm afraid that way I won't get to know you..."

"Could you really still stop now?" She has raised her head to look at me curiously. I think: the seduction of this woman is the way she does not seduce. Her mystery a clarity so rare it becomes in the next instant a great secret, what she has been through to make it possible?

"Yes, I could still stop," I say, because I feel, growing with the inclination of my hands to close around her, an even stronger desire not to do it in the old way. "Yes, I could still stop now if you asked me."

But my hands have begun to act according to their own wisdom, opening her scarf, touching her neck with a growing certainty, her neck keeps arching back beneath my hands, in that unmistakable arc of a woman giving herself so that something in me finally moves and bends me over and I am unbuttoning her blouse.

I do not know how she has come to be undressed, on another night I will undress her, touching her skin with my mouth as her jeans are drawn down over her stomach. This first night I wouldn't have dared. Somehow her blouse is off and the black strap of her chemise has been slipped down over her shoulder and then her breasts are bare and I have my hands on them. Then she is completely naked, standing while I am clothed, kneeling on the bed. I say, taking her hand to bring her down next to me: "How do you manage to disguise it? I'd never believe it." And she, laughing at my surprise, knows immediately I mean her body. It is more voluptuous, rounder, than one could possibly guess from her short hair, wearing jeans, disguised as a boy.

There is another gap. Both of us are naked now, we are sitting opposite one another, our foreheads touching, two candles are burning on the floor below the long window and beyond Paris, inescapable, reduced now to a single, old stone wall.

And now I, with the sense that I am letting myself grow down into a greater depth of myself than I had before now known existed, draw back from her and let myself be seen. "I see a fear of death in your eyes," she says, making me understand, for the first time, what it means to be naked. "A fear of death and sadness."

I sit very still, very cold, there is sweat on my forehead, she is seeing me as a small child watching my sister die. This fear I bring to whatever I love. Something inside me shaking itself open. Tears come out of it. "You have another face too," I say. "It is more than sad; there is in it an utter despair, a bleak desolation. . .terrible exhaustion." I am terrified by what I hear myself saying, surely she will draw back now to hide this true face of the self never shown to another person?

We hold still, neither of us knowing if we see only self in the other. Or see indeed the other? The difference useless, it will later be clear to us. We can see in the other only what each is able to know in herself.

The room is dark in spite of the two candles. I look out into the darkness, not really able to believe that my eyes are open. I want to go back into hiding, into an impersonal desire, but it is too late. I know now how to smell, to taste, to touch, to breathe her in, to make her cross the boundaries of self, to enter me through every pore and sense and mouth and opening long before her fingers enter. We are whispering something, back and forth, in this rhythm we do not create, from which the new selves still not born, still entangled together here, will be created out of the promise of that hot summer day, that seemingly casual meeting of strangers. "Yes, this," she says, "tenderness, this is the way, like this, like this."

And now I come to her with the entire history of my loves and heartbreak, vulnerable, unprotected, shaking in the naked revelation of self. I know the way to make love to this woman, my hands respond now to the silent calling of her body. Infant screeching for breast, small child raped in the cellar, young girl reaching out with very cautious hand to touch the naked belly of another girl.

Stroking her under her arm, kissing her left ear, studying each place from which the quick intake of breath arises, hollow of waist, curve of thigh, asking for me. The bed is crowded now. There is scarcely room for us here. I have brought into this room my mother, every woman I have ever wanted and feared to love. Breast against breast, how do I find her? This body almost my own, how tell her from the woman who did not call back, the woman who begged for love I could not give, the woman who grew cold, the woman who could never forget me?

My mouth feeling its way, her thighs grow from my lips. My tongue says this is what flesh means dissolving between us. Is she Lindenbaum, blue gate on its hinge, fountain overgrown with wanderer's sorrow? Will I be small enough to fit into her hands? Large enough to forget: adolescent love. Insane after a year of separation. Woman with flea powder in her hair. Woman loved and lost the eve of my wedding.

Her hands in my hair, closing around my head, her hands making their way, neck, shoulders, taking hold there, waist, hips, finding their handhold, growing up out of my skin.

We have gone back to origins, the forced passage, cave of myself in which I find her, putting my mouth to her, down in the wet salt heat of our beginnings. Woman with the name of mother.

There is no need to weep, I am wet with love, she takes me in the same act by which she gives herself to me, rocked out together on strange seas of forgiveness and redemption, forehead to forehead, mouth to mouth in this act of mutual surrender, later we call it intimacy. Tonight, falling into the self of the other, we say: Let it be love.

Spring Blossoms

TEE A. CORINNE

SPRING WAS A FEAST this year: waxy snow drops first and violets, pink and white and many purples, then yellow daffodils and small translucent white ones and creamy ones with egg-yoke yellow centers. Tiny spring beauties sprouted near the mailbox, vinca minor turned their small cobalt faces up from rich greenery. Flowering quince exploded overnight into labia-orange rays.

I reached for you in the morning, every morning, feeling myself flowering too, my own sap rising and spilling over into an excess of energy, of passion, of sheer exhuberant good spirits.

Sometimes you responded. Sometimes you nuzzled and went back to sleep. Sometimes I masturbated there in bed beside you, then you'd come wide awake, helping, rolling against me, rubbing, laughing until pleasure would take us, pulling us into its own rising currents, making us move in jerky, syncopated movements, clutching and breathing hard.

Springtime came that way too, bursting up with bright bobbing blossoms, then sweeping through in unusually warm days scented with heather, narcissus, plum cherry, apple and peach. Your hands would sweep over my body, into my body, brushing the hairs, holding my shoulders tight. Your lips would open my lips and your tongue would take me teasingly, gently, then with greater and greater insistence. "Now," I would cry and you would speed up just that fraction and hold the rhythm you knew would carry me up and out into bright explosions of color and sound.

Springtime markets were filled with fresh produce: kale and asparagus and those first incredible strawberries. I fed you the strawberries one by one, your fingers planted deep inside me. We ate grapes together and loved and talked about the past, dreamed about the future, expanded the propitious present in all directions.

Your lips were parted there above me, cranberry and rubies, your lips and the faun grey hairs along your temples filled my gaze. Your fingers moved inside me and I closed my eyes following the movements, the pauses, the sigh of want, the opening and spreading of desire.

The wisteria opened and spread across the porch, clematis in a white radiance wavered above the door. Spicy madrone perfumed the evening air. Early butterflies appeared darting among magenta shooting stars, lavender trillium and chocolate lillies speckled with yellow and brown. Manzanita dripped with blooms clustered like milky, rosy chandeliers.

Sometimes I say it's unreasonable that I'm so happy. That I work so hard and still I'm happy. Tired often, yes, but joyous, celebratory. Love can do this to me, lust too. How nice to have them combined.

Combined like our bodies rubbing and blending last night, late, both of us tired yet stirred by longing, me sliding my body down yours, feeling the hair of your legs against my crotch, against my breasts, the feel of your crispy hairs against my mouth, your odor, so delicate, so distinctly yours, fruity, earthy, pine forests in the late afternoon heat.

I rub my way into you searching for your softness, for your wetness, nest my way in and stay, dreaming of the mists rising in the mornings, of trees hidden and exposed.

I lick upward, springtime rain on my face, streams moving swiftly, rivers swollen and rich with silt. I lick upward, moisture poised on every leaf and stalk, glittering on the dandelions and buttercups, on wild strawberry blooms.

I tongue you, your liquid splashing my cheeks, subtle perfumes rising, your cries in my ears. I tongue you until you cry out and heave yourself into my face and grab my hair and then I move more slowly, gently, focusing love.

Each year with you the springtime enters differently yet each one buds and finds us open. Early greens expand through a mist of russet and rose, yellow greens and mint tones, chartreuse and emerald hues.

Each April the fiddle heads of the bracken fern push up and unfurl. Vetch and lupin open out with the dogwood, with Indian paint brush. I spread beneath you, skin on skin, mouth on mouth, I spread and rise. Spring's heart throbs in the screaming cerise of black current blossoms, in the faultless yellow of Oregon grape. And I come, and I come, and I come.

Each year, my love, your body close, your caring touch, each year in bursting glory, I feel the fluids rise.

The Confrontation

JUDY FREESPIRIT

MALKA WAS SHIFTING her weight on the toilet seat in order to get a better reach when she simultaneously heard and felt a snap. She stood up to inspect the pink oval and there it was: a hairline break just at the place where her right thigh had rested.

Now I've done it. Not ten minutes in my parents' new apartment and I've broken the toilet seat. I wonder if they'll notice it. Maybe if I just keep quiet about it...or maybe it was broken already and I just think I broke it. Of course I did it, and of course they'll notice. Shit, how could this be happening? I haven't visited since they moved here two years ago and I'm destroying the place before I've even had a chance to unpack.

Even though the air conditioning was set at 75 degrees Malka was soaking with perspiration. She grabbed the cool pink sink with one hand and leaned over to splash cold water on her face. Then, sitting on the edge of the matching pink tub she dried herself with the plush green guest towel.

I should just go out there and tell them what happened and offer to pay for it. Damn! Mom will use this as one more proof that I should lose weight. I can't stand this feeling like a little kid. I'm 47 years old and I'm acting like I'm 7 and just knocked over the cookie jar. I'm in a fucking panic over a toilet seat! This is just too ridiculous for words. Pull your self together, Malka, you have four whole days to get through and you have got to be more in control of yourself or you'll be...destroyed. That's how it feels...destroyed. Over a goddamned toilet seat yet!

Malka gritted her teeth, squared her shoulders and walked out of the bathroom into the hallway. This apartment was almost an exact replica of the one her parents lived in before they moved here from Los Angeles. Same cheap green shag wall-to-wall carpet; same square rooms with sliding glass windows; same off-white draw drapes; and, of course, the same furnishings, right down to the five foot tall plastic rubber plant in the corner. The only difference was that one wall in the living room of this apartment had alternating squares of cork and gold marbled mirrors which gave the room an extra sleazy appearance. There was something about her parents' taste in apartments that reminded Malka of a cheap motel.

The hexagonal mirrored coffee table in front of the mirrored wall reflected the dime-store knicknacks which were placed on it: the bowl of plastic fruit, the ceramic Chinese boy and girl sitting with their legs dangling over the edge of the table. Malka noticed that one of the teeth on the ceramic tiger was chipped, but other than that everything seemed to be just as it had been in L.A.

Malka and her parents were very polite with one another, and the evening passed quickly. There was homemade chicken soup for dinner and then a few hours spent visiting one of the nearby casinos. But even at night the air was hot and sticky and at ten o'clock Malka fell exhausted on the couch. She lay awake for two hours before finally falling into a fitful sleep. That night she dreamed that a volcano burst open, spewing boiling lava at her as she fled in terror.

Her heart beat wildly as she ran a zig-zag pattern in an attempt to escape. But no matter how fast she ran the hot mass pursued her, licking at her heels, always just a few seconds away from devouring her.

Howard Moskowitz groaned slightly as he sat up. Then he gently folded back the blankets so as not to awaken Hannah as he swung his thin, chalk white legs over the side of the bed and slipped his feet into the soft, navy blue slippers. Another groan as he stood up. His bones were aching. As usual he hadn't slept very well. All night long the radio beside the bed had been serenading him with music, and some of the night he had dozed, but not much—not enough. He was tired all the time, and nauseous from the chemotherapy. Lurching stiffly out of the room he closed the door behind him, relieved himself in the bathroom and shuffled into the living room where Malka was sitting on the couch, leafing through a magazine.

How can it be? Is this fat, middle-aged woman sitting there on the couch the same child I loved so much? Why do I feel so bad? I was a good father, even if I wasn't perfect.

It was always hard for Howard when Malka came to visit. He was glad to see her, and at the same time anxious for her to leave. It was all very confusing, the same way he had felt about his mother when she was alive.

This was not the first time he had realized how much Malka reminded him of his mother, but he didn't like to think about that.

Malka isn't irresponsible like my mother. She's just. . . too strong, too different, too loud, too opinionated and somehow uppity. Yes that's it. They both think they're better than me. How did Hannah and I go wrong in raising this only child? Didn't we give her everything we could? A nice place to live, food and clothing. Even sent her to college so she could find a good husband. Was it our fault she picked that well-educated schmuck she married? At least she got married and gave us a grandchild, for all the good it does us. Another disappointment, a grandson who never writes or calls. Kids these days have no sense of responsibility. And now she's gay. What's

*this world coming to? I did my best and look what it's gotten me.
If only I were healthy it wouldn't matter so much. If only*.... Howard
had a lot of "if onlys" these days.

Malka's gaze followed her father as he shuffled slowly across the
living room. "Good morning Daddy." Just a hint of a smile crossed
her lips.

"Hi, honey, was the couch comfortable?"

"It was all right. How about you? Did you sleep well?"

Howard shrugged and sighed. "You know how it is, I don't sleep
very much."

He walked stiffly into the kitchen and poured himself a glass
of orange juice before offering one to Malka.

"No thanks, I don't want anything yet. It's only 6:30. Do you
always get up so early?"

"It varies," he answered, after polishing off the last of the juice.
Then he returned to the center of the living room and began swinging his arms in circles.

"I do exercises twice a day," he told her. "It makes me feel a
little better to get the old juices flowing."

Malka watched as her father jumped up and down. He looked
funny standing in the middle of the room, bending over his scrawny,
bird-like white legs to touch the floor with his fingertips. Up and
down, up and down he went, like those toy birds that sit on the edge
of a glass, bobbing for water.

He felt her eyes on him as he worked up a sweat. *She thinks
I'm ridiculous. Well, that's just too bad. Wouldn't hurt her to exer-
cise a little bit.*

When he finished, Howard sat down on the couch leaving one
pillow's space between them. Malka seemed anxious, he thought,
as though something was on her mind. Well, she'd just have to tell
him what it was. He ground his teeth and waited through the long
silence before she began to speak.

"I need to talk to you about something," she said haltingly. Then
more firmly, "I need to talk with you about the incest."

Howard felt a current of electricity surge through his body. *After all this time I should have expected it. Of course I always knew that some day this would happen.* The thought of it had gnawed at his intestines for years. *Maybe it's just as well to have it out in the open. How much worse can the reality be than the anticipation?*

He steeled himself before saying the words he had thought about saying to his daughter for so many years. "I don't know why I did it. Maybe it was hereditary, I don't know. But I'm sorry. I really am very sorry."

Malka didn't seem to be paying any attention. "I don't care about *why*," she was saying, "what I care about is that you own up to what you did and acknowledge that you hurt me. I need some information from you. I have questions to ask you so I can work this through for myself."

"Honey, I'll try to answer any questions you have," he said softly, but his eyes refused to look toward her, fixing themselves instead on a dark area on the carpet. *I'll have to take some Energine to that spot as soon as this conversation is over.*

"Well," Malka continued, "I need to know how old I was when it started. I can remember it happening when I was five, but somehow I have the feeling it might have been earlier than that and I really need to know."

Howard cleared his throat before speaking. "Um, how old? Well, uh, I don't know. It was earlier than five but how much I really don't know." His voice was barely audible. *Why is she dredging up all this old stuff? What's done is done. What does she want from my life?*

Malka persisted. "Sometimes, in therapy, I've gone back to a time when I was very little, maybe so little that I couldn't talk yet and I feel very frightened. I seem to be in a crib or playpen or something like that with sides and I'm scared. Is it possible I could have been very young—young enough to still be sleeping in a crib?"

It took him a long time to answer. "Well, it could be. I just can't remember. I know it was younger than five but just how young I can't say for sure." *What does she need to know all this for? I said I was sorry.*

"OK, I'll let that go, then. It helps to just know that it was younger. Now for my other question. I need to know if Mom knows about this."

Howard's face turned ashen and little bubbles formed in the corners of his mouth. Ice water seemed to be running through his veins as he turned toward his daughter. "No, your mother doesn't know and she doesn't need to know! I don't want you telling her, do you hear me?" he hissed. "It would ruin our marriage." *Oh God, don't let her tell Hannah.*

Malka was stunned. So her mother didn't know. That meant she couldn't have done anything to stop it. With a sigh of relief Malka looked at her father who was hunched over, staring at the carpet in front of him. "No," she decided out loud, "I won't tell her if she doesn't know. There would be no point now."

Howard's body relaxed, but his eyes remained fixed on the stain in the carpet, which he stared at hard, as if his very look could make it disappear. Finally he sighed deeply and said, "I'm sorry. What else do you need to know?"

Just then the bedroom door opened and Hannah stepped into the hallway, looked into the living room, smiled and finally shuffled into the bathroom.

"Listen, Dad," Malka was in a hurry now, "I'll want to talk more about this later. When can we have some time to be alone to finish this conversation?"

"Don't worry, Baby," he said softly, "we'll find some time before you leave."

Father and daughter sat in silence for a few minutes before Hannah came bustling into the room saying, "Howard, we'll have to call the apartment manager. The toilet seat's cracked and I think it's dangerous."

Malka broke into a cold sweat. *Oh God, I forgot about the fucking toilet.* "I think I may have broken it, unless it was cracked before I came. Was it?"

"No, you didn't break it." Her mother brushed the idea aside with a wave of her hand. "They don't make things like they used to. I'm sure it was just shoddy materials, there's no reason why a toilet seat should crack like that."

Malka was on the edge of tears. *What a sweet woman my mother is. Even if she was thinking it was my fault she isn't going to say anything. I've misjudged her.*

As the two women discussed the problems involved in getting apartment managers to make needed repairs, Howard Moskowitz slipped quietly out of the room. It was 7:00 a.m. and the June Las Vegas heat was beginning to bother him already. He would wear one of his light, short-sleeved golf shirts today, he decided, and the shoes with the air holes in them for ventilation.

On the fourth day of Malka's visit, Hannah Moskowitz awoke from a fitfull sleep, then lay awake for half an hour before getting out of bed. A deep sadness had overtaken her. *Today Malka is leaving. Who knows when I will see her next?* She slipped her feet into the backless, pink terry cloth slippers. *It's amazing how quickly the four days passed—poof just like that. Today we should do something special.* She slipped the lightweight robe over her sleeveless cotton nightgown. *We've been to the casinos every day, taken her out to our favorite buffets. It's too bad about the review at the Silver Slipper. That was a disappointment to say the least. I was certain she would enjoy* Boylesque *as much as we did the two times we saw it before. Those men dressed up like women are so pretty, and funny. But Malka just seemed insulted by the whole thing and was sullen for the entire evening after the performance. Well, there's no accounting for taste.* Sitting on the edge of the bed for a few minutes Hannah mulled it all over. *Malka is more than usually tense this trip. I just don't understand her.*

Howard's breathing was uneven as he slept in the big, king-sized bed. Every so often he would clear his throat or grit his teeth. *Poor man, how he suffers.* She walked quietly to the door so as not to disturb him. Hannah stepped out into the hallway and peeked into the living room where her daughter was waiting. Malka was using her asthma aspirator.

"Hi, honey, having trouble breathing this morning?"

Her daughter nodded.

"It's after eight o'clock," Hannah exclaimed as she caught sight of the plastic wall clock in the kitchen. "Most days I'm up and out of the house hours before this. Dad and I usually take a three mile walk and have our breakfast by seven o'clock. I don't know why we've slept so late today. Do you want some coffee or juice or anything?"

"No thanks, not yet."

"Did you sleep well?"

"Yes, fairly well," Malka yawned. "It cooled off a little bit during the night and I slept pretty soundly."

Her wheezing eased slightly as she watched her mother busily puttering around the small kitchen.

"Mom," she said uneasily, "you never seem to ask me anything personal about myself. Don't you want to know more about me, about my life?"

Hannah felt a tight knot in her stomach as she sat down at the dining room table with her coffee.

"What do you mean?" she asked.

"I mean we talk about the weather and my job, but you don't ask me about my personal life. Don't you want to know?"

Hannah looked hard into her coffee cup. For a moment she struggled with the idea of changing the subject. Then she decided to get it over with.

"We know you're. . .uh, gay, and we don't like the idea."

Hannah was amazed at the shocked look on her daughter's face. *Why does she look so surprised? Didn't she think we read that book she gave us seven or eight years ago, the one she had written an article in, where it says in the back how she's an organizer for lesbian and gay rights? What does she think we are, stupid?*

"Mom," Malka was saying. "You know I'm a lesbian and you never said anything about it before?"

Hannah pursed her lips into an expression which made her look like she had eaten something that had gone bad. "We think you have the right to live your life the way you want to, but we feel very badly about it. It makes us feel awful for you that you're so unhappy."

Malka shook her head in disbelief. "What makes you think I'm unhappy?"

"Well, how can you be happy living like *that?*"

The pitch and volume of Malka's voice were rapidly rising. "What do you mean *like that?* How do you think I live?"

Hannah sighed deeply, "Well, you know it's just that it's *unnatural*. It's your life, but it's not right." The knot in Hannah's stomach was getting bigger and tighter and she felt a band of pain tightening across her chest. *She had to bring it up! I could have let it go but she pushed and now it's out in the open. She's the one who insisted I tell her what I'm thinking. So why does she have to look so hurt and shocked? What did she expect me to say, for God's sake?*

A loud belch preceded Howard into the room. He looked pale and haggard, his shoulders slumping more than usual, but he wasn't too exhausted to notice the tension between the two women.

"What's going on here?" he asked with a slight, nervous laugh. "You two having a little girl talk?"

Malka's voice was tense with anger. "No, we were just talking about the fact that I'm a lesbian and you and Mom think it's unnatural."

"Speak for yourself, Hannah," he said in that familiar put-down tone he reserved especially for his wife. "I don't think it's unnatural."

"Well," Hannah sniffed, "nobody in our family has ever been like that. I don't think she needs to go upsetting everyone with that information."

"Don't be foolish, Hannah," he snarled. "Do you want her to have to stay in the closet?"

Malka couldn't believe her ears. *How the hell does he know about closets? It must be the television. He probably saw a talk show about gays, or maybe a situation comedy. That had to be it.*

She decided to let her father's comment pass and concentrate on her mother. Mustering up her kind-but-firm attitude Malka plunged in. "Mom, I'm not willing to keep this a secret any more. It's too painful for me. I just can't stand it. And furthermore, I'm happy with my life. It's the most natural thing in the world for me," Malka shouted.

"Don't raise your voice like that to your mother," Howard snapped.

"I'm sorry if I raised my voice, but this is really upsetting. You have no right to tell me I'm not natural. Fifteen percent of all people in the entire world are homosexual," Malka retorted.

Hannah was on the verge of tears. *What does she want from us? Does she have to spread the dirty wash all over for everybody to see?* Hannah's voice was barely audible as she spoke through tight lips. "Malka, you don't have to tell everyone about this do you?"

"Mom, who is it you don't want me to tell?" There was just an edge of frustration in her voice.

"Well, Aunt Ruby for one. She'd never understand. It would kill her. You were always her favorite niece."

Her mother's response didn't come as a surprise. After all, it was the same one she had used herself all these years, when she was avoiding coming out to her parents. "It would kill them." She remembered herself saying that, over and over during the past ten years. Yet here she was, telling them and they were anything but dead. In fact this was the first real conversation they'd had in as long as she could remember.

"OK," Malka said reluctantly, "I won't tell Aunt Ruby, but I won't guarantee that I'll keep it a secret with all the family. Secrets keep people separate from each other and I don't want my lesbianism to keep me from other members of the family like it has up to now."

Hannah's face was pinched and gray as she slowly walked over to the easy chair and sat down heavily. "Malka," she said wearily, "we just don't. . . I just don't like the idea, that's all. I still think it's unnatural."

"Mother, do you feel somehow. . . responsible?"

"Well, yes, as a matter of fact I was thinking that maybe if I had stayed home with you more when you were younger, if I hadn't worked so much...."

"It's not your fault. I'm a lesbian because I love women. You have nothing to do with it." A brief smile crossed her lips, "So don't try to take any credit."

Hannah failed to see the humor. "Well, I just thought...well, maybe it isn't our fault."

"Oh Hannah!" Howard did not attempt to conceal his agitation. "Will you leave her alone already? She has her life to live and we have ours. You're not responsible for anything, and neither am I."

"Not responsible?" Malka snapped at him, "I can't believe you just said that."

"Why are you getting so upset with your father?" Hannah's confusion was profound. "After all, it's me who's getting yelled at, not you." Then she sighed deeply. "I still don't like the idea, but you know we still love you and want you to be happy. If you're satisfied with your life I guess that's your business. Does Aaron know his mother's a...about your...lifestyle?"

"Yes, and he feels fine about it."

"When did you tell him?"

"Actually I told him four years ago, when he was seventeen. And do you know what he said? He said, 'Mom, I don't know how to tell you this, but some of my best friends *really are gay*.' Isn't that a riot? I hadn't thought much about it, but of course growing up in L.A. right on the border of Hollywood, it was no big deal to him. He tells all his friends about me and I think he's really proud of his political dyke mother."

Hannah sighed again. "Well, like I said, we only want you to be happy. If that's the way you want to live, what more can we say?"

"Mom," Malka's voice was firm, "I don't want you to just be resigned to my lesbianism. I'm going to keep talking to you about this until you see my life as it really is. I know you've been fed a lot of misinformation. I'm going to tell you and tell you and tell you until you hear me. I'm not going to be silent anymore or let things pass. And sooner or later you're going to change your mind about me, and about what it means to be a lesbian."

"Well, we'll see." Hannah's jaw shut tightly. It was clear that for the moment that was all there was to be said about that subject. She stood up stiffly and headed for the bedroom to lie down.

Howard and Malka sat in tense silence. After several minutes Howard clasped his bony hands in front of him and leaned forward, resting his elbows on his knees. His head was lowered and his eyes closed. Malka was as conscious of him sitting there as she was of the pounding of her heart and the difficulty of her breathing, which was shallow and wheezy. The asthma medicine wasn't going to be much help this time. She looked at the sick old man who was her father and felt the urge to let him off the hook. After all, wasn't this enough for one day? Then, remembering her resolve and the years of pain she had suffered, she changed her mind. Why blow it now when there were only another six hours left before a plane would take her back to San Francisco? She wasn't finished with her business here. Who knew if he would live long enough for her to have another opportunity?

"Dad," she began softly, "it's been four days and we still haven't found the time to have that talk."

Howard spun around and glared at her. "I'm not going to talk to you," he snapped. "I don't have to talk to you."

"Why? I don't understand! What do you mean you don't have to talk to me? You promised we'd finish our conversation. What's going on?"

"I changed my mind, that's all," he sputtered, his teeth tightly clenched. "I don't owe you anything."

"The hell you don't! You owe it to me to hear me out. You're being impossible." She couldn't conceal her exasperation, didn't even want to. "A few days ago you thought you owed me that much."

"What's wrong?" Hannah's voice was edged with fear as she came into the room. "What's going on? I was just in my room for a minute. . . ."

"Tell her to leave me alone, Hannah."

"What are you doing to your father? Don't you know he's a sick man?"

"I need to talk with Dad alone, and he won't talk to me, that's all." Malka managed to keep the whine out of her voice, but she was feeling like a little girl who was being chastised.

Her mother was pleading now. "What do you want to talk with him about that I can't hear? What's so important? We can all talk together, can't we?"

Malka stalked angrily across the room. "There are things I just need to say to him alone. You and he are two people, for God's sake. 'We' this. 'We' that. That's all I ever hear from you. Mom, I get to talk to you alone, but Dad doesn't want to do that with me and I *need* to talk with him. It's *important*."

Hannah hesitated for a moment. Maybe she could convince him, but did she really want to? "Howard, why don't you just talk with her? I'll go for a walk."

"No, I'm not going to talk to her and that's that."

"But why not?"

"I just won't, that's all. You keep out of this Hannah. It's none of your business."

Hannah felt totally powerless. Nothing like this had ever happened before between the three of them. She was losing control. The room was beginning to spin slowly and she felt as if she were going to vomit.

"Malka, can't you just respect your father's wishes? What's so important you have to talk with him about it and make all this fuss? Can't you see he's upset? He's a sick man."

"Mother, I have to talk to him and I'm really not feeling comfortable with you being in the middle of this. It's between me and him, OK? I'd like you to stay out of it and I mean it."

The look on Hannah's face made Malka want to cry. *Poor Mom. She's always taking care of everyone else and settling for what she gets. But I haven't come all this way after so long to leave without finishing my business with Dad. He has to talk with me, that's all there is to it.*

There were several long minutes of dead silence. Finally, Hannah could not stand it any longer. She turned on the television, and for the next half hour they sat, each lost in his or her own thoughts, pretending to watch *Different Strokes*. When it was over Hannah rose to change the channel saying, "There's a talk show I like to watch at this time."

"Dad," Malka pleaded, "will you talk with me in your room?"

"No!" he answered sullenly. "I told you to leave me alone about this."

All she could do was glare at him. Then the announcer's voice caught her attention. "Our topic for today's show is a sensitive one. For too long the subject of incest has been taboo. Now there is a growing awareness of the problem and concerned adults are taking steps to stop this all-too-common occurrence. Our guest on today's program is a woman whose job it is to go out into the schools and educate children about their rights and options."

Malka could not believe what was happening. The three members of the Moskowitz clan were sitting in the living room, watching a program on *incest*.

There was nothing being said that she hadn't heard before, many times, from her friend who was doing incest prevention work in San Francisco. All she could do was sit there, stiff and miserable, through the program. *What is he thinking now? This is too bizarre. It's just too much of a coincidence.* Deep inside a giggle started tickling her. She wanted to laugh, to roll on the floor, roaring. Instead she bit her lower lip. Things were bad enough without *that* kind of a scene. She kept her face as stony as her parents' and for a grueling half hour watched the show. Then, when it was over, Howard slowly and deliberately stood up and walked to his room, shutting the door loudly behind him.

"I just can't stand the tension," Hannah announced. "I'm going to do the laundry."

As soon as her mother had gone, Malka knocked on the bedroom door.

"What do you want?"

"I want to talk to you."

"I told you I don't want to talk to you."

"Mother is doing the laundry and I want to talk to you *now*."

Howard opened the door and pushed past her into the living room, where he plunked himself huffily into the easy chair.

"I don't understand what's happening," Malka began. "You said the other day you would talk with me and now you're saying you won't. You're acting like. . . I don't know, I've never seen you like this before."

"You want to break up my marriage," he shouted at her, his white face turning a fiery red. "You want to break up my marriage."

"No, that's not true. I want to tell you how I feel, how your behavior has effected my life. I told you I wasn't going to say anything to Mom and I won't. But you owe it to me to listen to me for a few minutes. I'm not going to let up as long as I'm here, so you might as well get it out of your head that you're going to shut me up with this behavior."

"You have no right to demand anything from me."

"I have every right in the world. You owe me that much."

"What are you trying to do to me?" he yelled at her. "What do you want from me?"

"I want you to listen to what I have to say to you. Don't you see, this isn't really about you at all. It's about me. I have to do this for me. It's about my need to say, finally, what I have to say to you after all this time."

Before he could respond, the front door opened and Hannah, empty plastic laundry basket in hand, entered the apartment. She stood looking back and forth between her husband and daughter when Howard announced, "Hannah, we're going into the bedroom to talk for a few minutes. She's not going to leave me alone till I talk to her, so I might as well get it over with."

"Fine, take your time."

Malka followed her father into the bedroom. Now that she had his attention she couldn't remember what she had wanted to say. Maybe she was making too much of a fuss about this. He certainly wasn't helping her any. He was just sitting on the edge of the bed, waiting for her to speak, looking like a puppy anticipating a beating for some infraction he didn't quite understand.

She breathed deeply before beginning. "Dad, I've kept your lousy secret for over forty years. What makes you think I want to break up your marriage now?"

When he didn't respond it suddenly hit her. "When I was talking about secrets keeping people apart this morning, did you think I meant that I was going to tell her about us?"

Howard wouldn't look at her, but his head bobbed slightly in affirmation. *How could he think that? Doesn't he know by now that I keep my word?*

Then her father raised his head and faced her with tears streaming down his cheeks. He looked so pathetic, so completely helpless. Malka's strongest reaction to his tears was fury, not at her father, but at herself. *I can't believe I'm feeling sorry for the bastard. . .sorry for him!* She wanted to scream, to tell him to stop looking like that. She wanted him to be angry and hostile again so she could be angry and hostile back.

Finally she took a deep breath and forced herself to look at her father, without being distracted by his tears and his trembling.

"Dad, I don't want to take care of you any more. I need to start taking care of myself and I'm going to do that no matter what I'm feeling for you at this minute. This is what I want to say to you: I'm not going to tell Mother about you because there's no point in hurting her like that and I don't want to after all these years. I've had a lot of pain because of what you did to me and you need to know about that. You were responsible for causing that pain. The worst thing for me when I was growing up, was that I felt there must be something wrong with me, that I was dirty. It's been hard for me to trust other people and let them love me, but I'm finally learning to do that. I'll probably have to be working on this for a long time, but I don't hate you or want to punish you. I just need you to know that I'm not going to pretend any more that you didn't do those things to me. I'm not responsible for what happened. I was just a child and you abused me. You'll have to find some way to deal with that. It's not my problem. Don't expect me to forgive you. You can only do that for yourself. I need to put my energies into working on myself—into loving, and healing myself."

A calm settled over them both as Howard looked at his daughter's face and nodded that he heard and understood her. She watched him standing before her, arms hanging limply at his sides. Then with full knowledge that she was doing it for herself, Malka reached out and hugged her father goodbye.

Flossie's Flashes

SALLY MILLER GEARHART

FLOSSIE YOROBA WOKE for the third time that night with the tingling at her hairline skipping around to the nape of her neck. "Here she comes!" she thought, opening herself to the gathering explosion of pleasure. She grinned in the dark. "It's from the bones tonight."

Always it was one of two sources. She called the first "Volcano." In an increasingly urgent rhythm it would rise from the spot directly behind her navel, erupting in bursts upward to her arms and head, downward to her legs and feet. It moved patiently, irrevocably, relentlessly, inevitably, over muscle and bone, nerve and tendon, capturing layer after layer of forgiving flesh under its flow of molten energy. Then, in its surges toward freedom, it would strike the wall of skin and burst free of its encapsulation through welcoming pores, transforming itself always at that last second into ten thousand rivulets of pure sweat that sang and danced their way up and down her body.

Or across and under it, depending on whatever position that body occupied at the moment. Her toes and fingers always got it last, just about the time the sweat on her back was beginning to cool.

The other kind, and the ones she was waking with tonight, rose from a different place, from the geometric center of each part of her body, simultaneously from thigh, elbow, backbone, phylanges, the middle of her head. This kind she called "Hot Seep," oozing as it did from the marrow of each bone outward toward the skin, not in waves but at most in small eddies, all pacing themselves according to the thickness of the flesh they sought to conquer, all carefully timing their emergence from the body to be a synchronized drench, all at once and altogether, over her whole being, top to bottom, back to front, spilling out at precisely the same instant from her big toes and her nipples, her shoulder blades and her waistline, the palms of her hands and the caverns of her ears.

This Seep was seconds short of emergence. She reached for her clitoris, carefully avoiding its tender, aggressive tip. She pressed it gently side-to-side, then up-from-under. Once. Twice. Then with a whoop of joy she flung off the quilt and arched her back into a long stretch of denouement, collapsing at last into inert flesh, drenched and dazzled in the frost-filled air.

A high wind was outflanking the protective eaves of her cabin. It drove a deluge of snow through her window and onto her naked skin. Sweat met flake in a mighty clash of elements. Flake melted. But flake won, cooling the seat in an embrace both familiar and triumphant.

Flossie whooped again. She stretched wide another time and urged more of her undaunted wetness into its stark encounter with the cold. She smiled and shuddered as she sucked a raging winter into her lungs. She felt the air transfer itself from lungs to bones, there to entrap the heat and follow its path, moving on it from behind until now her skin felt downright crisp, crisp and encased in what she knew must be a thin sheath of ice. She whooped a third time and catapulted to the window, drawing it tight against the storm.

Back under her quilt she subsided, giving thanks to Whoever Was that Daaana had decided not to stay over with her tonight. She preferred not to share a bed these days, much less Spoon, what with this waking up four and five times a night to sizzle and freeze, sizzle and freeze.

Though as for that, she thought, marvelling at the completeness with which the quilt encased her, cuddled her—though as for that, Daaana was a great bedpartner for flashes. She actually envied Flossie, and advertised her in public to be better than Solar Central, hottest woman in the Grand Matrix, north-south-east-or-west.

Even from the depths of an early-dawn Spoon Daaana could sometimes feel the moment coming before Flossie knew it herself. Then she would chuckle and cling to Flossie, holding her close in anticipation of the explosion of heat. Flossie, torn between the loving clasp of a good woman and her desire to leap to cold freedom, would throw the covers at least from her own burning flesh and lie only tokenly connected to Daaana by finger or kneecap. That, of course, threatened to deprive Daaana of one of her greatest pleasures: the slick sensuousness of their undulating sweat-bathed bodies. It led, usually, to loud laments as Daaana protected herself from the window's blast and Flossie, naked as a jay to the churlish chiding of the wintry wind, inhaled there like a card-carrying health freak. Sometimes it all led to a tussle that ended in shouts and uncontrolled laughter.

Flossie loved her nights with Daaana and sometimes missed the dreamwalking that Spooning could bring. But right now, these months, these years, she was exhilarated with her changes and often sacrificed the adventures of Spooned sleep for a night of solitary encounter with the elements. Since childhood she had loved the run from the sweat tent to the waterfall, the smell of hard-worked body dripping in pungent clothes and the subsequent dunk into an icy mountain stream. She craved the contrasts, the sudden changes, the jig that her feet danced and the thanks that her heart sang every time she gifted them with those extremes.

Under the cover now she stroked her ample body, drawing her knees to her chest and lying Spoon with a phantom self as she cozed back into sleep. Not only did she get these wild free swings of heat and cold, but several times a night now she got to fall asleep again. Falling asleep, she thought. Sheer contentment, always, even with another Spooned body. But, she mused, there's a special balm to doing it in a wide bed all alone, with the margins of your body quite unbounded. . . .

Alien androids were attacking the cabin, rattling the windows and whipping the roof with giant rubber hoses. They were calling her name. "Flossie! Flossie, open up!!" She clamped her legs together. She heaved her extra pillow over her head, dug deeper into the tired old foam that supported her. "Stick it where the sun don't shine," she mumbled, trying for her gentle drop back into dreamland.

"Flossie! Get the bar off this door! I gotta talk to you!" More beating on the non-offending cabin. Flossie turned her face to the foam and smothered her breath. She willed the androids back to their planet of sterile basalt. She held her breath.

"Floss, dammit, it's me, City Lights! I'm freezing my butt off out here! Flossieeeeee!!"

Flossie breathed. No fun to wake up this way, she thought. She hauled her bare feet to the floor, feeling for her nightgown. Where had she left it? More banging. "I'm comin', I'm comin'!" she croaked. The banging stopped. Fighting her way into the warm flannel she reached the door and drew back the bar.

City Lights, No Bigger Than A Minute And Twice As Frail, stomped into the room and kicked the door back into place. She dumped a large patch of snow onto the floor with her jacket and laughed a greeting. Then she made for Flossie's stove. "You still got fire," she warbled. "How about a lamp?"

"City, I'm a gin day short of lacing you good. What you want?" Flossie cut the damper and opened her stove door. She lit a candle from a twig.

City shook possible spiders from some kindling and forced the wood under the smouldering logs. She looked over her shoulder at the flannel-clad figure, its arms akimbo, and got to the point.

"We got to Spoon, Flossie. You and me."

"You and me? City, your peanut butter's slippin' off of your bread. Last we Spooned was five years ago. . . ."

"We can do it." The younger woman sank to a stool in front of the fire and held out her hand to Flossie. "I'm not proposin' wild abandoned sex. Only a sweet gentle little Spoon. . . ."

"You proposin' — !"

"Not that I wouldn't love it, Floss. In fact. . . ."

Flossie let out her breath. "Wait 'till I get my socks." She threw the quilt from her bed around City's shoulders. Then on her knees she strained to rescue one wool sock from under her bed, another from her boot. She sat on a straight chair by City. "Coldest night in a universe and you got to come knockin' your way into my sleep."

She felt a reassurance, a satisfaction, as the sock stretched itself around her leg. When nothin' else helps, she reminded herself, pull up your socks. It always worked. She cut her eyes toward City. The tiny woman was intent on moving a log to catch the center of a volunteer flame. Still pretty, Flossie thought, the girl's still pretty, else the fire's makin' a lie of her face. Flossie pulled up her second sock and resigned herself to a conversation.

"City, I'm bound to tell you I won't try that flyin' again if that's how come you want to Spoon."

City wove her hand up through folds of quilt and held it out to Flossie a second time. "No," she urged, "I just need to dream-walk. All the demons been visitin' me lately. Like when I go to the lake where Eleeea died. You know?"

Flossie knew. She wanted to reach for her pipe, light it up and stay safe behind a cloud of smoke. Instead she took City's hand. "Umm-hmmm," she said.

"I just need you to hold me, Floss. You always been the best for walkin' together with me and findin' healin' waters. I can do a new incantation I made up for right after the master chant. It'll take us so deep, so easy." City Lights, No Bigger Than A Minute And Twice As Frail, raised the soft brown openness of her eyes to the soft brown openness of Flossie's. "Will you Spoon with me, Floss?"

There was never any brittleness to be found anywhere in Flossie Yoroba, and at this moment, she was sure, there wasn't even a trace of solid bone or cartilage. She harumphed her way toward a response. "Well, we might be ridin' a lame donkey," she growled. "It's not for certain I can stay down long enough to dreamwalk anywhere."

She was about to say more but at that moment her forehead began to tingle, just around her hairline. Her eyes grew a millimeter bigger. She stood up and wiped her brow. "City," she said, "City, come here to me." She pulled the small woman to her feet. "How come you got on so many clothes?" She turned toward the door, heaving the quilt onto the bed as she slid the bar closed.

City Lights knew when she'd been blessed. Move, girl! she admonished herself. Don't let your coattail touch the ground! She began peeling off her clothes, struggling all the while to meet the swell of primordial earthpower that was emanating from Flossie's body. She was just working her way out of her last pant leg when Flossie flung off the flannel nightgown and stood before her, wet and shiny in the candlelight, exuding wave after wave of unquenched fire.

First it was the warmth, then it was Flossie's arms that encompassed her. As she sank onto the bed, City Lights, No Bigger Than A Minute And Twice As Frail, heard the big woman say, "They's good Spoonin' tonight, girl. But first you got to let me show you what a hot woman is all about."

The candle, outdone in both heat and light, guttered, and then courteously extinguished itself.

Tommy

ELSA GIDLOW

THEN, IN THE YEAR 1924, on a soft, rainy weekend, I got married. Quite unintentionally. Tommy said, "Marry me for tonight." The ring was slipped on my finger without witness or benefit of clergy. Who could imagine we would be together for thirteen years—"till death did us part."

Tommy—Violet Winifred Leslie Henry-Anderson—was for years an almost mythical character. I used to hear spoken of by my Montreal friends Estelle, Roswell, and Harcourt. Actually, it was "Tommy and Mona." They came into conversation paired, like salt and pepper. But Tommy, in the comments and gossip, seemed to call forth more admiration than her companion. I had never heard anyone refer to her with other than pleasure and respect. I used to think: Why can't I meet a woman like that? I never thought I should meet her. She had moved far across Canada to British Columbia, and was in an apparently indissoluble bond with the younger woman, Mona.

95

Both had lived in Montreal for a short time, when Tommy left Edinburgh after the breakup of her home due to some unfortunate defection of her barrister father and subsequent loss of fortune. Her elder sister, Joan, moved to London, her two elder brothers migrated to different parts of Canada. Tommy chose Montreal at the start because her money would take her no further. She had never expected to work. She was born to ease, had devoted herself to sports and books, was a golfer, and had played in women's amateur championships. When disaster struck the family, she was world runner-up and aiming at top honors.

Instead, she had to consider how to earn her living. She knitted ties of a kind that were worn by upper class men and women. British women wore tweedy and tailored suits until it was time to "dress for dinner." The knitting earned her enough, along with what her family could contribute, to put her through secretarial school. Recommended by her father's associates, she found work in law offices as a legal secretary. In a few years she became expert and felt confident enough to dare the new world. She was as knowledgeable in law as many of the lawyers for whom she worked. In our day she would have become a lawyer. At the beginning of the century, such a step was unheard of.

Tommy and Mona Shelley met in Montreal. Mona wanted to go on the stage. She was a protege of Harcourt Farmer, and had acted in some of his productions surviving somehow in the Bohemian circles. Then Tommy fell in love with her, and they left together for Vancouver seven or eight years before my time. They were a legend by then, lingering in my thoughts wistfully as the only living lesbians anyone I knew had known.

Later, in New York City, Harcourt had written that Mona would be arriving any day. Still stage-struck, she intended to remain there and try to break into acting. The inference was that Tommy might follow, but I learned later that had been Mona's hope, not Tommy's. Roswell had brought Mona to meet me one evening. She was a cuddly, puppy-like young woman, maybe a few years older than me, outgo-

ing and physically energetic. Except for her good voice, I could not
see her as an actress. She was convinced there were parts she could
take and was haunting managers, producers, and casting agents.
Roswell and Mona went to plays together, and she was frequently
at the studio. I was surprised when she made advances to me. This
was shortly after my breakup with Muriel. Roswell may have told her
about it.

I asked her about Tommy. "Oh, she wouldn't mind if we made
love. She never wanted to bind me."

"Is Tommy coming to join you?" I had no wish to cut in to their
relationship, which had always been referred to as ideal.

"She might if she could get work."

Mona and I did kiss and cuddle and make superficial love a few
times. I was very lonely. Mona never meant much to me. I liked her
as one would a kitten that purrs her way into your affections. Mona
was living with a teacher named Miss Jonas. I never heard a first
name. Miss Jonas was "in love" with Mona but adamantly refused
to make love. This was all becoming very complicated. Once more
I asked, "But what about Tommy?" Tommy, she said, knew about
Miss Jonas.

I was in my last months with *The New Pearson's* when we needed
a secretary to help me with my many new duties. Mona asked eagerly:
"May I tell Tommy? Would you—they—consider her?"

I certainly would. *Pearson's* management left it to me. Violet
Winifred Leslie Henry-Anderson arrived with excellent credentials
and joined the staff. During the months before the magazine's move
to Chicago, she was "Miss Anderson" to me, one who "belonged"
to Mona. She found a place to live. Mona was with her when she
was not with Miss Jonas. I did not know what was transpiring or
if Miss Anderson would remain in New York. Our association in the
office was strictly business. In a sense I was immune to a new relationship by my continuing pain over Muriel's defection. The abys-
mal depression I have described was gathering and efforts to "save"
the magazine were absorbing my remaining energies. When it be-

came certain that *The New Pearson's* would move to Chicago, I felt very badly about telling Miss Anderson. She was so efficient, had such good recommendations, I was sure she would have no trouble finding a new job if she decided to remain in New York. She said, quietly, she thought she would—until Mona "made up her mind."

The best I could do to help her was to introduce her to the editor of *The Forum,* who later gave me freelance work. It turned out that his secretary was leaving, and he immediately engaged Miss Anderson. Ultimately, Mona refused to go back to Vancouver. She was sure of at least two acting prospects. And she was in love with Miss Jonas. She seemed to have the idea that she could keep Tommy as her physical lover and Miss Jonas as her "pure beloved." Neither Tommy or Miss Jonas would have any of it. Tommy was very quiet, but I knew felt deeply betrayed at being enticed to New York, which she immediately disliked. She loved and needed outdoor life, where she could play her beloved game of golf. She was living in an expensive, cramped little room. She had not decided whether, with or without Mona, she would return to Vancouver. She had friends of many years there and was a member of a club. At the moment, she wished to find a better place to live.

Roswell was by now established with Khagen in Brooklyn. I had the studio to myself. I asked Tommy if she would care to share it, taking over Roswell's half. She immediately accepted. At the time we came to live together and become friends, I was working with Gough in the bookstore. There is no doubt that from our first meeting I had felt a strong attraction for Tommy, but as I said, I regarded her as committed to Mona. Now that was ended. Tommy, it turned out, had been equally drawn to me. But, with English reserve and quixotic propriety, we both behaved as though we had no interest in one another beyond what the business of the day required. Until that rainy weekend.

We had been sharing the studio for a few days, bringing in Tommy's possessions, mainly clothing, golf clubs, a suitcase of books. I had made dinner one evening. She couldn't cook, it turned out,

and disliked doing it. The next evening she invited me out. We found
a place where we could order bootleg wine served in demitasse cups.
For the first time we talked frankly about ourselves, our lesbianism,
our commitment to women. She told me about her life in Scotland,
mourning for the beauty of the Highlands. She discussed a little of
her early love life there: a disastrous love for a woman she had never
ceased to love, who was committed to men, although as girls they
had been lovers. She said little of her disappointment over Mona,
enough for me to know that it cut deep, more for the way the break
had been handled, than for the loss itself. Suddenly she looked
straight at me, an altered expression in her grey-green eyes:

"But if she had not deceived me about her intentions in bringing me here, I should have not met you."

"Is—that important?"

She put out her cigarette in silence, reached across the table
and took my hand. "It could be."

That was all. Then we both became silent and shy. I do not know
if her heart was beating as mine was. The waiter came and took away
the dishes, poured more wine into the coffee cups from a disguised
container and asked if we would like dessert. Soon we went home,
that night each to our own beds.

It was the next evening, Friday, that she took from her finger
one of three gold rings she wore, and placed it on the traditional
"engagement" finger of my left hand, saying, "Marry me for tonight."
Her two remaining rings were on the little finger of her left hand.

The woman whose eyes I looked into as she held my hand with
her ring seemed to have been long known: that I knew so little about
her was of no significance. She *felt* familiar when her arms went round
me and we held one another close. I responded to the gentle strength
of her athletic body. When I opened my eyes, I liked the honesty
of her fine-featured face, the wide clear forehead from which the light-
brown, wavy hair was drawn back to a knot at the back of her head.

I do not remember our first kiss: there were so many as we lay
together on my couch that they merged as if into one continuous

kiss I had waited for a long time. And the love-making was different from what had transpired with Muriel. More *real* is the only way I can put it, than the almost disabling excitement of that brief romantic affair. I was not only transported as then, but satisfied.

Is there any better way to become deeply familiar with a new lover and friend-to-be than to spend two rainy days and nights alone? We were body to body in bed exploring passion and satiety, now held close in sleep or half sleep, now in dressing gown or pajamas beside the fire laughing over an improvised meal, or enjoying toasted English muffins with Dundee ginger marmalade. Tommy had brought a gift of the Scotch marmalade.

Whether we lay touching or caressing one another, or quietly talking, she was equally easy to be with. I liked her matter-of-fact self-acceptance. It reinforced or corroborated my own deep conviction that I had a right to be, to love, according to my nature.

Tommy was able to tell me more than I had ever suspected of women's passionate, romantic involvement with one another. In the Edinburgh upper classes and among her golfing associates, there were many such liaisons, she said.

"Did they make love?"

"Of course—those who did not get married, and even those who did for economic or family reasons. An heir was needed. Or they did not like being 'old maids.' Once married they were freer anyway. The men went off to posts in India, Africa, or the Colonies."

"And when they were left alone?"

"Some quietly turned back to one another."

"No one criticized or condemned?"

"People may not have thought, or known, there could be anything to condemn. Some people imagine women have no bodies below the navel."

We drew closer to one another—"below the navel," laughing. She asked me if I had heard the story about Queen Victoria's response to women's relationships. As we lay beside one another listening to the gentle rain, she told the following story. A proposed law concerning sexual practices between men, then called buggery or sodomy, was set before Queen Victoria for approval. Then someone asked if women should not also be included in the legal strictures. "Women!" she is reported to have laughed, "what could the poor things do?"

Little did she know. Throughout the European continent and in England, even among Victoria's own court ladies, women were finding and loving each other, some in lifelong relationships.

"In talking with Frank Harris I had learned a little about that," I told her.

"You discussed that with him!"

"He guessed about me, probably from reading my poetry to women, and from what he considered my 'boyishness.' He sometimes called me *androgyne*. He thought I should write about it frankly, in prose as well as poetry."

Tommy wasn't sure that would be advisable. "You probably wouldn't get it published." Tommy's general feeling was, then and later, what the average person did not know wouldn't hurt them.

"Remember the Oscar Wilde-Alfred Douglas affair? They were welcome in all the best homes in London until Queensbury precipitated the scandal. Most people were aware in those sophisticated circles what was going on. You know the British attitude: keep the small conventions, maintain the proprieties, and you can break the large ones. If you tell people and they are forced to recognize what we are doing, or even thinking about, they imagine we are obliging them to accept what they may consider, or believe others may consider, unconventional—or worse. If superficial decorum is kept, they can be spared that responsibility, and we'll not be bothered."

"You mean we are the beneficiaries of a tacit innocence or ignorance, but not real good will or tolerance?" She wasn't sure, but felt it was unwise to test the average person too far.

Tommy had had no trouble as a lesbian, even in western Canada. Friends in Vancouver all knew that she and Mona were together and had lived so for years. The couple did not conceal their affection or commitment. If Tommy arrived alone at a gathering or sports event, one friend, Sir George Bury, an executive on the Canadian Pacific Railway, would unfailingly ask in railroad language, "Where's the second section?" Everyone would laugh. It was all done in a friendly, jocular way like one referring to the member of a married couple.

However, a story appeared in the Vancouver newspaper about an individual presumed to be a man, but who was found to be a woman working at a man's job, and with a "wife." Discovery had come when she had a heart attack and died in the hospital. Vancouver was scandalized and indignant. Tommy remarked, "If she hadn't died I suppose she could have been put in prison. According to the news report, many people knew she was a woman masquerading as a man, but as long as there was no publicity they didn't care."

It was from Tommy I first heard the term "Boston marriage," as applied to households where two women lived together in life affinity. I was most curious about her experiences in Edinburgh and in London, and about women's love alliances other than her own. Did they conceal their attachments? "Not at all," she said, "they were quite affectionate with one another. None of us thought it was anybody's business."

I realize now that a certain arrogance of class pervaded European society with respect to individual behavior rights. The King can do no wrong, and the aristocracy, taking their cues from royalty, evidently found a wide range of amatory and sexual mores acceptable. The permissiveness stopped at the middle class, at least so far as open behavior went. The bourgeoisie seemed to need the bulwark of respectability for status.

Where did artists fit in? Tommy remarked that many of these were "pets" of the court or of other patrons with power and full purses. This was corroborated in my reading of the flowery and toadying dedications in some of the old books I was working with at Gough's. But it was also true that artists were usually able to transcend class, even as "pets" of privilege or as entertainers. Prevailing authority was often indulgent toward artistic sensibility, idiosyncrasy, and morality.

Perhaps, I suggested to Tommy, partly to tease her but also somewhat seriously, Frank Harris had therefore been correct that I as a poet might be able to write frankly about women loving women. In fact, I had already done it—and often. "The *average* person does not read poetry," she responded.

By dusk of our first weekend together, the falling rain had ceased. We decided to go out and find a restaurant where we could have a good meal. But we did not do so immediately. It was hard to break the spell of our new-found delight in one another. Presently we did wash and dress, then walk into the mild, moist dark in search of a place to eat.

Looking at her in the bright restaurant as we waited for our orders, I thought what a lovely woman she was and of my good fortune in finding her. Our coming together struck me as miraculous. I said something of the sort to her. She said:

"I'll be forty in December."

"What of that?"

"You told me you were twenty-five."

"Why should that matter?"

"It doesn't matter to me. If it doesn't to you—"

"I've always liked friends older than myself. They know more, have had more experience. I can learn much from them besides. . . ."

"Besides?"

"Loving."

She noticed my eyes resting on the ring she had slipped on my finger. She told me it was made for her and placed on her finger by her first love who had left her for marriage and whose loss had caused an abiding pain.

"Take it off—" she began.

"You mean the night it was to marry us is over?" I was sure she did not mean that; but smiling, half playful, held the ring out to her across the table.

"No, no, you are to keep it—as long as you wish to stay with me. But—" with a searching look into my eyes she said, "Love not only joy and happiness. There are hard times. We may have then Look inside, at the inscription."

It was hard to read but I made out the engraved words: *Vinci qui patitur.* She translated: "She conquers who endures."

I remarked on the beauty of the ring's design: three braided strands. She told me it represented the indissoluble bond of body, mind, and spirit and then placed the ring back on my finger.

When we were back in the studio she took me in her arms. "There is something I should like you to know as long as we are together. . . ."

"I hope it will be a long time."

"You are free. I shall not bind you. If you should ever desire to make love with anyone else, or wish our relationship to end, all I ask is that you be honest about it. Tell me. Dishonesty is the most destructive thing in love and in friendship. Do you agree?"

I said I did, wholeheartedly.

Within myself I prayed that I might be worthy of the affirmation.

Excerpted from *ELSA: I Come With My Songs, The Autobiography of Elsa Gidlow* (Booklegger Press)

Don't Explain

JEWELLE L. GOMEZ

Boston 1959

LETTY DEPOSITED the hot platters on the table, effortlessly. She slid one deep-fried chicken, a club-steak with boiled potatoes and a fried porgie platter down her thick arm as if removing beaded bracelets. Each plate landed with a solid clink on the shiny formica, in its appropriate place. The last barely settled before Letty turned back to the kitchen to get Bo John his lemonade and extra biscuits and then to put her feet up. Out of the corner of her eye she saw Tip come in the lounge. His huge shoulders, draped in sharkskin, barely cleared the narrow door frame.

"Damn! He's early tonight!" she thought but kept going. Tip was known for his generosity, that's how he'd gotten his nick-name. He always sat at Letty's station because they were both from Virginia, although neither had been back in years. Letty had come up to Boston in 1946 and been waiting tables in the 411 Lounge since

'52. She liked the people: the pimps were limited but flashy; the musicians who hung around were unpredictable in their pursuit of a good time and the "business" girls were generous and always willing to embroider a wild story. After Letty's mother died there been no reason to go back to Burkeville.

Letty took her newspaper from the locker behind the kitchen and filled a large glass with the tart grapejuice punch for which the cook, Mabel, was famous.

"I'm going on break, Mabel. Delia's takin' my station."

She sat in the back booth nearest the kitchen beneath the large blackboard which displayed the menu. When Delia came out of the bathroom Letty hissed to get her attention. The reddish-brown skin of Delia's face was shiny with a country freshness that always made Letty feel a little warm.

"What's up, Miss Letty?" Her voice was soft and saucy.

"Take my tables for twenty minutes. Tip just came in."

The girl's already bright smile widened, as she started to thank Letty.

"Go 'head, go 'head. He don't like to wait. You can thank me if he don't run you back and forth fifty times."

Delia hurried away as Letty sank into the coolness of the over-stuffed booth and removed her shoes. After a few sips of her punch she rested her head on the back of the seat with her eyes closed. The sounds around her were as familiar as her own breathing: squeaking Red Cross shoes as Delia and Vinnie passed, the click of high heels around the bar, the clatter of dishes in the kitchen and ice clinking in glasses. The din of conversation rose, levelled and rose again over the juke box. Letty had not played her record in days but the words spun around in her head as if they were on the turntable:

". . . right or wrong don't matter
when you're with me sweet
Hush now, don't explain
You're my joy and pain."

Letty sipped her cool drink; sweat ran down her spine soaking into the nylon uniform. July weather promised to give no breaks and the fans were working over-time like everybody else.

She saw Delia cross to Tip's table again. In spite of the dyed red hair, no matter how you looked at her Delia was still a country girl: long and self-conscious, shy and bold because she didn't know any better. She'd moved up from Anniston with her cousin a year before and landed the job at the 411 immediately. She worked hard and sometimes Letty and she shared a cab going uptown after work, when Delia's cousin didn't pick them up in her green Pontiac.

Letty caught Tip eyeing Delia as she strode on long, tight-muscled legs back to the kitchen. "That lounge lizard!" Letty thought to herself. Letty had trained Delia: how to balance plates, how to make tips and how to keep the customer's hands on the table. She was certain Delia would have no problem putting Tip in his place. In the year she'd been working Delia hadn't gone out with any of the bar flies, though plenty had asked. Letty figured that Delia and her cousin must run with a different crowd. They talked to each other sporadically in the kitchen or during their break but Letty never felt that wire across her chest like Delia was going to ask her something she couldn't answer.

She closed her eyes again for the few remaining minutes. The song was back in her head and Letty had to squeeze her lips together to keep from humming aloud. She pushed her thoughts onto something else. But when she did she always stumbled upon Maxine. Letty opened her eyes. When she'd quit working at Salmagundi's and come to the 411 she'd promised herself never to think about any woman like that again. She didn't know why missing Billie so much brought it all back to her. She'd not thought of that time or those feelings for a while.

She heard Abe shout a greeting at Duke behind the bar as he surveyed his domain. That was Letty's signal. No matter whether it was her break or not she knew white people didn't like to see their employees sitting down, especially with their shoes off. By the time

Abe was settled on his stool near the door, Letty was up, her glass in hand and on her way through the kitchen's squeaky swinging door.

"You finished your break already?" Delia asked.

"Abe just come in."

"Uh oh, let me git this steak out there to that man. Boy he sure is nosey!"

"Who, Tip?"

"Yeah, he ask me where I live, who I live with, where I come from like he supposed to know me!"

"Well just don't take nothing he say to heart and you'll be fine. And don't take no rides from him!"

"Yeah, he asked if he could take me home after I get off. I told him me and you had something to do."

Letty was silent as she sliced the fresh bread and stacked it on plates for the next orders.

"My cousin's coming by, so it ain't a lie, really. She can ride us."

"Yeah," Letty said as Delia giggled and turned away with her platter.

Vinnie burst through the door like she always did, looking breathless and bossy. "Abe up there, girl! You better get back on station. You got a customer."

Letty drained her glass with deliberation, wiped her hands on her thickly starched white apron and walked casually past Vinnie as if she'd never spoken. She heard Mabel's soft chuckle float behind her. She went over to Tip who was digging into the steak like his life depended on devouring it before the plate got dirty.

"Everything alright tonight?" Letty asked, her ample brown body towering over the table.

"Yeah, baby, everything alright. You ain't workin' this side no more?"

"I was on break. My feet can't wait for your stomach, you know."

Tip laughed. "Break! What you need a break for, big and healthy as you is!"

"We all gets old, Tip. But the feet get old first, let me tell you that!"

"Not in my business, baby. Why you don't come on and work for me and you ain't got to worry 'bout your feet."

Letty sucked her teeth loudly, the exaggeration a part of the game they played over the years. "Man, I'm too old for that mess!"

"You ain't too old for me."

"Ain't nobody too old for you! Or too young neither, looks like."

"Where you and that gal goin' tonight?"

"To a funeral," Letty responded dryly.

"Aw woman get on away from my food!" The gold cap on his front tooth gleamed from behind his greasy lips when he laughed. Letty was pleased. Besides giving away money Tip liked to hurt people. It was better when he laughed.

The kitchen closed at 11:00 p.m. Delia and Letty slipped out of their uniforms in the tiny bathroom and were on their way out the door by 11:15. Delia looked even younger in her knife-pleated skirt and white cotton blouse. Letty did feel old tonight in her slacks and long-sleeved shirt. The movement of car headlights played across her face, which was set in exhaustion. The dark green car pulled up and they slipped in quietly, both anticipating tomorrow, Sunday, the last night of their work week.

Delia's cousin was a stocky woman who looked forty, Letty's age. She never spoke much. Not that she wasn't friendly. She always greeted Letty with a smile and laughed at Delia's stories about the customers. "Just close to the chest like me, that's all," Letty often thought. As they pulled up to the corner of Columbus Avenue and Cunard Street Letty opened the rear door. Delia turned to her and said, "I'm sorry you don't play your record on your break no more, Miss Letty. I know you don't want to, but I'm sorry just the same."

Delia's cousin looked back at them with a puzzled expression but said nothing. Letty slammed the car door shut and turned to climb the short flight of stairs to her apartment. Cunard Street was quiet outside her window and the guy upstairs wasn't blasting his record player for once. Still, Letty lie awake and restless in her single bed. The fan was pointed at the ceiling, bouncing warm air over her, rustling her sheer nightgown.

Inevitably the strains of Billie Holiday's songs brushed against her, much like the breeze that fanned around her. She felt silly when she thought about it, but the melodies gripped her like a solid presence. It was more than the music. Billie had been her hero. Letty saw Billie as big, like herself, with big hungers, and some secret that she couldn't tell anyone. Two weeks ago, when Letty heard that the Lady had died, sorrow enveloped her. A refuge had been closed that she could not consciously identify to herself or to anyone. It embarrassed her to think about. Like it did when she remembered Maxine.

When Letty first started working at the 411 she met Billie when she'd come into the club with several musicians on her way back from the Jazz Festival. There the audience, curious to see what a real, live junkie looked like, had sat back waiting for Billie to fall on her face. Instead she'd killed them dead with her liquid voice and rough urgency. Still, the young, thin horn player kept having to reassure her: "Billie you were the show, the whole show!"

Once convinced, Billie became the show again, loud and commanding. She demanded her food be served at the bar and sent Mabel, who insisted on waiting on her personally, back to the kitchen fifteen times. Billie laughed at jokes that Letty could barely hear as she bustled back and forth between the abandoned kitchen and her own tables. The sound of that laugh from the bar penetrated her bones. She'd watched and listened, certain she saw something no one else did. When Billie had finished eating and gathered her entourage to get back on the road she left a tip, not just for Mabel but for each of the waitresses and the bartender. "Generous just like the 'business' girls," Letty was happy to note. She still had the two one dollar bills in an envelope at the back of her lingerie drawer.

After that, Letty felt even closer to Billie. She played one of the few Lady Day records on the juke box every night, during her break. Everyone at the 411 had learned not to bother her when her song came on. Letty realized, as she lay waiting for sleep, that she'd al-

ways felt that if she had been able to say or do something that night
to make friends with Billie, it might all have been different. In half
sleep the faces of Billie, Maxine and Delia blended in her mind. Letty
slid her hand along the soft nylon of her gown to rest it between
her full thighs. She pressed firmly, as if holding desire inside herself. Letty could have loved her enough to make it better. That was
Letty's final thought as she dropped off to sleep.

Sunday nights at the 411 were generally mellow. Even the pimps
and prostitutes used it as a day of rest. Letty came in early and had
a drink at the bar and talked with the bartender before going to
the back to change into her uniform. She saw Delia through the
window as she stepped out of the green Pontiac, looking as if she'd
just come from Concord Baptist Church. "Satin Doll" was on the
juke box, wrapping the bar in cool nostalgia.

Abe let Mabel close the kitchen early on Sunday and Letty looked
forward to getting done by 10:00 or 10:30, and maybe enjoying some
of the evening. When her break time came Letty started for the juke
box automatically. She hadn't played anything by Billie in two weeks;
now, looking down at the inviting glare, she knew she still couldn't
do it. She punched the buttons that would bring up Jackie Wilson's
"Lonely Teardrops" and went to the back booth.

She'd almost dropped off to sleep when she heard Delia whisper her name. She opened her eyes and looked up into the girl's
smiling face. Her head was haloed in tight, shiny curls.

"Miss Letty, won't you come home with me tonight?"

"What?"

"I'm sorry to bother you, but your break time almost up. I wanted
to ask if you'd come over to the house tonight...after work. My
cousin'll bring you back home after."

Letty didn't speak. Her puzzled look prompted Delia to start
again.

"Sometime on Sunday my cousin's friends from work come over
to play cards, listen to music, you know. Nothin' special, just some
of the girls from the office building down on Winter Street where

she work, cleaning. She, I mean we, thought you might want to come over tonight. Have a drink, play some cards. . . ."

"I don't play cards much."

"Well not everybody play cards. . . just talk. . . sitting around talking. My cousin said you might like to for a change."

Letty wasn't sure she like the last part: "for a change," as if they had to entertain an old aunt.

"I really want you to come, Letty. They always her friends but none of them is my own friends. They alright, I don't mean nothin' against them, but it would be fun to have my own personal friend there, you know?"

Delia was a good girl. Those were the perfect words to describe her, Letty thought smiling. "Sure honey, I'd just as soon spend my time with you as lose my money with some fools."

They got off at 10:15 and Delia apologized that they had to take a cab uptown. Her cousin and her friends didn't work on Sunday so they were already at home. Afraid that the snag would give Letty an opportunity to back out Delia hadn't mentioned it until they were out of their uniforms and on the sidewalk. Letty almost declined, tempted to go home to the safe silence of her room. But she didn't. She stepped into the street and waved down a Red and White cab. All the way uptown Delia apologized that the evening wasn't a big deal and cautioned Letty not to expect much. "Just a few friends, hanging around, drinking and talking." She was jumpy and Letty tried to put her at ease. She had not expected her first visit would make Delia so anxious.

The apartment was located halfway up Blue Hill Avenue in an area where a few blacks had recently been permitted to rent. They entered a long, carpeted hallway and heard the sounds of laughter and music ringing from the rooms at the far end.

Once inside, with the door closed, Delia's personality took on another dimension. This was clearly her home and Letty could not believe she ever really needed an ally to back her up. Delia stepped out of her shoes at the door and walked to the back with her same, long-legged gait. They passed a closed door, which Letty assumed to be one of the bedrooms, then came to a kitchen ablaze with light. Food and bottles were strewn across the pink and gray formica-top table. A counter opened from the kitchen into the dining room, which was the center of activity. Around a large mahogany table sat five women in smoke-filled concentration, playing poker.

Delia's cousin looked up from her cards with the same slight smile as usual. Here it seemed welcoming, not guarded as it did in those brief moments in her car. She wore brown slacks and a matching sweater. The pink, starched points of her shirt collar peeked out at the neck.

Delia crossed to her and kissed her cheek lightly. Letty looked around the table to see if she recognized anyone. The women all seemed familiar in the way that city neighbors can, but Letty was sure she hadn't met any of them before. Delia introduced her to each one: Karen, a short, round woman with West Indian bangles up to her pudgy elbow; Betty, who stared intently at her cards through thick eyeglasses encased in blue cat-eye frames; Irene, a big, dark woman with long black hair and a gold tooth in front. Beside her sat Myrtle who was wearing army fatigues and a gold Masonic ring on her pinky finger. She said hello in the softest voice Letty had ever heard. Hovering over her was Clara, a large red woman whose hair was bound tightly in a bun at the nape of her neck. She spoke with a delectable southern accent that drawled her "How're you doin' " into a full paragraph that was draped around an inquisitive smile.

Delia became ill-at-ease again as she pulled Letty by the arm toward the French doors behind the players. There was a small den with a desk, some books and a television set. Through the next set of glass doors was a livingroom. At the record player was an extremely tall, brown-skinned woman. She bent over the wooden cabinet searching for the next selection, oblivious to the rest of the gathering. Two women sat on the divan in deep conversation, which they punctuated with constrained giggles.

"Maryalice, Sheila, Dolores. . .this is Letty."

They looked up at her quickly, smiled, then went back to their pre-occupations: two to their gossip, the other returned to the record collection. Delia directed Letty back toward the foyer and the kitchen.

"Come on, let me get you a drink. You know, I don't even know what you drink!"

"Delia?" Her cousin's voice reached them over the counter, just as they stepped into the kitchen. "Bring a couple of beers back when you come, OK?"

"Sure, babe." Delia went to the refrigerator and pulled out two bottles. "Let me just take these in. I'll be right back."

"Go 'head, I can take care of myself in this department, girl." Letty surveyed the array of bottles on the table. Delia went to the dining room and Letty mixed a Scotch and soda. She poured slowly as the reality settled on her. These women were friends, perhaps lovers, like she and Maxine had been. The name she'd heard for women like these burst inside her head: bulldagger. Letty flinched, angry she had let it in, angry that it frightened her. "Ptuh!" Letty blew air through her teeth as if spitting the word back at the air.

She did know these women, Letty thought, as she stood at the counter smiling out at the poker game. They were oblivious to her, except for Terry. Letty remembered that was Delia's cousin's name. As Letty took her first sip, Terry called over to her. "We gonna be finished with this game in a minute Letty, then we can talk."

"Take your time," Letty said, then went out through the foyer door and around to the livingroom. She walked slowly on the carpet and adjusted her eyes to the light, which was a bit softer. The tall woman, Maryalice, had just put a record on the turntable and sat down on a love seat across from the other two women. Letty stood in the doorway a moment before the tune began:

"Hush now, don't explain
Just say you'll remain
I'm glad you're back

Don't explain..."

Letty was stunned, but the song sounded different here, among these women. Billie sang just to them, here. The isolation and sadness seemed less inevitable with these women listening. Letty watched Maryalice sitting with her long legs stretched out tensely in front of her. She was wrapped in her own thoughts, her eyes closed. She appeared curiously disconnected, after what had clearly been a long search for this record. Letty watched her face as she swallowed several times. Then Letty moved to sit on the seat beside her. They listened to the music while the other two women spoke in low voices.

When the song was over Maryalice didn't move. Letty rose from the sofa and went to the record player. Delia stood tentatively in the doorway of the livingroom. Letty picked up the arm of the phonograph and replaced it at the beginning of the record. When she sat again beside Maryalice she noticed the drops of moisture on the other woman's lashes. Maryalice relaxed as Letty settled onto the seat beside her. They both listened to Billie together, for the first time.

My Subway Lover

WANDA HONN

I GOT UP in the morning looking forward to my new life. I wasn't exactly anxious to go to work, but I felt confident in a desire to put more into my vocation. I would try to be there more for the patients and really start exerting my knowledge and ability. I'd try harder to rekindle a friendship with Janey and start looking at all the women more platonically and with less lust. I would free myself from the confinements of my sexual desire.

As I walked to the subway, the air was crisp and clear. The sun was just coming up, slightly softening the barren, gray, winter environment of the city. I arrived at the platform with the other early morning rush hour people. I was always amazed that in New York morning rush hour seemed to start at 6 a.m. and last until almost noon. The platform was crowded as the train pulled up. I saw that it was going to be one of those days when I had to cram myself into the car. I squeezed through the throng and pushed my way to the

117

area by the door that separates the cars. I leaned my back against the door for support.

As the car started moving I noticed, standing very close to me, a very beautiful woman. She was slightly shorter than I, with a soft, full face, shoulder-length curly brown hair, and a body that wouldn't quit. She had gorgeous large breasts that stood out firmly. Wow! Well, I can't help looking, I thought.

Soon the train stopped to let out a few and to take in even more. My friend got pushed in closer to me and was standing with her lovely bosom pushed up against my arm. I stiffened with embarrassment but also secretly felt delighted. The train moved on. I was immediately aware that the woman's breast rubbed up and down against me with the bouncing of the train. She smelled fresh from a morning shower and was wearing neat, clean clothes. Her hair radiated a flowery shampoo fragrance. I closed my eyes, felt her body moving against me, listened to the click-uh click-uh click-uh of the train. I was getting warm.

While absorbing these sensations, I noticed she had adjusted her position. Opening my eyes, I saw that what I had felt was true. She was facing me squarely, our bodies shoved together, front to front. She looked at me and smiled slightly. My face must have reddened deeply, and I thought she sensed what I had been feeling.

Then I felt something on my outer thigh. She was touching me with her hand. Oh, glorious, wonderful life! I knew then that she probably did know my mind and had one like it. Subtly, I put my own hand over hers on my thigh and led it in towards my center. She caught her breath, inhaled long and deeply. Our two hands began to move up and down my zipper, dipping in between my legs. Still leaning against the door, I spread my legs a little more. We bounced with the movement of the train, and giggled. The noise of the train seemed to be getting louder. She pressed her body hard against mine and continued to rub my crotch. Her breasts squished into me, the train's movement causing them to rub and tease my own. My clit was titillated and extremely sensitive; I began to rock towards her, our bodies grinding together quietly. I felt my underpants getting wet.

The train came to another stop, tossing people about. The woman had been pushed away from me slightly. As everyone regained their balance, I spread my legs a little more, and she, amazingly, unzipped my pants and slipped her hand inside. With one movement, while pushing up against me again, she wiggled her fingers underneath the leg band of my underpants and we were flesh on flesh. She made a slight noise, exhaling air quickly, and I began to sweat and tingle all over. The train started up with a jolt, and she pressed her fingers hard against me. I jerked with the shot of pleasure that ran through me. The train was moving smoothly again, and she kept her fingers held against my clit, with the rest of her hand cupping my bush. As the train rocked us, her hand and body moved up and down, pressing and relaxing in rhythm. My pelvis was throbbing. I felt the rush coming on. Oh, please don't stop, I thought. I began to tremble. My knees got weak. I wanted to pull her to me tightly and jump on her hand. Water dripped from my armpits and brow. I struggled to stifle grunting noises that began to force their way out of my throat. My thrusting became more pronounced. I held on to the door of the car with my hands. The noise of the moving train seemed to pound in my skull.

Suddenly we screeched to a halt. At that moment, she pushed hard against me and moved her hand rapidly and with force against my saturated groin. A flash went through me. I shuddered all over, my legs and pelvis twitching. A hot sensation of mounting pleasure drained me. I clenched my teeth and groaned softly. Shivering, I caught myself from sliding to the floor.

As the train resumed its journey, she slowly removed her wet, shaking hand from me. Regaining my composure, I looked around us nonchalantly, trying to determine from people's faces whether they had noticed anything. Everyone seemed to be looking away or downward and gave no indication of interest in me or my friend. But I still worried that some of them might have seen it all. Oh well, I thought, I'll probably never see any of them again in my life; I hope. The cynical part of me said, yeah, one of them will probably end up being your new nursing supervisor or something.

Then I gazed into my friend's eyes. They were dancing as she smiled and blushed. I wanted to say something but I didn't know what. I was still trying to find words when the train stopped again. Oh, no, my subway lover was moving to get off. As she turned to leave, I grabbed her arm quickly and said, "Thank you."

She turned her head, smiled fully, and said, "Any time."

I dropped my hand from her arm, and she rushed out of our rumbling, crowded boudoir.

Excerpted from *Rapture* (a Wanda Honn Publication).

Vacation Pictures

MELANIE KAYE/KANTROWITZ

WE DRIVE SOUTH through a Vermont blizzard that turns into vicious sleet in Connecticut, blinding rain as we pull into Brooklyn, where we sleep at Shelly's, and by the time we leave the next day, it's another goddam blizzard. First we get stoned at my suggestion and then you're pressing to leave and I want to stay until you coyly tell me it's my turn to feed the meter. I'm in the middle of talking to Shelly—*my* friend—and why the fuck are you so hellbent on measuring *turns* and I suddenly see our life together as coy, gamey, and tightassed. I don't want to go with you, I want to stay in Brooklyn with Shelly.

So that's how we drive off on our vacation. We're heading south and get about 30 miles, as far as New Brunswick, New Jersey, where we are forced to pay $50 for a motel because driving's impossible, and the only good thing that has happened is the drive over the Verrazano Bridge, my first time—yours too, but then you are not a New Yorker. I am wondering if I am still, did the first twenty years mark me indelibly as I like to think, even now when people say I've barely got an accent any more, and I don't know how to respond after years trying to shed it and more years trying to take it back.

Anyway, the Verrazano Bridge, silvery, technological beanstalk, only we land in New Jersey and the expensive motel. We're both stopping smoking today after a solid week of puffing our brains out, and we are on edge. I don't want to go on this stupid vacation, I'm bitter and resentful, the time, the money. I want simply to stay home and get some work done.

All week before we left, snow and ice made our road virtually unpassable, and every day one or the other of us stayed home waiting for Nancy, the friend of a friend who was supposed to animal sit the dog and four cats. The question was, would Nancy's car make it up the road? But every day for a different reason she couldn't come—except one day she got as far as the next town when her tire went flat, and another day her car absolutely refused, practically slid backwards down the hill. The last ditch hope was to see if snow tires made a difference.

All week, while you were getting more and more deeply depressed at the idea that we wouldn't be able to go, I was positively gleeful, trying to act subdued, until an hour before it was time to leave, we heard Nancy's car chugging up the driveway, and I said to myself, *Jessica, for once in your life think of someone besides yourself* and I tried to be glad for you.

And even am sort of glad, until you start being coy and measuring at Shelly's and insist we leave right that second, right into a snowstorm that is dangerous and costs us extra money, and we're irritable and I wonder how I came to be with you and how I will survive this vacation I don't want. But the next day, the snow, if not entirely melted, has stopped falling and we keep driving south and by the day after we can see grass and then flowers, in January. We eat in restaurants where white people talk like the white parents I saw interviewed on the news when I was nine years old, *how do you feel about your child going to an integrated school?* Customers seem almost equally Black and white, the workers also mixed, not evenly but ten times more than when I'd worked in Virginia twenty years ago teaching at a now historically, then totally Black college and when I'd walked downtown with a Black co-teacher, male, who was not then but did in fact later become my lover, a carfull of white men with that accent chased us and we had to run, breathless and terrorized.

The third day from Brooklyn we come into Florida, shed our sweaters and corduroy pants, walk along the beach and feel hot sun pouring down over our pale deprived skin. Finally I am glad to be here. I sit in the sun to read the news for the first time in days and learn about a march planned in a county just north of Atlanta to protest segregation. I want to be part of it. History is happening and we are on a frivolous bourgeois vacation. I try to talk you into leaving Florida the next day to drive to the march. You, exhausted from endless weeks of work, relaxing finally into sun and sleep, refuse: you're not leaving. You say we'll never get there in time and if I want to go, I can. But I'm afraid to go alone (of course I don't say this), and I'll never make it in time driving by myself, and besides I suspect you'd be furious at me for abandoning our vacation. I give up the idea, blaming you for my passivity. We don't even fight about it, I just take your reluctance as law and resent it. You don't know how it sets you up in my mind as superficial and materialist: *A vacation,* I think scornfully, until months later we talk about it. You had not known how deeply I felt nor did I realize you were somewhat open to negotiating. Though I wonder still if this is revisionist history. I know how people use each other as excuses.

The truth is we've been together two years and we're right in between being new lovers and old ones. Will it stick? "When we were in Florida," months later you will say, "remember you worried that I thought you were weird and I worried that you thought I was superficial. . .and the truth is, you *were* being weird and I *was* being superficial." When you say this, I will feel intense relief.

But right now you seem strange to me except you can always make me laugh. You keep making the same jokes because they set me to gasping helplessly, convulsively, knowing I shouldn't, jokes about how ugly you are—which you aren't—like *I'd better not go in the water, I'll scare the fish*—but funny. I want you just to be easy and accepting of how you look (so I can be easy and accepting of myself?). But you're not.

And I wonder: is this who I want to be with? Do I love you? What is love? etc.

On Wednesday we take mushrooms together, a gift from one of our favorite students. I'm sitting on the blanket, frightened, the drug just coming on, and you want to go to the bathroom but you say, *I don't want to leave you alone.*

Words come strangely to my mouth, as from some other larynx, some other brain center: *Yes, that's a good idea,* I smile weakly.

Jessie mustn't be alone, you say so gently sunglasses hide my tears, springing from the mere thought that someone, you, would take care of me, make sure I am not frightened, not abandoned.

Suddenly I love you. *If there were time, I'd have babies,* I say profound and thick-voiced, grasping mortality.

After a while we walk into the shimmering Atlantic, circles of golden light dancing over the green transparent water. We play in the ocean, and fear stabs me, dispelling the golden light, the cool joy: *Will we drown? Is this dangerous? Will the car keys get stolen, and the car, our money . . .*and all at once there comes a shocking thought and I say, speaking very slowly, and I don't think you realize what a bold thing this is for me to imagine: *I'm contemplating the possibility that the universe is not actively malevolent.*

Not *actively,* I'll think later, backsliding. But passively? The underlying principle is, after all, constraint, as now we have only three days left on the beach, lazy days, swimming days, walking days, shrimps and oysters and take-out from a Thai deli, and making love not so often as you'd think, considering it's vacation, but a couple of times anyway and we are more or less liking each other (except once walking along the beach I'm trying to explain about a poem I'm writing and you don't understand or aren't interested and I think, *maybe I don't want to be with her,* and am flooded by such terror and guilt I say to myself immediately, *swallow it, deal with it later).*

We drag the camera out only once, to a fishing pier, and when the pelicans swoop in close with their huge wings and expandable bills, you take pictures and I think, *if I could be any bird, I'd pick this one,* for the freedom of those vast swoops. I want desperately to fly, at the moment even more than I want to live forever.

It's not until we're leaving that we take out the camera again. We check the corners of our little efficiency apartment to which I am by now fiercely attached, pack the car and drive to the beach for our last walk before heading day by day back into hard winter. We're taking pictures of each other, I shoot as you walk towards me, the ocean at your back, your hair blowing, you're wearing a turquoise T-shirt with pandas on it, climbing bamboo. We are both especially fond of pandas since learning that all they ever do is eat bamboo shoots and fuck, continually. I try to imagine life without the need to dent some surface. I try to imagine I don't know I'll die some-time, maybe even soon, and you will too.

I take your picture as you walk towards me, you're laughing, the shirt is just a shade bluer than the ocean, a shade greener than your eyes. You flip up the T-shirt and flash your breast at the camera, mugging a wide funny mouth as if to get back at me for taking pic-tures of you when you think you are ugly and should not be pho-tographed. In fact you are a beautiful and sexy woman, but there is nothing sexy about the gesture or the photo. It reminds me what I do and don't love about you and it's the same quality: you'll make fun of anything. I love how you goose the prig in me who learned young to shrink—along with my mother and all other women who married a half-class down—from my father's very occasional dirty joke; I hate how you sometimes seem to value or respect nothing. Sometimes your mocking voice seems crude, embarrasses me, and I look around to see who's listening. I hear the snob in me when

I say this and am ashamed.

After the breast-photo and probably one or two others you say finally, brash, the way you get when you're embarrassed and pushing ahead anyway, *I know you're above all this, but I'm still subject to vanity, could you take a couple of me after I comb my hair?*

These words, and the sight of you, slightly embarrassed, combing your hair to pose, touches something raw in me. Your vulnerability, the simple thing you want: *to feel pretty.* Is that it? Or is it your failure to treat this want as I do, because I am not above it, in fact I am an extremely vain person, catching a glimpse in every store window or mirror I pass, checking, checking—how can you not know this? But I would never never ask to comb my hair, my vanity consists partly of pretending not to care, refusing to compete, *take me as I am.* How did I convince you I am above it and you should be embarrassed to want to feel like a pretty woman? I think of our familiar joke:

Two women, sitting up in bed, both speaking at once:
But I thought you *were butch!*

We resolve this joke intermittently by repetition, by making other jokes, by recognizing we are both butch, both femme, and it's the uneasy lack of distinction that sometimes catches us up in competition instead of compassion. I think of Otis Redding, killed in a plane crash that summer I taught in Virginia, his throaty sobbing voice instructing, *when that girl gets weary/ young girls they do get weary/ wearing the same old shabby dress*—image of a woman worn down by ordinary life which in no way cherishes her. Butch knows how to cherish: *Try a little tenderness,* Otis urges eternally on my *Best of Otis Redding* cassette, and I pledge to try.

But something more. The loved one as all-powerful, needs nothing, gives everything. I forgot you are vulnerable. Forgot. It scares me, the responsibility of loving you, caring for you. I want only to be the frightened small one on the blanket: *Jessie mustn't be alone.* Must I be the large soothing one, the one who says effortlessly: *Of course comb your hair, do whatever you want—I'll love you.* What if I fail, do not love enough?

You comb your hair and smile shyly for the camera, and no one but me (and other women who love you?) would recognize the smile as shy, but it is. In your smile I see my own tentative assertion: *Here I am, am I pretty?* I feel pain for your vulnerability and your failure to see mine, and swimming around the tender place is the mirror we make for each other, even though you don't see it and I don't show you, around the raw, painful place which is not easy, accepting, natural or anything but the cost of love.

New Year's Eve
At a Bar

LEE LYNCH

"WHAT A WAY to start the New Year," said Sally the bartender after another earth-shaking sneeze.

Tall, thin, she leaned over the bar, blonde head in her hands, and massaged her temples. Against the plate glass window which read CAFE FEMMES, tiny pellets of sleet cast themselves from the grey afternoon sky like so many chilly dykes just off to work, and impatient for the warmth inside.

"Why don't you go home?" asked Gabby, busy behind the food counter. "Look it," Gabby said, gesturing to the empty tables, "I can handle the hordes till Liz gets here."

"It's New Year's Eve," complained Sally. "I always work New Year's. You know that, Gabby."

"Come back later, when it's time, then," Gabby suggested. She worked cheerily enough, slicing her cheeses and chopping her fruit, but there was an exasperated edge to her voice.

129

"I know I'm being a crab," Sally admitted.

Gabby looked at her without expression. "Aw, Sal. Only for the last two months or so."

Sally closed her eyes. Her whole body felt as if it bore a weight much too heavy which pressed down and down and down. She had been depressed as long as Gabby said, and fearful to the point of being unable to handle her day-to-day life. It isn't liquor, she thought again. She'd stopped drinking altogether some time earlier. It isn't menopause; Dr. Stern had said she was too young. Her greatest fear was that it might be mental illness. Look at her mother, on tranquilizers for twenty years now. Look at her little sister, too zonked out on drugs to do anything but live off that terrible man. Was it Sally's turn?

She ignored Gabby's truth-filled sarcasm. "But, jeeze," she said, "the singer's not even here yet and who wants to go out into this weather just to be sick someplace else?"

It was true. Compared to the outdoors, the bar seemed like a haven. Liz, Sally's partner both at work and at home, had lately installed floor lamps here and there, from the Art Deco store up on Christopher Street. On a dark afternoon like this, their pools of light gave Cafe Femmes the look of a fifties living room—her fifties living room?—or, at the least, a basement playroom complete with flashing jukebox, beeping electronic game and, at long last, a pool table. Sally was especially proud of the pool table, placed in an alcove they'd knocked into the back room, and glowing green now, its own circle of hanging lamplight accenting it. There was something in the sight that awoke the dreamer in her, and she'd travel back to the roots of her imagination to drift into and out of reality.

"You think that's one of those made-up names these new little dykes are taking for themselves?"

Sally started. She must have the beginnings of a fever, she thought, to be *this* dreamy and lost. "Who?"

"Curly Singer, this *singer* you've got on tonight."

"I don't know. Could be. She's Julie's ex. Ask her. Anyway, we're lucky to get someone at all with Sappho's Swingers breaking up at the last minute."

"I just worry," said Gabby, moving to the bar. She pushed herself up on a stool and swung back and forth, her short legs sticking straight out. She seemed to be admiring from every side her orange polka dot high-top sneakers with their red and orange checked laces. "Just because she's hot in Denver—and Julie's bedroom—is no guarantee she'll go over in the Big Apple."

"New York dykes are too insular. A little new blood will be good for them. Besides, this is just her first stop. She's booked all up and down the east coast." She sneezed again. It felt as if she was rattling her brain. What if Gabby was right and Curly Singer was a flop?

"I wouldn't want you mixing *my* drinks," said Gabby, as Sally mopped her nose with a clean bar rag.

"All right, already. I'll go get some Contac. But you know I hate taking drugs."

"So who told you to? I said go home."

The drugstore was two blocks over. Sally girded herself against the weather and bent into the sleety wind, hunched over, hands fisted in the pockets of her old fleece-lined jean jacket. She even put the hood of her sweatshirt up. Hardly aware of the elements or the transaction in the drugstore, she daydreamed as she walked, of summer nights, softball in the park, enough heat for the whole city. She was soaked and freezing when she got back to the bar. She felt as if she were stepping from one cloudy otherworld into another. Through teary eyes she saw Amaretto, Gabby's girl.

"Don't we look in the festive spirit," Amaretto said. She wore high heels and a shiny red dress with shoulder straps.

"Yikes!" Gabby cried. "Who let that wet mop inside the door? Quick!" and she rushed toward Sally. "Help me wring it out before it drips all over the floor!"

Sally dodged Gabby, trying to laugh. She went for water to wash down her cold pill. "Any word from the singer?"

"This place has been deader than a —"

"Rusty skillet?" suggested the taller, long-haired Amaretto as Gabby backed up against her, rubbing bottom to pelvis.

"—than a—" Gabby went on.

"—empty jar of Miracle Whip?"

"Ugh," Sally said, trying again to laugh.

"—than a—"

"Doorknob!"

"That's it, Amaretto! Perfect! Brilliant!" cried Gabby, burrowing more deeply back.

Sally blew her nose mightily. The cold, on top of the depression, gave a nightmarish mien to the bar. She wanted to burrow deeper and deeper into something, anything, till she was totally protected from the world.

"Deader than you're going to be if you don't go home for a while," Gabby predicted.

"Can't," Sally replied, indicating the clock. "Liz is late. What if—"

"Never mind what if. She'll walk through that door any minute. As usual."

The pay phone jangled just then. Its sound filled Sally with dread. She'd been unable to bring herself to answer a phone all week, afraid of what would be on the other end, afraid she wouldn't be able to handle whatever demands it put on her.

Gabby saw her hesitation and went. After a moment she asked into the phone, "Where are you, Liz? JFK? *No*body's landing?"

"Shit," Sally said to Amaretto. "I *told* her to let the woman grab a limo into town."

"No," Gabby was saying. "I'll stay. You can't leave the airport. What if all of a sudden they let her land? Yeah, Sal's here, but she should be in bed. I'll try, but you know how she is."

Gabby hitched up her purple painter's pants, though the lavender suspenders gripping them appeared to work perfectly well. It was one of her gestures of self-importance.

"A disaster," Sally said when she'd heard the whole story.

"Be grateful the plane didn't crash."

"So I'm grateful. What are we going to do for New Year's Eve entertainment? Why did we ever let Julie talk us into this? There must be other ways to get to see an ex."

Gabby did a small leap into the air, then tapped and shuffled across the floor, bowing when she stopped. Amaretto curtsied to her. They began to dance in ballroom fashion. "I have often walked," they crooned in unison, "down this street before—"

"Am I glad my ears are plugged up," Sally complained, groaning. "You're not hired."

"I don't think she appreciates us," Gabby said.

The sound of sleet grew louder as the door opened. A little couple rushed in, as if propelled by the wind. They shot shy glances at the staff as they removed their coats and stamped the wet off their feet.

"Happy New Year," Sally told them at the bar. She rubbed the area before them with a clean white bar rag. "What'll it be?"

"Do you have something *hot*----?" asked one. "We came all the way in from the Island." She'd worn a rain hat over her tight curls and now tried to fluff them.

Even Sally could smell the new perm. She made them Jamaican coffees. "How was the driving?"

As if they'd been waiting for this cue, words began to spill from the women. Bumper to bumper. Accidents. Gusts. Good thing they took the whole day off. Missed their matinee. Never get home tonight. Worth it—

"For what? Are you going to watch the ball drop in this weather?" asked Sally.

"Oh, no. We came in for Curly Singer. We saw her at the New England Women's Music Retreat last summer and she was fabulous."

Sally sighed, and found she could just about breathe again, although the pills had made her head feel huge and stuffed, especially around her cheek bones, which seemed to be stretched beyond the splitting point.

Gabby was eating an enormous dill pickle, and transferring others from a barrel to a tray with stainless steel tongs. Amaretto had closed the costume shop she owned at five o'clock, having sold out of funny hats and oversized diapers with giant safety pins. She rubbed Gabby's back. Sally told them what the Islanders had said.

"What time is the first show scheduled for?" asked Amaretto.

"Seven, believe it or not. Liz wanted a dinner show." Her heart was fluttering with anxiety. The night was ruined. Their reputation shot. The business would sink beyond recovery. Liz would slide off the Long Island Expressway into a pole—

Two more couples came in and she shook herself out of her bad dream. The couples were dressed to the nines, and took a table right up by the tiny stage.

"Shit. What am I going to do?"

Amaretto, ever cool and practical, went to call the airline. While she was on hold, three more tables filled up. Gabby, who served her delicacies cafeteria-style on busy nights, loudly sang behind the counter. Finally, someone thought to drown her out with the juke-box. The bar had come alive.

Sally served drinks and watched as Amaretto left the phone. There was a sick feeling clutching at Sally's insides as Amaretto approached, but she couldn't tell where her apprehensions started and the cold medicine ended. Possible solutions darted around in her mind, but none would settle long enough for her to examine them. Maybe Liz would walk in any minute and she could stop thinking for awhile.

Amaretto shook her head. "Everyone was landing in Newark for a while, but now Newark's shut down too."

"You mean she could have landed in Newark already? We don't even know where our star performer is and it's 6:15." They looked at each other. "At least we're not too crowded. This weather's keeping the audience away, too."

Sally began to pace. That smell peculiar to colds had invaded her nostrils. It was a familiar, even comforting smell, and her colds carried it whether she was in the smokey bar or in a flower garden.

Something like mushroom soup, with the more attractive parts of cigarette smoke mixed in.

She drifted again and came out of it when she realized it was 6:30. She had to make a decision. She couldn't bear to disappoint the kids. Besides, fifty percent of them were new customers. They'd never be back if she didn't soften the blow somehow. She wanted nothing so much as to go curl up on the pool table, which looked warm and clean under its glowing lamp. To use all the customers' coats as a blanket, like a little kid dragged to an adult party and put to sleep in the host's bed.

Two of the women were playing pool, cueing up and posturing, clicking the balls, swallowing their smiles of triumph, squinting down their sticks like professionals. Two more were waiting to play, watching this game as if the world depended on it. Sally checked her register, then Gabby's. She pulled five of the newest, crispest twenties out, shut off the jukebox, and made her announcement.

Curly Singer was a little like Bob Dylan, Sally thought, listening to "Singin' Curly Blues." At the same time, she put Sally in mind of Gene Autry, in her cream-colored cowboy suit, fringe and all, her white guitar, her pointy-toed boots and her rhymes and country rhythms. Despite the conflict, it was foot-stomping music which threatened to lighten Sally's mood from the first song.

> My woman is a guitar
> And we lie beneath the stars
> Makin' melodies and reveries
> Pluckin' songs from memories.

Sally noted the way the musician's hair glowed at its edges like a halo. Amaretto had done a good job setting up the lights.

> I'm a buckin' lesbian bronco
> Kickin' about my rights.
> I throw every macho honcho
> And fight every woman's fight.
>   But nothin's as lonesome to this girl

As buckin' the whole damn world.

Maybe, Sally thought, she just liked Curly because she was corny and fun. The audience sang an enthusiastic yodeling cowboy chorus along with Curly. The Islander with the new perm watched her with adoration in her eyes. Liz took Sally's hand and they slipped into the back room. Liz lay her head against her lover's shoulder as they caught up on each other's day.

"I'm just grateful I didn't put a scratch on Dad's car with all the icy driving."

"I was worried about you. Especially when Curly showed up without you."

"As soon as the sleet stopped, the temperature went skyhigh. It felt like spring, not New Year's Eve. When the airline announced her flight had landed at Newark I almost cried. I thought she'd never get here unless I drove down for her." Liz's eyes were full of light. "How about you?" she asked, buttoning Sally's button-down collar. "Your cold sounds better than it did this morning."

"Pills," Sally answered, unbuttoning her collar again.

"I'm sorry I wasn't here to help with the crowd."

"We were lucky. It was slow."

"You call this slow?"

"These, my dear, are the 7:00 and 10:00 audiences. Together." Liz looked at her, eyes darkening.

Sally had the urge to float into a dream. Instead she said, "Why should they leave? It was awful out there." She looked down at Liz's breasts, swelling against the velour V-neck shirt that was as green as the felt on the pool table.

"Sal, is that *all* that kept them here?"

"Well, I held a little tournament."

"Your pool tournament?" Liz looked agitated. "So you finally found an excuse to hold it." She tapped a foot. "Sal, we've talked about how we don't want to be known as a seedy lesbian pool bar."

"They loved it! Some of them had only come to hear Curly, but they got so involved in the game, I swear they didn't care if she never—"

"How much, Sal?" Liz's hands were on her hips now, her foot still tapping.

"Huh?"

"What did this little pool tournament set us back?"

Sally told her.

Liz's lips were tight. She was staring at the breast pocket of Sally's white shirt. Sally stuck her hands into her jeans pockets and jingled the change. Eventually, Liz's shoulders relaxed and a smile came over her face. She shook her head. "Thank you," she whispered, "for saving the night. For keeping the customers."

"It *was* the right thing to do? I was afraid I was crazy. You know how I've been. I thought maybe my mind had snapped from this depression, but I wasn't scared anymore once I'd made the decision. It felt good."

"You know what, Sal? You needed to make a crazy decision. I thought I'd walk in here and find you climbing the walls. Or sick, or crying in the back room." She hugged Sally. "I'm proud of you."

The guitar was commanding attention. Liz and Sally moved back behind the bar.

"I understand we've got a winner here tonight!" Curly announced. "And I have the honor of awarding the prize!"

In the background, Gabby made trumpeting sounds as Curly called out the winner's name. With a flourish, she presented the five crisp twenty-dollar bills to the small woman with the perm. The woman whopped with excitement when Curly, who showed no sign of her rough trip, swept her off her feet in a hug.

Half the bar took up Gabby's trumpeting sound, then, and the noise opened some long-locked door in Sally. She could feel her spirits fly out and up, up as high as they wanted to go. The dreamer inside her took a bow.

"What a way to start the New Year!" Liz shouted over the exhuberant din.

Sally let out a whoop like the Islander's and pulled Liz into an impassioned, reckless, dizzying whirl.

Out of the
Frying Pan

HARRIET MALINOWITZ

FOR A MINUTE, as Paula watched Lee crane her neck and squint
at the figures on the gas pumps, she thought she looked like a dino-
saur. Lee's neck seemed to be divided into sections, the long upper
part projecting from the base which rose up from her shoulders.
Her body radiated indecision, clearly trying to do several things at
once: get nearer the pumps to read the prices, go into the office
to ask for a map of Connecticut, and return to the car, where Paula
sat in the passenger seat behind ten other cars waiting to be serviced.

Paula tried to imagine how Lee looked to other people: a tall,
tanned woman who zig-zagged her way up from feet to hair, with
angles formed at the ankles, knees, waist and neck—someone who
slumped more than was necessary, visibly trying to minimize the ef-
fect of her presence. A nice-looking person—too nice—absolutely
candid, almost gullible. Paula watched Lee's body move in sequence
in three directions, un-selfconsciously fighting with itself, and then

attempt a fourth—the women's bathroom. Paula instinctively drew in her own small body even more tightly, refusing to be associated with this person whose uninhibited bursts of motion revealed all.

Then, with a flash of relief and pain, she remembered that she wasn't responsible for Lee anymore.

When she remembered this, a scrim seemed to drop down in front of Lee, so that Paula's vision of her became muted, softened around the edges. Shocked at her thoughts of a moment ago, she felt ashamed, as if she'd insulted someone else's family with the words that were only permissible for her own, in whose foibles she was clearly implicated.

Once, when they were still lovers, she had taken Lee to a party given by friends she had met working in an environmental activist coalition. Lee, not knowing anyone, had felt uncomfortable. Towards the middle of the evening Paula had overheard her say to someone, intending humor, "Maybe it's just our conservatism that makes us hold onto our concept of what humans should look like. We're not used to sudden leaps in evolution, but what would be so bad, after all, if we went through mass mutations and a new species evolved with, say, two heads?"

"That wasn't funny," Paula told her later, angrily. "You embarrassed me." And that was enough—Lee understood. Paula had the right to demand that Lee's behavior not violate the rules which governed her own, just as Lee could demand it of her—for as lovers they were responsible for each other. They had chosen one another, and in time their tastes, attitudes, idioms, even mannerisms had blended, so that criticism of one implicitly reflected upon the other. But because Lee was large, Paula small; Lee candid, Paula guarded; Lee expansive, Paula compressed; because Lee stood up at a podium and delivered art history lectures, while Paula furtively and methodically edited copy; because Lee liked to throw parties, and Paula waited to be invited—the social risks of their merging were mostly Paula's.

Lee's six foot frame kept no secrets. Paula could read every emotion, every conflict in the unbridled movements of her body. When people laughed at Lee's jokes, her mouth twisted violently with the effort to appear nonchalant, and her legs would cross and re-cross themselves rapidly in delight. Paula knew when she had hurt her because the foot of her crossed leg would jiggle up and down, and she had been known at such times to stand up, walk across the room, pivot, and return, muttering, "Huh. Huh," to herself, as if pieces of a difficult equation were falling into place.

Paula often wished, uneasily, that she could keep Lee under wraps, as she had seen Bedouin women in the Sinai desert kept by their men, draped in black fabric from head to toe so that the sunlight never touched their skins. She would peer inside at her regularly, bringing nutrients and private love.

"A dollar twelve a gallon," Lee said, gathering herself into the car and pulling the door shut behind her. She opened the sun roof and began switching the radio dial from station to station, drawing loud bursts of static. This had long been a source of argument between them: Lee changed the station every time a song she didn't like came on, optimistically searching for something better, while Paula liked to find one station and stick to it, stoically enduring the loud rock or bubblegum music, sure that something appealing would be played in due time. When Lee flicked the dial Paula would sit very still, tight-lipped, as a wave of heat rose slowly from her groin to her face. Usually Lee wouldn't notice right away; she would go on talking, perfectly content in her world where the conversation was good, the music was in her control, and Paula was beside her. Sometimes Paula would count to herself, deliberately ignoring Lee, and then later she would tell her her score.

"Five hundred and sixty two before you woke up," she'd say, forcing a laugh. "A world record."

Lee would be contrite when she realized Paula's annoyance. "Oh, I'm sorry," she'd say, her hand jumping guiltily off the knob to hug the steering wheel. Finally they had agreed that whoever drove controlled the air waves.

Now Lee absently drummed her fingers against the steering wheel, and Paula knew that if she counted to a thousand there would never come that moment when Lee would look at her with her quick, hungry look, her brown eyes trusting and honest against all probability. Paula's irritation didn't matter anymore; it exploded into a vacuum. There was nothing left to threaten, no bond to sever.

Lee had moved completely beyond her jurisdiction. She hadn't any idea what Lee's habits were now—whether she still read late into the night and slept till ten o'clock, whether the bathroom in her Park Slope apartment still smelled of Irish Spring soap, whether she still put raw peppers and onions in her salads and chewed Rolaids for hours afterwards. She wondered if Lee lay in bed with her new lover, her ear pressed against the wall, listening to the couple next door, who owned a catering business, discuss the nuances of cheesecake. Lee used to repeat their conversations to her, speaking with the skill of a simultaneous translator. "They've tried a new ambrosia cake," she'd whisper as Paula lay beside her, her hand thrown across Paula's stomach. "Used a little Mateus in it—it was perfect." Paula would imagine the couple next door also lying in their bed, middle-aged, plump, joined together by a grand passion, like the Curies or the Brownings.

Lee had introduced her to new habits, like taking long, hot baths together in Paula's deep, claw-footed tub, and reading the business section of the *Times* to trace the entrepreneurial journeys of competing candy bars. And she had broken some of her old ones. The morning after the first night Paula had spent with Lee, Paula padded into Lee's bathroom and called out, "I don't have a toothbrush!"

"Use mine!" Lee had called back, and Paula had stood there, stymied, convinced that sharing toothbrushes guaranteed death as surely as playing transistor radios in the shower or sitting directly on public toilets. Lee had reappeared at the door. "What's the matter? It's brand new, medium hard. It does a great job, and it takes Crest."

"But it's *your* toothbrush."

"So? Do you think it has any germs you haven't already acquired straight from my mouth?"

So she'd brushed her teeth with Lee's toothbrush, and after that it became completely normal to keep only one brush in each apartment. It elevated brushing teeth to more than just a ritual function—it became a path to liberation, an act of breaking old taboos.

She had taught Lee new habits, too. She refused to touch in public, but she liked to be held while she slept, her body forming a "Z," her angles tucked into Lee's. When one of them tired of lying in the same position they would both turn over, Lee's broad back now crushed against her breasts, Lee's buttocks warming her legs. Many times they never woke up all night, but learned to respond even in sleep to each other's movements, never losing the thread of their touching.

And it was Paula who had started the tradition of eating bagels on Sunday mornings as they caught up on the back sections of the Sunday *Times* that she kept stacked in her non-working fireplace. If they were at Lee's apartment Paula would run out to the small bagel store around the corner. If they were staying at Paula's apartment on the Lower East Side, Lee would bring them the night before in a paper bag, wrapped in plastic to keep them fresh—a poppy seed bagel for Paula, an onion bagel for Lee, and a cinnamon raisin bagel that they would share sometime in the afternoon, dripping butter on the *Times* crossword puzzle.

But there had been other habits, too, the sort that went barely noticed until they became suddenly obtrusive, like dust which had accumulated on a windowpane. Paula could not say exactly when Lee's habit of talking loudly in restaurants and on buses had begun to bother her. There had been the Sunday evening on the quiet, echoing subway platform when Lee told her, her voice richocheting off the cavernous walls, of how Stephen Gordon's first frustrating relationship in *The Well of Loneliness* bore parallels to their own. Had that, too, been a liberating moment, or had she sucked in her breath as if to somehow enshroud Lee's words in the silence of her non-breathing? She only knew that one evening, looking at her across a table, it seemed that Lee's atoms had suddenly shifted around, so that she looked slightly grotesque—like one of the faces in the deodorant commercial where a voice in the background intoned dolefully, "Your inlaws are coming to dinner," and disembodied heads with distorted features floated toward the camera. Watching her with detachment, Paula understood that she had had this sensation before, perhaps many times, and when she recoiled from Lee slightly, this too felt familiar, though she could not specifically name another occasion when it had happened.

Gradually she had come to view them both more and more in caricature, Lee absurdly large, she excessively small, so that their lovemaking seemed to verge on burlesque. And as she lived more and more in her thoughts, regarding Lee silently and critically, she felt Lee in turn scrutinizing her as if she were a slide under a microscope, a property too infinitesimal to be perceived by the naked eye.

Once in February, as they both sat cross-legged on Paula's rug, Lee leaned over on an impulse to hug her, and Paula, with one quick practiced motion, snatched up her coffee cup in the instant before Lee would have knocked it over. Paula heard, with as much surprise as Lee, the sound of her tongue clicking against her teeth—it escaped without her own volition, like a hiccup. At the noise, Lee stopped, several inches short of her, and they looked at one another— Paula holding the cup like a shield in front of her, Lee poised at an awkward tilt.

Finally, Lee rocked back over her crossed ankles and, grounded, surveyed Paula from a speculative distance. "What?" she asked.

Paula opened and closed her mouth, making aborted attempts with her throat and looking troubled, as if she could not quite articulate the complexity of what ailed her.

And then, in the same week, Lee had made an omelette which Paula had refused to eat. When Paula made omelettes she cooked the vegetables slowly, allowing the fresh zucchini, mushrooms, and peppers to soften lazily in herbed butter; then she would pour the eggs on to settle over a carefully controlled low heat. Later she would life the edges gently with a spatula, letting the liquid run to the bottom of the pan. When the eggs were cooked she would meticulously fold them over to form a neat crescent-shaped pancake. Sometimes Lee would bring exotic or mundane cheeses, as the mood struck her, which Paula would cut razor-thin and lay in the skillet with slices of apple.

But Lee, even while she admired Paula's results and was eager to imitate them, had no patience. Her vegetables remained hard, her shortening evaporated when she wasn't looking, and in her fear that the omelette would burn she would try to fold it too quickly, causing it to break into sections which she helplessly scrambled.

And although Paula had conceded to eat these messes before, with wry humor and reproach, one day she simply felt that she could no longer do it. The room had become smoky, and when Lee finally filled her plate and handed it to her, she stared down at lumps of yellow burned a brownish color on one side and running watery on the other. On top of them, dished out as an afterthought, were little shreds of fry—not fried anything, but pure fry.

"I'm not eating it," she said, pushing away her plate.

"All right," Lee agreed. Without hesitating, she took Paula's plate, and then her own, over to the garbage. She scraped the eggs off rapidly so that they fell over the empty milk and egg cartons. Then she grabbed her bag and left.

Paula sat listening to the garbage bag make soft crinkling noises as its contents readjusted their weight. Tears came into her eyes; she thought of children starving in Cambodia and women on stools in Chock Full O'Nuts, spooning pea soup into their mouths from styrofoam bowls.

Two weeks later Lee had met Ellen.

Later on Paula would count back, trying to match up each of the days in those weeks with particular expressions on Lee's face, things Lee had said, the precise tenor of her voice. Like a doctor doggedly reviewing the same symptoms, hoping they would reveal some pattern which had heretofore eluded her, she sorted through those days again and again. She knew—she *thought*—that on the day of the eggs all had been as usual. They had fought before—and if Lee was the one who usually got scarred, it was only because they both knew that she was the one who would come back. Paula wouldn't. If she had lived in another century she would have died for honor; if she had been a plant she would have died from refusing to bend toward the sun. Lee had always been the active solicitor, Paula the acquiescor, the conciliated. Lee invaded; Paula braced herself against those invasions but expected them regularly and even depended on them. It was as if they had come to be pushing on opposite sides of a wall, each counting on the continued pressure of the other. This, more than anything, was the essential element between them, the force that kept them locked—the sport in the middle of the large stadium, the solid core at the center of soft fruit.

But suddenly Lee had stopped pushing, leaving Paula pressing against air, causing her to fall over from the force of her own unblocked thrust.

The actual ending of it was a formality, inevitable as speeches delivered after an election—the statement of new policy, the gracious concession. When Lee called and said quietly, "I'd like to come over tonight and talk to you," Paula quietly submitted. When Lee came, Paula was sitting on the floor of her studio apartment, leaning on a cushion propped against the wall.

She was glad to have the pillow behind her head. When she was upset she often became convinced that her head was falling off her neck. She had devised ways to rescue it, holding her cheek in her palm if there was a high surface to brace against, or by casually pulling taut a strand of hair, keeping her head aloft by tension. She had confided this to Lee at the time in their relationship when such confidences were customary: "I've always been afraid of...", "I feel most vulnerable when...", "I pretend to be..., but I'm really...." Now Lee would abscond with this information, to become one of the mob from whom she had vowed to protect her.

Lee sat slumped forward, her chin planted soberly on her knuckles. Paula wondered how Ellen felt about posture. She had met Ellen three days before at a party. She remembered watching from across the room as Lee opened a bag of potato chips and proferred them to Ellen, who stood beside her talking to someone else. Lee had swooped down in her clumsy, zealous way, and she, Paula, had flinched, expecting to see Ellen shrink back with the same instinct. But Ellen had calmly put in her hand, extracted a chip, and gone on talking.

Paula remained very still as Lee talked, her eyes fixed on a patch of eczema which had begun to grow on her toe. Lee's voice filtered through to her sporadically: ". . .not good for either of us that way. . .couldn't go on forever. . .you must agree. . .just one of those catalytic things. . .didn't take much at this point." Paula had heard these words before—in movies, on soap operas, in books. Rhett Butler had said them to Scarlett O'Hara scores of times, until the pages had frayed and fallen out of her book. She knew them by heart, knew that in a moment would come the part where her eyes misted over.

"I wouldn't ever want to let you out of my life completely," Lee was saying. "Although I can't renege on what I've said."

"Renege," Paula thought. A good word for six-letter jotto. It had three vowels, but they were all the same, which was tricky, and an opponent with all the right letters might easily get stuck re-arranging them. Some of the likely configurations were: energe, greene, gneere, genere, reenge, engree. By the time she had run through them all, the way she might silently recite multiplication tables in the dentist's chair, Lee was finished. It wasn't until she had gone, pulling the door closed softly behind her, that Paula let her head fall forward so that it dangled loosely, and cried.

Now, six months later, Paula sat in the car at the gas station looking at Lee. They had kept minimal contact—Lee had called from time to time, suggesting they meet for coffee, or for breakfast. "It just takes time," Lee had said. Wounds would heal, things would change—Lee believed they could be friends.

Paula had been sickened at the new equanimity in Lee's voice. She did not know what to do with her when she did not insist or demand anything—did not, in fact, seem to want anything. She was behaving exactly as Paula had always said she wanted her to behave, and it was unbearable. Paula didn't initiate any phone calls. She met Lee in coffee shops, moved by a fatalistic compulsion, but Lee's idle friendliness crushed her. She would stretch her face into appropriate shapes, and afterwards she would lie in bed for hours, unable to move.

But now they were spending their first full day together. Lee had asked her to come up to Connecticut to visit her brother, David, and Diana, her sister-in-law. David had been dying of Lou Gehrig's disease for five years. She had called Paula and said, casually, "I'm going up on Saturday, and I thought maybe you'd like to come. David and Diana have been asking about you." Paula had held the mouthpiece of the phone above her nose so Lee wouldn't hear her breathing, returning it to its normal position in time to remark, her voice equally casual, "All right, that sounds nice."

It was October, the right weekend to see the leaves at their peak. "We'll only stay a few hours," Lee had said. "Then we can do what we want, drive around, have dinner somewhere." Paula had been overwhelmed by the breadth of this proposition, which seemed to encompass so much in the way of time and events. They had done this so many times before that their old intimacy seemed destined to creep up through the vinyl of the seats in Lee's car, appear at every toll booth where they had once given out Toll House cookies with their change, signal them from the highway exit at Darien, Connecticut, where they used to stop at the Driftwood Diner for coffee and bran muffins, listening to the truck drivers and waitresses enthusiastically insult each other.

Of the seasons, fall had always seemed the most emotionally manipulative to Paula. The needs that came out in the spring were frivolous—very pleasurable when fulfilled, frustrating but not fatal when thwarted. In the fall love was mandatory, insurance against death. She had been aware of death in the fall since she was very young, running home from school panicked with the sudden realization that someday her parents would die, and that she would remain marooned on earth, an orphan. Later on the fall had intimated her own death—sometimes a dry-mouthed, nuclear holocaust sort of death, and sometimes a death with a sad euphony, a nineteenth century kind, personal and enduring, with leaves falling on a graveyard, ghosts, and the inconsolable grief of someone whispering into the ground where her physical self slowly fell away.

Lee had rolled down her window, resting her elbow on the ledge. Her fingers curled around the molding at the top of the door frame, and her shirt sleeve blew taut like a sail in the wind above the place where she had rolled it up.

"Are you cold?" she asked, raising her eyebrows courteously. Paula shook her head, but Lee didn't see. "Hmn?" she inquired, withdrawing her arm and moving to roll up the window.

"No!" Paula shouted.

"OK," Lee said, resuming her position with an ease far removed from her old hasty eagerness to please. Paula watched the small brown hairs on her forearm stand up in the breeze, angled sharply like an inside-out umbrella. She felt jealous and resentful of this limb which could enjoy the brisk weather without regrets. Lee's skin could rise responsively and still not have to endure a minute's solitary aching. It wouldn't have to cancel out the feeling from its cells one by one.

"Be forewarned," Lee said. "David's much worse than he was the last time you saw him." She said it matter-of-factly, in the tone Paula remembered her whole family using when they spoke of David. She might have been saying, "By the way, you'll notice they've redecorated the bathroom." Paula was still amazed at their bluntness, even in front of David himself. In her own family, death, pain, and suffering were all couched in euphemisms. "He's uncomfortable," her mother had said of Paula's grandfather, stuffed with tubes the day after his open heart surgery. "It's unpleasant," had been the tribute to her aunt's mastectomy. Lee's mother wrote poems about the family's ordeal which she published in the Amyotrophic Lateral Sclerosis Newsletter.

When Paula went with Lee, David, and Diana to a restaurant, none of the other three seemed to mind the stares of the other diners as they rolled David in in his wheelchair, his torso drooping off to one side, his face devoid of expression because he'd lost the muscle control to form one. And Paula would be shocked when Diana, feeding him lukewarm soup through a straw, would drop the fork with which she was simultaneously feeding herself and groan, "Oh, he's *wet* himself again."

"He was still talking the last time you saw him, wasn't he?"

"Barely."

"Well, Diana says now he blinks in Morse Code."

Paula could chart the key points in her relationship with Lee by the progress of David's disease. They had met when David was in his third year, a full year after he was supposed to have been dead. He could still walk then, if someone grasped him under each armpit. By the time they had become lovers, David couldn't stand up at all. The summer they talked about living together his words had grown slurred, and when they decided not to he was spelling things, the letters easier to distinguish than the complicated polysyllables and diphthongs.

They arrived at the house in time for lunch. David lay in the hospital bed they kept in the living room, fully dressed in a T-shirt and slacks, with loafers on his feet. Lee went over right away and hugged her brother, her elbows sliding into the crevices formed where David's shoulders met the pillow, her hands meeting each other where the thin black hair was combed back at the crown of David's head.

Paula realized, as she did afresh each time she came here, how alike Lee and David looked. Both were dark, large-boned, and lean, although all of David's weight had dropped below his waist, leaving loose flesh hanging from his neck and arms, and they had the same

fullish lips and heavy eyebrows. For a moment Lee imagined the
two reversed—that David bent over the bed and that Lee was the
one who lay helplessly looking up at the rest of them. Involuntarily
she shivered, feeling waves of the same queasiness she always felt
with David but could usually push aside, like a friend's baby's dirty
diaper. There was a certain horror in the vision of such stark need
demanding assistance that went beyond pity, beyond fear. It was
embarrassment—the same that she had once felt at Lee's unmasked,
self-revelatory love—a shame that she had alchemized into anger,
venting it upon Lee until she had withdrawn her offensive need. She
had felt this shame for herself sometimes, too, when the vulnerable
lines had crept into her own face, and, in the dim streetlight from
her window, she had gazed with awe at Lee's parted lips drawn back
from hers. At these times she felt both released and endangered,
with the sensation of a bound foot that has had its bandages finally
removed and flexes painfully, its bones twisted, its skin white and raw.

She felt embarrassed—and yet, she was jealous of Diana. She
realized this with the surprise of discovering a piece of a puzzle which
she had believed until this moment to be complete. She was jealous
because Diana could pour love into David like gas into a car's empty
tank during an oil crisis, love that he could never reject, abuse, pity,
laugh at, or trivialize. It was secret love, safe love, love with a war-
ranty. David would never stop needing Diana, and thus he would
never leave her. He would die, true, but that was different.

"And see, I've brought Paula," Lee was saying, cutting into her
thoughts. She dutifully stepped forward.

"Hello, David," Paula said. David stared impassively back at her.
"How are you? Have you been out yet today?" She paused, pretending he had answered, and rushed on, "The colors were wonderful
along the highway. Later on we're going to drive along some back
roads and—" She searched for things to say, hating herself for her
evident confusion.

While she talked to David, Lee and Diana disappeared into the
kitchen. For a minute or so she continued with her monologue, rub-

bing the undersides of her fingers back and forth along the metal railing of David's bed. Then, in the middle of a sentence, she stopped. She looked into David's soft brown eyes, so much like Lee's—and yet so unlike them, because they looked at her steadily, penetrating as Lee's didn't anymore. Suddenly, on an impulse—because he couldn't tell anyone, and would die with this knowledge in his head—she reached out her hand and touched his cheek. His skin was warm under its stubble of beard, and seemed to grow warmer under her touch. She wondered whether he liked it—whether her gesture moved him, or embarrassed him, or angered him. His eyes continued to look directly at her, blinking occasionally. Because he was the helpless object of her affection, she continued to let her hand rest where it lay.

Once, when she had come home late at night after a long vacation, she had tumbled into bed in her empty apartment and fallen into a deep sleep. In the morning she woke to find Lee kneeling beside her, her hand on Paula's hair. Lee had let herself in with her key, and had quietly watched Paula until her eyes opened. Her hand continued to gently massage Paula's head, as it had done even while Paula had slept, and the look Paula had caught in her eyes in that first moment upon awakening did not change. Lee's eyes were limp with adoration; they might have been regarding a relic from the Renaissance behind bullet-proof glass. For several minutes neither of them spoke. Lee stroked her, and Paula lay still, watching Lee, feeling a sort of admiration that she could stroke her so boldly, in a way that she, Paula, would only venture to stroke a cat. This admiration bordered on envy—it was as if Lee had a special talent whose apparent simplicity masked underlying deftness and expertise—and yet mixed in with it, was contempt. "You are foolish," Paula thought, looking at Lee. "You are foolish, you are foolish," and the conviction grew insistently as Lee's expression remained unaltered, oblivious of the accusations raging in Paula's head.

But now, this October day in David and Diana's living room, she was careful to recompose herself. It would be just this side of

tragic for Lee or Diana to walk in and find her touching David like
this. It made her want to throw up just thinking of it.

Over lunch they talked of Lee's and David's parents, of news from
their sister in Oregon, of the few relatives and fewer friends who
still came to visit. Paula felt like an outsider, as she always did during these conversations. She was given all the facts, but not included
in the family experiences, like a cleaning woman who touched intimate trinkets every week for years but didn't get invited to the wed-
dings and funerals. Diana spoke of Lee's and David's parents as "Mom"
and "Dad," with the authority of the initiated. Paula watched her
feed David, wipe his chin with a napkin. "Would you like some apple juice, honey?" she asked, speaking the dialect of marriage. Paula
pretended that she and Lee had been married and were now divorced.
Looking around the table, she imagined the room throbbing with
acknowledgement of her pain, different from but equal to Diana's.
She would be the ex-wife, the still fiercely beloved sister-in-law. They
would cling to a silent hope that she and Lee might "work it out,"
that this cleavage in their network might still be repaired.
How comprehensible and how intolerable it would be if she were
titled: "wife." How comforting and yet how awful it would be to have
a name for her rejection—"divorced"—a legal, public, social name,
a name that would tell everyone—friends, family, people in banks,
courts, law firms, strangers who read job applications—that she had
loved and lost. At least now people she met need not be told that
Lee had ever existed for her, they might easily never even imagine
that she had recently been a part of a Couple, that unit that ran
abreast through life like two strands of recombinant DNA. And people
who had known could be deceived with an ironic shrug, the shrug
of a woman who inhabited a world where monogamy was serial, where
relationships strove to be honest and were thus, regretably, transient,
and where family pressure to stay together was virtually nonexistent.
She could easily lie or omit or shrug as people often claimed to sniffle
with colds when in fact they were crying, or sat with stiffly averted

eyes beside fellow airline passengers who had, with unpleasant consequences, forgotten to lock the bathroom door.

"Don't touch me!" Diana cried suddenly. Paula jumped. Lee jumped too; and probably something inside David jumped, though he was not allowed the relief of a true human reflex. It was revealed that Lee had accidentally bumped Diana's knee under the table with her own, and that Diana had forgotten to tell them she had poison oak. "I'm very contagious," she explained. "I've been putting sheets between David and me at night, so he won't catch it. It itches like hell, and you're not supposed to scratch it—but I have no control, I do anyway. Poor David would go crazy, he couldn't scratch at all. Well, actually, that might make him a model victim!" She laughed at this, and Lee laughed, too. Both of them put down their forks and laughed long and hard, leaning on each other for support, until Diana cried again, "You're touching me!" and they burst forth with fresh peals. Finally Lee bent forward, and her arm pitched out and accidentally knocked over a water glass, which sent water dripping into David's lap. This was the cause for fresh hilarity.

"You haven't changed a bit!" Diana guffawed. "My little sister-in-law still has the grace of a dump truck!"

Lee, looking anything but little, pushed back her chair with a loud squeak and ambled off to the kitchen for paper towels. She returned and mopped them about the table, the wheelchair, the floor, and David's lap, awkwardly crouching before her immobilized brother and patting his legs. "Sorry about that, Dave," she said. Diana sat with her head thrown back, holding her stomach as laughs came shaking out of it.

Paula watched them with furtive glances; her eyes kept returning to her plate. She felt the way she had once felt in France in a room full of people who were making jokes rapidly in French. She, not understanding, had debated whether it would be more inappropriate to sit poker-faced in frank ignorance or to fake laughter which everyone would know had no source. There had been no satisfactory solution. The problem was that she did not belong among that group.

Now, she couldn't force herself to laugh. It was difficult enough to conceal her discomfort and disapproval. She didn't see how they could draw such *attention* to David's helplessness, how they could make *jokes* about it. It didn't even matter that if David could laugh he would probably be laughing too. These people were absolutely raw, uncooked in any opaque sauce that might hide their primitive nakedness. She wondered how they could come together so openly diseased, infectious, clumsy, and put these deficiencies right on the table, right there beside the guacamole salad and the cold chicken and the wine. She didn't understand how they could like each other so much, and continue liking each other year after year, never re-evaluating, but always coming back for more as if on automatic replay—when Lee had stopped liking her, Paula, or at least she had stopped loving her, had stopped looking at her as if Lee were an explorer and Paula were a new land which would soon reveal its port of entry. Why had Lee stopped loving her when she kept herself so neat, clean, restrained, undemanding, disciplined, so completely inoffensive in every way? When she didn't make any trouble, as some other women did, calling their lovers in the middle of the night to see if they were alone, requiring explanations for inattention and lapses of memory, demanding time, money, energy, declarations of love, accounts of the details lodged among the facts of their lovers' lives like dust between toes?

Why?

When Paula and Lee left, Paula had an old, familiar sense that this would be the last good bye—that David wouldn't live until her next visit. It had always seemed so; she had never at any time since she'd known him been able to imagine him descending any lower on the scale of the living and still remain alive. And yet he did; he seemed to constantly invent new ways to be a person. Now she thought that even if David lived for another five years, perhaps Lee would never ask her to come here again; and if she did, perhaps

Paula would say no. She was not like David; she could not watch her bond to Lee deteriorate indefinitely and still be willing to call it a bond.

Yet she pretended that she would see David again soon. "Take care," she said, kissing his cheek as form prescribed and made easy, as she kissed Diana's. "It was good to see you. Maybe we'll be by again soon for some cross-country skiing." As if she and Lee would naturally welcome this weather together. As if people could retrieve each other as certainly as the snow would fall.

They drove along country roads until the sun went down. They looked at leaves and stopped at antique stores and shops. Later they drove back to Manhattan and ate at a small Indian restaurant on East 6th Street where they used to go often. The waiter remembered them and brought an extra order of paratha bread, for two. Then, just when Paula thought Lee would drop her off at home, Lee said tentatively, "How would you feel about going dancing?" and Paula, surprised, said, "All right," unable to resist protracting the day a little longer—as if something might yet be discovered, changed, advanced.

They went dancing at a place they used to go to on the West Side. There weren't any slow dances, just hard rock and disco, but they kept within each other's locus, moving close and then away without touching. It seemed that they each held an end of a cloth that sometimes went slack, sometimes pulled taut between them, neither letting them come together nor separate, as Paula had seen Hasidic dancers do at Lower East Side dance festivals. She thought: this is what it's all come to. All this time, and here we are, dancing together. Together. Like two eyes in the same face, spaced slightly apart but collaborating with each other in order to see the world in three dimensions.

And all the while she kept thinking. If this is happening, then what could have been so wrong? Could she really have stopped loving me? And if she did, then why?

She kept asking herself "How?" and "Why?" all the way home

in the car. She kept her face down, her eyes fixed on her hands in her lap, because suddenly she felt she might cry, and she had to think of some way of postponing it. Lee was quiet, too; perhaps she sensed something was wrong, or maybe she was just absorbed in her own thoughts. Paula started thinking hard of other things so that the tears would change their minds, turn around and head back down past her nose, past her throat where they would take the terrible ache with them, the ache that would block her voice and give her away, past her chest which needed room to expand, and down to her stomach, where they could rest until she was ready for them.

Thinking about her tears made her think of Muriel, a friend from junior high school who had been born without tear ducts. At all sorts of odd moments tears would spill down Muriel's face—in classes, in assembly, in stores, in the subway, in ordinary conversations. People would put their arms around her and say, "Muriel, honey, what's the matter?" and she'd have to explain about her tear ducts. Muriel had told Paula that when she was little she'd been given hundreds of lollipops, pieces of bubble gum, and toys by adults who thought she'd been crying. But when she really *was* crying, she could still say, "It's just my tear ducts," and people would believe her.

Paula had been jealous of Muriel's remarkable ability to keep the truth about her emotions private, to divulge it only at will, and she'd prayed that her tear ducts would vanish, too. But they hadn't. She'd had to run into the bathrooms, closets, out of rooms, sometimes out of buildings into bitter cold air, so that people wouldn't see her face when it crumbled—so that she could remain unfurled and unrevealed, and unpitied.

Once, though, the worst had happened. She'd been twelve years old, and some girlfriends had come over to her house. She'd been sitting in the den with two of them, watching a program on television, while the other two talked in her bedroom. When the program was over the three in the den had gone into the bedroom, where they found the others poring over her diary. She'd tried to grab it, but they wouldn't let her have it. They had held her back, while one of them, a big girl named Evelyn, read out loud, "I think if I get my ears pierced I'll be popular. I'm scared to get them pierced, but I'll do anything to be popular." On and on Evelyn read, revealing everything that Paula had taken great pains to conceal, the things that she'd only had the nerve to write down on paper because something inside her would have exploded if she hadn't, and because she'd promised herself that *no one* would ever read it; she would burn it and herself first.

She had screamed and bitten and kicked and spat at them, desperate to get her diary out of their hands, but they wouldn't let go of her. Finally, she had cried in defeat, heaving sobs of despair that she could afford to heave only because her life would have to be over; she couldn't continue beyond this. And miraculously, when she cried, they stopped. They stopped giggling and squealing and Evelyn stopped reading. She said, "All right, that's enough," and put the diary back under the mattress, where she had found it.

Paula thought that she would mutilate herself if she had to, not to have to go to school again; she couldn't ever, ever live by breathing the air in a room with these girls again.

But, strangely, they had liked her better after that. There was no way to stop living that she could bring herself to elect; and in the aftermath they became gentle with her, and invited her to sleep over at their houses, and confided things to her that they told no one else.

Now, a decade and a half later, one block from her apartment in Lee's car, she felt the child who had existed then still raging and crumbling inside her. The girl who would have destroyed herself before seeing her secrets destroyed, who refused to surrender the intricate code of her thoughts and feelings, who lived inside them as if they were amniotic fluid, guarding her against bumps and jolts—that girl still hid, still huddled like a fetus refusing to be born.

But holding back her tears would not make Lee turn to her. It would not bring the avid, inquisitive tenderness back into Lee's eyes. Paula imagined them both in another minute. Lee would drop her off in front of her building and say, in an offhand way, "Well, this was nice. We should get together again sometime," and she would agree, virtually outdoing Lee's casual friendliness. They would kiss, their lips popping off each other the way friends' lips did, and when she got out of the car she would shut the door—not too softly, like a woman in wet, gentle love, and not too hard, like a woman in furious love, but in a carefully medium way, the way the middle bear would do it—not very this or that, but indifferent, just right.

"Well—" Lee said, pulling over to the curb. Paula turned to half face her, her hand already on the doorknob. She looked at Lee's long, awkward, vulnerable neck, which used to stick itself far out for her. She thought of how many times she had cringed for that neck even as it had connected her to life like an umbilical cord, while she had held her own drawn in, like a turtle. And suddenly it felt almost blasphemous to bury the day with a medium ending, to close the door behind her with a noncommital push, to walk into her building with moderately paced steps. She had done these things thousands of times before. Whatever comfort they brought was as gratifying as eating sand, as worth holding onto as a watch that had lost its hands.

For once she'd have to risk her own neck. It occurred to her that if she really wanted to know how Lee had stopped loving her, and why, and if she might ever love her again, there was a way to find out. She could ask.

Trespassing

VALERIE MINER

EXHAUSTED FROM four hours of traffic, Kate and Josie almost missed seeing the two doe and their fawn drinking at the pond. The women waited in the car, cautious lest the noise of opening doors disturb the animals. The deer lingered another five minutes and then stepped off gracefully into the wings of sequoias. Last sun settled on the golden hills. Night noises pulsed: Frogs. Crickets. Mallards. Wind whispered across dry grass. Jays barked from the top of the hill. As the sky grew roses, Kate and Josie watched Jupiter blaze over the Eastern mountains.

They unloaded the Chevy quickly and sloppily, eager for the comfort of the compact wooden cabin they had built with their friends over five summers.

Josie opened the gas line outside the house. Kate lit a fire, reflecting on the joys of collective ownership when the rest of the collective was absent. She could hardly believe it—two whole days away

161

from Meredith High School; forty-eight hours of privacy and peace.

Suddenly starving, they decided to eat right away. Afterward they would sit in front of the fire and read to each other. Kate chopped salad while Josie made pasta and whistled. The sky got redder and then, abruptly, the cabin was dark. With heavy reluctance, Kate walked around and lit the lanterns.

"Oh," Kate said.

Josie turned and caught a flick of brown before her, like an insect crashing on a windshield.

"Damn bats," Kate shook her head and picked up the broom.

"Bats!" Josie screamed. "I thought Iris got rid of those gruesome things last month."

"Must still be some holes in the sun porch," Kate shook her head.

A dark object dropped beside Josie, like a small turd falling, from the eaves. It disappeared. She fretted the wooden spoon through the pasta, watching another tiny brown mass cut its fall in mid-air and swoop across the room. It was too much. "Bats!"

Josie ran outside. She felt safer in the dark.

Kate stayed in the house, sweeping bats out of the windows and back door.

Staring up at the stars, so benign in their distance, Josie considered vast differences between Kate and herself. Rational, taciturn Kate was probably calculating the increasing velocity of wing movement as the bats ignited to wakefulness. Josie, herself, still cringed at Grandma's tales about bats nesting in little girls' hair. And raised as she was in a willful family where intentionality was more important than action, where danger didn't exist if one closed one's imagination to it, Josie was given to the substitution of "good thoughts." Let's see, she forced herself to concentrate on a pleasant memory: how she and Kate met. It was a miracle if you thought about it; *who* would have expected romance at the school xerox machine? But there was Kate copying quark diagrams for her Physics students while Josie waited to xerox a new translation of "La Cigale et La Fourmi." If Kate hadn't run out of toner, they might never have become acquainted.

"All clear," Kate called. There was no disdain in her voice for she had always envied Josie's ability to show fear. She should tell Josie this.

Josie craned her neck and stared at the sky. "Glorious night," she called back. "Wanna see?"

Ducking out the front door, Kate ran through the pungent pennyroyal to her friend. Josie took her hand. Together they stood quietly until they could hear the frogs and the crickets once more.

They slept late and spent the next morning eating eggs and fried potatoes and rye toast. Josie noticed some wasps dancing around the table, so they cleaned up and went outside to lie on the warm deck.

Later they spent an hour fitting moulding around the edges of the sun porch's glass door, sealing the house seams against nocturnal trespassers.

At noon the women drove five miles to town for forgotten country necessities—ice, water and flashlight batteries. Josie secretly checked the grocery shelves for bat killer, but she didn't find any and she knew Kate wouldn't approve.   As they drove back to the land, Josie tried to renew her enthusiasm for the weekend. She stopped in front of the cabin. Kate, now completely restored by country air, bounded into the house with the grocery bag.

Josie moved the Chevy into the shade of an oak tree which was being gradually occupied by Spanish moss. As she locked up the car, she saw a fat man with a rifle, waddling out of the forest. He wore a yellow cap, a striped T-shirt and bluejeans.

A giant bumblebee, she thought. Then she warned herself to get serious. The land was clearly posted, "No Trespassing. No Hunting." A shiver ran along her collarbone. They were half-a-mile from the highway here. It could be weeks before anyone investigated.

Josie decided to be friendly and waved.

"Hello there," he was winded, hustling to meet her.

Josie closed her eyes and hoped Kate would stay in the house until it was all over.

"I got lost," he said, nodding his whole body. "How do you get back to the highway?"

"That direction," Josie tried to calm herself. "Up the road there."

He looked her over. "You got any water? A glass of water? I've been walking for hours."

Biblical tales filled her head. The Woman at the Well. The Wedding at Cana. The Good Samaritan. "Sure," she said as noncommitally as possible. "I'll be right back."

"Who's that?" Kate greeted her.

Josie tried to be calm. "Water man. I mean, a lost man who needs water." She watched Kate's jaw stiffen. "Now let me handle it. He just wants a glass of water and then he'll be on his way." Josie poured water from a plastic jug into an old jam jar they used for drinking.

"Water, my foot, what is he doing on the land? It's posted 'No Trespassing,' for godsake."

"Listen, Kate, he was hunting and. . . ."

Kate took the glass and poured half the water back into the jug. "Don't *spoil* him. He may return."

She stalked out to the man, who was leaning on their car, his gun on the ground. Josie stood at the door, watching.

"Thanks, Mam," he reached for the water.

"No shooting on this land," Kate said as she released the glass.

"Sorry, Mam. I was hunting up there on the North Ridge and I hit a buck. But he got away. I followed, to make sure I got him good. Then I got lost and I guess I wound up here."

"Guess so," Kate said. She held her hand against her leg to stop it from shaking.

"I'll be off your land soon's I finish the water," he promised.

"That's right," she kept her voice even.

"But I'll need to be coming back to get the buck. See, I finally did get him. But since I was lost, I couldn't drag him all over tarnation."

"We don't want a dead buck on the land," Kate conceded.
"When're you coming?"

"Tomorrow morning?" he asked. "About 8:00?"

"Fine, and no guns," she said.

"No Mam, no guns."

"Right then," she held her hand out for the jam jar. "Road's
that way."

"Yes, Mam."

Kate watched him climb the hill and walked back to the house,
shaking her head. Josie reached to hug her, but Kate pulled away.
"God damned hunter." She was on the verge of tears.

"How about some coffee or lunch?"

"Naw, are you nuts, after all we ate this morning? No, I think
I'll just go for a walk. See if I can find the buck. If there *is* a buck."

Josie nodded. "Want company?" She wasn't keen on viewing
a dead animal, but she didn't care to admit being afraid to stay in
the house alone, not after her melodramatic performance with the
bats last night.

"Sure," Kate was grateful. "Let's go."

Josie locked the ice chest and dropped the jam jar in the brown
paper garbage bag on the way out.

It was hotter now, about 85 degrees. The pennyroyal smelled
mintier than last night. The day was dry and still—bleached grass,
golden hills scumbled against teal sky. A turkey vulture glided above
the oak grove. As they walked around the pond, they could hear
frogs scholop into the water. Kate stopped to inspect the eucalyptus
trees they had planted in the spring. Four out of five still alive, not
bad. Further along, a salamander skittered across their path. Josie
felt cool even before she entered the woods. In a way, she hoped
they wouldn't find the buck. But if there was no buck, who knows
what the bumblebee man really wanted?

The woods were thick with madrone and manzanita and poison oak. It was always a balance on the land, Kate thought, pleasure and danger.

Josie wished she had worn sneakers instead of sandals. But Kate didn't seem to be bothered about her feet as she marched ahead. Right, Josie reminded herself, this wasn't a ramble. They continued in silence for half-an-hour.

"'Round here, I guess," called Kate, who was now several yards ahead. "See the way branches have broken. Yes, here. Oh, my god, it's still alive. God damned hunter."

They stared at the huge animal, its left front leg broken in a fall, panting and sweating, blind fear in its wide eyes.

"I told Myla we should keep a gun at the house." Kate cried, "What are we going to do?"

Josie didn't think about it. She probably wouldn't have been able to lift the boulder if she had thought about it. But she heard herself shouting to Kate, "stand back," and watched herself drop the big rock on the buck's head. They heard a gurgling and saw a muscle ripple along the animal's belly. Then nothing. There was nothing alive under the boulder.

Josie stared at the four bullet wounds scattered up the right side of the buck. The animal's blood was a dark, cinnamon color. She noticed sweat along the hip joints.

Kate walked over to her quietly and took her hand. "Good, brave," she stuttered. "That was good, Josie."

"Yeah, it seemed the right thing."

Kate hugged Josie and gently drew her away from the dead buck and the broken bush.

They walked straight out to the trail. Neither one seemed to want to stay in the woods for their customary ramble. Kate watched her friend closely, waiting for the explosion. This silence was so uncharacteristic of Josie. Soon, soon, she would erupt with anger and aggravation and guilt and a long examination of what she had done in the woods. For her own part, Kate could only think of one word. Brave.

"Let's go swimming," Josie said, trying to focus on the trail. It'll cool us off."

The two women stripped on the makeshift dock and lay in the sun beside one another. Kate was slim, her legs long and shapely. She didn't think much about this body which had always served her well. She never felt too thin or too plump. Josie, in contrast, fretted about her zaftig breasts and hips. Her skin was pinker than Kate's, a faint pink. Kate curled up beside Josie, her legs across Josie's legs, her head on Josie's shoulder.

Josie closed her eyes and told herself it was over. They were all right. She had never killed anything before and she felt terribly sad. Of course, the animal had been dying. It was a humane act. Still, her chest ached with a funny hollowness.

"What's that?" Kate sat up.

They listened, Josie flat and Kate leaning forward from her waist.

The noise came again.

A loud whirrr.

Like an engine.

Whirrr.

"Quail," Kate relaxed back on her elbow. "Come on, let's wash off the feeling of that creepy guy."

She lowered herself into the water from the wooden ladder, surprised as Josie jumped in.

"Freezing," Josie laughed, swimming around her friend and noticing how Kate's blond curls sprang back the minute she lifted her head from the water. "Freezing!"

"You'll warm up," Kate said, herself breathless from the cold.

"You're always telling me to stop daydreaming, to stay in the present. The present is freezing." Josie giggled and splashed her friend.

Kate laughed. She ducked under the water, swimming deep enough to catch Josie's feet, which were treading earnestly.

"Hey, watch it." But Josie called too late. Now she was below the surface, tangled in Kate's legs and the long roots of silky grass. It was green down here and very cold.

They dried out on the sunny dock and dressed before starting

toward the house. Often they walked naked across the land, especially after swimming when they didn't want to wear sweaty clothes.
Today that didn't feel safe.

Back at the cabin, the afternoon grew long and restless. Both
women felt fidgety. Kate put aside her equations and washed all the
windows in the house. Josie couldn't concentrate on her translation,
so she worked up lesson plans for the following week.

About five o'clock, she glanced at Kate, stretching recklessly to
the skylight from the top of a ladder.

"Careful up there."

"Sure, hon."

"What did we bring for dinner?" Josie's mind was blank.

"That beef chili you made last week. And rye bread."

"Why don't we go out?" Josie paced in front of the wood stove.
God, she wished Kate would be careful on that ladder.

"Out. But the whole point of being here, oops," she tipped precar-
iously and then straightened. "Hey, just let me get one more lick
in her and we can talk. There." She started down the steps. "But
the whole point of being in the country is to retreat together in solitary bliss. And what's wrong with your chili? I thought this batch
was perfect?"

Josie shrugged and looked out the big bay window across the
grass. She told herself to watch the horses ambling along the ridge
or the hawk hovering over the pond. Instead she was caught by a
line of lint Kate had left in the middle of the frame. "I don't know.
Not in the mood. Guess I'd like vegetarian tonight." Her eyes stung.

Kate stood behind her; still Josie could sense her nodding.

"Why not," Kate said. "Be nice to take a ride this time of evening."

Edna's Cafe was practically empty. But then—Kate checked her
watch—it *was* only 5:30. Edna waved menus from behind the counter.
Josie and Kate said yes.

"Coffee, girls?" Edna carried the menus under her arm, pot of
coffee in one hand and mugs in the other.

"Thanks," Josie said.

"Not just yet," Kate smiled. Edna reminded her of Aunt Bella who worked in a coffee shop back East.

While Kate studied the menu, Josie excused herself to the restroom.

Kate breathed easier when Josie returned to the table looking relaxed. She felt a great surge of affection as her companion intently appraised the menu.

"I think I'll have the chef's sald with Jack cheese," Josie decided.

"Sounds good," Kate nodded. She was relieved to see Josie looking happy. "Two chef salads, with Jack cheese," she called over to Edna.

They talked about plans for the following summer when they could spend four consecutive weeks on the land.

"You two girls sisters?" Edna served the enromous salads.

"No," laughed Kate. "Why?"

"Don't know. You kinda look alike. 'Course when I stare straight at you like this, there's not much resemblance. I don't know. And you always order the same thing."

"In that case, I'll have tea," Kate laughed again. "With lemon."

They ate silently, self-conscious of being the only ones in the restaurant. Kate could hardly get down the lettuce. She'd feel better after she made the phone call. She wouldn't tell Josie, who would get nervous. But it was responsible to report the intruder to the sheriff. "Excuse me. Now I've got to use the bathroom," she said to Josie. "Don't let Edna take my salad."

"I'll guard it with my life," Josie grinned.

The sheriff's number was posted beneath the fire station number. She dialed and heard a funny, moist sound, as if the man were eating or maybe clicking in his dentures. She concentrated on the sturdy plastic of the phone.

"Hello," he said finally.

She began to report the incident.

"Listen, you're the second lady to call me about this in twenty minutes. Like I told the other one, there's nothing I can do unless the man is actually trespassing on your land. Since you've invited him back tomorrow, he ain't exactly trespassing."

"We didn't exactly invite him."

"OK, if it makes you feel easier, I said I'll swing by about 8 a.m. That's when the other lady said he'd be coming."

"Thank you sir."

"Sir," she shook her head as she walked back to the table. She hadn't said "sir" in fifteen years.

Josie had finished her salad and was doodling on a paper napkin. Definitely signs of good mood. Kate sat down and stared at her until she looked up. "So I hear you have a date with the law tomorrow morning."

Josie smiled. "Hope you don't think I'm stepping out on you."

By the time Kate finished her salad, the cafe was getting crowded.

"Refills?" Edna approached with a pot of coffee and a pot of hot water.

"No thanks, just the check," Josie said.

"Guess you girls didn't mind my asking if you was sisters?"

"No, no, not at all," they spoke in unison.

It was a warm, richly scented evening and they drove home with the top down. Jupiter came out early again. Josie thought how much she preferred Jupiter to the cold North Star.

They were both worn out as they collapsed on the couch together. Their feet on the fruit crate coffee table, they watched pink gain the horizon. It was almost pitch dark when Josie reached up to light the lanterns.

She hesitated a moment, remembering last night, and then proceeded. Light, voila, the room was filled with sharp corners and shiny surfaces. Kate picked up her book, but Josie drew it away, cuddling closer.

"Here?" Kate was surprised by her own resistance. After all, they were alone, five miles from town.

"Where then?" Josie tried to sound like Lauren Bacall.

Kate sighed with a breath that moved her whole body, a body, she noticed, which was becoming increasingly sensitive to the body next to her. "Mmmmm," she kissed Josie on her neck, sweet with late summer sweat.

When Josie opened her eyes, she thought she saw something. No, they had sealed off the sun porch this morning. She kissed Kate on the lips and was started by a whisssh over her friend's head. "Bats," she said evenly, pulling Kate lower on the couch.

"Don't worry," Kate said. "I'll get rid of him."

Worry, Josie cringed. She wasn't worried; she was hysterical. Calm down, she told herself. Think about the invasion of Poland. This was her mother's approach to anxiety—distract yourself by thinking about people with *real* problems. Worry is a perversion of imagination.

Kate opened the windows and set forth again with the broom, but the bat wouldn't leave. Eventually it spiralled upstairs into the large sleeping loft. Kate shook her head and closed up the house against further intrusion. She shrugged and returned to the couch, where Josie was sitting up, considerably more collected than the previous night.

"It'll be OK," Kate said. "It'll just go to sleep. You know they're not really Transylvanian leeches. They're harmless little herbivores. And rather inept."

Herbivores, Josie thought about eating salad for absolution after she murdered the buck.

Kate reached over and brushed her lover's breast, but Josie pulled away. "Not now, sweetie. I can't just now."

Kate nodded. She picked up her book. Josie fiddled with a crossword puzzle. About 10 o'clock, Kate yawned, "Bed?"

"OK," Josie was determined to be brave. "I'll go up first."

"Sure," Kate regarded her closely. "You light the candle up there. I'll get the lantern down here."

They settled comfortably in the double nylon sleeping bag. Kate blew out the light. She reached over to rub Josie's back in hopes something more might develop. Suddenly she heard a whissh, whissh, whissh.

"Looks like our friend is back," Kate tried to keep her voice light.

"Just a harmless little herbivore," Josie rolled to her side of the bed, putting a pillow over her head.

That night Josie dreamt that she had become Mayor of Lincoln, Nebraska.

Kate slept fitfully, hardly dreaming, and waking with the first sun. She lay and watched Josie breathing evenly, blowing the edges of her black hair, her body ripe and luscious in the soft light. If she woke up early enough, they could make love before Mr. Creepo arrived. And the sheriff. Had they made a mistake in phoning the sheriff?

The loft grew lighter. Kate lay on her back with her head on her palms, wondering where the bat had nested, about the reliability of her research assistant, whether she would go home for Christmas this year. Then she heard the noise.

Her entire body stiffened. No mistaking the sound of a car crawling down the gravel road toward their cabin. She checked her watch. 7 a.m. Shit. The sheriff wouldn't arrive until their bodies were cold. Maybe Josie would be safer if she just stayed in the house; maybe she wouldn't wake her. Yes, Kate pulled out of the sleeping bag. She was grabbed by the nightgown.

"Not so quick, brown fox," Josie said sleepily. "How about a cuddle?"

She was adorable in the morning, thought Kate, completely "dérangé" as Josie, herself, would admit, before two cups of coffee.

The noise outside grew closer and Kate tightened.

"Don't you even want to hear how I got elected Mayor of Lincoln. . . ."

"Not now," Kate couldn't stem the panic in her own voice.

Josie sat up. "What is it?" Then she heard the truck's motor dying.

"I'll just go check in with him," Kate said nonchalantly. "You wait here and I'll come back to snuggle." She pulled on her clothes.

"No you don't, Joan of Arc." Josie stood up and tucked her night-shirt into a pair of jeans.

The two walked downstairs together.

The fat man was approaching the house empty-handed. His friend, also bulky and middle-aged, stayed behind, leaning against the red pick-up truck.

Kate called out to him when he was three yards from the house. "Back again."

"Sorry to bother you, Mam. As you can see we didn't bring no guns. We'll just get that deer and then git offa yer propert'y as soon's we can."

His friend shuffled and looked at his feet.

"OK," Kate said gruffly. "We don't want dead animals on the land. By the way, we finished him off for you yesterday."

The man opened his mouth in surprise. His friend moved forward, tugging him back. They closed up the truck and headed into the woods.

Josie watched until they were out of sight. Kate went inside to make coffee.

Half-an-hour later, as they sat down to breakfast, another vehicle crunched down the hill. Josie looked out at the black and white sedan. "Our hero, the sheriff."

They walked over to greet the sheriff, a solid man, who looked them over carefully.

"You the girls who called me yesterday?"

"Yes, we did," Josie smiled.

"Yes," Kate nodded, the "sir" gone as quickly as it had come. She didn't like his expression.

"Only ladies listed on the deed to this land, I see. Looked it up last night. All schoolteachers. Some kind of commune? Something religious?"

"Just friends." Kate stepped back.

"Edna says she thought you was sisters." He squinted against the bright sun. "One sort or another."

"Just friends." Kate's voice was more distant.

"Soooo," the sheriff held his ground. "You want to run through the nature of that problem again?"

As Kate talked with the sheriff, Josie inspected the hunters' pickup truck. The bumper sticker read, "I live in a cave and one good fuck is all I crave." Inside dice hung from the rearview mirror. On the seat were a parka and two empty cans of Dr. Pepper. The dashboard was plastered with several irridescent signs. The sun glared so that she could read only one. "Gas, Ass or Grass—No one rides for free."

The sheriff noticed her and observed, "Leon's truck. Just as I figured. Leon Bates, a local man. He's, well, he's strayed off the hunting trail before."

"Isn't there something you can do about him?" Josie felt the heat rising to her face. "He might have killed one of us. On our property. With a gun."

"Today," the sheriff's voice was cool, "today your friend tells me, that he has no gun. That in fact, you said he could come back here to get his buck. That right?"

Josie closed her eyes, feeling naive for imagining this man might protect them. Now bureaucracy seemed the only recourse. "Right. Can't we make some kind of complaint about what he did yesterday?"

"Sure can," the sheriff nodded. "If that's what you want."

"What do you mean?" Kate's back tightened.

"You're weekend folks, right?" He lit a cigarette.

"We work in the city, if that's what you mean," Kate spoke carefully, "and don't live here year around."

"None of my business what you all have going on here. None of Leon's business either. But if you file a complaint and we take it to court, well, he's bound to do some investigating and. . . ."

"There's nothing illegal about our land group," Josie snapped.

"Miss, Miss, I never said anything about legal, illegal, but you know there are natural pests the law can't control. And it's better maybe not to get them roused."

Kate and Josie exchanged glances. "Well, perhaps we'll check with Loretta; her sister's a lawyer. We'll get back to you."

"Yes, Mam," he grew more serious. "That about all for today, Mam? I mean you said they didn't bring no guns with them. You feel safe enough on your own?"

"Yes," Josie said. "We're safe enough on our own."

"Then if you'll excuse me, it's almost 8:00 and services start early around here," he stamped out his cigarette and softened. "Church is always open to outsiders and weekend people, by the way. Just three miles down, on the road by the gas station."

"I know where it is," Josie said. "Good-bye, Sheriff."

They watched him roll up the hill, then returned to the house for breakfast. They were both too furious to talk. Kate hardly touched her food, watching out the window for the trespassers.

About 10 o'clock, she saw two pregnant-looking men pulling a buck through the dust by its antlers. Her first thought was how powerful those antlers must be. She tightened and Josie looked up from her book. "At last."

It took the men ten minutes to reach the truck. They were huffing and sweating and Josie had to resist the urge to bring them a pitcher of water. She followed Kate out on the front porch.

Leon Bates glowered at them, as if weighing the value of wasting breath for talk. He and his friend heaved the buck into the truck. On the second try, they made it.

Leon's friend wiped his hands on his jeans, waiting with an expression of excruciating embarrassment.

Leon straightened up, drew a breath and shouted. "That'll do it."

"Good," called Kate.

"Gotta ask one question," Leon leaned forward on his right leg. "What'd you have to go and bust his head for? Ruined a perfect trophy. Just look at the antlers. Would of been perfect."

"Come on, Leon," his friend called.

Kate stood firmly, hands on her hips. Josie tried to hold back the tears, but she couldn't and pivoted toward the cabin.

"The road's that way." Kate pointed. "Only goes in one direction."

Kate stamped into the house. "Damn them. Damn them!" she screamed.

"Hey, now." Josie reached up to her shoulders and pulled Kate toward her. "Hey now, relax love."

"Don't tell me to relax. This man comes on our land, shoots living things, threatens us. And you tell me to relax." She banged her hand on the table.

Josie inhaled heavily and pulled Kate a little closer. "They've gone now." She looked over Kate's shoulder and out the back window, which gleamed in the mid-morning sun. "See, they're over the hill."

"Out of sight, that's what you think, you fool," Kate tried to draw apart.

Josie held tight, hoping to melt the contortions from her friend's face.

Kate pushed her away. Josie lost balance, hitting her head against a pane of glass in the sun porch door.

The glass cracked, sending a high-pitched rip through the room.

Josie ducked forward, her eyes tightly shut, just in time to avoid most of the showering glass fragments.

Drenched in sweat, Kate shook her and shouted, "Josie, Josie, are you all right? Oh, my god, Josie, are you all right?"

"We'll never keep out the bats this way," Josie laughed nervously, on the verge.

"Josie, I didn't mean it." Tears welled in Kate's eyes. "I love you, Josie, are you all right?"

Josie nodded. They held each other, shivering.

Josie stepped forward, "OK, yes, but I feel a little like Tinkerbell. Scattering all this glitter."

"Tinkerbell!" Kate laughed and cried and choked. The room

seemed to be closing in on them. Hot, tight, airless. She could feel herself listing.

"But you, hey," Josie frowned, "Let's go upstairs and have *you* lie down."

They sat on the bed, holding hands and staring out at the land. The day was hot, even dryer than yesterday and the golden grass shimmered against the shadowy backdrop of the woods.

"We really should go down and clean up the glass, put a board over the shattered pane." Kate whispered.

"Yeah, if we don't head home soon, traffic's gonna be impossible."

Kate rested her head on Josie's breast. She smelled the musk from the black feathers beneath her arms. Her hand went to the soft nest at the bottom of Josie's generous belly. Josie slipped off her clothes. Kate followed. They sank down on the bed, swimming together again, sucked into the cool sleeping bag.

"Home," Josie murmured.

"Hmmmm?" Kate inhaled the scents of Josie's sweat and sex. Forcing herself to be alert, she pulled back. Was her friend delirious? Maybe she had a concussion.

"Home," Josie kissed her with a passion so conscious as to take away both Kate's concern and her breath.

"Yes," Kate moved her fingers lower, separating the labia, swirling the honey thicker. "Yes."

Josie crawled on top of Kate, licking her shoulders, her breasts; burying her nose in her navel; kissing her thighs. Then she was distracted by a slow fizzzz, as if their airmatress were deflating.

Josie looked up. Two wasps hovered over them, bobbing and weaving and then lifting themselves abruptly out of vision. Maybe if she just continued Kate wouldn't notice. But it was too late.

"They always come out in the middle of the day," Kate said drearily. "For food. For their nests."

Josie shook her head, staring at the unsteady, fragile creatures.

"What the hell," Kate shrugged, inching away from Josie.

"What the hell," Josie whispered seductively. They returned to the pleasures between them. When they finished making love, Josie curled around Kate. She explained how she had been elected Mayor of Lincoln, Nebraska.

The wasps wove over and around the two women. Even as they fell asleep.

Silver

MERRIL MUSHROOM

I NEVER IN A MILLION YEARS would have thought that something like this could happen to me. I mean, I am just not that type of person. I am a mature woman, fifty-five years old, sixteen of which I have been living in a committed relationship with my lover Sarah (along with our cat, dog and canary). I am well-established in a career that I created for myself through years of hard work and many disappointments. I am respected in the Huntsville community (where I am, of course, in the closet) and am on several boards of directors. Nevertheless, it happened to me, and I had no control over it—I, an old-timey butch, a used-to-be tough bar dyke who turned respectable in my later years, had gone and flipped totally out of my gourd over a weird, arrogant, blatant, lesbian teenager!

It happened when I went to Chicago to speak at a NOW event about the processes involved in building my advertising business. I planned to spend several days there and visit with some old friends, eat city food, and go to the lesbian bars. I'm still a bar dyke at heart, and I like going to lesbian spaces when they're far enough away from Huntsville for me to feel at ease being open about who I am. Sarah, who is even more closeted than I am, does not like the bars, and does not care for large gatherings, stayed home.

My talk—to a packed auditorium—went well, and I had a wonderful time with my friends, visiting, talking, eating, laughing, and going to the bars. On my last night in town we went to The Fruitie Bar, a new place in the city that was supposed to be a lesbian alternative to the bars.

The Fruitie Bar was a big barn of a place with chairs and tables, a dance floor, snacks, and a juice/soft drinks/coffee/tea bar. It was an altogether delightful space. The walls were decorated with visual art by lesbian artists, and potted plants were everywhere. Some evenings there was live music or readings. Tonight, we were entertained by recorded music, dancing, and our own conversations.

I was sitting with my friends, joking and laughing, when this very young-looking woman rose from a table nearby and came over. Without asking or even excusing herself, she slid her little backside onto the chair next to me that my friend Sue had just vacated when she left to go to the ladies room. "Hi," she said.

"Hello," I responded rather cooly, looking her over. She did look a sight, I must say. She wore hand-embroidered blue jeans and a purple tie-dyed T-shirt which was tight enough to reveal that she wore no brassiere. I stared at her breasts, perhaps a bit crassly, but there they were, so I figured I might as well. I could tell by looking at them what they'd feel like. They would be firm, somewhat hard, very smooth-skinned, with ripe, pliant nipples. They would be unlike Sarah's breasts which were low and pendant, covered with unbelievably soft skin that slipped easily over her flesh; nor would they be like the small, somewhat sagging tautness of my own.

Between the breasts hung a crocheted pouch, and several strands of beads rested above that. One necklace, longer than the others, was centered with a large carved piece of wood that looked suspiciously like a vulva. The girl had several holes in each ear from which hung an assortment of earrings, and a tiny pearl on a post was impaled through the crease of her right nostril. Her long, thick, kinky dark hair appeared not to have been brushed in days. Her skin was very pale and smooth, and somewhere behind the art work that coated the area around her eyes, really pretty bright green irises called for some attention.

The girl cleared her throat. "I heard you talk at the NOW meeting the other night," she began, which I was not especially thrilled to hear. "I'm from Huntsville too," she went on, which was worse yet. She kept talking. "I really enjoyed your speech. I think you said some very important, practical things about how to start up a small business."

"Yes?" I couldn't quite believe someone who looked like *that* would be interested in business. I had no need for her compliments, and I really didn't want her to settle in on Sue's chair. "Good," I said briskly, as I saw Sue returning from the bathroom. "Now why don't you go on back to your table?"

Her color rose slightly. Without saying another word, she departed. I wasn't meaning to be cruel, but I had very little time left to be with my friends, and I wasn't willing to waste any of it in conversation with this kid. Even so, throughout the evening, I remained aware of her. From time to time I could sense her gaze on me, and whenever I looked her way, she was watching me; and she didn't even look away when she saw me looking back at her. She began to talk very loudly to her companions, laugh loudly, and I felt that she was showing off for my benefit, seeking to attract my attention. At one point, I looked over to see that she had moved to another table where she was sitting on the lap of a girl dressed very much like herself but whose long, blond hair was strung with beads. She was bouncing on the blond girl's knee, showing obvious affection; and I was surprised that a little pang ran through me at the sight.

She was back at her original table again when I decided to go to the ladies' room myself. I had to pass her and as I did so, she reached out and touched me on the hand. I stopped and she gripped me by the wrist, brushed her other hand against my hip. Her friends had gotten up to dance, and she was alone at the table.

I was nervous. Why should I be nervous? The thought made me even more nervous. I had to do something. I loomed over her, standing close, so she had to lean back to look at my face. "What's your name, sugar?" I asked.

She puffed herself up, raised her chin. "They call me," she paused, "Silver," she said, her voice swelling with pride.

"Silver?" I repeated. I couldn't believe this. I wanted to put her down, lash her for her affectation over something so silly. I chuckled. "Where'd you get a ridiculous name like that? Silver's the name of a horse!"

She flushed. "It. . . it was Given to me," she stammered, and I figured that she most likely Gave it to herself. I also realized that she probably had no idea who Silver the horse was. I suddenly felt embarrassed for both her and for myself, and I was glad that her friends were not at the table. I continued on to the bathroom then; but I did not feel good about my encounter with Silver, and I wondered why I had wanted to be so unkind to her.

I did not behave any better when we left. I let my friends go ahead of me, and as I passed her table, I stopped for a moment. She looked up at me and half-smiled. "Good night, Silver," I said, using that silly name. On impulse, then, I bent, grasped her beneath the chin, and kissed her on the mouth, giving her little lips a good hard grab with my own, smooching her just like I would have in the old days. Then I pulled away and, without another word, without a backward glance, I left the building and crossed the street to meet my friends at their car, trying not to dwell on thoughts of Silver's soft, warm lips that had been so terrifyingly responsive against my own.

I was very relieved to get home to dear, familiar Sarah, my girl, the woman with whom I'd made a life, shared the past sixteen years, and intended to share the future. Sarah was a schoolteacher, as respected a citizen of Huntsville as I was. Some of our colleagues knew that we lived together, but if they thought anything further about it, they kept what they thought to themselves.

She welcomed me home with a favorite meal and good sex, and we laughed together over the precious humdrum of our lives, how predictable we both were to each other, how comfortable that was for each of us. I told her about my presentation, gave her news about our mutual friends, and talked about my adventures in Chicago. She asked questions, made comments, and became involved. She was delighted that I'd enjoyed myself, and I was delighted to be able to share with her that pleasure, loving her so much because we could do things separately as well as together and be glad over it.

I did not tell her about Silver.

Every now and again, over the next few days, I'd find myself thinking about the girl. Impatiently, I'd push away those images, forcing my attention back to whatever I had been doing. One afternoon, while I was working at my desk, my concentration was suddenly disrupted by a vivid memory of Silver's face, her dark hair and green irises, the multitude of holes in her ears and the one in her nostril, her soft lips and firm breasts. I was glad when the phone rang, startling me away from those images. I reached for it. "Hello. This is Regina Black."

"Hello. This is Silver."

I suddenly got such a rush I felt dizzy. *What is that crazy kid doing calling me here at work? What is she doing calling me at all?* I immediately assumed the worst, that she was on the make, chasing me, a woman old enough to be her mother, hell, probably even her grandmother! "Yes?" I responded as calmly as I possibly could, wondering if she had the nerve to assume that I remembered who she was.

She did. "I want to meet you for coffee after work. I'd like to ask you some business questions."

Now I *really* felt huffy. Not so much as an "if you don't mind" or "please, if you'd care to." I opened my mouth to say, *Sorry, Baby, that would be impossible,* but, to my horror, I found that what came out sounded more like, "Alright. Meet me at 5:30 at Lousiana's on 23rd Street." Then I hung up, not even bothering to find out if she knew where Lousiana's was on 23rd street. *Let her call back if she doesn't know,* I thought spitefully.

She didn't call back, and I was tempted to stand her up, but I am not the type to do that or even to be late. *I should have asked her what she wanted over the phone,* I thought. *What the hell is with me, anyhow?* Warning bells were ting-a-linging, albeit faintly, through the turmoil of my thoughts. I began to reason with myself: *What could be wrong with meeting the kid for coffee?* I argued. *She looks up to me. She could do worse for a role model. I mean, it's not as though we were going to engage in adult/child sex or anything. She's probably older than she looks, anyhow.* I began to relax, to feel better. I left the office at 5:20 so as to be sure to arrive at Lousiana's at precisely 5:30.

I spotted Silver as soon as I walked through the door. She was seated at a table for two near the window, and for a moment I was sorry that I'd asked her to meet me at a place where I sometimes came with clients. Her get-up was worse than the first time I saw her—an Indian print top studded with mirrors and bright red bell-bottom pants that were short enough to display her coarse, dark leg hairs. She was barefoot. A different earring dangled from every hole in each ear, and that awful pearl was still impaled through her nostril. I wondered what she did when she had a cold.

Gritting my teeth, I remembered the multitude of statements that I was trying to live by about acceptance and loving my sisters and the wonderfulness of differences and how strong we were in our diversity, and then I walked over to the table and sat down. She hadn't seen me come in. Now she turned toward me, and her face lighted with a smile. Her "green-means-go" eyes were merely circled with black today, and little dimples twinkled on her chin. I noticed how nice her teeth were, and I remembered how soft her mouth had felt.

I nodded to her, very aloof, and then the waitress came over. "I'll have coffee and a cheese danish, please." I said.

Silver was reading the list of hot drinks on the menu. "I'd like a cup of the mulled cider." Then, without preliminaries or niceties, she began to ask me questions, business questions, most of them quite well thought out. She was trying to start a mail order line of women's greeting cards and craft items, and her ideas were interesting. We talked for an hour. I learned that she was eighteen years old, was raised in Huntsville where she had just finished high school, and that she came out as a lesbian at the age of fourteen with her best friend, the beaded blond from The Fruitie Bar who now lived in Chicago.

I don't remember the bulk of our conversation, but I do remember how cute her chin looked flashing dimples as she spoke, how surprised I was at her intelligence and serious approach to her business. I answered her as best as I could and encouraged her to enroll in a business class at the local community college. What I really wanted to do was tell her to scrub her face and shave her legs and put on a proper dress, and she might find it easier to make her way in the professional world, but I didn't.

I did not tell Sarah that I had met Silver for coffee.

All this was most disturbing to me. In the past, I never had any problem in talking with Sarah, even the most difficult discussions about the most touchy matters. But I could not discuss this with her. I could not broach the subject of Silver or these strange feelings that I was having. I did not know what was going on with me, but one fact was undeniable—I was definitely and hugely attracted to this hippie kid who was thirty-seven years my junior.

I could see the scenario unfolding: Silver calls again, we go to lunch. I never call her, of course, but she continues to call me. We lunch together more and more frequently under the guise of discussing business. Then we begin to meet for dinner. I offer her the benefit of my experience and knowledge. I give her the support and information she needs to make her business a success. I am her role model, her teacher, her advisor. She adores me. Eventually, we end up in bed, consummating our attraction. We end up doing it, having sex, making love.

Now the scenario grows wilder: She is delightful. I am smitten. She washes her face and combs her hair and shaves her legs just for me. She wears matching pairs of earrings, and never more than two pair at a time. She removes the pearl from her nostril and lets the hole close up. We like each other, we have fun together, and the sex is great. The thirty-seven year age difference does not matter. We run off together, passionately in love, and prove that anything can succeed if the right people are involved.

But from here on, the scenario becomes bleak: Sarah is alone with dog, cat, canary, and home. She tries to be understanding and accepting, but she is devastated. We lose contact with each other. The last I hear, she is with someone else. Silver does not like my long hours at work. She wants me to spend more time with her. This begins to pall on me. We begin to run out of things to talk about. She has a crisis. I stick with her through it. I have a crisis. She is not able to cope with it. She wants to spend more time with her friends. So do I, with mine, those who are left. I think her friends are wild and crazy. I cannot relate to them. She thinks my friends are old and stodgy. She becomes outspoken, rude, crass. I become embarrassed. She stops shaving her legs and starts mixing her earrings. The joy of sex begins to wear off.

There is another scenario: Silver and I have an affair, an intense experience of each other on many levels. It is wonderful. I tell Silver all about Sarah. She respects that. I do not tell Sarah about Silver. Silver and I see each other now and then. The sex is great. I feel guilty.

What was going on for me? Was this a midlife crisis? Was it due to a shortage of hormones? Was it caused by an organic dysfunction? Or was it a desire to regain my own lost youth? Did I need more excitement, stress, chaos in my life, or had I been overachieving all this time and now was on the verge of a nervous breakdown? Was I secretly dissatisfied with my life with Sarah? Was something critical missing from our relationship? Was I attracted by the bizarre, by a twisted fascination with Silver's differentness? Or was it simply a matter of pheremones? Was it old karmic baggage, or was it a long-time connection that Silver and I were re-experiencing in the New Light of Now?

In the long run, it didn't matter; my primary consideration was not why this was happening or even that it was happening. At this point, what was called for was nothing more than my decision about how I would act. I could think about the reasons, about the motivation, over time. I could self-examine, talk with friends, go to therapy. I would work it out later, for sure, and, in time, discuss it with Sarah. What mattered in the here-and-now, in the world of present-time reality, was Sarah and our relationship together, Sarah and our life together; and because of this I knew that I could not let things with Silver go any further. There would be no more meetings to discuss business. There would be no lunches, no dinners, and no sexual seductions. I would not tempt fate, nor would I put myself to any test. What mattered was my life as it now stood, my life with Sarah, and I knew, at least for now, I would have that, and I would keep it.

My Woman Poppa

JOAN NESTLE

YOU WORK AT A JOB that makes your back rock-hard strong; you work with men in a cavernous warehouse loading trucks while others sleep. Sometimes when you come to me while I work at home, you fall asleep in my bed on your stomach, the sheet wrapped around your waist, the flaming unicorn on your right shoulder catching the afternoon sun.

I just stand and look at you, at your sleeping face and kind hands, my desire growing for you, for my woman poppa who plays the drums and knows all the words to *Lady in Red,* who calls me sassafras mama, even when I am sometimes too far from the earth, who is not frightened off by my years or my illness.

My woman poppa who knows how to take me in her arms and lie me down, knows how to spread my thighs and then my lips, who knows how to catch the wetness and use it and then knows how to enter me so women waves rock us both.

189

My woman poppa who is not afraid of my moans or my nails but takes me and takes me until she reaches far beyond the place of entry into the core of tears. Then as I come to her strength and woman fullness, she kisses away my legacy of pain. My cunt and heart and head are healed.

My woman poppa who does not want to be a man, but who does travel in "unwomanly" places and who does "unwomanly" work. Late into the New Jersey night, she maneuvers the forklift to load the thousands of pounds of aluminum into the hungry trucks that stand waiting for her. Dressed in the shiny tiredness of warehouse blue, with her company's name white-stitched across her pocket, she endures the bitter humor of her fellow workers, who are men. They laugh at Jews, at women, and when the Black workers are not present, at Blacks. All the angers of their lives, all their dreams gone dead, bounce off the warehouse walls. My woman grits her teeth, and says when the rape jokes come: "Don't talk that shit around me."

When she comes home to me, I must caress the parts of her that have been worn thin, trying to do her work in a man's world. She likes her work, likes the challenge of the machines and the quietness of the night, likes her body moving into power. When we go to women's parties, I watch amused at the stares she gets when she answers the traditional question, "What do you do?" with her nontraditional answer, "I load trucks in a warehouse." When the teachers and social workers no longer address their comments to her, I want to shout at them, where is your curiosity about women's lives, where is your wonder at boundaries broken?

My woman poppa is thirteen years younger than I, but she is wide in her woman-loving ways. Breasts and ass get her hot, that wonderful hot which is a heard and spoken desire. I make her hot and I like that. I like her sweat and her tattoos, I like her courtliness and her disdain of the boys, I mother her and wife her and slut her, and together we are learning to be comrades.

She likes me to wear a black slip to bed; to wear dangling earrings and black stockings with sling back heels when we play. She

likes my perfume and lipstick and nail polish. I enjoy these slashes
of color, the sweetened place in my neck where she will bury her
head when she is moving on me. I sometimes sit on her, my cunt
open on her round belly, my breasts hanging over her, my nipples
grazing her lips. I forbid her to touch me and continue to rock on
her, my wetness smearing her belly. She begins to moan and curves
her body upwards, straining at the restrictions.

"Please baby, please," my woman poppa begs. "Please let me
fuck you." Then suddenly, when she has had enough, she smiles,
opens her eyes, says, "You have played enough," and using the power
she has had all along, throws me from my throne.

Sometimes she lies in bed wearing her cock under the covers.
I can see its outline under the pink spread. I just stand in my slip
watching her, her eyes getting heavy. Then I sit alongside her, on
the edge of the bed, telling her what a wonderful cock she has, as
I run my hand down her belly until I reach her lavender hardness.
I suck her nipple and slowly stroke her, tugging at the cock so she
can feel it through the leather triangle that holds it in place.

"Let me suck you," I say, my face close to hers, my breasts spilling out on hers. "Let me take your cock in my mouth and show
you what I can do." She nods, almost as if her head is too heavy
to move.

Oh, my darling, this play is real. I do long to suck you, to take
your courage into my mouth, both cunt, your flesh, and cock, your
dream, deep into my mouth, and I do. I throw back the covers and
bend over her carefully so she can see my red lips and red-tipped
fingers massaging her cock. I take one of her hands and wrap it
around the base so she can feel my lips as I move on her. I give
her the best I can, licking the lavender cock its whole length and
slowly tonguing the tip, circling it with my tongue. Then I take her
fully into my mouth, into my throat. She moans, moves, tries to watch,
and cannot as the image overpowers her. When I have done all that
I can, I bend the wet cock up on her belly and sit on her so I can
feel it pressing against my cunt. I rock on her until she is ready and

then she reaches down and slips the cock into me. Her eyes are open now, wonderfully clear and sharp, and she slips her arms down low around my waist so I am held tight against her. Very slowly, she starts to move her hips upward in short strong thrusts. I am held on my pleasure by her powerful arms; I can do nothing but move and take and feel. When she knows I have settled in, she moves quicker and quicker, her breath coming in short hard gasps. But I hear the words, "Oh baby, you are so good to fuck."

I forget everything but her movements. I fall over her, my head on the pillow above her. I hear sounds, moans, shouted words, know my fists are pounding the bed but I am unaware of forming words or lifting my arms. I ride and ride harder and faster, encircled by her arms, by her gift.

"Give it all to me, let it all go," I know she is saying. I hear a voice answering, "you you you you" and I am pounding the bed, her arms, anything I can reach. How dare you do this to me, how dare you push me beyond my daily voice, my daily body, my daily fears. I am chanting; we are dancing. We have broken through.

Then, it is over. We return and gently she lifts me off her belly. I slide down her body, rest and then release her from the leather. We sleep.

Yes, my woman poppa knows how to move me but she knows many other things as well. She knows she will not be shamed; she knows her body carries complicated messages. My woman poppa, my dusty sparrow, I know how special you are. Your strength, both of loving and of need, is not mistaken for betrayal of your womanness.

The Dating Game

LESLÉA NEWMAN

I
The Party

"MAZEL TOV" Chelsea leaned over and kissed Darlene on the cheek, handing her a big bouquet of wild irises. "Where's the other half of this celebration?"

"She's in the kitchen getting more burgers. These are beautiful. Thanks, Chelsea."

"Sure." Chelsea sat down on the chair nearest Darlene. "Irises are for seven years. Your next anniversary you get mums." "What's after that?" Rachel called from across the yard. "Roses?"

Chelsea looked up. "I don't know. I'm running out of kinds of purple flowers."

"How about violets? Those are pretty," Jessie said, flopping onto a lawn chair holding a paper plate full of food.

"Chelsea, do you know Jessie? Jessie, Chelsea. Chels, Jess."

"Hi." Jessie balanced her plate on her lap and reached over to shake Chelsea's hand.

"Hi yourself." Chelsea smiled.

"You know everyone else, Chelsea, don't you?" Darlene asked.

Chelsea looked around. Phyllis and Rachel were playing frisbee and Sunflower was turning some tofu hot dogs on the hibachi. "This is nice Darlene. I think it's great that you and Alice are throwing a party for your seventh. It should only happen to me."

"It will." Darlene patted her arm. "Have some food, Chels." "Right. A girl's got to keep up her strength."

"That's right. You don't want to be all skin and bones when Ms. Right comes along."

"No, you wanna be big and tough like me," Phyllis said, coming over to the picnic table and picking up a paper plate. "You gotta be strong enough to sweep her off her feet, scoop her up in your arms. . . ." Phyllis made a muscle, first with her left arm and then with her right.

"Oh Phyl, you're so butch." Rachel said, coming up behind her and squeezing her biceps.

"So that's why you study karate," Darlene said.

"Sure," Phyllis said, heaping a small mound of potato salad onto her plate. "Watching those girls change in the dressing room every Thursday is the high point of my week."

"I'm telling your Sensei," Sunflower said, putting a plate of tofu dogs on the table. "Who wants one of these?"

"No thanks, Sunflower, I'm waiting for the chicken," Chelsea said.

"Got any burgers for us real dykes?" Phyllis asked.

"Coming right up," Alice called, walking across the yard with a paper plate covered with tin foil. She squatted down and put some hamburgers on the hibachi.

"Oh there's the other anniversary girl. Mazel tov."

"Thanks, Chelsea."

"Hey you shouldn't be cooking, Alice. It's your party," Jessie said.

"Go sit down next to your girl. I'll watch these."

"Yeah, Honey. Come sit next to me."

"Okay." Alice sat down on the grass in front of Darlene's chair with her back leaning against her lover's legs.

"Look at that. The happy couple. Smile now." Sunflower held up her hands and pretended to click a camera in front of her face.

"A match made in heaven." Chelsea sighed wistfully.

"How did you two meet, anyway?" Phyllis asked.

Alice swiveled around to face Darlene. "How did we meet, Sweetheart?"

"You don't remember?" Darlene folded her arms. "Cancel this party."

"Now now, just wait a minute. Let me think. It was in Michigan, wasn't it, at the Butch/Femme workshop, no, no, that was Emily. . . ."

"Alice!" Darlene leaned forward, threatening to spill her beer over Alice's head.

"Only kidding, only kidding." Alice covered her head with her hands. "Of course I remember where we met. It was at Annie and Ellen's fifth year anniversary party."

"Tell us what happened," Sunflower said.

"Yeah, did you know right away?" Chelsea asked.

"Well, I definitely thought Alice was cute right away," Darlene said, running her hands through Alice's hair. "She was wearing these tight black pants and a white button down shirt, with her brown shoes and one rhinestone earring in her left ear."

"You remember what I was wearing?" Alice turned sideways and leaned her elbow on Darlene's knee.

"Of course I do, Sweetheart," Darlene said lovingly. "You've worn that outfit to practically every party we've been to since in the last seven years." She laughed. "Of course I didn't know that then." Darlene paused. "Don't you remember what I was wearing?"

Alice ate some coleslaw, trying to think. "No."

"Well I do," Darlene said. "I was wearing my black sequin top and my hot pink skirt, you know the one that goes straight down, and black fishnet stockings and high heels."

"Wow." Phyllis rolled her eyes. "Too bad I wasn't at that party, Darlene. I would have snatched you right up."

"I had a date for the evening anyway," Darlene said.

"Well that usually doesn't stop Phyllis," said Rachel.

"What do you mean?" Phyllis asked, indignant.

"Go on with your story," Chelsea said. "So you met at this party, then how did you two get together?"

"Wait a second, I want to hear this." Jessie came over and set a plate of burgers down in the center of the circle of women. When everyone had their food, Darlene continued.

"Well as I remember it, I called up Alice and asked her on a date."

"You did?" Rachel asked.

"That was brave," Sunflower said.

"But did she know it was a date-date, or did she just think it was a date?" Chelsea asked.

"How do you know the difference?" asked Phyllis.

"What is dating anyway?" Jessie asked.

"Dating means no sex," Sunflower said.

"Not always," Phyllis said.

"Especially in Phyllis's case," Rachel added.

"I think you're dating someone until you have sex with them," Chelsea said thoughtfully.

"Then what happens?" Jessie asked, looking interested.

"Then you're going out with them."

"What does seeing someone mean?" Sunflower asked.

"That definitely means sex." Chelsea nodded her head.

"But how do you know if you're having an affair or a relationship?" asked Jessie.

"Or a non-committed relationship," Chelsea added. "I've had plenty of those."

"Alice, did you know it was a real date when Darlene asked you?" Rachel asked.

"Well, yeah, sort of," Alice said.

"There's a definite answer." Phyllis said.

"I always know when I'm going out on a date," Chelsea said.

"How?"

"Well, I have two barometers."

"Oh yeah? Do you keep them in your living room?" Alice asked.

"No Alice, listen. The first is how old I feel before she gets there. If I feel between 12 and 16, it's a sure sign. And the second is, how many times I change my clothes before I go."

"It's all in the inflection of your voice when you ask," Jessie said. "Like for example, you could say, 'Would you like to go out on a date,' " Jessie said this without expression, as if she was asking if you thought it was going to rain today, "or," she continued, "you could say, 'Would you like to go out on a *date*,' " she repeated, this time in a low Marlene Dietrich type voice.

"Ooh, I like that, I like that," Chelsea said, turning towards Jessie. "Say that again."

"Oh I couldn't." Jessie looked down shyly.

"I went out on a date a few months ago," Rachel said.

"You did, Rach? You didn't tell me. That's great," Darlene said.

"What happened, Rachel?" asked Alice.

"Well, we went out for a drink, only she doesn't drink, so we had seltzer," Rachel said. "Then afterwards we took a walk down by the river and the moon came up and it was really romantic."

"Ooh, sounds hot!"

"Then what happened?"

"Then she took my hand and we stopped walking," Rachel said. "So there we were by the river, listening to the water and looking at the stars, not another soul in sight. Then she turned to me and I shut my eyes, all ready for her kiss. . . ." Rachel shut her eyes and tilted back her head.

"And then what happened?"

Rachel opened her eyes and threw her hands up in the air. "Then she told me she was committed to being celibate for a year."

"Oh no!"

"Yep." Rachel sunk back into her chair.

"Only us lesbians," Sunflower said, shaking her head.

"And she wanted to keep dating," Rachel added.

"What did she mean by celibate? No sex, no kissing, what?" Darlene asked.

"No nothing," Rachel said gloomily. "Just seltzer."

"I had a date recently," Chelsea said. "I didn't really know it was a date until the middle though."

"What happened?"

"I bumped into this friend of mine at the bookstore. She wasn't a good friend really, just a casual friend, you know? And we were both reading this notice about a Ferron concert and I said 'Wow, I'd really like to go to that,' and she said, 'Wanna go together?' and I said, 'Sure.' "

"So?" Darlene said.

"So halfway through the concert she just reached into my lap and started holding my hand."

"Oh no!"

"What did you do?"

"I didn't know what to do. What would you do?" Chelsea asked looking around. "I waited a minute and then I let go of her hand to scratch my face and then I folded my arms."

"Did you talk about it?"

"Of course not. Then she called me the next day and we had to process the whole thing for two hours."

"Oh no. Yuk," Alice said.

"That's weird," Phyllis said, "when friends start having crushes on you. That's happened to me."

"Everything's happened to you," Rachel reminded her.

"Well I can't help it if I'm so charming, right?" Phyllis shrugged her shoulders. "It was a woman on my softball team. She kept asking me for a ride home every Tuesday night after practice. And every week she'd sit closer and closer to me in the car."

"And then what happened?"

"Well, I didn't want to assume anything."

"Phyllis never assumes anything," Rachel said.

"Well maybe her car was broken."

"All summer?" Darlene asked. "C'mon, Phyllis."

"Well I wasn't sure. You know."

"Did she ask you to come in when you dropped her off?" Sunflower asked.

"Yeah, she always wanted to fix me dinner or something to drink, but I don't know, maybe she was just trying to be friendly."

"You don't fix someone dinner at 9:30 just to be friendly," Darlene said.

"Especially after you've gone out for pizza already," Rachel added.

"Did you ever go out with her?" Chelsea asked.

"Well, then softball season ended. But she did call and invite me to go out to Tanglewood with her next week."

"Yeah, lying on a blanket under the stars, listening to music—that's really romantic."

"Yeah, she's making a whole picnic—wine, cheese, apples. I don't know, though. You guys really think she's interested?"

"I'd say she's pretty interested," Sunflower said.

"I'd say she has a pretty high interest rate," said Chelsea. "But I don't know. I can't imagine sleeping with friends."

"That's what I always do," said Sunflower.

"Then what happens?" asked Chelsea. "I mean, do you stay friends with them?"

Sunflower thought for a moment. "No. Then we become lovers."

"And then what?" Chelsea asked. "I mean assuming you break up eventually."

"Not everyone breaks up eventually," Alice pointed out.

"That's right, Sweetheart," Darlene added.

"Wow," Jessie said. "Do you realize that all of us, except you two are single. That's pretty rare at a lesbian party."

"I rest my case," Chelsea said, brushing a potato chip crumb off her skirt. "So, Sunflower, do you think it's easier to remain friends with someone after you break up if you were friends first?"

"Well, let's see. Yes. No. Well, not necessarily," she said. "I guess it depends."

"On what?"

"On how clear you were from the beginning about what you both wanted. Like if one of you wanted to have a fling and the other one of you wanted to get married, it could be trouble."

"It's hard to have a fling in this town." Jessie sighed and rested her chin on her fist.

"You have to go out of town for a fling," Phyllis said.
Rachel looked at her. "You don't."

"Tell us, Phyllis." Chelsea leaned forward in her chair. "Have you really had an out of town affair?"
Rachel choked on her beer and Phyllis glared at her. "Yeah, I've had maybe one or two."

"One or two?" Rachel gasped.

"Tell us about one. The last one."

"Well, let's see." Phyllis thought for a minute. "It was at this teacher's convention in Minneapolis last year."

"Minneapolis? I thought we were talking Boston here."

"Or New York."

"Or Northampton. I can't afford to go all the way to Minneapolis."

"So what happened?"

"Well, you know how these things are. We sat at the same table the first night at dinner, and it was pretty clear we were the only dykes there, so we took a walk after dinner and then we just slept together."

"Wait a minute, wait a minute," Chelsea said. "What do you mean, you just slept together?"

"Well we were in a hotel already, you know for the convention. So one thing just led to another, you know. . . ."

"No I don't know," said Chelsea. "That's the problem."

"It's just an organic process, Chels," Sunflower said.

"You mean like gardening?"

"Yeah, sort of." Sunflower picked a dandelion from the lawn and started playing with it. "I mean first you have this feeling and then another feeling grows, and then another one grows, and then. . . ." she shrugged her shoulders. "And then you just know."

"I disagree," Chelsea said. "I mean this just knowing stuff assumes an awful lot. I went to the JoAnn Loulan workshop last week, you know, she wrote that book *Lesbian Sex*?"

"Ooh, that was brave of you to go," Darlene said.

"Yeah, tell us about it," said Phyllis.

"Well," Chelsea said, "she said that lesbians have to talk to each other more about sex and dating. I mean, straight people always know when they're going out on a date, right? So she had us practice by having lunch with three women we didn't know and talking the whole time about what we like in bed."

"Over lunch?" Darlene asked. "How did you eat?"

"Very s-l-o-w-l-y," Chelsea said with a laugh.

"I can tell you what I like in bed," Jessie said. "Soft flannel sheets, my teddy bear, a nice hot cup of tea. . . ."

"No, she means sexually, don't you Chelsea?" asked Phyllis.

"Give us an example, Chelsea," Rachel said.

Chelsea looked down into her lap. "Oh no, I couldn't."

"Oh c'mon."

"Yeah, c'mon Chelsea. You're among friends."

"Okay, let me think." Chelsea took a deep breath. Then she took another one. "Oh I can't."

"I know," Jessie said. "If Chelsea says something, we all have to say something."

"Yeah," Chelsea said. "That's fair. Okay you guys?"

"Okay."

"Okay." Everyone nodded.

"Well," Chelsea looked down into her lap again. "Someone in my group said, she said . . ." Chelsea paused and then her words came out all in one breath very fast, "she-said-she-liked-having-both-her-breasts-sucked-at-the-same-time. Oh my God, I can't believe I just said that." Chelsea covered her face with her hands.

"Can you do that?" Darlene asked, looking down at her chest.

"Obviously some of us can," Jessie said, staring at Chelsea who was blushing furiously.

Phyllis squeezed her breasts together, under her T-shirt which said "An Army of Ex-Lovers Cannot Fail" on it, trying to get her nipples to meet a mouth's width apart. "Of course, you could be in bed with more than one person," Phyllis said, failing at her attempt.

"Only you would think of that," Rachel said, shaking her head.

"You could be nursing two babies," Sunflower added.

"Or you could suck one of your own breasts and have your lover suck the other one," Alice said.

"Okay, okay, who's next?" Chelsea asked.

"Wait a minute, you said it was someone in your group. You didn't say it was you," Jessie said.

"Come on Jessie." Chelsea gave her a long look until she too was blushing. "Besides the workshop was confidential. I couldn't tell you what anyone else said."

"I think Phyllis should go next," Rachel said. "She's had the most experience."

"Oh c'mon Rachel. It's been a long time."

"How long?"

"I don't know. Let me see." Phyllis started counting backwards on her fingers. "August, July, June, May, April. Five months. No, wait a minute. Do one night stands count?"

"I think Darlene and Alice should go next," Sunflower said, turning towards them. "Let us in on some secrets about how you two manage to stay together."

"No way!" Darlene said.

"Well, first of all, Darlene likes her back scratched," Alice said with a little smile. "And then she likes me to. . . ."

"Alice!" Darlene clapped her hands over Alice's mouth. "Is nothing sacred?" She looked up at the darkening sky. "Hey, do you think we could get in one more game of volleyball before the sun goes down?"

"I'm too full to move," Rachel said.

"I gotta get going," said Phyllis.

"Got a date?" Sunflower asked.

"I'll never tell." Phyllis stood up and threw her paper plate in the trash.

"Hey, wait a minute. You guys promised." Chelsea folded her arms.

"Uh-oh. Now she's going to pout," Alice said.

"At our tenth year anniversary party, Chelsea," Darlene said, patting her on the shoulder. "I promise, everyone will tell all."

"Great," Phyllis said. "That gives us plenty of time to practice."

"Thanks for the party," Sunflower said, giving Darlene a hug. "It was really fun."

"Hey, it's only 9:00. How come everyone's leaving so soon?" Chelsea asked.

"Pssst. This is an anniversary party, Chelsea," Rachel said in a stage whisper. "Darlene and Alice want to do a little private celebrating."

"Oh, I get it." She got up from her chair and straightened out her skirt. "Well, come to think of it, I've got to get going myself." She hugged Alice and gave Darlene a kiss on the cheek. "See you."

"'Bye."

Chelsea walked across the lawn and paused for a minute, leaning back on her car. The stars sure are pretty tonight, she thought, trying to pick out the Big Dipper.

"Hey, there's a girl with stars in her eyes," Sunflower said, putting her pack in the back seat of her car. "See you, Chelsea." She pushed the driver's seat forward so Rachel and Phyllis could get into her car.

"Goodnight."

Chelsea watched them drive off, then reluctantly got into her own car. Just before she pulled out of her driveway, she was startled by Jessie tapping on her window. She rolled it down and smiled.

"I just wanted to tell you," Jessie said, leaning her forearm along the car door, "I thought it was really brave of you to say what you said, and I'm sorry no one else said anything after they promised that they would."

Chelsea looked up into Jessie's eyes. "Thanks." She paused. "Do you think I made a fool of myself?"

"No. Sometimes it's important to take a risk, that's all." Jessie kicked at the driveway with the toe of her sneaker without saying anything. Chelsea waited for a minute, feeling that Jessie wanted something, but she didn't know what. "Well, goodnight, Jessie," she said.

Jessie didn't move. "Chelsea," she said softly, staring down at her own arm. "One thing I really like is sucking both women's breasts at the same time, too. I mean one woman's both breasts. Ah, you know what I mean." Chelsea looked up to see Jessie blushing furiously before she turned and disappeared into the night.

II
The Phone Call(s)

It was Sunday morning around 11:00. Chelsea sat at the kitchen table staring blankly into her bowl of yoghurt and rubbing her eyes. She hadn't slept very well. All that sexual energy had followed her home, and there wasn't much to do with it there. She'd tossed and turned, tried counting backwards from 100 and drinking catnip tea (one of Sunflower's suggestions for insomnia). Then around four in the morning she'd finally given up, snapped on the light and began to read. The words swum around the page though, and rearranged themselves into the profile of a face that looked remarkably like Jessie's.

"That woman is completely cute," Chelsea said aloud, dribbling some honey from a plastic bear into her yoghurt. "God, I'd love to ask her out on a date."

"Do it," a voice inside Chelsea's head urged her.

"But I don't have her phone number," she answered it.

"Ever hear of the phone book?" the voice shot back.

Chelsea abandoned her yoghurt for the moment, walked into the living room and picked up the phone book from the telephone stand. She started flipping through it and then remembered she didn't even know Jessie's last name. "Damn." She put the phone book down and went back into the kitchen. I could always call Darlene, Chelsea thought, as she started to eat. She glanced up at the clock above the kitchen table. It's only 11:20 though. She's probably still in bed with Alice. That's what girls with girlfriends do on Sunday mornings.

Chelsea ate slowly, thinking about last night's part. I can't believe I said that about my breasts in front of everyone, she thought, staring at her rounded reflection on the back of her spoon. "So much for my reputation," she told herself. And what about what Jessie had said? Was she being nice, or was she interested? She certainly didn't have to say what she said, Chelsea pointed out to herself. And furthermore, she went out of her way to say it. "And furthermore," Chelsea told the Swedish ivy hanging in the window, "I just love it when a tough butch blushes like that."

Chelsea looked up at the clock again. All of seven minutes had passed. Almost 11:30—how to fill up the day? Sundays were hard on a single girl living alone. I wonder what Jessie's doing right now—just getting up, going out for a run . . . she seemed more the athletic type than the sit at home with bagels and the New York Sunday *Times* type. Though she did seem pretty intellectual too. Or maybe it was just her wire-rimmed glasses.

Maybe she's thinking about me this very second, Chelsea thought. Maybe she's even contemplating giving me a ring. I'll send her some vibes. Chelsea closed her eyes and placed her hands on her lap, palms facing up. Earth to Jessie, earth to Jessie, she mouthed silently. Call Chelsea Klein. Call Chelsea Klein. 555-2370. That's 555-2370. Chelsea waited but the phone didn't ring. She opened her eyes and sighed. "Oh well," she said.

Chelsea finished her yoghurt, went into the living room again and dialed Darlene and Alice's number. The phone rang and rang.

They must be either fighting or fucking, Chelsea thought, remembering her last relationship. Of course there always was the remote possibility that they really weren't home.

Chelsea took a shower, watered the plants, putzed around the apartment for a while, and tried to call some friends to see if anyone wanted to go swimming. Since there was no one around to play with, she decided to be productive. She did her laundry and her food shopping for the week, and even wrote a few letters, one to her brother who lived in New Jersey, and one to her Great Aunt Rose.

At 6:30 Chelsea tried Darlene again. After the third ring she answered.

"Hello?"

"Hi Darlene."

"Hi Chelsea. What'cha doing?"

"Oh nothing much. Just sitting her fantasizing about that Jessie girl."

"Really? Do you have a crush on her?"

"I got it bad, Darlene. You know me, I always go for those strong silent butchy types." Chelsea paused. "I was, uh, thinking about asking her out on a date."

"That's a great idea Chelsea. You want her phone number?"

"Oh I thought you'd never ask." Chelsea balanced the receiver between her ear and shoulder and picked up a pen. "Got it?"

"Wait a minute, I'm looking. Hey Honey, guess what?" Chelsea heard her call, "Chelsea's going to ask Jessie out on a date."

"Alright—way to go Chelsea!" Alice's voice came through the receiver.

"Darlene, for God's sake, don't tell anyone," Chelsea said.

"Why not?"

"I don't know. You know how rumors spread all over this town."

"Faster than peanut butter," Darlene said. "Oh here it is. 555-3221. Are you going to call her right now?"

"I guess so."

"Well call me right back and tell me what she says."

If you only knew what she said, Chelsea thought, but she couldn't bring herself to say it. Instead she said, "Darlene, what if Jessie doesn't want to go out with me?"

"Why wouldn't she? You're a wonderful woman, Chelsea. She'll probably be flattered that you asked. And besides, Jessie's nice. You don't have to be afraid of her."

"But is she the kind of nice person who would go out with me just because she feels sorry for me?"

"Chel-sea," Darlene moaned. "You are being ridiculous."

"Okay, okay. Listen, I better call now before I lose my nerve."

"Okay. Don't forget to call me back."

"I won't. 'Bye." Chelsea hung up the phone and started pacing around the apartment. What should she say to Jessie on the phone? "Hi Jessie, this is Chelsea and I'm calling to ask you out on a date." That sounded pretty good. A little formal maybe. Maybe I shouldn't say it right off, Chelsea thought. Maybe I should make a little small talk first. You know, how'd you like the party last night, what'd you do today, wanna come over and suck both my breasts?

Chelsea walked back over to the phone, picked up the receiver and dialed. After one and a half rings, Chelsea heard a click and then Jessie's voice.

"Hi, you have reached 555-3221. . ."

Oh no, Chelsea thought, not an answering machine. Maybe I'll just hang up. No, I can't do that, I'm sure she'll know it was me. Oh my God, what should I say?

". . . and leave a message after the beep. Beep."

"Hi Jessie, this is Chelsea and I'm calling to ask you to go out on a date. With me, I mean. That's date as in date, capital D-A-T-E, date. My number is 555-2370 and I'll be home all night. 'Bye." Chelsea hung up the phone and immediately called Darlene back.

"Hello?"

"Hi, it's me again. I did it."

"So fast? What happened?"

"She wasn't home, but I left a message on her tape."

"Did you say you were calling about a date?"

"Yep."

"A date-date?"

"A date-date."

"Good for you. Well let me know when she calls you back."

"Okay, I will. 'Bye."

"'Bye."

Chelsea hung up the phone again and stared at it. Now what should I do? Suddenly she felt very hyper. I could go for a walk, she thought. Or a bike ride. But I told her I'd be home all night. If she calls and I'm not here, she might think I'm a pathological liar or something. Then again, if she knows I'm just sitting here waiting by the phone, she'll think I'm a real jerk. I mean, that's about the most politically incorrect thing a feminist can do. Chelsea settled herself down on the living room couch with a new collection of lesbian short stories to try and distract herself. Every once in a while she'd look up at the clock. 7:30, 7:45, 8:15, 8:35. . . .

At 9:40 Chelsea got into bed. So don't call me back, she thought, taking off her turquoise earrings and setting them down on her night stand. See if I care. Just as she got all settled in and cozy, the phone rang. "Coming, coming," Chelsea called, leaping out of bed, half excited and half annoyed. She picked up the phone anxiously.

"Hello?"

"Hi, is Chelsea there?"

"This is me."

"Hi Chelsea, this is Jessie."

"Hi." Chelsea wondered if Jessie could hear her smiling.

"Well I got your message. You're a pretty brave woman."

"Well, you're not so timid yourself." Chelsea said, twirling the telephone cord around her finger. "So, um, would you like to go out on a date with me?"

"Yes, I'd love to."

"You would? Really?"

"Sure I would. Why do you act so surprised?"

"Oh I don't know. You really want to go?"

"Yes, I really do. Do you?"

"Yes." Steady now, Chelsea old girl, she thought to herself. Just try and hold it together here. Details, she reminded herself. Time, place, activity. "Well, what's your schedule like?"

"Pretty booked until the end of the week. How about Saturday night?"

Bingo—date night. "Let me look in my calendar," Chelsea said, glancing around for her purse. Her Great Aunt Rose always told her to play hard to get. She flipped through her calendar to the current week and saw what she already knew; Saturday night was completely empty.

"Looks good," Chelsea said. "I'm writing you in."

"What should we do?" Jessie asked.

Chelsea sighed. "Oh God, I don't know. I didn't get that far."

"What do you mean?"

Chelsea ran her fingers through her hair. "Just thinking about calling and asking you out on a date took most of the day," she said, thinking, why am I telling her this?

"I love how honest you are," Jessie said.

Oh, that's why. "Thanks," said Chelsea. "Well, what do people do on dates? They eat dinner, they go to the movies. . . ."

"I don't want to go to the movies," Jessie said. "That's not a good way to get to know each other."

She wants to get to know me, Chelsea thought happily. "Want to do dinner then?"

"Okay."

"I'm a lousy cook though."

"Me too."

"Wow, we have so much in common," Chelsea said with a laugh. Then she blushed, remembering what else they had in common. "Let's go out then. How about 6:30?"

"Fine. Should I pick you up?"

"That would be great. I live at 16 Grove Street. A big brown house, second floor."

"Got it." Jessie paused. "You know, Chelsea, I was thinking of calling and asking you out on a date myself."

"You were? You really were?"

"Yes I really was. Why do you sound so surprised again?"

"You really were? You're not just saying that?"

"No. Why would I just say it?"

"To be nice. Darlene said you were nice."

Jessie laughed. "I'll have to thank her next time I see her."

"Oh I feel much better now," Chelsea said.

"Why?" Jessie asked. "Didn't you know I'd say yes?"

"Well, I didn't want to assume anything."

"Like Phyllis," Jessie said and they both laughed. They talked a little longer then, about work, about what they'd been doing all summer and before Chelsea knew it, it was 11:15. Jessie was really easy to talk to, and besides, her voice was incredibly sexy. She could seduce me by reading me her shopping list, Chelsea thought, as Jessie went on about a canoe trip she'd taken a month ago. Pomegranates, Chelsea thought. Strawberries, whipped cream. Dried pears. Cat food. Applesauce. There was a pause and Chelsea realized Jessie had stopped speaking and was waiting for her to answer a question she hadn't heard her ask.

"I'm sorry Jessie, what did you say?"

"Am I boring you?"

"Oh no, not at all. I'm just sort of spacey. I didn't get much sleep last night."

"Me neither. Well, I guess I'll let you go then. Sweet dreams."

"Yeah, see you Saturday. Thanks for calling back."

Jessie laughed. "Well thanks for calling."

"Okay, 'bye."

"'Bye." Chelsea hung up the phone and drifted back to bed as though she were walking on stars.

III
The Pep Talk

Darlene sat on the edge of Chelsea's bed watching her friend rummaging through her closet. "How about this?" Chelsea asked, turning around to face Darlene with a red jumpsuit in her hands.

"Ooh, that's nice, Chels. But do you want to be that dressed up?"

"I don't know, Darl. Is Jessie the dress up type?"

"No, not really. I mean, she'll look nice and everything, but she won't be dressed up. She'll probably wear jeans and your basic white button down shirt. Ironed though. She's a great ironer."

"Oh God," Chelsea groaned. "Jeans and plain white shirts for the next twenty years?"

"Twenty years? Chelsea girl, get a grip. We're talking about one date, remember?"

"I remember, I remember." Chelsea hung the red jumpsuit back in her closet. "Maybe this then, what do you think?" She held up a bright blouse with flowers and tropical birds printed on it.

"Oh I like that. Try it on."

Chelsea slipped her arms through the sleeves and buttoned it up. "What do you think?"

Darlene stood up, walked over to Chelsea and straightened her collar. "Ooh, maxi pads," she said, squeezing the shoulder pads over Chelsea's shoulders. "Very convenient, in case you start to bleed."

"Or find yourself involved in a football game. Okay, now what pants?"

Darlene inspected Chelsea's closet. "These, I think," she said, taking out a pair of red pants, "and your red shoes."

"Okay." Chelsea unbuttoned the blouse and hung it back on a hanger.

"Now what accessories?" Darlene mumbled to herself as she opened the jewelry box on top of Chelsea's dresser. "Wow, look at these. Can I borrow them sometime?" She held some dangling rhinestone earrings up to her ears and admired herself in the mirror.

"Sure." Chelsea came over and stood behind Darlene. "I was thinking about these turquoise earrings," she said lifting them out of the box.

"Yeah, wear those," Darlene said. "Blue's her favorite color. Now what about underwear?" she said, stepping back and opening the top drawer of Chelsea's dresser.

"Underwear is irrelevant," Chelsea said. "We're not going to sleep together right away. We're just going out on a date to get to know each other better."

"To see if you want to sleep together or not," Darlene said.

"Right. Oh my God, is that what we're doing?" Chelsea began to pace around the room.

"Let's see now. How about these?" Darlene turned towards Chelsea and held up a pair of bikini underwear in a black and orange jungle motif with Garfield on the front of them, baring his fangs.

"Give me those!" Chelsea lunged for her underwear, which Darlene held high over her head, before tossing them over her shoulder.

"Or how about this?" Darlene pulled a black lace bra out of the drawer. "This is really pretty." Darlene put her hands in the cups of the bra to inspect the lace better. "My God, Chelsea, this is a cut out bra," she said, as her fingers slipped through the nipple hole. "You little slut! I didn't know you had one of these."

"Darlene! Give me that!" Chelsea's face was bright red as she grabbed the brassiere and shut the drawer. "Now come sit down with me before I have a heart attack." She pulled Darlene across the room and flopped down on the bed. "What time is it?"

"Three thirty."

"Oh my God, she'll be here in three hours. Darlene, I'm going on a date—a real date. How am I going to live through it?"

"Relax, girl. You've survived worse things."

Chelsea threw herself down flat on her back and flung one arm over her head. She stared at the ceiling. "Darlene, do you think Jessie is really interested in me?"

"Well, I didn't want to tell you this, but she did call me up to tell me you had asked her out."

"She did? She did? Why didn't you tell me?" Chelsea sat up and grabbed Darlene's arm. "What'd she say? Did she sound happy?"

"Yeah, she sounded happy. And she said she was scared."

"Scared? Why would she be scared?"

"I don't know. Because she's going out on a date with you."

"Well I won't bite her or anything. Not on the first date, anyway." Chelsea let go of Darlene's arm and lay back down on the bed again. "Now, if she said she was scared, that means she must like me, right? Because if she didn't like me, she wouldn't be scared."

"Such logical thinking." Darlene leaned back against Chelsea's pillow and stroked her friend's hair. "What are you going to do, anyway?"

"We're going out to dinner and then we're going to hear some music. That sounds pretty romantic, don't you think?" Chelsea asked anxiously. She reached for Darlene's hand and held it against her cheek. "Darlene, do you really think there's a teeny weeny chance that she just might be interested in me?"

Darlene shook her head. "We are hitting an all time low in the area of self-esteem here. No Chelsea, I don't think she's interested in you at all. I think someone is paying her off to go out with you. Probably your mother."

"Don't even say that!" Chelsea shrieked. "You know how paranoid I am."

"Okay, okay. Only kidding."

"Oh God, what are we going to talk about? What'll I do when she gets here? This is exhausting," Chelsea moaned, curling up on her side.

"She's picking you up, right?" Darlene asked.

Chelsea nodded.

"So, it's very simple. You open the door," Darlene stood up and pantomimed opening a door, "and you take the flowers she's brought you. . . ." Darlene reached for an imaginary bouquet of flowers.

"Darlene, she's not going to bring me flowers."

"What if she does?"

"What if she does?" Chelsea mumbled. "If she does, I say, 'Flowers for me?' " Chelsea spoke in a high pitched squeal. "But," she went on in a normal voice, "now I have something else to worry about. What if she doesn't bring me flowers?"

"You open the door," Darlene said, "and you say. . . ."

" 'Jessie, where are the flowers?' "

"Right." They both laughed.

"Okay, so we go out to dinner, we go hear the music, then what happens?"

"Then she brings you home."

"And then what? Do I kiss her goodnight?"

"It depends."

"Depends on what?"

"Well, do you think you'll hold hands?"

"I don't know." Chelsea moaned, moving over to rest her head on Darlene's lap. "So many decisions."

"Well you can't hold hands over dinner. You have to eat."

"Oh God." Chelsea looked up into Darlene's eyes. "What if I get food stuck in my teeth and I don't know it?"

"Well, you better not eat any corn," Darlene said. "Or chicken."

"No chicken or corn," Chelsea repeated. "What else is there?"

"I don't know, Chels. Bring lots of toothpicks and go to the bathroom frequently."

"Darlene," Chelsea asked anxiously, "is she the kind that would tell me if I had food stuck in my teeth? I'd be so embarrassed, I would die." Chelsea stared up at the ceiling thoughtfully. "But would she not tell me to be polite and then I'd have made a fool of myself the whole time? Oh God, Darlene, I don't know if I can go through with this."

"Of course you can, Chelsea." Darlene looked down at her. "Relax, girl. Let me rub your head a little." Darlene started massaging Chelsea's temples with her fingers in a small circular motion.

"Umm, that feels good. Now, what were we talking about?"

"Kissing goodnight."

Chelsea's body jumped. "What did we decide?"

"Well, you made the first move by calling," Darlene said, stroking Chelsea's forehead. "So it's her move. But then again, if you hold hands. . . ."

Chelsea opened her eyes to inspect her hands. "My hands are a mess," she groaned. "I knew I shouldn't have worked in the garden today."

Darlene ignored Chelsea's remark. "Let's say, for some reason, you go out to dinner, you go to the concert, you drive home, without holding hands. . . ." Darlene paused to think. "Got it." She looked down at Chelsea. "Listen. If she brings you flowers you can kiss her, but if she doesn't, you can't."

"Okay. Flowers, kisses, no flowers, no kisses. I can remember that." Chelsea furrowed her brow. "But I'll die if I don't kiss her."

Darlene smoothed Chelsea's forehead. "You won't die."

"Maybe I should kiss her when she comes to pick me up, just to get it over with?" Chelsea asked, hopefull.

"Nothing doing. God, it's amazing you ever got a girlfriend before you had me around to coach you."

"What if she honks? Is she the honking type?" Chelsea asked.

"She's not a goose, silly. She'll definitely come up. I don't know, Chelsea, you'll have to play it by ear."

"Do you think I should invite her up after the date, when she drops me off?"

"Depends."

"On what?" Chelsea threw up her hands in exasperation. "Everything depends on something."

"Well, it depends on whether she shuts the car off or not when she pulls into the driveway."

"Right. If she shuts it off, it's a good sign. What if she doesn't shut it off?"

"You tell her you had a nice time and you'd like to go out with her again."

"But what if we have a lousy time?"

"You tell her you had a lousy time and you don't want to go out with her again." Darlene gently nudged Chelsea's head off her lap. "Speaking of time, girl, it's getting late. I have to go. And you have a date to get ready for."

Chelsea sat up. "Don't remind me."

Darlene bent over and kissed Chelsea on the cheek. "Now call me Sunday morning and tell me everything. And don't worry. It'll be fine. Just be yourself."

"Okay I will. Thanks for coming over, Darlene."

"See you later."

"'Bye." Chelsea watched Darlene's back disappear through her bedroom doorway, then leaped up, grabbed her clothes and rushed into the bathroom to take a shower.

IV
The Date

Six o'clock. Chelsea stood in front of the bathroom mirror, inspecting her face. "Bags under my eyes," she moaned, staring at herself. "Well what do you expect from someone who hasn't slept all week?" Chelsea ran a brush through her hair, trying to tame it into some kind of presentable shape. "I knew I should have gotten my hair cut," she groaned, tucking a stray strand behind her ear. Chelsea's hair was at its unruly length—long enough to part, but not long enough to pull back into a braid or do anything else to keep it out of her eyes. "Oh well, too late now," she said. "And besides, what if they'd really butchered me? Then I'd have to call and tell Jessie I couldn't go out with her."

Chelsea sighed. "C'mon girl." She shut the bathroom light, took herself by the hand and sat down on the living room couch. "It's enough already. You'll make yourself sick." She had, in fact, had the runs twice this week, though she'd barely eaten a thing. "This is not normal," she told herself, hugging a lavender pillow to her chest. "Not that I ever thought I was normal," she went on, "but this is ridiculous. I hardly know this woman." Chelsea stood up and started picking dead leaves off the spider plant hanging in the window. Her apartment was immaculately clean. Maybe too clean. Chelsea looked around and frowned slightly. Maybe I should mess it up a little, she thought. I don't want her to think I'm compulsive or anything.

She walked over to her bookshelf. Maybe some books scattered around. That'll impress her. She's the intellectual type. Chelsea studied the titles: *Lesbian Psychologies*, no, sounds too dry and academic. *Lesbian Sex*—definitely not. How about some fiction, then? Dostoevsky? No, too morbid. Jane Rule, I think, but for God's sake not *Desert of the Heart*. That's too obvious. Chelsea selected a collection of Jane Rule's short stories and set it down on the coffee table.

Six-twenty. She'd be there in ten minutes. Chelsea wondered if she'd be on time. She seemed the punctual type. And Darlene said she wouldn't honk. What to be doing when she arrived? Listening to music? No, then she might not hear her knock. Oh God, music, Chelsea thought. What if she asks me to find a station on the radio and I pick out something nerdy? Chelsea walked back into the kitchen, grabbed a sponge from the sink and started wiping the table. I can always clean, she thought, picking at a drop of wax with her thumbnail. I could always scrub the stove. Or polish the toaster.

Six-twenty five. What if she was early? She could be here any second. Sit down, Chelsea, before you make yourself sick. Oh my God, what if I get car sick? she asked herself. What if I open my mouth to say hello and I vomit? Chelsea threw the sponge into the kitchen sink and sank down into a kitchen chair. Oh God, please just don't let me make an ass of myself, she prayed, holding her head in her hands.

There was a knock at the door. Chelsea jerked her head up and looked at the clock. Six-thirty exactly. She took three deep breaths which didn't calm her down at all, and ran to open the front door.

"Hi."

"Hi. Come on in." Chelsea stepped aside making room for Jessie to pass. She felt her face break into a wide open smile at the sight of her. She was wearing just what Darlene had predicted—jeans, a white shirt, and black Reboks.

Chelsea realized she was staring, and looked down shyly. Then she forced herself to look up. "Hi," she said, again, and then blushed. "Oh, I said that already."

"You can say it again if you want," Jessie said smiling at her.

"Oh I couldn't," Chelsea said, turning away shyly.

"Nice place you got here," Jessie said, looking around. "What a great toaster." Jessie walked over to the counter and inspected Chelsea's toaster. It was from the '40's and was the kind that had two side doors that opened and only toasted bread one side at a time.

Chelsea leaned her back against the stove and folded her arms. "Yeah, it was my mother's. She was gonna throw it away but I nabbed it. She couldn't believe I wanted it. My mother thinks the microwave is the greatest invention since the wheel."

Jessie made a face. "Yuk. I'm an old-fashioned girl."

Chelsea smiled. "Me too." They held each other's gaze for a moment, then at the same time started moving towards each other, stopping about two feet apart. Now what? I am going to die, Chelsea thought. Should I give her a hug? I have never felt so graceless in my entire life.

"Well, should we go?" Jessie asked, not moving any closer, but not backing away either.

"Yeah. I'm ready," Chelsea said, without moving. "Jessie," she said, taking a deep breath. "I'm really nervous. I mean really really really *really* nervous. I don't know why, and I probably shouldn't be telling you this, but I just wanted you to know."

"I'm so glad you said that." Jessie shoved her hands into her pockets and looked down at her shoes. "Listen, I probably shouldn't tell you this either, but I spent about two hours trying to decide whether to bring you flowers or not. I almost did, but then I thought it would be too obvious. Now I wish I had."

Oh no, Chelsea thought, remembering the guidelines she and Darlene had come up with: flowers, kisses; no flowers, no kisses. But she almost brought me flowers. Does that mean I can almost kiss her? "Well, it's the thought that counts," Chelsea said, trying to comfort them both.

"Next time, I'll bring a dozen roses," Jessie said, looking up. "How's that?"

"Great." Chelsea looked down shyly. She said next time. Does that mean there'll be a next time? "Well, I'm ready," Chelsea said, grabbing her purse. "Are you?"

"Yeah. Let's go." Jessie moved towards the door and Chelsea followed her out and down the steps. Once they were outside, Chelsea felt a little more relaxed. Jessie opened the car door for her which endeared her to Chelsea's heart forever. I love old-fashioned butches, she thought, as Jessie slid behind the wheel. They really know the right way to treat a girl.

"So, where are we going?" Chelsea asked.

"How about Monaco's? Do you like Italian food?"

"Yeah, that would be great."

Jessie backed out of Chelsea's driveway, looking over her shoulder and resting her arm across the back of the seat, letting her hand lightly touch Chelsea's upper arm. Oh my God, if she leaves her hand there I am going to die, Chelsea thought, scarcely daring to breathe. Luckily her life was saved by the fact that Jessie had to use her right hand to shift the car into first.

"So, um, how many times did you change your clothes before you came over?" Chelsea asked, staring at Jessie's profile as she drove.

Jessie laughed. "You sure don't pull any punches, do you?" She took her eyes off the road to look at Chelsea for a minute and Chelsea felt her belly jump. "Oh I considered, two, maybe three shirts. But I did spend about an hour ironing."

"You did a great job," Chelsea said, following the crease that ran down the arm of Jessie's shirt with her finger. Oh God, I'm touching her. Stop, she told herself, pulling her hand away and dropping it demurely into her lap. "Well, I'm not much of an ironer myself, but I did spend most of today trying on my entire wardrobe in front of Darlene."

"You look really nice," Jessie said, turning to look at Chelsea again. "Darlene's got good taste."

"So do you."

"Why do you say that?"

"Because you're going out on a date with me."

They both laughed. She's nice, Chelsea thought, as they pulled into the parking lot of the restaurant. She's really nice. I can be myself with her. Well who else would you be, asked a voice inside Chelsea's head. Greta Garbo? Amelia Earhart? Gertrude Stein?

They entered the restaurant and sat down. On their table stood a fat red candle and a small glass vase with a bunch of yellow zinnias in it. The restaurant was fairly empty, much to Chelsea's relief. She didn't want this hitting the dyke grapevine. Not yet, anyway, she thought, as Jessie handed her a menu. Now, nothing with garlic, she reminded herself. And no spaghetti, that's too hard to eat. And eat slowly. You don't want to burn your mouth.

Jessie watched Chelsea with a little smile. "You look pretty in this light," she said.

Chelsea forced herself not to lower her eyes. "You don't pull any punches either," she mumbled. "I mean, thank you."

"Thank you," Jessie said.

"For what?"

"For being pretty. For being you. For asking me out on a date."

"Thank you for coming. For coming out I mean. With me. On a date I mean. Oh, you know what I mean." Chelsea shook her head. "I feel so incredibly awkward, do you? I mean, why is this so hard?"

"Because we're being honest with each other," Jessie said.

"Because we're not jumping right into bed," Chelsea added, sort of wishing they were.

"Right," Jessie said, tapping her fork lightly on the table. "It's easy to just go to bed with someone."

"It is?" Chelsea asked.

"Yeah. I don't want to do that anymore."

"You don't?" Then why are we out on a date, Chelsea wanted
to add.

"No, I don't. I mean, I do. I'm very attracted to you Chelsea,
you know that don't you?"

Chelsea nodded, thinking, I can't believe she just said that.

"I just want to take my time and get to know you better, and
see what kind of relationship develops."

Chelsea gripped the table. Oh my God—the R word. She used
the R word. I am going to die.

"I really like courting," Chelsea said. "Flowers, love letters, you
know, the whole bit."

"Oh, so you're a romantic, huh?"

Chelsea nodded. "Incurably. Completely."

Jessie smiled. "A woman after my own heart."

"You'd better believe it," Chelsea said, looking right into Jessie's eyes.

Luckily the waitperson came just then to take their order, because Chelsea's smile was so big she was afraid her face would fall
off. Chelsea ordered a cold pasta salad and Jessie ordered shrimp
scampi. After the waitperson left, they sat in silence for a few minutes.
Chelsea sipped her water and Jessie fiddled with the perfectly ironed
cuffs of her shirt. Every time one of them looked up, the other one
would look away, only to look back again a few seconds later to see
the other one glancing away again. Finally Chelsea cleared her throat.

"So, um, do you come often? I mean, do you come here often?
To eat, I mean. You know, food. Oh God, Jessie, I didn't mean it,
it just slipped out, you know what I mean?" Chelsea hid her face
in her hands and took a deep breath before she dared look across
the table. "Am I impressing you with my articuless-ness? Is that a
word? I mean my ability to articulate? Or not articulate?"

Jessie laughed. "Chelsea, you're lovely."

Lovely. Had anyone ever called her lovely? It was such a, well, such a lovely word.

"I am?"

"Yes you are. Lovely and funny and charming and I really like you."

"You do?"

"Yes I do."

"I like you too." Chelsea reached across the table for Jessie's hand which was slowly sliding towards her. They held hands and gazed at each other until their food arrived. Thank God for food, Chelsea thought, spreading her napkin on her lap. She began to eat, and though the pasta salad was wonderful, it could have been sauteed wood chips, for all Chelsea noticed.

"So, um, what is your thesis about anyway?" Chelsea asked, remembering Jessie had told her over the phone she was a doctoral student.

"Spiders."

"Spiders?"

"Yeah. I mean, it's a little more complicated than that. That's my one word answer. I don't want to bore you about it."

"Oh, I wouldn't be bored," Chelsea reassured her.

"But I would. After five years, I get pretty tired of talking about it."

"Well I hate spiders myself," Chelsea said. "I try not to kill them, but they really creep me out. Do you do experiments on them and stuff? Oh, I'm sorry," she put down her fork. "Chelsea, the woman said she didn't want to talk about it. Don't you listen?" She shook her head. "Jessie, I really am a good listener and I do respect boundaries. Really. You can ask Darlene. She'll vouch for me."

"She already has."

"What do you mean?"

Jessie shifted her weight. "Well, I um, I called Darlene to ask her about something else, and we talked a little bit about you."

"You did? What did she say?"

"Let's see." Jessie paused, a piece of shrimp in mid-air. "Well, she said you were very funny, a great cook, and a lousy driver."

"A lousy driver? Oh no. Jessie, did she tell you how we met?" Jessie nodded. "Oh no, I am so embarrassed." Chelsea put down her fork and touched Jessie's arm. "It's not true. I'm not a lousy driver. I mean, I've never had an accident or anything. I'm just a lousy parker."

Chelsea had met Darlene four years ago when she was going to see Casselberry and Du Prée. She had pulled up in front of the theatre and spent about ten minutes in four vain attempts, trying to parallel park her little Toyota. Finally, Darlene had stepped out of line, rapped on Chelsea's window and volunteered to do it for her, and Chelsea had stepped out of the car, embarrassed, though grateful.

"She said the space was big enough for a bus," Jessie said.

"A bus? It was not." Chelsea frowned. "A small truck, maybe. Oh I am going to kill her the minute I get home. Well, maybe not the very minute," she added, remembering that she still didn't know what the night held in store for her. "But tomorrow for sure." She put a tortellini in her mouth and paused.

"So, um, Jessie, you were asking Darlene questions about me?"

Jessie swallowed a bite of shrimp and nodded.

"Well, I never assume anything, but could that mean that you were interested in me?"

Jessie took a sip of water. "I'd say there's a pretty high interest rate on this side of the table."

Chelsea laughed. "You really listen, don't you? God, I love being quoted to myself." She wrinkled her nose. "Do you think that's a really weird thing to say?"

They finished their dinner, eating slowly, talking and not talking, looking and not looking at each other. After they paid the check they left the restaurant and got into the car. Jessie hesitated before starting the engine.

"Chelsea, I have a confession to make."

Uh-oh. She has another girl friend. I knew it. Chelsea felt the pasta salad shift in her stomach.

"Well, there are two things. First of all, I didn't call Darlene to talk about anything else. I called to ask about you."

One down and one to go, Chelsea thought. "And?"

"And, I don't really want to go listen to music."

"You don't?" Oh well, Chelsea thought, glumly. The night is still young. Maybe I can catch a late movie on TV or something.

"No. Would you like to take a walk down by the river instead?"

Chelsea looked up hopefully. "And look at the stars maybe?"

"You have this knack for saying just what I'm too scared to say." Jessie smiled at Chelsea.

"What else are you too scared to say?" she whispered.

Jessie looked into her eyes. "Can I kiss you?"

"Yes."

Jessie moved towards her then and took Chelsea in her arms. They hesitated for a moment, each feeling the pounding of her heart. Then they moved at the same time and bumped noses.

"I don't believe this," Chelsea mumbled, tilting her head to the side and touching Jessie's lips lightly with her own. Gingerly at first, and then a little more forcefully, they kissed for a few minutes.

"Hey, I thought you were a lousy parker," Jessie whispered, pulling back a little to look at Chelsea.

"You're lovely," Chelsea answered, moving forward to kiss Jessie again. She felt electric desire shooting through her veins and pulled away gently.

"We better stop," she murmured, "or I won't be able to."

Jessie nodded. "Right. We're courting, remember?"

"How could I forget?" Chelsea took Jessie's hand and started playing with her fingers. Such strong hands, she thought. "Um, according to the official Guide To Lesbian Dating, how long does courting usually last?"

"About three hours." Jessie interlaced her fingers with Chelsea's.

Chelsea looked up. "You got a watch?"

"No," Jessie answered. "You got time?"

"I got all the time in the world, angel." Chelsea leaned back against the seat, so happy she thought she would burst. Jessie started up the car and pulled out of the parking lot, heading for the stars.

V
Three Years Later

"So that's how you two really got together? I always wondered," Sunflower said, chopping up a giant zucchini from her garden. "Because of Darlene and Alice's party three years ago?" She was standing in Darlene and Alice's kitchen along with Rachel, Phyllis, Chelsea, and Jessie. It was Alice and Darlene's tenth year anniversary party, and since it was raining, the party had to be indoors this year. Darlene was in the living room picking out some music to put on, and Alice was rummaging around the pantry, looking for a corkscrew.

"God, I remember that party," Rachel said. "I still haven't been able to find anyone to suck both my breasts at once."

"Watch your language," Alice said, emerging from the pantry, corkscrew in hand. "I am shocked."

"You could always do it yourself," Phyllis said.

Rachel nodded. "That's true. We lesbians are so independent. I should write the lesbian do-it-yourself sex book. God knows, lesbians do everything else themselves—tune up their own cars, build their own houses. . . ."

"Grow their own food," Sunflower held up a fat juicy tomato from her garden.

"DJ their own anniversary parties," Darlene said, coming into the kitchen, as Deidre McCalla's voice came blasting out of the speakers.

"Well, not everything," Chelsea said, putting her arm around Jessie's waist and kissing her on the cheek.

"You newlyweds are disgusting," Phyllis said, making a face.

"You're just jealous," Jessie said, squeezing Chelsea to her side. "And anyway, we're not newlyweds. It's been three years."

"And the honeymoon isn't even over," Chelsea said, looking directly into Jessie's eyes.

"Oh Goddess, gag me with an organic cauliflower," Sunflower said, breaking the vegetable up into little flowerettes.

"Just how long did you two actually court?" Phyllis asked.

"Oh, not long," Jessie said.

"Not long? It was practically forever." Chelsea disengaged herself from Jessie's embrace and started counting the months on her fingers. "Let's see. Our first date was in August. August, September, October, November, December. Five months."

"Five months! That's a world's record," Phyllis exclaimed.

"Who made the first move?" Alice asked.

"I did," Chelsea said.

"She said if she didn't make love by the end of the year she'd forget how," Jessie said.

Darlene hooted. "And you believed her?"

Jessie looked over at Chelsea. "Not really. But I didn't want to take the risk."

"How did you guys wait so long?" Phyllis asked, munching on a carrot stick.

"My God, Phyllis. Five months isn't all that long. Some of us have been waiting for years."

"We had a few things to work out first," Chelsea said.

"Like what?"

"Well, Jessie wanted a fling and I was looking to get married."

"So what did you do?"

Chelsea shrugged her shoulders. "Well, first we flung and then we got married."

"So much for dating," Sunflower said, setting a platter of chopped vegetables and hummus on the table.

"Who needs to keep dating when you've found what you're looking for?" Jessie asked.

"You two are really nauseating. That's the last time I ever match up two of my friends," Alice said.

"You didn't match them up. I did," Darlene said. "Anyway, they're just both hopeless romantics."

"We matched up ourselves," Jessie pointed out.

"And that's not hopeless. It's hopeful. Hopeful romantics," Chelsea added.

"Well, I'm still looking for Ms. Right," Sunflower said. "I hope I'm not the only single girl at this party next year."

"You won't be," Rachel said, handing out paper plates to everyone. "If I'm invited, that is."

"Rachel, of course you'll be invited," Darlene said.

"Well, I never assume anything," Rachel said. "I learned that at one of your parties."

"Wasn't that the party when Chelsea said she assumed that everyone broke up eventually?" Phyllis asked, piling some tabouli onto her plate.

"Phyllis, you know I hate being quoted to myself," Chelsea said, poking her with her elbow. "Besides, Alice and Darlene are still together."

"We sure are." Darlene handed Alice a plate.

"I rest my case," Chelsea said, filling a glass with iced tea.

"Well, I guess some couples do stay together," Phyllis admitted, sitting down with her plate.

"I think it's wonderful," Rachel said.

"A toast! A toast!" Sunflower popped the cork on the champagne, filled seven glasses and passed them around.

"To the happy couple," Sunflower said, raising her glass.

"To 38 more years of celibacy," Rachel mumbled.

"Rachel, it hasn't been 38 years." Phyllis laughed. "You haven't been celibate since you were born."

"It sure seems that way," Rachel said with a sigh.

"To our friends," Darlene said, looking around, smiling.

"Hear, hear," Alice added.

"And to true romantics, everywhere," Chelsea said, clinking her glass against Jessie's.

"I'll drink to that," Darlene said, clinking her glass against Alice's.

"I won't," Phyllis said.

"You will too." Rachel lightly punched her.

"To all romantics and cynics," Sunflower answered. "Is that better?"

"Yeah." Phyllis touched her glass to Sunflower's. "May they continue to keep finding each other."

"And may one of them find me," Rachel added.

Everyone laughed. "Here's to all of us, and our happiness," Jessie said. "Whether we're single. . . ."

"Or double," interrupted Sunflower. Then laughing, everyone clinked glasses, downed their champagne, and moved into the living room to enjoy dinner, the party, and the rest of their lives.

From a forthcoming collection of short stories titled *Secrets*.

Tell Me Where
The Road Turns

CAROL ORLOCK

JESSICA'S SKIN WAS SOFT and smooth and still a little warm.
Monica knew she should go before the sun left the high branches
of the tulip tree. By then Jessica would be cool, no, cold. Jess did
not breathe. She had not breathed for maybe an hour. Monica wished
she knew a lullaby that said any of this in it.

The sheets were crumpled where Jessica had griped them in
one fist when they made love. Lovemaking today was gentle, unex-
ceptional. Monica wondered idly, as she had wondered often over
the last year or two, if this was how old married couples felt, lust
building up over a week or so, the familiar haven of a lover's arms,
and then the sweet acquaintance, the knowledge of how that skin
would feel if she did this, or this, or this now. She suposed love grew
even more intimate, more ordinary, from here on in. Then she remembered. Jessica lay dead beside her. She had died of a stroke. Their
love would not grow more ordinary.

229

Monica had arrived at Jessica's small house at two. They planned a picnic out behind the abandoned army barracks off State Route 40. Of course there was danger in going anywhere together. There was danger they would be seen, danger they would be noticed, that anyone with a grudge, maybe the new nurse on Two West, would connect the dots and make a whisper that turned into a dishonorable discharge. They discussed it many times in the early years, turning the words over and over, handing them back and forth until they seemed like a stain, spread over each other each time they touched.

Dishonorable discharge. Jess would repeat it. The head nurse in gynecology dishonorably discharged. People would react, Jess always said, the way they did to a homosexual man caught working in a boy's school. People would make another horror story out of it.

For her own part, Monica did not care. If they threw her out, she would find a way to live elsewhere. The world should tolerate the differences. Maybe the world, Jess argued, but not the army.

And to Jess the army was everything. She was career army. The army was the world, the army and her family. She rose through the ranks straight and true, like her father hoped, and made head nurse two years ago.

He had looked so damn proud. And Mom couldn't figure it out, Jess had said the first time they were alone together after her trip home. Monica smiled, and wondered if Jess's joy felt any less for the secret she kept back, the old news Jess had never told them about her life.

For Jess's sake they kept apart, working the same ward and keeping the cool distance of professionals. Some patients sensed it, the drugged or crazy ones down in emergency. Like that one they had to manage together, Jess holding him down while Monica pulled and fastened the restraints. He howled and struggled, a scared animal, while they worked as one body. Then he suddenly stopped. He looked from one to the other, dazed, because he felt it too, their love flowing back and forth and into him.

"You two aren't sisters, right?" He stared, lucid for a split second. He looked at their faces, the tall blond Jessica and shorter, black haired Monica. "I give up. You know something I don't." Then he went limp while they finished him.

Or maybe it was simple paranoia. Maybe no one suspected. Maybe all their caution, the codes for when they would meet in the coffee shop, the seeming to shop separately at the same store then go home together, the weeks apart, the loneliness too, maybe all paranoia. But it was a small base, supply and munitions, and everybody knew everyone. And they all knew the retired general who was proud of his daughter. So Monica kept the secret for Jess.

Today was the same. Jess met her at the door and hurried to get inside, shutting it. Jess stood tall and thin in her gold bathrobe, the sun streaming through the window and glinting red on her thick blond hair. Her week-old permanent looked frizzy.

"I thought we were doing a picnic," Monica asked. Jess's face looked drawn, her blue eyes nearly gray with shadows of tension. She pulled her robe close, turned and led the way to the kitchen.

"I heard they're planning something, maneuvers or something, along State 40."

"So a couple of nurses happen by on a picnic. What's wrong with that?" Monica helped herself to a teabag from the glass bowl by the sink, took a cup and poured water from the kettle steaming on the stove.

"But it's probably Burdick. He's got maneuvers next week. Remember Burdick who we saw with his wife at Mario's last Wednesday?"

Monica set her cup across from Jess's, which was lukewarm and half-filled, on the kitchen table. The lid of the honey pot was askew and she straightened it. "So?" she said, but did not press. She could tell Jess was suffering another headache. That was reason enough not to go and she wished it were the real reason Jess still wore her bathrobe, unwilling to get dressed and go.

"You have another headache." She reached and lifted Jess's bangs back from her forehead.

"It's better. I was dizzy earlier." She lowered her eyes and her hand covered Monica's. She seemed small, childlike even though she was older, forty-six next winter and Monica turning forty. "It's been off and on, a couple days."

Cardiovascular, the word whispered in Monica's mind. She pushed it back. "You got checked?"

"Taylor looked me over Tuesday. Says it's the flu and everybody calling in sick because of it. He figures flu and the tension of working half-staff."

"He got it yet?" Monica laughed lightly.

"No, but it starts with a headache."

Monica tangled her fingers into Jess's and pulled them down to curl together on the cool table. The sun beat through the orange curtains, a hot August afternoon and no picnic. The room was starting to heat up.

The headaches had come off and on for two weeks now. Jess looked pale and drawn mornings on the ward, then perked up in the afternoon if the headache passed. One day last week she said she felt dizzy and lay down in the nurses' lounge for a half hour before it passed. Monica wanted to go to her, hold her, make her go home, but that broke the rules. It would frighten Jess.

"Who cares about an old picnic," she said and Jess brightened. She reached for Monica's other hand and drew them both to her across the table, nudging the honey pot aside. "Besides, what time do you have duty tonight?"

"Seven," Jess said, "and I want to lay in bed with the sun coming in all afternoon."

Monica left her tea cooling on the kitchen table and followed Jess. They lay propped on the pillows for a long time, talking, stroking each other. These last few years, more and more, Monica could not be sure which she loved most, this lean, big and graceful woman, or their beautiful ordinariness together. She loved the pillow her shoulder burrowed into because it was Jess's, loved the old flute Jess kept on the mantle and always dusted and never learned how to play, loved how her lips knew the chip on the edge of the cup that was hers in Jess's kitchen.

The first few years, when they argued and fought, meant less than this. They had taken a long time getting used to each other, beyond the curves and sensitivities in each other's bodies. That came easy enough because they wanted it badly. It was the silence that took longer, the drifting afternoons after childhood memories had been told, angry silences when Monica wanted to go out and Jess could not feel safe, the silence late one night when Jess had cried and cried and then lay on Monica's shoulder, shaking and finally still. They had argued the usual ground and Jess remained afraid.

Monica stroked the thick blond hair until Jess's head lifted. "Tell me," Jess said. "I want to know where the road turns."

"Look, you can say if you're sorry," Monica told her. "If you're sorry, then it's over, but you can say it. Say you made a mistake. Go back to men, or nobody. I should think I understand."

Jess's face was red from weeping, but shock drained the color away. She was not sorry, she could never feel sorry. They loved each other and that was fact. Plain and simple.

"I knew when we met, just the way I always knew the important stuff. Like about being a nurse. Like I knew I was army. But I knew the why of those things too. Not like this." Her shoulders loosened, sloping downward. "I'll never understand this."

Jess's big frame felt small then, no more weight than a child, and her voice was small with uncertainty. She whispered each word distinctly, "Just tell me where the road turns. I hurt, I need to know."

"The road we took into this? Or where we're going?"

Jess said she'd take either one, but Monica could not find an answer. Not that day, not in all the years since. Yet that day she stopped complaining about the secrecy. That day they began knowing how to keep silences, and the sweet secret routine began to weave, transparent between them.

She looked up now. She loved the tulip tree, the sun leaving its leaves, the older leaves deep in the trees turning brown already. Monica shifted the blanket she had draped between herself and Jess and eased her head down on it. She heard no heartbeat, nothing. She did not expect one, yet the silence disturbed her. She would go soon. At seven the hospital would call because Jess did not show up. They would hear the phone ring, but the ringing would make no sound here. The phone lay beside the bed, the box twisted from the wall. Later they would send someone to look for Jessica.

They had made love gently, taking their time. The sun glistened on Jess's pale skin. Monica held her, then felt herself tumble backward and Jessica's lips on her skin. They dawdled and enjoyed, playing for time, and the lovemaking drifted to its finish, meandering through a pause into the knowledge that it was over for this time. They settled backward on the pillows, Jess's eyes closed, Monica watching the paisley pattern the sun made between the shadows of leaves on the blanket. She must have dozed, must have slept not to have heard sooner. Suddenly she awoke with the bed trembling. Jess's body was shaking it.

Jess's head jerked back, her hand gripped to her eyes. Her head, it was her head, and from her cries it must have hurt fiercely. Monica pushed her back on the pillows, gripped the fingers to pry them loose and see Jess's eyes, terror-filled, twitching suddenly back toward the top of her head. A seizure. Not enough blood to the brain. Monica gripped her, held her head still so that its shaking did not hit the shelf at the head of the bed. She pummelled through the covers, hanging on to Jess's skull as the neck spasmed and bounced. Her other hand reached for the phone by the bed, punching buttons, but the receiver dropped clattering to the floor. She reached for it and felt Jess heave under her. She heard a voice on the line before it went dead. Jess's fist held the cord, falling backward again as the colored, electrical lines strained from the wall and broke.

For an instant Monica saw Jess's eyes. They opened slightly, like a child's last fight against sleep. They were clear and blue and seemed to plead for understanding. Even as she saw, Monica slid from the bed and was halfway into a step to the door. She was nude, she realized then, and understood what Jess meant, stooping back to sweep the gold robe from the side of the bed, pulling it over her. They would know why she was there. Dishonorable. She ran down the hall and pulled the front door open and almost ran from the porch before she realized her stupidity. The odds were ninety-nine to one against Jess surviving now. Minutes had passed, eight, ten, maybe twelve. Blood had been cut to the brain. One way in, one way out. Ninety-nine to one that Jess wouldn't make it, and with that look Jess asked to throw away the one.

Monica closed the front door and leaned against it, her pulse roaring in her ears. Then she made herself turn and go back. She checked the vital signs slowly, methodically, as she had been taught. They had both been right. When she was done she let the hard part of her mind go loose, let her arms circle Jess's waist, put her head into her belly and cried into the soft skin there.

Sunlight still came through the window, but the patterns of the leaves blurred away into shadows. It was time to go. Monica pulled the covers aside and smoothed her imprint from the sheet. They would think Jessica had tried to reach the phone. They would think she was alone. They must think that. Anger rose in her throat, the bitter taste of black tea. She pushed it down. It was Jessica's one chance in ninety-nine. She had chosen to throw it away.

Monica rinsed her cup in the sink and set it upside down on the drainboard. She wished she could take it with her, then decided she would. She carried it back to the bathroom where her clothes lay tangled on the floor.

The mirror reflected her body as she dressed. She thought of how Jess must have watched herself in this mirror. It had reflected them both younger. It probably saw the night they celebrated Jess's fortieth. Now it would not see either of them age or gain weight or go through menopause.

She walked slowly through the house to make sure nothing of hers remained. The cup rattled in her handbag as she opened the front door.

Jessica's key stood in the deadbolt lock. It had to be used to close the door from outside, but she had planned that when she lay beside her, loving her. It was dark now and she fitted the key by touch. The lock clicked and slowly, for silence, she lifted the frame of the window and reached in to the small table where Jessica's purse lay. She dropped the key inside and pushed the window closed.

Safe At Home

SHELLY RAFFERTY

SOMEHOW ANNA BLAMED the act of forgetting her car keys on Rebecca's insistence that they go to her class reunion. As she dug into her back pocket, her back arched and she stood up on the brake pedal. She realized her keys were still laying in her desk's top drawer. Suddenly, the hundred yards across the high school parking lot and back into that musty basement looked vast and unconquerable.

She pulled her reluctant frame out of the car and slammed the door shut.

Why couldn't Becca go to the reunion alone? As she crossed the deserted asphalt, Anna imagined Becca's former fellow students, coughing discreetly behind napkins and plates of baked beans and barbecued chicken, their curious eyes peering myopically through translucent cups of foamy, luke-warm beer: "That must be her lover. . . . I always knew she was a lesbian. . . . They live together. . . ." Becca could have pulled off the ruse; why not simply say that she was divorced (which was true) and leave it at that?

Earlier, over their morning coffee at home, Anna had been in-sistent about not going.

"Look at me! I know what I look like!"

"And what would that be?"

"I look like a dyke!"

"Goodness," Becca had teased, laying her hand along her cheek in mock dismay. "Darling, if only you'd wear that adorable summer frock I bought you at the boutique—'

"I'm going to work," Anna growled. She sauntered out the screen door.

Rebecca had followed her. "I'm not ashamed of you," she called after her from the porch. "I don't give a damn what they think. . . ."

"Then why are we going?"

"Because we can."

Two juniors nearly knocked Anna over as they pushed through the locker room door.

"Good night, Miss Carpenter!" they cried, nearly in unison. "See you tomorrow!" Their bumpy passing was a flurry of gangly limbs, softball gloves and nylon jackets.

"Good night, girls," Anna muttered.

In the inner office, Millie was slipping into her coat and sling-ing her purse over her shoulder.

"You're back," she observed, smiling.

"Forgot my keys," Anna gestured toward her desk.

"Your softball schedules came."

"Jesus, I've only been gone for five minutes."

"Lightning quick mail service from the central office; one of those detention deliveries from a delinquent freshman—check your 'in' basket. I'm gone."

"Good night, Mill." The office door closed with a gentle swoosh. Anna plucked the softball schedule out of the basket; this sheet of pink grid paper was to rule her life for the next 12 weeks. Seven games out of town, five at home, plus the double header with Rockland in three weeks. If the rain hadn't been so bad last year, they wouldn't have to double up this season . . . not to mention the fact that Anna was not looking forward to seeing Pat Conover again.

They'd had the misfortune to run into each other in a bar in Albany last January. Of course, Rebecca had been with Anna, but Pat hadn't bothered to introduce the young lady she'd left behind at her table. Introductions weren't necessary; Anna recognized her as the senior pitcher from the Rockland team.

Resignedly, Anna shook her head, and dropped the schedule back into the mail basket. Would she ever get used to this audacity? She moved toward the door and flicked off the lights.

The sudden darkness blacked out the office, opaquing the windows from the dim outer locker room. Anna reached in her pocket for her keys and realized they were still in her desk drawer. As she moved across the darkened room, she could hear the sound of a shower running. She paused. Could there still be students here? At the far end of the room a single overhead fluorescent light illumined the narrow passage between the gunmetal lockers, the distance between them severed only by a low birch bench.

Later, she would ask herself why she had lingered—no, waited— there in the darkness by the door, unseen by the students who were unaware of her presence.

"God, we're here alone! We must be the last ones!"

That was MacNamara, who played second base, dripping from head to toe, a towel loosely draped around her waist. Nothing else.

Kim Janacek, the scorekeeper, the quiet one, padded along behind her, more modestly attired. She held her towel over her breasts. It hung down to her knees.

"Too much Vidal Sassoon, that's your problem," she complained good-naturedly.

"But darling," chided Mac, flailing back her shoulder length brown hair, "my public expects me to maintain a certain standard."

"Get dressed. We should get out of here before the janitor comes."

Janacek turned to her locker and opened it, tossing jeans, under-shirt, underwear, socks and the rest haphazardly on the bench. Cu-riously, MacNamara settled back against her own locker and watched, unrushed, as Janacek organized her clothing.

"Did you see the double play, Wendle to Harrison?" she asked casually.

"Harrison made a nice snag," Janacek agreed. She was sitting on the bench now, drawing a wide-toothed comb through her dark, wet hair. "I heard Coach say she'd been recruited by Bailey *and* U of M."

Mac brushed at a few drops of water on her forearms, then read-justed the cinch of the towel at her waist. Slowly she turned and pulled a T-shirt out of her locker. Jeans followed, and socks and sneakers tumbled in a noisy clutter to the floor. The T-shirt slipped easily over her head. Then she sat down, shoulder to shoulder, next to Janacek.

"I got my acceptance from Westin yesterday," announced Mac quietly.

Janacek stopped combing her hair. "You did?"

The two stared at one another in a long, comprehending silence.

"You know I have to go, Kim."

Janacek shook her head slowly. "You don't have to, but you will."

Mac's arm slid gracefully around Janacek's waist.

"I'll be home at Christmas. It won't be so—"

"Don't," interrupted Janacek. "We don't know what's going to happen. Please don't make me any promises."

Mac pulled her closer then, and their arms found a safe, com-forting place around one another. But then, their cheeks touched, their lips met, their mouths and throats and breasts pressed together in a tender embrace.

Suddenly Janacek pushed her away.

"Mac. . . ."

"What? There's no one coming. . . ."

"It's not like we were at home."

"Whose home is that? We never have this much privacy at your place or mine. Either your father is yelling from downstairs or my mother's hovering outside my bedroom door." Mac placed her hands on her hips and imitated her mother's falsetto: "Are you girls studying in there?"

"Stop it!" Janacek's voice was angry. "It doesn't matter anymore."

"What are you talking about?" Mac defended herself.

Kim stared hard into her eyes.

"It doesn't matter. Don't you see that? You're leaving." She paused a moment. "Me," she added. "You're leaving me."

Then they were kissing, deeply, passionately, like lovers. . . . Their hands and mouths touched everywhere, each clearly familiar with the nuance of the other's body.

From her dark corner, Anna took a step back, ashamed of her witness, knowing that this moment was intensely private and should be protected. She turned her head. They didn't suspect her presence.

And Anna hadn't suspected them.

Certainly, there had been other dykes in the years before, but none that had surprised her—they were jocks, adulant adolescents, gung-ho team players who followed her down the halls and carried the bats and would have cut off their throwing arms for more than the most minimal encouragement her position allowed. One had even sent her love letters. She'd ignored them.

But these two did surprise her. MacNamara, with her easy charm and her graceful femininity, president of the French club; hell, she even sang alto voice in the church choir where Anna and Becca had been going for years. Not a bad ballplayer, either, but not like the little butches who had preceded her.

And Janacek, that mousy, quiet, junior whose distinct unathleticism had been the only thing which had impressed Anna. It was rumored that she was the poet laureate of her class, but she was also a loner who rarely spoke out in defense of anything.

But here Janacek was eloquent.

Here Janacek spoke words for many lesbians, spoke truth, spoke pain, alienation, loss and love. Anna grimaced with the sour regret of realizing that sixteen was too young to know already that others would not let her be the loving person that she was.

No fool, that one.

There, still, waiting in the darkness, Anna let herself sink down to the floor, pushing the young lovers out of her consciousness. After a while, she heard the locker doors slam, and the sound of the two girls push through the outer gym door. She waited even longer, until she heard the janitor make his rounds. Finally, he turned out the last light.

When she left, she could barely smell his cigar smoke, mixing faintly with the lavender powder that lingered in the air.

Later, turning the old Buick onto Cold Springs Road, Anna felt happy to see the porch lights on. Rebecca had gotten home early. In the comfortable reach of her mind, Anna imagined her in the kitchen, cleaning the carrots for the soup, or maybe folding the clothes off the line in back of the house.

They'd been together a long time, almost eighteen years, since graduate school. At times it hadn't been easy, holding the relationship together without the supports that would have been afforded them in a larger city, but they had endured it. In fact, things were going quite well these days. The little gourmet shop that Rebecca owned in Phillips was prospering; at last they seemed to have a little money, and time for each other.

Except that they didn't know anyone, really.

Rebecca didn't go to school functions; no faculty dinners or post-PTA cocktail parties.

Only occasionally she'd show up as a quiet, somewhat disinterested spectator at the softball games, hunched up in a corner of the stands, wearing sunglasses. She was careful not to sit where others would talk to her. She always left in her own car, cautiously reserving her congratulations or consolation for later, when Anna got home.

Anna pulled into the driveway and turned off the engine.

MacNamara would never come back for Kim. Surely, they'd see each other on school breaks, but the lure of the big city, the bars, the attractive women, the pressure of college life, all of it—no seventeen-year-old would be normal if she didn't fall into the trap of independence.

It would be harder for Janacek.

For her, there was still another year of high school, and then on to the local community college. Of course, she'd go on living at her parents' house, hiding, waiting, wondering if Mac would still want her, and then, when Mac didn't, she'd wonder about herself. . . .

"Planning to sleep in the car?" Becca was opening her door, smiling. She leaned in and kissed Anna briefly.

Anna stared at her a moment, as if mulling over the question. Becca's mood seemed appreciably changed since the morning. But no, that wasn't exactly accurate. Becca hadn't really been angry at all. *I was the angry one,* she realized.

"No, I don't think so," she answered simply.

"Hard day?"

Anna clambered out of the car and the two walked up to the house.

"Let's sit outside," said Anna suddenly, turning. She settled herself on the porch steps, and Becca came back and sat behind her, her strong brown hands resting gently on Anna's shoulders. Becca stroked her hair and kissed her.

"What's going on?" asked Becca.

Anna shook her head. She paused. "I caught two students making love."

"Where?"

"In the locker room."

Becca tapped the side of her head with her fingertip. "A-ha. Girls, then," she deduced, grinning slightly. "That's a tough one. What happened?"

"Nothing. I let them finish. Then they went home. They didn't know I was there."

A gentle breeze stirred through the spring grasses at their feet. Across the neighboring fields, on the western ridge of hills, the sun had nearly disappeared, and long shadows stretched up their yard from nearby trees. They stayed quietly there, on the porch, sitting, Becca's arms loosely around Anna's neck, rocking in silence, almost imperceptibly, for several minutes.

"Sorry about the fight—"

"Already forgotten," interrupted Becca.

"I want to go," added Anna. "To the reunion."

"You do?"

"Yes."

"Why the sudden change of heart?" inquired Becca.

Anna leaned away from her then and turned to look at Becca. For a moment, she took in Becca's beautiful face, her patient eyes and soft, graceful hands. She was lucky; she knew it.

Slowly, she crossed her fingers over her heart, and Becca's eyes followed. It was a gesture that meant, I can't explain how I love you. It also meant, this is a gift. It was a familiar gesture to them both. Then Anna leaned back into Becca's arms, and Becca pulled her closer.

"Thanks Anna," she whispered in her ear.

Anna nodded silently. *Thanks Janacek,* she thought.

Slumber Party

LOUISE RAFKIN

WE LIVED IN Rancho Del Mar, near the beach, but not everyone did. There were a whole mess of houses across the freeway, past the golf course, in what people called The Flats. The streets there were narrower and most were cracked and almost none had sidewalks. There were no patios for skateboarding or skating and the kids that lived over there mostly hung out outside at Al's market. Some people over there lived in apartments, some even lived in these old hotels that had dry swimming pools, like craters, in their middles. I didn't go over there much but some kids that lived in The Flats went to our school, and some were even my friends. Cassy McDaniels was one.

Cassy McDaniels came to La Playa, my school, at the beginning of the sixth grade from I don't know where. She had blonde hair that fell past her shoulders and sometimes she'd brush it over the back of her head and in front of her face so she'd look like "Thing" from the Munsters. We wore shorts under our dresses every day, so

245

when we hung from the monkey bars or played dodgeball no one could see our panties. Cassy never wore shorts and you could always see under her dress but she didn't notice or else didn't care. I had dreams about going to school and forgetting to put on shorts. I could never understand how Cassy made it through recess. But I always wanted to play with her.

By Christmas she was popular. She told us all about Slam Books. They had them at her old school. You would write your name in the front of them next to a number and then on every page there would be a question like, Who Do You Like? Or, Who Is The Best Kisser? Or, What Teacher Don't You Like? So then you'd fill out the questions and pass it around and then everyone would try to steal it and you'd slam it shut. None of us had ever kissed anyone so some of the questions we left blank. Lisa Medichi wrote on that one "None of your bees-wax!" but we knew she hadn't kissed anyone either. Cassy wrote the name of some boy from her other school and then she put three stars next to it because she said he was a real good kisser. I wondered what made someone really good or not.

It was hard to convince my mom to let me go to Cassy's slumber party. She didn't know the family. "And are Mr. and Mrs. McDaniels going to be there?" For about a week she said "We'll see" and "I'll discuss it with your father" and then Mrs. Larson called to invite her and Dad to a cocktail party and she said yes. Then it was easier for me to go than for them to find a baby-sitter, plus my older brother had a basketball game and she couldn't just dump me with him.

But I didn't *really* want to go. At slumber parties you don't get much sleep and I liked to sleep. If I didn't get enough sleep I'd wake up with a stomach ache. Mostly I worried about not getting to sleep, but if you went to sleep early the others were likely to put your hand in a cup of cold water. And then you'd wet the bed. Sometimes I liked to sleep over at someone's house, or better, have someone over to mine. But even though I went to slumber parties I was always scared.

What would you be asked to do? What would happen when they started to play "Truth or Dare"? What if boys came over and wanted to play spin-the-bottle? What if Cassy McDaniels started to strip— where would you look?

When we played Truth or Dare, I took dare. Luckily all I had to do was knock on Mrs. McDaniels bedroom door. She was in there with her boyfriend but the television was turned so loud she didn't hear, or maybe she ignored me. It was late and we had eaten a ton of caramel corn and then had started to make chocolate chip cookies but Cassy decided we should just eat the raw dough. After a while my stomach hurt. I lay flat on my back under my red and black flowered sleeping bag, hoping that perhaps the others would think I was asleep. Cassy was about to strip.

She turned the lights off, all except the kitchen light which spilled into the living room. She put some slow music on the Hi-Fi, something of her mother's, and hid herself in the living-room drapes. She folded into them like a caterpillar in a cocoon.

All of us ten girls were quiet. Everyone was into their sleeping bags and the floor looked like some sort of funny quilt. Most of the others were sitting up but I just peeked over the top of my bag.

The music started to swell and Cassy rolled herself out from the drapes. Her black pedal-pushers were tight on her already rounded hips, her dotted blouse was tied at her waist. She pushed her hair up and off her face like some sort of movie star. Her shirt hiked up and I could see a crescent of a shining white bra. Puckering her lips, she kissed at the air. Lila screamed and then everyone else did too. Then the others all tumbled to a heap at Cassy's feet giggling and laughing. Helen turned the stereo up.

At every overnight Cassy acted liked a stripper. Sometimes she just danced and moved around twisting from side to side like a snake. At Rachel Whitmore's party she had taken some of her clothes off. At the age of eleven she already had her period and already had breasts and most of the rest of us didn't have either. She started to bob and dip to the music, rubbing her hands along her thighs and then wrapping her arms around herself so that from the back it looked like someone was hugging and feeling her. The first song ended and she had only undone the top three buttons of her blouse. "More! More!" said Lila and then everyone else said it too. Cassy looked towards the back bedroom but there was just a faint line of TV blue glowing from under her mother's door.

The next song was faster. Cassy swung her hips and flipped her hair over onto her chest. Then she untied and peeled away her blouse. Her white bra shone in the half-light of the living room and we all hushed. Many of us still wore undershirts. Cassy flipped her hair back and laughed, then we did, too. I was sitting with the other girls now. I wore two-piece striped pajamas but some of the others, like Lila, had on babydolls. Cassy was standing with her shirt off. At Rachel's house she had stopped after taking her shirt off; it looked like she was going to go further.

I stared at her bra. Lumps of creamy flesh tucked into pointy cups almost like those cones you put in those plastic holders for drinking. I was warm. I tried to get into the middle of the others, to laugh and giggle but the strange feeling in my stomach just got worse.

Cassy had turned around and unzipped her pedal-pushers. She started to pull them over her hips. It looked like a banana losing its skin. The pants were tight and they got stuck on her thighs; she had to bend over to pull them down. The smile across the back of her white Carter's underwear made me gasp and I coughed to cover it up. Angela Ellis sat up and slapped Cassy's bottom when she was doubled over. "Bulls-eye!" she said. Everyone laughed. Cassy kicked off her pants and turned around facing us. She tried to pretend she was mad at Angela but when she turned and saw everyone smiling she smiled too, this long wide smile, slow-like. Her bikini underwear fell short of the tanned line where her bathing suit stopped, so a pale stripe, about the color of a tan Crayola crayon, circled her waist.

"Show us your boobies!" Melinda said and Cassy slid her bra

down her tanned arms. I could hardly breathe. White triangles of fless spotted with pink moons sat on her chest like targets and I couldn't take my eyes from them. The other girls started to horse around a little; I sat behind them and watched. Cassy touched the very tips of her breasts and started to moan.

"This is what they do down at the Cat 'N' Mouse," she said. The Cat 'N' Mouse was a bar near her house. "I know cause I went there with my mom." I'd walked past it before. The sign in front showed a cat chasing a mouse down a hole. The cat had long whiskers that flashed on and off.

I backed away from the other girls, all the way to the fireplace, scraping my legs against some ceramic logs stacked against the bricks. Cassy was standing half-naked in front of everybody talking about the Cat 'N' Mouse. "Well, they don't take everything off," she admitted. "But almost."

Melinda had moved up close to where Cassy was standing and she reached up and grabbed at Cassy's underpants, pulling them down past her knees. Cassy screamed and then everyone did too. I swallowed, trying to keep the air inside of me from coming out and making a noise. I didn't want anyone to look at me. I wanted to be invisible. In the light from the kitchen I could see a tiny triangle of dark hair like a small shadow between Cassy's legs.

Cassy tried to move but her panties were caught around her ankles and she toppled into everyone. There was a big tangle. I wanted to jump into the mess and touch her too, but I also wanted her to put her clothes back on. I didn't know what I wanted.

"What's the matter with you?" Cassy said. She was lying on her stomach over Lila's knees, her hair was all messy across her face. She looked right at me and I looked away. Someone pinched her bottom and she turned over and away from me. They were all laughing again.

I felt frozen to the fireplace and unable to move. My stomach was queasy and itchy. While they were still wrestling with each other I went to the bathroom. The crotch of my pajama bottoms was damp.

I touched myself and it was a little slimey. I felt afraid but somehow I felt okay, too. I grabbed a towel and started to rub myself dry.

A Perfectly Nice Man

JANE RULE

"I'M SORRY I'M LATE, darling," Virginia said, having to pick up and embrace three-year-old Clarissa before she could kiss Katherine hello. "My last patient needed not only a new crown but some stitches for a broken heart. Why do people persist in marriage?"

"Your coat's cold," Clarissa observed soberly.

"So's my nose," Virginia said, burying it in the child's neck. "It's past your bath time and your story time, and I've probably ruined dinner."

"No," Katherine said. "We're not eating until seven-thirty. We're having a guest."

"Who?"

"Daddy's new friend," Clarissa said. "And I get to stay up until she comes."

"Really?"

"She said she needed to talk with us," Katherine explained. "She

251

sounded all right on the phone. Well, a little nervous but not at all hostile. I thought, perhaps we owe her that much?"

"Or him?" Virginia wondered.

"Oh, if him, I suppose I should have said no," Katherine decided. "People who don't even want to marry him think this is odd enough."

"Odd about him?"

"Even he thinks it's odd about him," Katherine said.

"Men have an exaggerated sense of responsibility in the most peculiar directions," Virginia said. "We can tell her he's a perfectly nice man, can't we?" She was now addressing the child.

"Daddy said I didn't know who was my mommie," Clarissa said.

"Oh?"

"I have two mommies. Will Elizabeth be my mommie, too?"

"She just might," Virginia said. "What a lucky kid that would make you."

"Would she come to live with us then?" Clarissa asked.

"Sounds to me as if she wants to live with Daddy," Virginia said.

"So did you, at first," Clarissa observed.

Both women laughed.

"Your bath?" Virginia ordered and carried the child up the stairs while Katherine returned to the kitchen to attend to dinner.

Clarissa was on the couch in her pajamas, working a pop-up book of *Alice in Wonderland* with Virginia, when the doorbell rang.

"I'll get that," Katherine called from the kitchen.

Elizabeth, in a fur-collared coat, stood in the doorway, offering freesias.

"Did he tell you to bring them?" Katherine asked, smiling.

"He said we all three liked them," Elizabeth answered. "But don't most women?"

"I'm Katherine," Katherine said, "wife number one."

"And I'm Virginia, wife number two," Virginia said, standing in the hall.

"And I'm Elizabeth, as yet unnumbered," Elizabeth said. "And you're Clarissa."

Clarissa nodded, using one of Virginia's legs as a prop for leaning against or perhaps hiding behind.

Elizabeth was dressed, as the other two women were, in very well cut trousers and an expensive blouse, modestly provocative. And she was about their age, thirty. The three did not so much look alike as share a type, all about the same height, five feet seven inches or so (he said he was six feet tall but was, in fact, five feet ten and a half), slightly but well proportioned, with silky, well cut hair and intelligent faces. They were all competent, assured women who intimidated only unconsciously.

Virginia poured three drinks and a small glass of milk for Clarissa, who was allowed to pass the nuts and have one or two before Katherine took her off to bed.

"She looks like her father," Elizabeth observed.

"Yes, she has his lovely eyes," Virginia agreed.

"He doesn't know I'm here," Elizabeth confessed. "Oh, I intend to tell him. I just didn't want it to be a question, you see?"

"He did think it a mistake that Katherine and I ever met. We didn't, of course, until after I'd married him. I didn't know he was married until quite a while after he and I met."

"He was a patient of yours?" Elizabeth asked.

"Yes."

"He's been quite open with me about both of you from the beginning, but we met in therapy, of course, and that does make such a difference."

"Does it?" Virginia asked. "I've never been in therapy."

"Haven't you?" Elizabeth asked, surprised. "I would have thought both of you might have considered it."

"He and I?"

"No, you and Katherine."

"We felt very uncomplicated about it," Virginia said, "once it happened. It was such an obvious solution."

"For him?"

"Well, no, not for him, of course. Therapy was a thing for him to consider."

Katherine came back into the room. "Well, now we can be grownups."

"She looks like her father," Elizabeth observed again.

"She has his lovely eyes," it was Katherine's turn to reply.

"I don't suppose a meeting like this could have happened before the women's movement," Elizabeth said.

"Probably not," Katherine agreed. "I'm not sure Virginia and I could have happened before the women's movement. We might not have known what to do."

"He tries not to be antagonistic about feminism," Elizabeth said.

"Oh, he's always been quite good about the politics. He didn't resent my career," Virginia offered.

"He was quite proud of marrying a dentist," Katherine said. "I think he used to think I wasn't liberated enough."

"He doesn't think that now," Elizabeth said.

"I suppose not," Katherine agreed.

"The hardest thing for him has been facing. . .the sexual implications. He has felt. . .unmanned."

"He's put it more strongly than that in the past," Virginia said.

"Men's sexuality is so much more fragile than ours," Elizabeth said.

"Shall we have dinner?" Katherine suggested.

"He said you were a very good cook," Elizabeth said to Katherine.

"Most of this dinner is Virginia's. I got it out of the freezer," Katherine explained. "I've gone back to school, and I don't have that much time."

"I cook in binges," Virginia said, pouring the wine.

"At first he said he thought the whole thing was some kind of crazy revenge," Elizabeth said.

"At first there might have been that element in it," Virginia admitted. "Katherine was six months' pregnant when he left her, and she felt horribly deserted. I didn't know he was going to be a father until after Clarissa was born. Then I felt I'd betrayed her, too, though

I hadn't known anything about it."

"He said he should have told you," Elizabeth said, "but he was very much in love and was afraid of losing you. He said there was never any question of his not supporting Katherine and Clarissa."

"No, I make perfectly good money," Virginia said. "There's no question of his supporting them now, if that's a problem. He doesn't."

"He says he'd rather he did," Elizabeth said.

"He sees Clarissa whenever he likes," Katherine explained. "He's very good with her. One of the reasons I wanted a baby was knowing he'd be a good sort of father."

"Did you have any reservations about marrying him?" Elizabeth asked Virginia.

"At the time? Only that I so very much wanted to," Virginia said. "There aren't that many marrying men around for women dentists, unless they're sponges, of course. It's flattering when someone is so afraid of losing you he's willing to do something legal about it. It oughtn't to be, but it is."

"But you had other reservations later," Elizabeth said.

"Certainly, his wife and his child."

"Why did he leave you, Katherine?"

"Because he was afraid of losing her. I suppose he thought he'd have what he needed of me anyway, since I was having his child."

"Were you still in love with him?" Elizabeth asked.

"I must have been," Katherine said, "or I couldn't have been quite so unhappy, so desperate. I was desperate."

"He's not difficult to be in love with, after all," Virginia said. "He's a very attractive man."

"He asked me if I was a lesbian," Elizabeth said. "I told him I certainly didn't think so. After all, I was in love with him. He said so had two other women been, in love enough to marry him, but they were both lesbians. And maybe he only attracted lesbians even if they didn't know it themselves. He even suggested I should maybe try making love with another woman before I made up my mind."

There was a pause which neither Katherine nor Virginia attempted to break.

"Did either of you know. . .before?"

Katherine and Virginia looked at each other. Then they said, "No."

"He's even afraid he may turn women into lesbians," Elizabeth said.

Both Virginia and Katherine laughed, but not unkindly.

"Is that possible?" Elizabeth asked.

"Is that one of *your* reservations?" Katherine asked.

"It seemed crazy," Elizabeth said, "but. . ."

Again the two hostesses waited.

"I know this probably sounds very unliberated and old-fashioned and maybe even prejudiced, but I don't think I could stand being a lesbian, finding out I'm a lesbian; and if there's something in him that makes a woman. . . How can either of you stand to be together instead of with him?"

"But you don't know you're a lesbian until you fall in love," Katherine said, "and then it's quite natural to want to be together with the person you love."

"What's happening to me is so peculiar. The more sure I am I'm in love with him, the more obsessively I read everything I can about what it is to be a lesbian. It's almost as if I *had* fallen in love with a woman, and that's absurd."

"I don't really think there's anything peculiar about him," Katherine said.

"One is just so naturally drawn, so able to identify with another woman," Virginia said. "When I finally met Katherine, what he wanted and needed just seemed too ridiculous."

"But it was you he wanted," Elizabeth protested.

"At Katherine's and Clarissa's expense, and what was I, after all, but just another woman."

"A liberated woman," Katherine said.

"Not then, I wasn't," Virginia said.

"I didn't feel naturally drawn to either of you," Elizabeth protested. "I wasn't even curious at first. But he's so obsessed with you still, so afraid of being betrayed again, and I thought, I've got to help him somehow, reassure him, understand enough to let him know, as you say, that there's nothing peculiar about him. . .or me."

"I'm sure there isn't," Katherine said reassuringly and reached out to take Elizabeth's hand.

Virginia got up to clear the table.

"Mom!" came the imperious and sleepy voice of Clarissa.

"I'll go," Virginia said.

"But I don't think you mean what I want you to mean," Elizabeth said.

"Perhaps not," Katherine admitted.

"He said he never should have left you. It was absolutely wrong; and if he ever did marry again, it would be because he wanted to make that commitment, but what if his next wife found out she didn't want him, the way Virginia did?"

"I guess anyone takes that risk," Katherine said.

"Do you think I should marry him?" Elizabeth asked.

Katherine kept Elizabeth's hand, and her eyes met Elizabeth's beseeching, but she didn't answer.

"You *do* think there's something wrong with him."

"No, I honestly don't. He's a perfectly nice man. It's just that I sometimes think that isn't good enough, not now when there are other options."

"What other options?"

"You have a job, don't you?"

"I teach at the university, as he does."

"Then you can support yourself."

"That's not always as glamorous as it sounds."

"Neither is marriage," Katherine said.

"Is this?" Elizabeth asked, looking around her, just as Virginia came back into the room.

"It's not nearly as hard as some people try to make it sound."

"Clarissa wanted to know if her new mother was still here."

"Oh my," Elizabeth said.

"Before you came, she wanted to know, if you married her father, would you be another mother and move in here."

Elizabeth laughed and then said, "Oh, God, that's just what he wants to know!"

They took their coffee back into the living room.

"It must be marvelous to be a dentist. At least during the day you can keep people from telling you all their troubles," Elizabeth said.

"That's not as easy as it looks," Virginia said.

"He says you're the best dentist he ever went to. He hates his dentist now."

"I used to be so glad he wasn't like so many men who fell in love with their students," Katherine said.

"Maybe he'd be better off," Elizabeth said in mock gloom. "He says he isn't threatened by my having published more than he has. He had two wives and a baby while I was simply getting on with it; but does he mean it? Does he really know?"

"We're all reading new lines, aren't we?" Virginia asked.

"But if finally none of us marries them, what will they do?" Elizabeth asked.

"I can hardly imagine that," Katherine said.

"You can't imagine what they'll do?"

"No, women saying 'no,' all of them. We can simply consider ourselves, for instance," Katherine said.

"Briefly anyway," Virginia said. "Did you come partly to see if you were at all like us?"

"I suppose so," Elizabeth said.

"Are you?"

"Well, I'm not surprised by you . . . and very surprised not to be."

"Are you sorry to have married him?" Virginia asked Katherine.

"I could hardly be. There's Clarissa, after all, and you. Are you?" she asked in return.

"Not now," Virginia said, "having been able to repair the damage."

"And everyone knows," Elizabeth said, "that you did have the choice."

"Yes," Virginia agreed, "there's that."

"But I felt I didn't have any choice," Katherine said. "That part of it humiliated me."

"Elizabeth is making a distinction," Virginia said, "between what everyone knows and what each of us knows. I shared your private humiliation, of course. All women must."

"Why?" Elizabeth demanded.

"Not to believe sufficiently in one's own value," Virginia explained.

"But he doesn't believe sufficiently in his own value either," Elizabeth said. "He doesn't even quite believe he's a man."

"I never doubted I was a woman," Katherine said.

"That's smug," Elizabeth said, "because you have a child."

"So does he," Katherine replied.

"But he was too immature to deal with it; he says so himself. Don't you feel at all sorry for him?"

"Yes," said Katherine.

"Of course," Virginia agreed.

"He's been terribly hurt. He's been damaged," Elizabeth said.

"Does that make him more or less attractive, do you think?" Virginia asked.

"Well, damn it, less, of course," Elizabeth shouted. "And whose fault is that?"

Neither of the other two women answered.

"He's not just second, he's third-hand goods," Elizabeth said.

"Are women going to begin to care about men's virginity?" Katherine asked. "How extraordinary!"

"Why did you go into therapy?" Virginia asked.

"I hardly remember," Elizabeth said. "I've been so caught up with his problems since the beginning. The very first night of group, he said I somehow reminded him of his wives. . ."

"Perhaps that is why you went," Katherine suggested.

"You think I'd be crazy to marry him, don't you?" Elizabeth demanded.

"Why should we?" Virginia asked. "We both did."

"That's not a reassuring point," Elizabeth said.

"You find us unsatisfactory," Katherine said, in apology.

"Exactly not," Elizabeth said sadly. "I want someone to advise me. . .to make a mistake. Why should you?"

"Why indeed?" Virginia asked.

They embraced warmly before Elizabeth left.

"Perhaps I might come again?" she asked at the door.

"Of course," Katherine said.

After the door closed, Katherine and Virginia embraced.

"He'd be so much happier, for a while anyway, if he married again," Katherine said.

"Of course he would," Virginia agreed, with some sympathy for him in her voice. "But we couldn't encourage a perfectly nice woman like Elizabeth. . ."

"That's the problem, isn't it?" Katherine said. "That's just it."

"She'll marry him anyway," Virginia predicted, "briefly."

"And have a child?" Katherine asked.

"And fall in love with his next wife," Virginia went on.

"There really isn't anything peculiar about him," Katherine said.

"I'm sorry he doesn't like his dentist."

"He should never have married you."

"No, he shouldn't," Virginia agreed. "Then at least I could still be taking care of his teeth."

Barring that, they went up together to look in on his richly mothered child, sleeping soundly, before they went to their own welcoming bed.

Sapphire

CANYON SAM

KATE AND I had enjoyed many a day working on Mandy's hexagonal cabin. We'd work shirtless in the mornings on the building site that stood right below the crest of a long, sloped meadow overlooking the valley until about eleven, when the hot summer temperatures climbed to an uncomfortable level and we'd retreat to Kate's cool cabin on the next hill. It was there at Kate's place in the afternoons where I sipped homemade lemonade, curled up in the big armchair in front of the picture window, and soaked up Lesbiana. I read and read and read, choosing kernels from that treasure chest that was the Womanest library next door. I read *Well of Loneliness* and wept, read *Edward the Dyke* and chuckled, read back issues of *Quest* and pondered. I listened to their collection of women's music—Meg Christian, Cris Williamson, Alix Dobkin. Every poem, every photograph, every song a new discovery.

Kate was busy fixing up and making plans for the house—a cobwebbed, abandoned hunting cabin with only a rusty box-spring bed and two broken chairs to its name when we'd first stepped across its threshold two weeks earlier.

Now it was clean but still barren and Kate, who was not only energetic and talented, but a visionary, had great designs for it. She was also a wonderful cook and we ate heartily and smoked contentedly every evening in front of the fireplace.

I had quite a crush on my new friend the carpenter, who'd befriended me when I arrived and who, like myself, was a recent transplant to Oregon from San Francisco. The nights were especially endless and fitful because we shared the ancient mattress that sank in the center like a crater of the moon, continuously pitching us together as we slept. I couldn't even cling to my own edge of the bed and withdraw; I was compelled to lay right beside her in a quiet, frustrated frenzy of newly-awakened sexuality. I was much too shy and inexperienced to do anything about my crush, so most of the time I just looked upon Kate in the way of a young woman to an adored older buddy.

When I came out two months earlier in San Francisco, that spring of 1975, one of the things that was most important to me was to meet another Asian lesbian, of which there were scant few at the time. When I inquired one woman's name kept popping up over and over from many and separate quarters, but I never got a chance to meet this woman, Sapphire, before I moved out of the area. One evening I mentioned this to Kate and it turned out she had left not just a career behind in the city, but a five-year relationship with...can you believe?...Sapphire. Photo albums and stories poured out about this powerful, attractive Asian lesbian who was somewhat of a legend in San Francisco. Sapphire became larger than life.

These days Kate was in love with a carpenter from Sonoma who had traveled through Oregon that summer. So in love that after a couple weeks without seeing her Kate wanted to make a trip south to visit.

The morning Kate's red van, packed up and fueled, finally pulled away from the house a wave of emotion rolled across my stomach and flushed through my cheeks. My protection and my role model was leaving for two weeks. Suddenly I realized my isolation on this land, my newness to country living, and to the skills it required to survive. Mine was a generalized sense of abandonment at being left alone at this raw point in my struggle with my new identity. The cabin and the land were filled with her energy; when an occasional visitor came I would show them the plans for the second story addition, the new wood-burning stove, the kitchen table Kate had built— just like she did with guests—in my faded denim overalls.

Everyday I got up and went to work. I was building some scaffolding that we'd need to install the roof on Mandy's cabin and I was dismantling a fallen chicken coop by the side of the road on the Womanest land next door.

In my free time I embroidered patches for my overalls: impressionistic designs with neat patterned centers and etched stitches around the border. I sewed on scraps of Peter Max material—royal blue background with Sargent Pepper stars floating by wildly reflecting my new interest in astrology; swatches of leather and sheepskin fur; a beaded Indian talisman for the center of my back where the two straps crossed.

My overalls had been given to me by John, a dance friend in San Francisco after he'd returned from a trip to his native Texas. They had belonged to an 88-year-old farmer who'd just passed away and John bought them from the man's widow at a roadside sale. They were sun, wind, and field faded. . .and soft as a rag.

One afternoon I was at the chicken coop pulling out nails and sorting lumber when a big, long car came through the clearing at the bottom of the Womanest meadow. It was white and fancy and seemed to float like a boat. I smiled slightly: it was so easy to miss that turn; people came up here all the time looking for the MacCulloughs or Grant and Glenna's place, only to find women with crewcuts on a hilltop.

I knew this was the case here because this car was spanking new and late model deluxe with chrome so shiny sunlight spun off it, and one of those figurines on the hood like on a stretch limo or a Greek yacht. Glinting slivers of sunlight swirled through the cloud of dust fanning into the air as the automobile picked its way up the potholed path. Most of what we saw up this way were rusty VW vans and ten-year-old Valiants; this car was so wide it spilled off the sides of the road.

They saw me and stopped. I was about to tell them they'd taken the wrong turn and ask who they were looking for, when I saw behind the passenger window long black hair and an Asian face. There was a whirring sound like an electric can opener as the blue-tinted glass dropped and released a hit of frigid air, giving me goose bumps. I found myself looking face to face and exchanging words with this woman in a moment strange—not only because this was the only other Asian face I'd ever seen in the state, not even because I realized in a flash this was not a misdirected family but Sapphire come alive from the pages of Kate's photo album, but because I found her beauty undeniably captivating and her soft distant manner disturbingly intriguing in a way others had described, but I doubted *I* would ever feel.

I directed them back down and around the long way to Kate's, then scurried up the hilly shortcut to tidy up the house. Still being so new to lesbians, every time I met some it was an event of note and aroused great anticipation, fear, and excitement in me.

"We just moved in," I said, as they climbed out of their boat and looked up at the faded red cabin while I led the way inside.

Sapphire was an imposing figure with a stunning mane of thick, lustrous black hair that swept down the length of her full-figured back. Her presence commanded attention. (Since then I've actually discovered I'm taller than Sapphire but low cabin ceilings and my own sense of invisibility led me to believe that *all* lesbians I met that summer were taller and bigger than they actually were). Nancy, her lover, was heavy-set with brown hair and a down-to-earth manner. They were both in their 30's.

I showed them the house with the same pride and enthusiasm Kate did with visitors: the wood-burning stove we'd hauled from town, the stained-glass windows we'd hung, the kitchen table Kate built, the bookshelf I made.

Sapphire was curt—her eyes darting about taking in everything with sharp, tense glances.

"What did you say your name was?" she asked in a soft but pointed tone of voice.

Where are you from? Oh, the City. . . what part of the City? What high school did you go to? What year did you graduate? How did you get to Oregon? How long have you been here? How do you know Kate?

I thought we were conversing at first, but it quickly became apparent I was mistaken. My answers never seemed to improve her mood or serve as an entree to a friendly chat—as soon as I answered one question she drilled me with another, the whole time scanning the room like a cool spy in some dark European movie.

What was with all the questions? When would they be over? Why did she care what year I graduated from high school? (Whatever year it was, I suddenly felt like I was back there in the dean's office.) She obviously wanted to determine my age, get some sort of fix on me. When would she be the charming, charismatic personality I'd heard so much about?

After I said I'd attended Lowell, a college prep public high school in San Francisco, whatever sinking ship I unwittingly found myself on gasped its last breath. Whatever I thought *might* be happening before deepened, and a distinct and not kindly frost started to chill the hot summer temperatures inside the cabin.

Nancy was more friendly, albeit slightly anxious. I didn't have a clue as to what was happening: did I say something wrong? did something about the place offend Sapphire?

Their scruffy little black dog, snipping and growling underfoot and flinging himself around the floor like a flea, was starting to make me nervous. My ankles suddenly felt vulnerable and naked around him. Sapphire strode boldly into the kitchen as if she owned the place. The conversation was over.

Nancy suggested we leave Sapphire alone and take a walk outside. The afternoon was brilliant and warm, and the wild-grass hillside the color of straw.

Nancy was easy and engaging to be with and before I knew it I forgot the strained interaction indoors. I showed her where we planned to put the garden, introduced her to the prized manzanita tree, and then walked her out to the boundaries of the property, as butterflies danced like stained glass miniatures in the sunlight and bird songs whistled down from the pine trees. The sun shone through my soft denim overalls and warmed my bare brown arms.

When we got back to the house Sapphire said she had left a note and some boxes of food for Kate sitting on the pot-belly stove. Then without another word they left: climbed into the long white car, turned it around in the short rocky driveway, and descended down the road through the trees.

When Kate returned a few days later I told her how inexplicably cool Sapphire had been. . .that I was puzzled and troubled by it. . .and did Kate have any ideas about why Sapphire would have acted like that?

Kate looked at me a long minute with alarm growing in her bright hazel eyes.

"Canyon. . .Oh, My Gawwwd!" her long, lanky body drew back in shock and she stared at me strangely, as if she was suddenly seeing me in a new light. "Oh no!" she screeched in her hoarse smokers' voice, clasping her hand to her mouth.

"Canyon," she said finally, peeling her palm from her grimace of disbelief, her voice low and serious like we'd just made *big* trouble, "Sapphire and I fought and fought because I wanted to move to the country. . .I wanted her to come with me. She said 'no way!'

There was absolutely no way she'd ever move to Oregon. 'There are no *Asians* in Oregon!' she'd always argue.

"Now six months later she drives up to the sticks of rural Oregon. . .somehow finds her way back here. . .and I don't know how because she and I have not been in touch all these months; I've never given her my address. . . . And *who* does she find at the end of a twelve-mile dirt road when she comes calling unannounced?. . .This cute young *Asian* woman! *Living* with me! On my new land!"

I still didn't get it.

"She thought you and I were *lovers*! That's why she was acting so weird to you!!" She giggled throatily and popped open the tab of her beer can.

"Remember I told ja, Canyon. . ." she said, taking a sip, "Sapphire's the jealous type."

Since Kate didn't know I had a crush on her, I alone found particular irony in this.

I was sorely disappointed at not having made a better connection with Sapphire. She was the first other Asian lesbian I'd ever met. Actually, from what I was able to gather, she was the only one around *to* meet. I thought we'd have an instant rapport—based on our common upbringing in the San Francisco Chinese-American community, based on the voluminous reading I'd done about lesbian feminism. . .about The Movement. . .reading poetry about us being common loaves and an army of lovers. The concept 'Sisterhood is Beautiful' was an ideal we strove for in all parts of our lives, like seminarians for virtue. I had harbored secret hopes that I'd find in Sapphire a fascinating, powerful, older Asian sister to look up to. . .or at least make a friendly acquaintance with.

I pointed out to Kate that she and Sapphire were broken up. . .they'd split up their property in the city months ago and gone their separate ways. Sapphire had a new lover. They even lived together. So why was she so upset when she met me?

Somehow none of that seemed to matter. Kate shook her head resignedly like she'd seen it all before.

But it was all new to me: I was 19...they were Real Lesbians—26, 28, even 30. I'd never even had a genuine love affair...they had Relationships.

Thus my first meeting with another Asian lesbian took place not in San Francisco where there were hundreds of thousands of Asians and tens of thousands of gays, but in the quiet foxtailed hills of backcountry Oregon where I was just getting my first taste that summer of Lesbian Drama.

A Special Evening

ANN ALLEN SHOCKLEY

SATURDAY—WHY DID IT have to rain? Toni thought, gazing out the water-smeared windows. March was so unpredictable. The morning had been bright and clear, but in the afternoon, the sky's glaze grew shrouded with warning signs. Still, despite the threatening clouds, she held to the hope that the somberness would eventually lift.

In the evening, after seeing the last patient in her office and going home to bathe and dress, the rain came. There was a crash of thunder, the switchblade flash of lightning, and the rain descended in a torrent of swift heavy release.

A week of anticipation and preparation for the dinner engagement was now marred by ugly weather. An evening she had looked forward to and planned for with such carefulness. It should have been beautiful with silver stars and a full benevolent moon christening the sky, for wasn't an evening such as this supposed to be designed by poets? The way Sappho would have made it?

269

She turned from the window, hoping that Letia wouldn't change her mind. Some women just didn't like to go out in the rain. Another worry to vex her. As yet, the telephone hadn't rung, and it was six p.m. She had better hurry. Letia was expecting her at seven and the drive across town would be slower because of the rain.

In the bedroom, getting her car keys off the bureau, Toni glanced into the mirror. The expensive black tailored pants suit, trimmed with white braid, fitted neatly, camouflaging the slight bulges of late middle age. A hint of natural lipstick was applied just right to the strong mouth, and deft touches of powder gave the broad handsome face a touch of softness. Vanity, she admonished herself—no one was completely without it.

She had collected her keys, annoyed at the way her hands shook, like a teenager's on a first date. Ridiculous. But this was a special night with a special person. She hoped it would go well.

She rang Letia's doorbell exactly on time, in spite of the blinding rain that the windshield wiper could hardly cope with. Letia opened the door and said, with concern: "You're almost drowned!"

"Not quite—" she smiled at Letia, who was wearing a long multi-colored hostess gown that fell in waves over her slim figure down to her ankles. Her thick dark hair was swept up in spiraling tiers above a too-thin pale face. The sight of Letia caused a lonely pearl to form a knot in Toni's throat and turn to stone in her stomach. To conceal the way her eyes had been embracing Letia, Toni said hurriedly and a little fearfully: "You aren't going out in *that*, are you?"

Letia laughed as she closed the door behind them, barring the world. "Of course not! Here, give me that wet coat. You need to dry out. Go over by the fireplace, Toni—" A small question anxiously pocketed her mouth. "You don't mind my calling you Toni, do you? Doctor Reis for office hours."

"No, certainly not, please do. I'd like it very much." She crossed over to the fireplace to focus her gaze on something else—anything except Letia who was hanging her coat and hat in the closet. The apartment was small, tastefully furnished in delicate soft feminine appointments, but functional.

"I thought since it was so messy out we could just stay here and I'd cook something," Letia said from across the room.

Toni turned the suggestion over in her mind. The rain's hoof-beats against the window galloped in tune with her heart. How many times in the short while she had known Letia had she wanted this? Thinking about it alone at home during the nights, after the endless parade of patients who needed healing, consoling, attention. Can a dream distilled suddenly come alive?

At her silence, Letia said quickly: "I *can* cook, you know." A smile's hint covered her lips.

"I believe it," Toni laughed reassuringly. "It's just . . . well . . . wouldn't you prefer going out? After all, I *did* invite *you* to have dinner with me."

"It won't be any bother—cooking for you," Letia said, watching for an approving response.

Toni turned her gaze back to the fireplace to grasp a newly feigned interest in the bright flames. What did she mean? *Cooking for you.* Or had she misinterpreted the meaning? The words caused a shiver to run a fine sharp line through her.

She couldn't afford to misjudge. She had been hurt before. It was so easy to fashion other peoples' words into meanings you wanted. That was the trouble with being like she was: it was terribly difficult sometimes to really know. With some, the signs were apparent—by a glance, gesture, intoned word, thought perception. She couldn't afford to make any more mistakes. She was getting older. She had learned from the mistakes of the past—only a few—but enough. Enough to have left a bottomless reservoir of hurt inside her brimming with the painful words: *I'm not like that.*

"Well—" she faced Letia again, "if you don't mind. I'd enjoy having a good home-cooked meal. I usually eat out. Too tired to cook after work."

"Good!" Letia's face brightened, pleased.

"May I use the phone? I'll have to cancel the reservations."

"It's by the couch. What would you like to drink? Scotch, bourbon? A martini? I'm an awful drink mixer."

"Scotch on the rocks will be fine," Toni said, going over to the telephone. Perhaps that was what she needed to relieve the tension. She called the Ledo and cancelled the reservations. Wearily she sat on the sofa near the wall with the shelves of books. A large desk was opposite her, cluttered with paper, a typewriter and pencils. This was probably where Letia did her writing. Children's stories. That was what she had said when she'd wandered into her office one night suffering from gastritis.

"I write children's stories . . . when I'm well," she had added facetiously.

"Here's you drink—" Letia was back.

Toni thanked her. "Anything I can do?"

"No," a shake of the head. "There really isn't that much to do." She sat down beside Toni with her drink.

Toni smelled her perfume like roses on a fresh morning. She tasted her drink. The scotch spread warm tentacles through her.

Letia reached for a cigarette and automatically Toni picked up the table lighter and flicked it alive. Letia bent to the flame, cupping her hand lightly around Toni's. She breathed in the smoke, and then blew it out in a gray wavering stream.

Toni set the light back on the table, thinking, now wasn't that butch? But it was instinctive with her. One of her give-away features, she concluded wryly.

"It was really lucky for me to have walked into your office that night," Letia began conversationally. Then narrowing her eyes thoughtfully: "It was raining that time too."

"Yes, it was," Toni said softly, also remembering. Was the rain an omen?

"I was so sick. I was coming from my agent's office, and luckily saw your office sign. It was very kind of you to look at me when you were ready to close up. I felt like a fool after I found out you were a noted surgeon."

"I'm not noted," Toni protested modestly.

"Anyway," Letia smiled, "I'm glad I was sick. I got to meet you." She paused reflectively, flicking ashes in the tray. "I don't know anyone whom I've felt so comfortable with in a long time."

Toni looked across the room. Be careful how you answer, she warned herself, wanting to say one thing, but instead, she said: "I'm glad. I like your company, too."

She thought about the few times in the past two months when they had chatted over the phone. The first time she had called was on the pretense of finding out how Letia was. Afterwards, the calls were mutual ones that consisted of sharing of interests and thoughts, and above all, discovery.

"Do you?" Letia half-turned to face her, drawing her gaze back. Her brown eyes met, held and searched Toni's questioningly.

Toni wondered if she were looking for a sign. "Yes, you know," she went on briskly, "I'm quite fortunate. I have a rapport with most of my patients."

"Patients—" Letia tested the word, while putting out the cigarette. "Am I not a friend too?"

"Certainly," Toni replied softly, raising the glass to her lips. The social helpfulness of a drink. It occupies the hands and elasticizes strain. "I consider you a friend. Didn't I invite you to dinner?" she smiled.

Letia was silent as she sipped her drink. "How long have you been in practice?" she asked abruptly.

"Too long, I'm beginning to think. I'm getting old and tired. I think it's about time for me to fold up and have some fun before I get much older."

"You aren't old—"

"Aren't I? I'm a few years ahead of you," she sighed, running her long fingers through the short black hair sprinkled with silver.

"It's beautiful—" Letia murmured, watching her, "your hair. It looks so soft. Is it?" She touched Toni's hair, her fingers as gentle as a feathery wind. "It is—" she laughed shakily, scattering the fragile moment into a thousand broken pieces.

Toni felt warm icicles pricking her skin. *Please don't touch me again, she cried inwardly, for I won't be able to stand it.*

"Have you been doing any writing lately?" Toni asked, fumbling for normalcy again.

"Uh-huh. I'm finishing a story about a little girl who didn't like Christmas."

"Did you know a little girl who didn't like Christmas?"

"Yes—" Letia's fingers toyed with the purple sash of her gown. "I had a very close friend once whose little girl didn't like much of anything." Quickly she finished the remains of her drink. "My friend did everything in the world to get her to like things."

"Did she—finally?"

"No, not until I left. You see, she didn't like me. Thought her not-for-real Aunt Letia was a threat between her and her mother." Suddenly she laughed bitterly, not wanting to talk about it anymore. "I'm going to check on dinner. I don't want you sitting here starving while I bore you with segments from my past."

"You aren't boring me. I want to know—about you." And she did.

Letia's eyes fastened upon her. "You—what about you?"

"There's nothing to tell about me. Except hard work to get where I am in a field where males dominate. A double hard road for one to travel from a poor Minnesota family of five children."

"Any special friends?" Letia asked quietly.

Toni ran her thumb up and down the sides of her glass. A question harmless to many, but for her, one that could trap, ensnare—betray.

"Well, did you?" Letia persisted.

"What?" Toni sparred.

"Have any special friends," Letia repeated impatiently.

"It depends on what you mean by special. Friends are special for special reasons."

Frowning, Letia got up suddenly. "How do you like your steak?"

"Medium."

Letia gathered the empty glasses, signs of not enough or too much. "Would you like to watch TV or listen to some music?"

"Tonight, I'd rather have music," Toni said, looking up and seeing the frown still there. The fine lines between her wide-spaced eyes were almost permanent now. She would have liked to erase each with a kiss. But can one erase time?

"What do you like? I have an assortment. Pops, blues, show tunes, symphonies, jazz," she announced gaily, waving her hand in a mountainous brush. "Which?" Then, without waiting for an answer, she pulled out an album. "You look too pensive tonight. I'll put on some jazz. This is Jonah Jones. I like his style."

She placed the record on the turntable and the muted trumpet of Jonah Jones softly assailed the room. Toni leaned back, giving up her thoughts to the music. It was then she began to feel tired, drowsy. The patient load had been heavy for the day, and the suspense of tonight had added to the strain. She closed her eyes.

Something cold touched her hand, startling her. She had almost fallen asleep, and Letia was standing above her holding a fresh drink.

"Here's another one to wake you up. Dinner won't be long."

"Thanks—" she grinned sheepishly, accepting the drink. "Guess I'm not used to such carryings on."

"Stick around. It might even get better," Letia retorted saucily. "If you'll excuse me, I'm going back to the galley."

Toni sipped on the drink. It was short on ice and long on scotch. Her thoughts focused on Letia. Was she or wasn't she? Almost like the hair rinse commercial, she smiled to herself. She wanted so much to hold, touch, and caress her. Say the things she wanted to say. Males had no problems such as she. By role playing, they were the aggressors, and an approach was not an indictment, but something expected if the time, place, and moment were right. With her, a direct approach could be quicksand. There was so much to lose.

The drink was making her more sluggish, too musing. She stood up and stretched. Perhaps she should offer to help again. After all, she *was* to have treated Letia to dinner.

She heard the rain vying with the music, drumming steadily against the window.

Toni decided to take her drinkk and go through the door where Letia had gone. Letia had an apron on now and was standing on a stool reaching into the cabinet. Not hearing Toni behind her she backed down and bumped against her.

"Oh!" she gave a gasp of surprise as Toni's arm instantly reached out to steady her. A little of Toni's drink spilled on her suit.

"I'm sorry," Toni apologized quickly. "I thought you heard me come in."

Her arm was still around a startled Letia who was loosely holding a forgotten wooden salad bowl, and suddenly she was aware of Letia's face so near and the warmth of Letia's body. She dropped her arm limply to her side.

Letia stayed in the circle, invisible now, that Toni's arm had once made. The warmth of her breath lightly touched Toni's chin as she stared up at her intensely. There was a smudge of flour on the tip of Letia's nose, and Toni wanted to wipe it off with a kiss she did not give.

"Next time, doctor, rattle your scalpels," Letia laughed shakily.

"I'll remember," Toni promised, backing away. "I just wanted to know if I could help with anything—" And be with you.

"No, thanks. I have the operation well under control."

Letia busied herself at the sink, breaking crisp lettuce into the bowl. Toni found herself staring at her—the way her head tilted to the side, the slight slump of the small shoulders, her concentration on the task before her. A rend like a sharp ache seared through her. She wanted so much to brush her fingers across Letia's face, to know, trace and remember. And last, to cup her chin in the palm of her hand and lock her eyes with hers.

She would have to wait until she was sure, and sometimes one was never sure.

Outside the rain's sounds had grown softer, sounds of slow

diminishing. Jonah Jones' *Cherry Pink and Apple Blossom White* surfed the apartment in a misty musical spray.

"I'm glad it rained," Letia said, slicing tomatoes over the lettuce. "I like it here better with just the two of us."

"I like it too—" The words escaped before she could stop them and form others. She became aware that she was still holding her glass. The ice had melted and the drink was warm. Politely she finished it and set the glass on the sink.

"If you really want to be useful," Letia said, "fix two more drinks. The liquor's in the buffet in the dinette. You might as well learn where I keep it."

"All right." Toni picked up their glasses and went into the dinette off the side of the kitchen. A round table was covered with a white linen cloth and glistening silverware. Two bronze candle holders in the center flanked a floral piece. It looked intimately inviting. She got out the scotch and carefully measured out two jiggers each.

"Get some ice out of the refrig—" Letia directed when she returned.

Toni filled the glasses with ice cubes and watched as Letia slid two thick red steaks under the broiler. She handed Letia her drink, fingers brushing her, and quickly withdrew her hands as if from fire. Letia cast her a quizzical look, then smiled: "Here's to—us."

She lifted her glass in the toast, feeling a little tight already. Not real high, but nice and mellow and happy. Watching Letia bending over the steaks, she suddenly felt hungry.

Her gaze swallowed Letia's movements and came to rest on the small cleft in the back of her neck where lips could fit. A glow began to spread warmly through her. She could wait, for wasn't waiting and wishing and hoping the vine of life—in the life?

Mixing Business
With Pleasure

JUDITH STEIN

SHE HAS JUST FINISHED brushing her hair, and sits on the bed resting for a minute before she gets dressed. She hasn't had a single quiet moment all day to renew her self-esteem in the face of the world's hostility. Now, even though she knows she will be late, Claudine sits very still, reflecting on the pleasures to come.

She is about to meet her lover, Clotilde, for a special dinner. They are celebrating two things: the completion of Clotilde's long and difficult divorce, and the sale of Claudine's designs to a major couourier. Just the slightest hint of pride in her work begins to show on Claudine's face. She is doing very well, especially for such a newcomer.

Slowly Claudine relaxes, dropping the persona she must project every moment of her work day. She begins to release the tension that tightens her body, remembering that at home she needn't prove herself to anyone. In the fashion world she must prove herself constantly: as a woman without money or connections, and especially as a fat woman, designing beautiful clothes for fat women.

Brushing her hair, Claudine smiles as she remembers the first day she met Clotilde. The ad looking for large models had run in *Le Monde*. Although Clotilde had sounded pleasant enough on the telephone, her lack of modelling experience had made Claudine hesitate to set up an appointment. But Clotilde's self-assurance had convinced Claudine to take the chance. She had not regretted that decision for a single moment.

She could still picture every detail of Clotilde's arrival at the salon. As she heard the door open, Claudine looked up to see a stunning middle-aged woman. As Clotilde introduced herself, Claudine extended her hand and mumbled her name. All the while, she stared with professional admiration at the woman in front of her. And, to be honest, with more than just a little lust.

Clotilde was just under six feet tall, with short-cropped, wavy black hair streaked with silver. Her fair skin was emphasized by thick black eyebrows and long eyelashes which framed eyes of the deepest brown. She was quite large, perhaps 300 pounds, and carried herself with the assurance of a woman who knows her own beauty. Her full-cut, teal-blue cotton trousers and tailored ivory silk blouse might have been too severe on someone else, but they seemed to emphasize the natural beauty of Clotilde's face and figure. She wore no make-up, and little jewelry.

Claudine gestured towards the seating area, but she had no memory of performing the social amenities. For a few minutes, there was an awkward silence, finally broken by Claudine's stammered apology for staring. Then, without intending to, she blurted, "But you are even more beautiful than my fantasies. . . ." As Clotilde blushed and looked away, Claudine recovered her composure. She knew the signs of her own infatuation, and struggled to suppress the heat rising within her.

Claudine blushed at the memory of what followed, and that sudden heat startles her back into the present. As she notices the time, she knows she should finish dressing immediately, but a quiet dreaminess keeps her seated on the bed, remembering the slow beginnings of her love affair.

She had asked Clotilde a few questions about her previous work, her interest in modelling, and then had asked her to stand and walk across the room. Clotilde's walk was so poised that Claudine began to think she had found the perfect model for her new designs. Asking Clotilde to sit, stride, turn, and bend produced only graceful, easy movements. Claudine became suspicious of Clotilde's supposed lack of experience, and fearing a spy, asked her sharper questions about her previous work. Finally, Clotilde sighed, and said, "I must tell you the truth, I see. I really haven't worked as a model before, but I used to be a dancer. You see, before I married I worked as an exotic dancer in a burlesque show in Montmartre." She paused, looking at the floor, "Oh, I might as well say it all...before I married, I worked as a stripper. I think that's why I'm so comfortable presenting my body as a model would."

Claudine felt a sharp pang and realized how upset she was to hear that this beautiful woman was married. She chastized herself for letting her fantasy life run wild, and gave herself the usual lecture about how her personal life must come second to her work.

At the same time, Claudine began to talk to Clotilde, to reassure her that her previous work was an asset, not a liability. She told Clotilde how difficult it had been to find fat women who were good models, how impressed she was with Clotilde's self-confidence and self-assurance, how elegant she thought her designs would look on Clotilde. Realizing she was babbling, Claudine excused herself for a moment, ostensibly to get a drawing.

She returned a few moments later, all business. She remained cool and business-like throughout the interview. Clotilde's experience was perfect; Claudine was thrilled when Clotilde accepted the job.

Claudine had made the right decision; Clotilde was a wonderful model whose presentation greatly enhanced Claudine's designs. As they worked together over the drawings, with the seamstress, or in a showing, theirs became a highly complementary relationship. Buried deeply under her cool professionalism, Claudine's passion grew feverishly, but she let no hint of this show to the woman she assumed to be happily married.

For almost six weeks their partnership developed, with a speed and comfort at which they both marveled. Claudine was happy, certainly happier with her work than she had ever been. She began to hope that this could continue for a very long time, and secretly, despite her better judgement, made long-term plans for the salon which included Clotilde. It all seemed so perfect until that day almost a year ago when Clotilde burst into tears, and bolted towards the door. "Claudine," she sobbed, "I am too miserable. I simply cannot continue this way. . . ." Claudine was shocked into silence as she watched the weeping Clotilde run from the salon.

Looking back now, things must have happened quickly, yet Claudine couldn't forget the agony of her emotions those next long days. Clotilde did not return, and there was no answer when Claudine telephoned, even in the early morning. Claudine's concern grew with each passing hour. She decided that she must put aside her horror of meeting Clotilde's husband; she simply had to see her again.

Claudine drove to Clotilde's apartment. The first two rings of the doorbell produced no response. After the third ring, she heard Clotilde's voice, small and tinny through the intercom. Claudine's words tumbled out, "Clotilde, it's me, Claudine, I just had to come. I've been so worried about you, there's been no answer when I telephoned. I care for you so much. I haven't slept, I keep seeing you in tears running from the salon. I haven't been able to work. . . I must know what is wrong, I'll do anything for you to return to the salon. Clotilde, what is it, please, you must tell me. . . .Clotilde, please. . . . Clotilde?"

Panic overtook Claudine as she realized that Clotilde wasn't listening at the intercom. As she turned to pound on the door, she berated herself for hiding her true feelings, thinking perhaps she had been too cold. Then she berated herself for having had those feelings, fearing that Clotilde had been frightened away by a passion which she had unsuccessfully hidden. As she raised her fist to begin knocking, she saw Clotilde rushing down the stairs toward the door.

Clotilde opened the inner door, and pulled Claudine into the building. Tears were streaming down her face. "You said you care for me," she cried, "but I had no inkling of your feelings. Even now, I don't know what you mean. I only know that I'm in love with you, and you've never given me the slightest hope that you might return my feelings." She sobbed, and took a deep breath, "That's why I ran away from the salon, because the agony of being so close to you without touching you, without kissing you, without. . .ah, Claudine, I couldn't bear it. . . ." Clotilde's words stopped, but her tears continued.

In one brief moment Claudine realized what Clotilde was saying, and she, too, began to weep. But her tears were mixed with laughter as she pulled Clotilde into her arms. "Clotilde, I've been in love with you from the first moment you entered my salon. But you said you were married, and I made myself hide my passion for fear of driving you away. I told myself that business must come first, that you were too important to the salon to risk our work together. Perhaps I seemed cold then, I only know that I burned with a passion for you which I struggled to ignore. Ah Clotilde, the effort was so great. . .I've wanted you so much, I had no idea that you were wanting me."

As their tears mingled, their embrace became more heated, until Clotilde finally said, "My darling, will you come upstairs with me now. May we begin again? I have no husband anymore, I have only myself, and my love for you. . . ." Claudine nodded, and arms entwined, they began the climb upstairs, their love and desire climbing with them.

Deep in her memory of those next glorious days, Claudine is startled into the present by the doorbell's insistent ring. She pulls on her red silk slip, and runs to greet Clotilde. As they meet in a passionate embrace, memories of past pleasures fade to make room for the delights of the present.

Why The Milky Way
Is Milky

KITTY TSUI

A LONG TIME AGO when the mountains were young there were two friends who dwelt in a cave by the side of a river. Crane Woman and Dragon Woman had lived together for many years in a wilderness world of animals and birds, rock and water. They passed the days swimming the deep pools and racing up and down the familiar slopes of the mountain. Dragon Woman could fly on the wings of the wind, and the two friends would take trips to the ocean and lands far from their mountain home.

For nourishment they made love in cool pockets of moss under redwoods and drank the pure water of the river. On some days they ate fruit: oranges, melon and kiwi. For companionship they had each other and traded stories and songs with hawk and raccoon, hummingbird and coyote.

Summer was passing. Leaves turned red, yellow, and brown and fell from the limbs of trees like rain. Only the magnificent evergreens

285

remained verdant on the mountainside. Mornings and nights became bitterly cold. Crane Woman and her friend, who was also called Siew Lung, stayed inside the cave. The nights grew longer and colder. The sun rarely showed her face. The two friends stayed close together, warm on their bed of pine needles.

"In all the time I have lived, I cannot remember a time as cold as this," said Crane Woman, burrowing deeper into the bed. "Even my feathers do not help."

"Sweet Crane Woman, would you like me to give you some heat?"

Crane Woman replied with a smile and turned onto her stomach. Siew Lung blew air onto her hands and rubbed her long fingers together vigorously. Then, with lightning speed, she rubbed her hands up and down the length of her friend's body from her toes to her shoulders. She did this until she was exhausted. Then she lay down beside her friend and sank into sleep.

Crane Woman lay awake throughout the night. Though her body was warm from Siew Lung's touch, she did not understand why she felt cold; she had slept through many a chilly month. She even toyed with the thought of flying somewhere for the winter, knowing it might not be possible for her to survive a journey through the cold air. She fell asleep at dawn and dreamt of the sun beating down on her body.

The next weeks were hard ones for Crane Woman. Wind whipped the mountainside. The days became as cold as the nights. Siew Lung, being a creature of the air as much as of the land, did not feel the biting cold. Crane Woman could not go outside, she could not sleep and she had no appetite to eat. Soon she grew pale and listless. Dragon Woman unearthed some walnuts from their storage place and juggled them in the air.

"Look, see this! Now look, one hand!" she called in a voice as bright as stars.

"My friend," whispered Crane Woman, "something feels not right. I am always cold and I cannot sleep. I have no dreams. What is wrong?"

Siew Lung could not answer her. She could only hold her close.

The next day Dragon Woman awoke from her dreams to an unusual calm. Except for the voice of the river, all was quiet. The wind had died down. She rolled over, looked at her friend and was relieved to see that she was asleep. She yawned, stretched, and sat up in bed. She tried to recall her dreams but they were too vague. She got up and walked to the mouth of the cave. She was startled to see a strange tree with three bare limbs silhouetted against the sky. Siew Lung blinked to be sure she was not in a dream.

The tree had no leaves and the bark was peeling off in long, curly slivers. Siew Lung reached to touch one but it broke off into her hand. She drew it close to her face to examine. As she did so, one end of the bark glowed bright orange, and a sensation of warmth traveled up her fingers. She waved it in the air. With each movement she felt warmth from the glowing tip.

Overjoyed with her discovery, she ran inside. Crane Woman had not stirred. Siew Lung did not wake her. Instead, she waved the glowing bark close to her friend's face. Currents of warmth pulsated in the air. Crane Woman opened her eyes.

"Look at this! I found it growing outside. It gives off warmth. Here, see!" said Siew Lung excitedly. Crane Woman reached toward it and touched the glowing tip. She immediately cried out and jerked away her hand.

"Eeeehh, it hurts!" she shouted.

"Don't touch that end. Here, hold it like this. Feel the warmth!" Crane Woman took it gingerly. It glowed from the movement.

"I don't feel cold," she exclaimed, running it along one arm.

"There's more outside, enough to keep you warm all winter!" shouted Dragon Woman as she ran outside.

When Siew Lung came back inside the cave, she found Crane Woman blowing on the bark.

"Look, this lights it up too!"

They both laughed. Dragon Woman was glad to see her friend lively for the first time. Crane Woman held the bark to the light and looked through one end, then the other. With the tip away from her, she held it up to her lips and blew. Warmth came whistling out.

"Siew Lung, if I can blow warm air out, I can suck warm air in! Then my inside will be warm too!"

"Wait," cautioned her friend. Something did not feel right to her.

"I am cold inside," Crane Woman insisted, "as cold as if my heart were left out in the night." And with that she put the bark to her lips and inhaled deep.

Siew Lung was so startled by the sight in front of her that she jumped to her feet. Crane Woman's chest was lit up like a cloud passing in front of the sun. Dragon Woman could see her spine and her rib cage.

"Aiiieee!" she screamed.

As Crane Woman exhaled, smoke came out of her mouth. She closed her eyes and smiled, "I am warm, so warm."

Quick as lightning, Siew Lung snatched away the bark and told her friend what she had seen.

"But it feels good. I am warm for the first time. You know I was suffering. This is from a tree, you say. It is of the earth. How can it be bad?"

Siew Lung did not know how to answer her friend. Something bothered her but she did not know what.

"Why don't you use it close to your body," she said as she reluctantly handed it back.

"It heats me from the inside out and I feel so much better," replied her friend, inhaling with relish.

"There, see yourself," Siew Lung said.

Unconcerned, Crane Woman replied, "I feel so good."

The cold remained unchanging. The days passed but things were not the same. Crane Woman stayed in bed with the bark.

"Come with me to the river. The sun is shining. Our bird friends say they miss you."

"I am happy to stay here. I am warm, I am happy. Have some of this with me." She held out a piece of bark to Siew Lung.

"No," she snapped. "It is not good. See what it does to your chest."

Crane Woman shrugged. "It is good. It keeps me happy." She turned her back on her friend and continued her daily ritual of smoking the bark.

Siew Lung took some empty gourds and walked to the river. She was worried about her friend but she did not know why. Everything seemed clear: Crane Woman was sick with cold, the tree appeared, the bark gave warmth. But she did not like the way her friend had become, always in bed with a distant look on her face and a fixed smile on her lips. They no longer shared each other's warmth and conversation. She could not understand the change in her friend. She picked up a stone and threw it into the air, straining to hear the sound of it crashing through the trees. But all was quiet except for the river. Then she thught she heard the sound of many voices whispering: "Firebark, danger, danger."

Summer came at last; the days were long and the sky clear. Siew Lung walked alone on the mountain. Crane Woman would not leave the bed or the bark.

"It is hot," said Dragon Woman, "why do you still use the bark?"

"It makes me happy. I don't have to go outside. I am happy here."

"Don't you miss the rainbow? The air after rain? Your friends, deer and sunflower?"

"No, dear friend, I have them right here." Crane Woman closed her eyes.

Siew Lung surfaced from the water and tossed the hair from her eyes. She climbed onto a huge white rock and dove into the river. Underwater was green and clear. Sun on the surface threw webs of light onto the riverbed. She swam strong, seldom surfacing for air. She swam round and around, on the surface and underwater.

Siew Lung surfaced from the water and lay on the shore. Soon she drifted into sleep. She dreamt of a purple koi in a turbulent river, swimming upstream.

◆

Crane Woman was jerked from sleep by a fit of coughing. Her chest was tight and gripped by spasms. She lifted a heavy hand and brushed the hair from her face. Her head felt as if it were made of wet clay. Her mouth was dry and her memory was a blank. Where was she? Why did she feel so drowsy and sluggish? She coughed again, tried to swallow, couldn't, and started to choke.

Siew Lung ran in, pulled Crane Woman to a sitting position and thumped her on the back.

"You are not well, my friend, you sound terrible."

"What is wrong? I cannot breathe."

"It is the smoke, the firebark. You must stop. You are a changed person, not the little crane I met and loved."

"I need the bark. It will make me well. Get me some."

"No," replied her friend firmly, "no more bark."

Crane Woman struggled to get up. "I want the bark . . ." She got to her feet, took three steps and fell to the floor. Siew Lung picked her up and settled her back into bed. She got water, wiped her face and forced her to drink. Siew Lung worried frantically about what to do. All of a sudden, she heard voices saying: "Follow the koi, follow the koi."

While Crane Woman slept, Siew Lung filled gourds with water. She cut some rosemary from the bush next to the firebark tree and tied the sprigs around her waist. On impulse she also took some bark from the tree. When her friend woke up, Dragon Woman told her they were going on a journey. Despite her protests, Siew Lung took her friend on her back and leapt into the air.

After traveling for some time, Dragon Woman sighted a grassy area and stopped to rest. Crane Woman looked pale and felt cold as a rock.

"I need the bark. I am cold. I will freeze."

Siew Lung took a piece of bark and waved it along her friend's body.

"Give it to me. My inside is cold."

"I cannot. You are sick from smoking the bark."

"No, I am cold from flying in the air. Give me the bark. This cold is hurting me," she cried.

Crane Woman's voice made Siew Lung grow soft toward her, but she did not relent.

"It is your fault I am cold. What are we doing here? Where are we going? I was warm and happy in the cave. Why did you drag us out here?" She started to cry and beat her hands on her friend's back.

"You are not well. We are going to find a cure."

"Let me have the bark and I will be warm and well. Have some with me, then you will know."

Dragon Woman stayed firm. Night fell heavy on two distant friends.

The next day Crane Woman refused to continue.

"I am cold. I never wanted to leave the cave. Go if you wish. I will stay here."

"Little crane, you cough all night long. Your skin is white from not seeing the sun. Please, come with me," she begged.

"Where to?"

"To a place upstream."

"I am tired and I want to go home. If you want me to go, give me the bark."

"No, no bark."

"Then go alone," snapped Crane Woman in a voice as cold as ice.

Siew Lung wanted to cry. She did not know what to do. In all their years together they had never fought. She walked to the river and sat on a rock. She closed her eyes and listened to the river-song. After a while she heard a strange gurgling sound. She opened her eyes and saw a purple koi floating belly-up in the water close to her feet. She reached into the water and turned the fish over. She saw bubbles of air coming from the koi's mouth.

"What is wrong?" She put her head into the water and strained to hear against the sound of the rushing river.

"I am sick," came a small voice.

"What can I do?" offered Siew Lung.

"You must take me to God's Hand or I will die."

"Where is God's Hand?"

"Follow the river. . ." The fish could not continue.

Dragon Woman ran back to her companion and told her of the koi.

"You want to help a dying fish? What about me?" Crane Woman retorted.

"Let us take the koi to the place of God's Hand. Then we will see."

Her friend agreed reluctantly. "But," she said, "I will not speak to you until you let me have the bark."

Siew Lung took one of their gourds and broke off the top. They went to the river and scooped the koi into the bowl. Following the river, they flew in silence. When night fell, they stopped to rest.

"Speak to me, my friend, I feel so alone. Why do you cut me off?"

But Crane Woman would not speak.

The next day they flew on. After a time, Dragon Woman decided to change the water in the bowl. When she did so, the koi, who had been very still the whole way, started moving her tail. Siew Lung shouted with glee.

"Look, little crane, the koi is stirring. And this water is warm!"

Her stubborn friend stuck to her silence.

They walked on in shallow water that became warmer and warmer. All of a sudden, they approached a place of great beauty. A sheer cliff face rose to the sky. Two huge bowls were cut out of the rock, and water ran from the larger to the smaller. It was as if God had stretched her arm down from the sky and scooped out the rock with her hand. The water was very warm. Dragon Woman lowered the purple koi into the water.

"We are here," she said. The fish slipped into the water. It seemed to Siew Lung that the koi suddenly grew in size.

"Kind one, I thank you for my life," the koi said. "Before I take my leave, I wish to ask another favor."

"What is it? I will do anything you want."

"First you must get a sharp stone."

Dragon Woman hunted around and found a pyramid-shaped stone with a jagged edge. She returned to the river.

"Take me in your hand and turn my belly to the sky. Say a prayer of thanks to the wind. Then take the stone and cut me open."

Siew Lung gasped. "I cannot." She dropped the stone into the water and turned to find Crane Woman. But she was nowhere to be seen.

"But, koi, I cannot do what you ask."

"Siew Lung, you must."

Dragon Woman looked at the fish. "You are beautiful. You are alive. You are my friend. I cannot cut you open."

The koi swam around the woman, her purple body glistening in the sun.

"You say you are my friend. Then you must prove your friendship by trusting me. Do what I ask you."

Siew Lung picked up the stone. She took the koi and held her to her stomach. She took a deep breath and whispered a prayer. Then she took the stone and slit open the fish. From out of the belly jumped many koi with white bellies: orange and black koi, golden koi, purple koi. Dragon Woman dropped to her knees and let out loud whoops of joy.

Crane Woman had been sulking and silent for days. She craved the bark but could not get it. High above her she saw an indentation in the cliff wall. Feeling an urge to release her pent-up frustration, she scaled the cliff. Its face was sheer but pitted with holes. She climbed slowly, her breathing hard and irregular, sweat running from her pores. She had never felt so tired and weak; the firebark was taking its toll on her body. She looked up and saw the hollow place within reach. All of a sudden, her foothold gave way. She grabbed at an out-jutting rock and hung suspended in the air.

Crane Woman hung from her fingers high above the water, straining to keep a hold on the ledge. She opened her mouth to shout for Siew Lung, but no sound came from her lips. Suddenly, she felt herself slipping. Her life passed in front of her: her mother, her friend, herself. I cannot die, she thought. I will stop smoking the firebark. I must live, I must live. With a mighty effort, she hoisted herself up onto the ledge and collapsed in a heap.

The hollow place was dry and warm as a nest. Crane Woman closed her eyes and heard the riversong. After a while she thought she heard the sound of many voices singing in harmony. She opened her eyes and looked around her. There was not a bird or a creature in sight. She could not even see her friend. She closed her eyes. Again she heard the sound of many beautiful voices. Music engulfed her being, and before she knew it, she was singing too.

Dragon Woman held the skin of the koi in her hand. She tied it around her waist with the rosemary. High above her, she saw her friend. She felt a strong urge to wave and shout but instead dove head-first into the rushing water.

Music engulfed her being. Crane Woman sang as she had never sung before. Her lungs opened and filled with song. Her head cleared and her heart soared in the sky. Her whole being radiated with warmth. Before she knew it, a new chant was spilling from her lips: *azu, azu, azu.*

Siew Lung was floating on her stomach when she heard a clear, strong voice singing a chant. She turned over and saw Crane Woman high above her. She waved both arms. Her friend waved back. Then Crane Woman leapt into the air. Her body arched, straightened out and disappeared like an arrow into the river.

The two friends found each other in the water and surfaced together.

"I heard voices up there," Crane Woman said excitedly, "beautiful voices singing. Then I heard a chant. And when I repeated the chant, something told me it was my name. Siew Lung, I was given a name!"

"What is it?" asked Dragon Woman.

"Azu."

"Azu!" Siew Lung shouted, "Azu, Azu, Azu!"

They laughed. Azu took Siew Lung in her arms. They kissed and held each other for a long time. Azu touched Siew Lung's breasts, lingering over each nipple. She turned her onto her stomach and kissed her back. She caressed the inside of her thighs. They made love for a long time on the banks of the river and fell asleep at dawn.

They stayed by God's Hand for many moons. Azu soaked in the warm water and lay in the sun. She slowly regained her color and her spirit. On some days she craved the firebark but resisted the temptation, knowing how it slowed her spirit and changed her person. She sang her chant every day in the high place above the river. The scorching dry pain inside her chest felt less intense. She slept without coughing.

One morning black clouds darkened the sun. Wind shook the trees and rain poured from the sky. Siew Lung had flown off earlier in the day and had not yet returned. Azu ran for cover from the cold rain. A gust of wind chilled her to the bone. Suddenly, she thought of the warmth of the firebark inside her. She ran to the place under a rock where they had stored it. She withdrew a sliver and held it to her lips. The bark glowed red. She felt its warmth. She was about to inhale but stopped in mid-air. I cannot do it, she thought, I almost died that day on the cliff. I made a promise to myself. The water is healing me. Quickly she replaced the bark and ran to the river. She dove in and warmth enveloped her.

The sky cleared. All of a sudden, a huge bird dropped from the sky and landed on the water by Azu. It was a magnificent creature with orange and yellow feathers. On its head were three long red plumes.

"Greetings," said Azu. "I have never seen a creature as beautiful as you."

"I am Phoenix," replied the bird, "here with a message. The spirits of the sky gave you the firebark tree so you could be warm. Now they want something from you."

"I will surely give them whatever they wish."

"The white feathers that cover your body."

Azu froze in shock. "My feathers?"

"Yes. Go to the high place on the cliff and make your offering."

"But they are part of my body. How can I give them up?"

"Your friend, the dragon, will know." And with that, the bright bird flew off.

When Dragon Woman returned, Azu told the story. Siew Lung did not speak.

"What shall we do? The phoenix said you would know. Tell me, why do you not speak?"

Dragon Woman went to her friend. "Maybe we can pull out the feathers without hurting you. Let us try it." She took a long feather in her hand and pulled. Azu screamed in pain. Still the feather would not loosen from her body.

"Little crane, I have something to tell you." Siew Lung told of the purple koi and how she had slit her open. The two friends fell silent. Finally Azu said, "Let us sleep close this night. When morning comes, we will go to the hollow place."

When the sun rose over the cliff, Azu embraced her friend.

"Siew Lung, I will love you for all eternity."

Dragon Woman hugged her tight. "I love you as I love myself. How can I do this?" Tears flooded her eyes.

"We must trust in our love, then," Azu replied. She kissed her again.

They both stood on the edge of the high place overlooking the river. Siew Lung held the sharp stone with a shaking hand.

"I love you forever," Azu whispered and closed her eyes.

Dragon Woman stood over her, stone poised and ready. In a quick movement the stone sliced into her friend's breast. The feathers fell from Azu in a heap to the ground. Azu opened her eyes. Her body was smooth of feathers. She had no wound where Siew Lung had plunged the stone.

The two friends stood in the high place together and sang their joy. Azu held the feathers outstretched in her arms. Then she threw them up into the air. A mighty wind roared and carried the white feathers high into the sky.

And that, my friends, is why the Milky Way is milky.

Two Willow Chairs

JESS WELLS

THIS IS A LESBIAN PORTRAIT, I tell my friends, pointing at the photo in a silver frame on my desk, but they don't understand. To them, it's just a snapshot of two empty chairs, and they cock their heads at me, wondering why the photo has a place of honor and the chairs are the subject of such elaborate plans.

I took the picture when I was 17, which made the chairs brand new, my mother's sister Ruth and her lover Florence in their fifties, and their relationship in its fifteenth year. Flo's chair is made of willow branches, twisted into locking half moons, a rugged chair that somehow looks like filigree. Next to it on their lawn—a secluded, overgrown stretch of grass and overhanging vines—is Ruth's willow chair, a simpler one with a broad seat and armrests that circle like a hug. All around the chairs are flower beds, usually gone to seed, and grass that was "never properly cut," my step-father would growl in the car on the way home from visits, grass thick like fur that Flo

299

would wiggle her toes in, digging into the peat until her feet were black and she would hide them inside their slippers again.

The year of this snapshot, Aunt Florence was "struck with spring" as she used to say to me. We arrived on the Fourth of July to find blooming peonies and iris and marigold ("always marigold against the snails," she would whisper to me, as if imparting the wisdom of womanhood). Florence and my mother wandered the garden, pointing at stalks and talking potting soil, promising cuttings to each other and examining the grape vines up the trellis, while Ruth and my step-father faced each other silently, she slumped in the willow chair like a crest-fallen rag doll and he sitting rigid, twisted sideways on the plastic webbing of a broken chrome chair. I wandered the yard alone with the garden hose. After ten minutes of listening to the women's voices but not hearing anything, Ruth got up and slouched into the house to start bringing out the beers, calling in an overly-loud voice, "So, Dick" (everyone else called him Richard), "how's business?"

Talking commerce was a great diversion for him, and my mother was already occupied with explaining her begonias, which left me to be the only one in the place grappling with the realization that this lesbian child was being deposited for the summer with the family's lesbian aunts because a new step-father, two brothers and a male cat were more than I could possibly stand. It was the first of many such summers, visits that after a few years turned into summers with autumns and then special Christmases and soon all important holidays and all important matters of any kind. That first summer, nervously pacing the backyard, I knew it would develop into this and when my parents finally left, Ruth and Florence and I stared at each other with wonderment. They'd never had a family before and all of a sudden they had a daughter, full-grown and up in their faces feeling awkward. Since my mother was straight, there was something I could dismiss about her, but here were these two, with the weight of maturity *and* the righteousness of twenty years of lesbian lifestyle behind them. Now *that's* what I considered authority.

Aunt Ruth breathed a sigh of relief after the car had pulled out of the drive. Florence let some of her gaiety drop but turned to me, ready to fulfill her last social obligation of the day.

"Beetle," as she had called me since the time I was a baby with big eyes, "Welcome." There was so much hesitancy in her voice, fear almost, as if this child, who did not really know about being a lesbian, were looking at a lesbian who did not really know about being in a family. I dropped the garden hose and wiped my hands on my pants, trying to smooth my carrot-red hair that was frizzy in six different directions. Florence strode over and gathered me in her arms.

"I don't know about these chairs," Ruth said, getting up and yanking one out of the grass. "Let's take them back by the trellis," she said to me, "Florence's favorite spot." And we all grabbed chairs, me taking my mother's chrome one since it was known to all but Richard that his was the only broken chair in the place. We settled into the afternoon, our conversation picking up pace while Florence shuttled lemonade and beers. That's when I got my first photo of the chairs.

Ruth was sitting sideways, her leg slung over the arm of the chair, head thrown back, her whole big body lit by a streak of afternoon sun. Florence was struck by spring only in selected places, and the back of the yard was not one of them: the grape vines behind Ruth's head dangled low and free, the grass crept up around her chair even though it was early in the season.

We had become very quiet for a moment and Ruth turned in her chair to talk privately to Florence. My camera caught her in midsentence, her mouth open, hand reaching for her lover's knee, her eyes still not aware that Aunt Flo was in the house and that she and I were alone. Her face showed all the tenderness, history, trust in her femme as she turned to ask, "Wren, what was the name of that. . . ."

Ruth looked back at me. "I wish you'd quit with that camera," she growled weakly as I laid the photo on the tops of the tall grass to develop, already sensing that I had exposed her. And in a way, she was right. Until then, I had used this camera as a form of self-defense, silently proving to my brothers that they looked stupid, threatening to catch them in the act, snapping photos of my mother as if to prove to myself that she wasn't just a phantom woman. But this day, this photo of Ruth and the empty willow chair was the first photo I had ever taken in an attempt to preserve something beautiful.

I handed the photo to Florence first as she returned with two beers and a lemonade. She stared at it a long time, seeing the look on Ruth's face.

"Oh God, Wren, get rid of that! I look like a jerk," Ruth protested, but Florence held the photo close to her.

"You look wonderful. Besides, I want a photo of my chairs. Here Beetle, take a picture of the chairs for me. Rudy, get up. God, I wish the garden looked better."

Florence kept the two photos in her jewelry box for years. The two willow chairs stayed in their places in the back of the yard and whenever I would visit (on leave from the Army, or home from another city) we would first convene at the chairs, even during the winter when we would huddle in big coats, and share important news like a ritual before rushing inside for the evening.

Years later, when Florence gave the photos to me, there was one take of myself and Flo sitting on a porch step, our pant legs rolled up from gathering mussels in the tidepools. Florence is gesturing to me, her arms in the shape of a bowl.

"Now look, honey," she said that day, "don't give up. Love is just a matter of the right recipe: a cup and a half of infatuation, a pinch of matching class status, two tablespoons of compatible politics and three generous cups of good sex. Mix. Sprinkle liberally with the ability to communicate and fold into a well-greased and floured apartment. You bake it for at least six months without slamming the door and pray you have love in the morning. And it works—when you've got the right ingredients."

Of course their relationship was a serious one, so I have photos of times when the recipe wasn't quite right with the two of them, either. In the package with the other photos is a black and white from the 50's of Florence in a wool suit and a hat with a veil, standing at the rail of an ocean-liner. She and Ruth put all the money they had into a ticket for her to go to Europe and even though it was the best trip she'd ever taken, she looks miserable in the picture. The veil is down over her face, almost to her lips that are thick with lipstick, and she's wearing kidskin gloves but not waving. She looks very tight and cold to me in this picture, but Ruth liked how smart Flo looked. Aunt Florence would stand in front of it, holding my hand (even though I was home on leave for the third and last year) and say, "Beetle, I keep it because it reminds me of when I was less frightened of running and being alone than of staying and loving." She turned to me, one hand on her hip. "Now isn't that ridiculous, to think that it's less scary to have a lousy relationship than a good one? That intimacy is more terrifying than loneliness. God, the world is so crazy, Beetle. It's like saying garbage is more delectable than food." Well, I stood in front of that photo with her, looking up at her glowing face, then back at the picture of that sunken young thing and it seemed her face now wasn't wrinkled by age, just stretched from being so open. I thought about my latest crush in the barracks and how good Florence's choice seems to have been (after all, here was home and warmth and Ruth lounging on the sofa throwing cashews to the dog), but I looked back at that picture, those eyes big and scared and I knew that's where I was, a veil over *my* face. I turned from my aunt and thought, 'Oh Jesus, somebody send me a ticket and point me towards the ocean.'

Ruth kept the photo at her side of the bed, as if to remind herself of how far Florence had run and how close she now lived.

On Florence's side of the bed was a photo taken the summer after she returned. The two are in funny brown swimsuits with pointed bras, Ruth sleeping in Florence's arms. Flo is bending to kiss her on the neck and years later, she related to me that, lying in the sand with her lover in her arms, Florence could feel the years passing. She could feel Ruth getting older even though she was in her thirties, feel her getting heavier through middle age, belly growing across her hips, feel her shift in her sleep from an injury to her shoulder that she didn't have yet, see the scars she would have in the future, Ruth getting smaller and more frail as she aged, wrinkling into buttery skin. And all the time, holding Ruth encircled in her arms, Florence knew that this would be the progress of her world, that this was her future and her life, that this woman between her arms was her home.

Of course Flo had pictures of her Mom and Dad, who have been dead for nearly two decades now, and the family at picnics, Ruth playing horseshoes on her sixtieth birthday and pictures of me when I was a kid with teeth missing, though we won't go into that. There's another lesbian portrait in this stack from Flo—it's a picture of a dog.

Clarise was the spaniel Florence had when she was lovers with the woman before Ruth (which is how she was always referred to, she never had a name) and Flo kept the photo on top of the television for years after she had left the woman and the dog. The little thing was sitting attentively on the beach, clumps of dirt hanging on its paws. It was the first dog Florence had ever learned to love, and every year, with a far-away look in her eyes, Flo would ramble on about how special and psychic and beautiful and protective it was. It was everything a dog should be. Just a few years ago, Ruth, sick and lying on the couch, threw off the afghan and snatched the photo off the T.V.

"For Godsake, Florence, it's over, and it's okay that it's over," she shouted, starting to cough. "The dog wasn't the only thing good and the woman wasn't the only thing bad. Now c'mon."

Florence went into the back yard and sat in her willow chair. It was her 70th birthday and she should have a jacket on, I thought.

"Stay here, Beetle," Ruth said.

"I don't see why you're jealous of a dog, Rudy. For Christsake, it was years ago."

"I'm not jealous. Florence doesn't know what to do with all those years she spent with that woman and so she puts them here," she said, tapping the glass frame. "When you're consumed with bitterness, where do you put all the good times? The dog. The only reason I'm even saying it is because she knows it herself. A couple of months ago, we went to Bolinas, remember the spot. . . .?"

"Where we used to gather mussels?"

"Right. Well, Wren thought the air would make me feel better or something, but who should come trotting up but the spitting image of that dog. Splatters mud all over Wren's newspaper, knocks the damn iced tea into the potato chips and rolls over to stick up her tits, I mean it. Well, it finally dawns on Wren, 'Goddamn, maybe that Clarise was just a fucking dog, too.' "

Now I have the photo of Clarise. I keep it with a bunch of others Florence gave me in a white, unmarked envelope. These are the painful pictures, the ones that bring floods of heat to your face, pictures you look at and smell perfume.

There's a picture of Florence pointing at the flowerbeds with her cane, trying to get *me* to be struck with spring and do some planting while we waited for Ruth to get well. Then there's Ruth lying on the couch covered with the afghan, looking tiny and angry, and after Ruth died, a photo of Florence looking remarkably like her picture in the hat with the veil. Florence never went back to the chairs, never went into the back of the yard, only stared at it from the kitchen window, stricken now that Ruth, love, hope and future were dead and decaying, confused by the sight of the grass and the flowers blooming, as if life were threatening to overtake her when she knew it was death that was the encroacher. The grape vines grew lower, entwining with the boughs of the willow chairs, as if threatening to scoop them into a cluster and throw them up to the sun to ripen, while the grass underneath fought to drown the chairs in green. I took a picture of the chairs last year in this condition but I conveniently lost it. I do have a snap of me, fifteen pounds thinner from not sleeping while Florence lay dying, and one of my Mom at Flo's wake, crying like she couldn't at Ruth's. Maybe someday I could frame them and hang them and still be able to walk through the room, but I doubt it. Right now all I can manage is that first snap of the two empty chairs. My friends don't understand it. Nor do they understand why I'm borrowing a truck and calling around for a hack-saw.

"I have to save the chairs," I tell them, slamming down the phone on my mother and dashing for my jacket. The house has been sold, finally, my mother tells me, and the new owners are sure to throw Wren and Rudy's chairs into the dump—if there's anything left of them. They were nearly part of the grape-vine forest last year when Florence died. First thing in the morning I'll cut the chairs away from the underbrush and drive them to a field near Bolinas. They can sit together and watch the unruly grass grow up around them, again.

We Didn't See It

BARBARA WILSON

GWEN WAS THE ONE everybody liked. She was short and chubby, with ringleted brown hair, round cheeks and innocent blue eyes, a natural performer. People looked up with a smile when she came into the room; they knew that she'd have some outrageous story, some hilarious joke to share, that her presence would lift and cheer them, make them remember the humor of being a woman, of being a lesbian.

"So I said to him." Pause. "What'd I say, honey? What would *you* have said? No, you're wrong. I didn't tell him to go stuff his balls in a garbage can and give it to the trash compactors. . . ." General laughter. "I said, I'm the assistant manager of this warehouse and if you keep sticking your little prick in my face, I'm going to put it in the paper-cutter and get rid of it for good." Gasps of hysteria.

"No, you didn't?"

"Hell, no man is going to push me around," she laughed, and

punched her right fist into the flat of her open left palm. Her hands were small and fat and ringed with intricately silver and turquoise bands. She waved them around a lot when she talked and was always punching herself playfully, the one hand into the other. It made a fast, threatening crack.

I admired her, but I didn't like her all that much. I guessed I was the only one who didn't.

I said to Miriam after a few visits to her new collective household, "I don't like the way Gwen talks to Amy."

Amy was Gwen's lover. She was tallish, quiet, studious-looking, with a brush of stiff blond hair and small, unobtrusive breasts. She was always wearing a different T-shirt, each one with a slogan about women or a women's event. Amy was friendly but remote, and at first I wasn't sure if she lived in the house or not. She smoked, and wasn't allowed to inside, so she was constantly slipping out to the front or back porch in the middle of conversations. Especially when Gwen was telling a story. "Goddamn cancer sticks," Gwen would throw after her, to the general amusement. "Well, don't think I'm going to take care of you when you get emphysema."

"Oh well," said Miriam, twining her long black hair around her wrist like a bracelet. "Couples, we all know how they get after a while. . . Amy probably doesn't like Gwen showing off. But she's so funny. I can't believe she talks like that to the guys at work. She's got spunk."

"Yes," I said, and nothing more. Miriam was new in the household and eager to be accepted. I was a recent friend of Miriam's and needed her approval.

Still, a week or so later, after spending the night with her for the first time, I said, "I heard Gwen just now, when I went to the bathroom. She was talking really loud, and her voice went on and on. . . I couldn't hear Amy." I paused and gazed, suddenly shy, at Miriam over in the bed. It was early morning and the light from the window settled on her face and shoulders like a soft yellow porcelain glaze. "Well, it just scared me somehow, that's all. The tone of it or something. . . ."

Miriam pulled the covers up and looked at me with sleepy exasperation. Her black hair hung over her shoulders in two ropes, touched with gold.

"Hey, come on, people have a right to their privacy, Diane. How do you know what they were talking about, arguing about? You shouldn't have listened, you wouldn't want anyone to listen to us, would you?"

"We haven't even had our first fight yet." I laughed uneasily and added, "I wasn't *really* listening. . . ." That wasn't true. I had heard the words quite clearly through the bathroom wall: "You goddamned lying cunt." And now they wouldn't leave me alone.

"What if it were a man?" I suddenly asked. "A man talking like that to a woman in this house?"

"Forget it, would you? Come on," Miriam said, and held out a hand to me, smiling. "There are no men here, thank god. Just lesbians."

After that I was often over at the house. I wasn't exactly in love with Miriam, but I thought she was beautiful, with her long black hair and green eyes, her forthrightness and challenging spirit. Here's a person I could fight with and feel good about it, I sometimes thought, remembering the sly digs and subtle jabs of Bev, the woman I'd been with for two years. But Miriam and I didn't fight, and I was just as glad. I didn't like fighting all that much.

It was summer and I was unemployed. Miriam, with a Ph.D. in Comparative Literature, got up early every morning to make croissants for a French bakery. It was pleasant to lie around in her cool dim bedroom after she left, reading her novels and books of essays, lingering in her scent, Hungary Water, she'd said it was. Later, I would sit on her front porch waiting for her to come home. I had plenty of time to get to know the women in the house: Nelda, the housepainter, Betty, the grad student, Karen, the waitress. I helped them water the lawn and weed the garden; they were always friendly and made me feel at home. Gwen did too.

Amy was the only one I couldn't get a handle on. I knew she worked with deaf children at a spacial school, and as far as I could tell, that's all she did, aside from smoke and listen and quietly clean up after the others.

"Here my Amy can sign and everything," Gwen said once, pushing Amy forward in the kitchen. "And she won't even think of volunteering to sign in concerts or lectures or anything. I tell her she's letting the women's movement down and she says she's *shy.*"

"It's the work I do all day," Amy protested mildly. "I want to do something different in the evening."

"If only you did!" Gwen seemed to be teasing; her blue eyes were merry, but her tone was sharp. "You let everyone else do the talking. Shy!" she repeated, throwing up her small fat hands so the turquoise and silver shivered under the light. "If I was like you the world would have run me over a long time ago. But then, I guess I didn't grow up on the Rancho Nuevo Estates, *my* father wasn't a bank vice-president...."

"I'm not shy," Amy said, and left the room for a cigarette.

"What do they see in each other? How did they ever get together?" I demanded later that evening. Miriam stood brushing her long hair in front of the mirror, dreamy.

"Opposites attract."

"Thank you, Professor."

Miriam laughed. "I suppose Amy calms Gwen down, lets her talk and act out. Gwen's under so much pressure at work—you've heard her stories, those guys are complete assholes, most of them. And she doesn't get support from the women either. But she won't quit, she won't back down. She's determined to control the situation. Of course it stresses her out." Miriam tugged at a knot, winced.

"So what does Amy get out of it?"

Miriam suddenly looked impatient. She threw down her brush and hopped into bed. "I don't know—excitement, maybe. Gwen's fun and lively to be around. How the hell should I know? You're always so fucking curious about other people. Leave them alone. They're together because they want to be. If they didn't want to be together, they wouldn't be."

"It's that simple, is it?"

"That's why we're together, isn't it?" Her lip curled up, ironic or nasty, I couldn't tell.

My heart pounded strangely, violently, and my skin flushed and froze. "Well, good-night then," I said, and turned out the light, getting in next to her.

We lay side by side and I smelled the sweet, nostalgic scent of Hungary Water.

"If you trusted me, would you fight with me?" Her voice floated above us like a balloon.

"I don't like to fight at night," I said. "It scares me."

It was the beginning of August. I'd been lovers with Miriam for a month. It had been exactly that long since I'd heard Gwen's raised voice through the bathroom wall. I hardly paid any attention to Amy now, made little or no attempt to get to know her. When Gwen made a crack about her I ignored it as the others did, keeping my uneasiness to myself. I had to admit that Gwen could be pretty funny sometimes.

I felt comfortable in the house, though Miriam and I had begun to have difficulties. We'd had our first fight, and then some. She thought I should get a job; she said it put too much responsibility on her. "I come home from work tired and want a little time alone. You've been doing nothing all day and want to go have fun."

"I've been working every summer for fifteen years," I defended myself. "I get laid off my job and decide to take a vacation. I can afford it, I deserve it. You sound like my mother."

"I feel sorry for your mother, that's all I can say."

"Yeah, well, what am I supposed to do—make croissants or something? I only have a B.A., maybe they wouldn't hire me."

"That's really below the belt, you know, that's really low of you. . . ."

Gwen passed by the half-open door of Miriam's bedroom and poked her ringleted brown head in. "Now, now, girls," she laughed. "So you're finally getting to be a couple. Congratulations. It's nice to see that other people have problems too."

I wanted to say, not like yours, and slam the door, but Miriam laughed and reached for my hand. I had the odd sensation that she was binding me to silence, that we were binding ourselves in a ceremony under the mocking, sympathetic gaze of Gwen.

"So, what do you think, Gwennie?" Miriam said. "When Nelda moves out, should we let this one here move in?"

It was the first time Miriam had suggested it and I should have felt pleased. I'd thought for a while that if I had a room in the house we'd both have more space, I wouldn't be so dependent. But somehow it didn't feel good to hear Miriam say it now, at this moment and in front of Gwen, especially when Gwen turned to me with her round face all smiles and said, "Yes, I think she'll fit right in."

Nelda left and I moved in later that month, and immediately everything began to go better between Miriam and me. She was offered a part-time teaching job for the fall and I started seriously reading the want ads. I felt more settled than I had since Bev and I had broken up, felt more certain that Miriam was committed to me and that I was to her.

Then, late one night, after Miriam had fallen asleep and I was going to the bathroom, I heard a voice coming out of Gwen and Amy's room. It was Gwen's voice, dry, hard, outraged, unstoppable.

And then, unmistakable, the words, "I'd like to kill you, bitch."

And equally as unmistakable, the sound of a fist cracking against flesh.

I didn't think about it. I threw open their door, saying, "No, please."

They were in bed, in pajamas. The table lamp was on; its small light illumined Amy, eyes closed, arms wrapped around her body.

Gwen said, "What the fuck are you doing in our room? Get out of here."

"You can't do this, Gwen."

"You just stay out of this. We're having a fight and it's none of your business." Her ringlets were askew on her head and her cheeks were flushed.

"But you hit Amy, you hit her, I heard you." I sounded almost hysterical. "I heard you."

"You're crazy," said Gwen, flatly and furiously. "Get out."

Amy didn't say anything. She suddenly got out of bed and walked past me, heading for the bathroom next door. I didn't dare touch her, stop her, hold her. Her face was as closed as a still-life behind glass; then I saw her eyes. Bewildered, ashamed, guilty, they caught mine and confirmed everything.

"You hit her," I said to Gwen again, my voice shaking. "You can't do that. You hurt her."

"What right have you to come barging into our bedroom in the middle of the night and tell us what to do? Have you got any idea what she said to me? You think she's so quiet and sweet, that's what everyone thinks. You don't know what she puts me through, it's emotional abuse, that's what it is. She was emotionally abusing me."

"You hit her," I said. "You called her a fucking bitch. You said you'd like to kill her."

"You goddamned spy," Gwen hissed, jumping out of the bed and beginning to cry. "You just heard me, you didn't hear her, you don't know what she did. I didn't hit her, you didn't see anything, we were just having a fight." She rushed towards me and I shrank back, but she was past and gone, down the hall, down the stairs and out the door. Her car started in the driveway.

I went to the bathroom door. "Amy," I whispered. "Amy?"

"I'll talk to you in the morning."

"But what if she comes back?"

"She won't come back tonight." Through the door her voice

sounded flat and distant. "Just leave me alone now, okay?"

I went back to Miriam's room, but she was deeply asleep. I turned off her lamp and went to my own bedroom. I was frightened but certain. Gwen had hit Amy and confirmed everything I knew was wrong about their relationship. Tomorrow I would talk to Amy, help her escape, move out, get out of the relationship and the house as fast as she could. I knew the others would support me, that they would be as shocked as I was as soon as I told them.

"It was really my fault," said Amy the next morning. We had walked down the street to a cafe for breakfast and she seemed willing, if not happy, to talk about it. "I know how sensitive she is about certain things, I just forgot. . . ."

Amy was wearing a Sweet Honey in the Rock T-shirt and her blond hair was slicked back damply. I felt as if I were seeing her for the first time: her clear, softly transparent skin, her wide, generous mouth, her warm hazel eyes. She would be good with kids, I thought, patient and kind.

". . . you know her warehouse job, and how bad it is. People can never find anything around there, they're always asking her. She's so tired of being asked where things are. Well, what happened is, she had given me a roll of film to be developed earlier in the evening, she'd sort of put it down next to me and said something, and I hadn't really been paying attention. So just as we were going to sleep, I said, hey, why didn't you give me that roll of film? That was such a stupid way to put it, I mean, it was as if I was doing what everyone at work does to her, making her feel crazy about where things are. See, I didn't just say, I don't remember—did you give me that roll of film today or not? I had to say, *Why* didn't you give me that roll of film today, like I was accusing her of not giving it to me. . . ."

"But Amy," I broke in. "She called you a fucking bitch, she said she'd like to kill you, she hit you."

Amy flinched slightly and looked down at her empty coffee cup and then over at the waitress. "We go back a long way," she said, as if in apology. "We've been together ten years, I cam out with her." Her hazel eyes were pleading. "I did something awful to her once, she can't forget. See, I slept with another woman, I had this affair, I *lied,* and she can't forgive me. She just gets worked up when she remembers. It's really my fault."

"I can't believe you're saying this," I exploded. "No one has the right to call you names and hit you, no matter what you've said or done."

"We went to a counselor once," said Amy, smiling gratefully at the waitress who filled her coffee cup. "I'm still going to her. I don't know—I've been going through kind of a depressed time, I guess. It's nothing to do with Gwen really, I love her, you know. It's just that I've been feeling bad about myself. I don't have any close friends, and I've sort of lost my momentum. I don't even know if I like my job anymore—it's so *silent.* But when I think of changing, I don't know. . . ."

"The reason you're unhappy is because you're in some kind of abusive relationship. You've got to get away from her."

Amy said nothing for a moment, then asked if I minded if she smoked. I asked if I could have one too. I'd given it up two years ago, but sometimes I still wanted one.

We smoked in silence, then she said, "I've thought about it sometimes, leaving. . . . I've thought about it because—because sometimes I'm afraid of her. Nobody else really sees that side of Gwen, they don't know how she can be sometimes. . . . Once, this is kind of funny, but anyway, we were in the car, I was driving and we were on our way to a potluck with some potato salad. And Gwen got mad about something I said and all of a sudden she threw the whole bowl of potato salad in my face. I couldn't see for a minute, I had to turn off the road. I was yelling at her too, she could have killed us. And it was a perfectly good salad, and then we couldn't go to the potluck." Amy laughed a little. "We call it the great potato salad war."

I felt cold all over. "It's not a joke, Amy."

"I know," she said. "I know, I should. . . . But she won't go to a counselor. . .she doesn't think anything is wrong. . . ."

"Then I'm going to talk to her," I said. "I'm going to tell her I won't stand to hear a woman called names and hit in the house where I live."

". . . And so," I finished, trying to stop my fingers from twisting themselves in my lap, my intestines from twisting in my abdomen, "it's just a personal decision I've made, to intervene in this situation, not to accept it. . . ." I stared almost imploringly at Gwen. "I can't accept it."

Her round face was kind, composed, as if she were a therapist listening to a hopelessly unaware client. By design I'd caught her alone in the house as soon as she came home from work and had forced my nervous prepared speech on her in the living room.

She nodded and smiled, but not in her usual jokey fashion. "There are a lot of things you don't understand, Diane," she said patiently, almost absent-mindedly, as she pulled a silver and turquoise band off one of her fingers and polished it on her sleeve. "Amy and I have a long history together. We recognize that we have a few problems and we're trying to work them out. When you've been together ten years like we have you have a tendency to push each other's buttons the wrong way. Amy just pushed my button, she can do that really easily—that's part of being a couple."

"But name-calling, violence," I interrupted, still not accusing her directly. I watched the fluid movements of her plump hands, watched how the silver and turquoise emphasized her gestures, finalized them somehow.

"When I called Amy from work today she told me that she was sorry she'd provoked me. I accepted her apology and I said I was sorry we'd had a fight, too. It was enough for me, it should be enough for you."

"You can't just hit people when they make you mad, you can't call them names."

"I want to tell you something, Diane," said Gwen, still in that eerily patient voice. "Amy has some real problems. Serious emotional problems. We were going to a counselor together to try to work things out and it just became apparent that Amy was in a deep, deep depression and that she really needed some professional help. The counselor said to me, Gwen, I see why you two have problems together, Amy has a lot to work out on her own—so she just started seeing Amy."

Had they told the counselor that Gwen hit Amy? I doubted it. My voice rose squeakily as I reiterated, "It's my personal decision. I'm going to intervene if this happens again. I won't live in a house where this is going on."

"And I'll just tell you to get the fuck out like I did last night," Gwen said firmly and flexed her hands so one of the big turquoise stones stood out like an extra knuckle. "I don't want to hurt your feelings, but I'll have to. What happens between me and Amy is private, just the way what happens between you and Miriam is private."

"It's not right," I said, like a child who keeps repeating the same answer even though the teacher had told her it's wrong. "I won't stand by and let it happen."

Gwen shrugged, weary of the discussion. "And I'll just tell you to get the fuck out."

The front door opened and Amy came in. She looked frightened, hesitant. Her T-shirt read, "A Room of One's Own," and had a silk-screened photo of the young Virginia Woolf.

"So come in already," said Gwen. "We're just finishing a little talk."

Amy avoided my eyes, went over to the stereo and started looking through the records.

"Put on Linda Tillery," Gwen said, and her voice was as cheerful as if nothing had happened.

I felt like a record myself, a record that's gotten stuck in the same place, that can only repeat the same refrain over and over until it seems to lose all meaning.

"It doesn't matter if you tell me to get the fuck out. I won't.

I'll stand there witnessing it, I'll try to stop it in any way I can, I'll tell other people. I won't ignore it. I won't stand to hear a woman called names and hit. I wouldn't allow it if it was a man doing it to a woman and I won't allow it if it's a woman."

Gwen didn't seem disturbed by Amy's presence; it seemed instead to make her more confident, as if she were certain Amy would support her. "Look, Amy told me she told you the story of what happened. She as much as accused me of lying about that roll of film. That's exactly the thing to push my button, and she knows it, too!"

"But you called her names, threatened to kill her. You hit her."

Amy said timidly, "It's really the names that hurt me."

And Gwen erupted. The calm patience that had ringed her anger snapped apart as she jumped up and screamed at Amy, "You lying bitch, you traitor. You told me you explained what happened to her, that it was your fault. You betrayed me, you traitor, you lying fucking bitch traitor."

Amy stood there, frozen, pleading, palms out. "Gwen, listen, I didn't, Gwen, I didn't. . . ."

But Gwen was gone, knocking over the rocking chair in her fury and haste to get out the door. Amy ran after her, ran out to the sidewalk, and down the block.

While I sat there, shaking.

Gwen didn't return home that evening. In the middle of the night she came and moved all her things out. Amy stayed. I don't know what was said between them.

Betty was shocked; she said she couldn't believe Gwen had really hit Amy. "Did you see it?" she kept asking me. "You know how Gwen punches her fist into her hand. It could have been that."

"I heard it. I didn't have to see it, I know what a punch sounds like."

Karen had been on a camping trip. After listening to the story on her return, she said, "And we never suspected anything!"

I wondered how true that could be; they had lived with Amy

and Gwen for months. "Didn't you ever listen to them?"

"Peoplee's fights are their own business. As long as they do it behind closed doors, who's going to pay attention?"

She looked guilty, then worried. "Does anyone know where Gwen has gone?"

Neither she nor Betty asked much about Amy, how she was feeling, if there was anything they could do for her. They didn't try to talk to her directly about it. They said things about being terribly sorry that it had all turned out like this. They didn't blame me specifically, but they made it clear I hadn't handled the situation very well.

Betty said, "Of course Gwen felt a little crazy when you said you were going to keep intervening. I'm sure she imagined you'd be standing over her all the time, watching her."

Miriam argued with me too, especially when I brought up the fact that we wouldn't stand to hear a man abusing or hitting a woman in our house.

"There you go again. I'm telling you, it's not the same. You can't talk about it in the same way, using the same terminology. Women are more equalized in terms of size and power; it's not the same thing when they fight."

"But they weren't fighting equally. Gwen was battering Amy."

"I didn't see it, I can't say," Miriam said flatly.

"Don't you believe me?"

"I believe that you've had something against Gwen ever since I moved into this house. You've been determined to find her guilty, and now you have. I just wonder why you've needed to make Amy into the victim and why you've identified with her so much."

I was encouraged that Amy didn't move out, that she stayed. For a week or two she became a kind of obsession with me. If I could only make her see what had happened to her, if I could only understand it myself. I went to the library and the bookstore and got books on wife battering, read them and gave them to Amy. She read them too and gradually began to talk about what had gone on between

her and Gwen. It upset me to find she still thought she was wrong
to have accused Gwen about the film; somewhere inside she thought
she'd deserved to be punished. She didn't deny that Gwen had hit
her, but she didn't seem to think it was that important.

"Hitting's the least of it," Amy said, at one of our by now daily
breakfast discussions at the cafe down the street. "My dad used to
beat me all the time. You just withdraw, you don't feel it. It's the
other stuff. You know, sometimes it's seemed amazing to me that
I could hold down a job at all, be helpful to people, do some good
in the world, when I felt so bad about myself all the time. This last
year has been particularly awful. I've just had no self-confidence at
all. It used to drive Gwen crazy. She thought I'd had everything in
life—grew up in a nice home, went to a good college, lived in Paris
for six months."

I accepted one of Amy's cigarettes, seeing her tall and thin with
her blond brush of hair, smoking Gauloises in a Parisian cafe.

"How did you meet her?"

"A women's self-defense class. She was my partner." Amy smiled,
aware of the irony. "She wasn't very graceful, but she put her all
in it. I thought she was so cute and energetic. I don't know, she
seemed so much braver than I was. She was calling herself a dyke,
was ready to take on the world. She's always been so verbal. I'm not
good at expressing myself."

"And that was ten years ago?"

"Yes. We became lovers. I think our first years were happy, more
or less. I learned a lot from her. Everybody liked her—suddenly, from
being a loner, I had a social circle. We were in the lesbian community. I wasn't an outsider anymore."

"But then you got involved with someone else."

"Yeah." Amy stubbed out her cigarette. "I don't know how it
happened; she was just a friend and then one day we slept together.
It was frightening to feel that strongly. I always thought I'd be with
Gwen, and then Marcia came along. I wanted to give up everything
for her. She made me happy."

"And she felt the same?"

Amy lit up again. "For a while. We kept it a secret, met each other secretly. You see, she had a lover too. And then her lover found out, and she told Gwen. It was a big mess."

"Why didn't you and Marcia go off together?"

Amy shook her head. "She didn't want to, couldn't in the end. She wanted to stay with her lover. And so I stayed with Gwen. She's never forgiven me."

"How long ago did it happen?"

"Oh god, it's ages—seven years ago, I guess."

Betty said she'd run into Gwen at a movie and that Gwen had told her side of the story. Betty emphasized "*her* side" with an accusing look.

"If you'd told me the whole story, Diane, about the film and everything, and about Amy's depression, I think I would have understood a little better."

I felt as if I were going crazy. "You mean it's all right to go around punching your lover and threatening to kill her because she didn't notice a roll of film you left?"

"I didn't see it."

"You're accusing me of lying then?"

"I only think you interpreted it the way you wanted to. You know how Gwen punches her fist into her palm. I'm sure that's all she did."

"But Amy said...."

"Amy is into this victim thing that I just can't identify with."

Karen said, "I think it's pretty presumptuous, your whole idea of intervening, Diane. I mean, are we moral policewomen or what? We need to be supportive of each other's weaknesses, not condemning. We get enough of that from the outside world."

I began to cry myself to sleep at night, lying beside Miriam, then, increasingly, alone in my room, grieving a sisterhood that was as illusory as anything else, doubting myself and all that I'd seen. I was irritable when I talked with Amy. What was wrong with her that she'd let this terrible thing happen to her? Why did any of us put up with less than what we could have?

Miriam suddenly accused me of using this situation to move in on Amy. She said I'd had my eye on her from the beginning. I said, so what if I had, it was none of her business. But I said that only to hurt her.

I dreamed that Amy and I were swimming in a warm sea that had begun to go cold, like bathwater, and that Amy couldn't talk, she could only sign and that I couldn't understand her. I dreamed I asked her again and again Why, Why, and she just stared and made gestures I couldn't comprehend, palms out, pleading. I dreamed she was drowning me, hanging on to my shoulders, pushing me down into the water that was so cold at the bottom. I dreamed of Miriam's body like an island, dreamed her long black ropes of hair were lifelines I could cling to, that they were a ladder I could climb.

Miriam came to me and said she'd overheard Betty telling Karen that Amy and I were having a relationship and she wanted to know if it was true. She said she was moving out; she said the whole thing had made her sick, she didn't know why things had to be so ugly and sad and hurtful. She said she'd given Betty and Karen her notice—but would I consider giving up Amy?

I said I'd never been involved with Amy, I never would be.

We cried. We held each other for a long time and we didn't want to fight anymore. We said we wouldn't fight anymore. We started sleeping together again.

One afternoon when I came home there was a little pile of books about battering on my desk and a note:

"Dear Diane,

Thanks for all your help. I've been seeing Gwen again—I was embarrassed to tell you—and we've worked things out. She didn't feel good about moving back into the house, so we've found an apartment together. I think it will be okay, we just needed a cooling off period. Hope to run into you sometime.

Love, Amy."

She didn't leave an address or a phone number.
And gradually life settled back to normal.

Postscript

It's six months later and winter now. Miriam and I are still together, still fighting. We both have jobs we like, that's not the problem; we both have our own rooms, that's not the problem, either. It's something deeper, something to do with power and dependency, something to do with respect, something that I don't understand. We know how to hurt each other now, and seem to want to.

We still live in the same house with Betty and Karen and a new woman that Miriam has slept with once. None of us ever sees Amy or Gwen anymore. I've heard they're planning to move to California. Occasionally someone will tell a joke or a story, maybe about a man they work with or a woman they dislike, and they'll be mocking or indignant or just plain mean, and again I'll see Gwen's ringed fingers and have the impression of someone with her hands full of silver and precious stones, flinging them away in gestures of contempt, as if they weren't valuable at all, as if it hurt to try to hold them.

When that happens I sometimes leave the room. I've taken up smoking again, and it's as good an excuse as any.

Contributors' Notes

GLORIA ANZALDÚA is a Chicana lesbian feminist poet and fiction writer from South Texas. She is the co-editor of *This Bridge Called My Back: Writings By Radical Women of Color* (Kitchen Table: Women of Color Press), which won the Before Columbus American Book Award. She is the author of *Borderlands/La Frontera: The New Mestiza* (Spinsters/Aunt Lute), selected by *Library Journal* as one of the best books of 1987. She is currently working on an anthology of creative, critical and theoretical writings by women of color, titled *Making Face, Making Soul: Constructing the Colored Self*, to be published by Spinsters/Aunt Lute in 1990.

ANTOINETTE (TONY) AZOLAKOV is a fourth-generation Texan, born in 1944, who lives and writes in Austin. "What's special about me?" she asks. "I'm just an ordinary dyke. What could be more special than that?" Azolakov's novels, *Cass and the Stone Butch* and *Skiptrace* are both available from Banned Books.

BECKY BIRTHA is a black lesbian-feminist author whose work has appeared in several anthologies, including The Pushcart Prize XIII (1988-1989). She is the author of two collections of her own work, *For Nights Like This One: Stories of Loving Women* (Frog In The Well) and *Lovers' Choice* (Seal Press). A recipient of a 1988 grant from the National Endowment for the Arts, she is deeply indebted to both the women's community and the feminist publishing network for their support of her work.

SANDY BOUCHER is the author of four books, the most recent being *Turning the Wheel: American Women Creating the New Buddhism*. In good crone fashion she has recently started a new life by becoming a masters student at the Graduate Theological Union in Berkeley, studying Buddhist Studies, Comparative Religion and Women's Spirituality. She lives with her lover and cat in Oakland, California.

MAUREEN BRADY is the author of the novels *Give Me Your Good Ear* (Spinsters/Aunt Lute), *Folly* (Crossing Press) and the short story collection *The Question She Put To Herself* (Crossing Press). She is currently working to complete her third novel. She teaches writing workshops and has been the recipient of numerous writing grants.

KIM CHERNIN is the author of books on mothers and daughters, women's spirituality, eating disorders, and ethnic identity. Her published works include *In My*

Mother's House: A Daughter's Story, The Obsession: Reflections on the Tyranny of Slenderness, Reinventing Eve, and *The Flamebearers.* She lives in Berkeley, California.

TEE A. CORINNE was born in 1943. She is a writer and artist whose published work includes *Dreams of the Woman Who Loved Sex* (Banned Books), *Yantras of Womanlove* (Naiad Press), the *Cunt Coloring Book* (Last Gap) and the *Sinister Wisdom* poster. She is the Art Books columnist for *Feminist Bookstore News* and documents lesbian writers in a photo series called "In Search of a Lavender Muse." For fun she swims and takes long walks in the country with her sweetie and her dog.

JUDY FREESPIRIT has published short stories and poetry in lesbian and feminist journals including *Common Lives/Lesbian Lives, Lesbian Contradiction* and *Sinister Wisdom.* She was a contributor to *The Tribe of Dina: A Jewish Women's Anthology* (edited by Melanie Kaye/Kantrowitz and Irena Klepfisz). *Daddy's Girl: An Incest Survivor's Story* was published in 1982 and is now part of a longer work, a collection of ten short stories about incest and its affect on different generations of the same family.

SALLY MILLER GEARHART lives on a mountain of contradictions in Northern California. She is the author of *The Wanderground: Stories of the Hill Women* and *A Feminist Tarot* (with Susan Rennie), both published by Alyson Publications. She has appeared in the documentary films "Word Is Out" and "The Times Of Harvey Milk" and teaches speech at San Francisco State University. She is active in the movements for lesbian/gay rights and animal rights; she works in solidarity with Nicaragua.

ELSA GIDLOW (1898-1986) was a poet-philosopher and lesbian-feminist pioneer. In 1923 she published *On A Grey Thread,* the first North American book to celebrate lesbian love. Her last book, *ELSA: I Come With My Songs* (Booklegger Publishing), is the first full-life, explicitly lesbian autobiography yet published.

JEWELLE L. GOMEZ is a poet, short story writer and reviewer whose work has appeared in numerous journals and anthologies including *Home Girls: A Black Feminist Anthology* (edited by Barbara Smith). She has published a book of poetry called *Flamingoes and Bears* and is currently working on a novel.

WANDA HONN is a pseudonym for Wendy Borgstrom who works in New York City. Wendy got the inspiration to write her erotic novel, *Rapture,* during a Gay Pride march, as a result of a conversation among friends who were bemoaning the lack of explicit lesbian erotic literature. Her novel is self-published and distributed to bookstores through The Inland Book Company.

MELANIE KAYE/KANTROWITZ is the author of a collection of short stories, *Some Pieces of Jewish Left,* and *We Speak In Code: Poems and Other Writings.* She is the co-editor of *The Tribe of Dina: A Jewish Women's Anthology* (Sinister Wisdom Books) and, from 1983-1987 she was the editor and publisher of *Sinister Wisdom,* a lesbian/feminist literary and political journal.

LEE LYNCH began to write lesbian literature for *The Ladder* in the late sixties. Since then she's written *Toothpick House, Old Dyke Tales, The Swashbuckler, Home In Your Hands,* and *Dusty's Queen of Hearts Diner* (all published by Naiad Press). Her columns appear in gay and lesbian publications nationally and have been published by Naiad Press as *The Amazon Trail.* She earns her living in the social services and lives in the rural west with four cats and her sweetie.

HARRIET MALINOWITZ has published fiction, articles and reviews in a number of feminist journals and anthologies including *Nice Jewish Girls: A Lesbian Anthology* (edited by Evelyn Torton Beck) and *Love, Struggle and Change: Stories by Women* (edited by Irene Zahava). She is currently writing lesbian stand-up comedy and teaching English in a New York labor college.

VALERIE MINER is the author of *All Good Women, Winter's Edge, Movement, Murder In The English Department* (all published by Crossing Press) and *Blood Sisters.* She is the co-author of *Competition: A Feminist Taboo, Her Own Woman, Tales I Tell My Mother* and *More Tales I Tell My Mother.* She has won numerous writing grants and awards and, for the past eleven years, has taught at U.C. Berkeley.

MERRIL MUSHROOM describes herself as a "tall, myopic, middle-aged, hot Jewish mama who loves to write about lesbians." Her work has frequently appeared in *Common Lives/Lesbian Lives.* She was a contributor to *We Are Everywhere: Writings By And About Lesbian Parents* (edited by Harriet Alpert) and *The Coming Out Stories* (edited by Julia Penelope and Susan J. Wolfe, reissued in 1989 by Crossing Press). She has written a fantasy novel called *Daughters of Khaton* (Lace Publications).

JOAN NESTLE is co-founder of the Lesbian Herstory Archives, author of *A Restricted Country* (Firebrand Books) and a teacher of writing in the SEEK Program, Queens College, CUNY, N.Y. The Lesbian Herstory Archives, a fifteen year old institution, has just launched a building fund so that this immense collection of lesbiana, the largest in the world, can have a permanent home. For more information write: Lesbian Herstory Archives, P.O. Box 1258, New York City, New York 10116.

LESLÉA NEWMAN is the author of a short story collection, *A Letter To Harvey Milk,* a novel, *Good Enough To Eat* (both published by Firebrand Books) and a collection of poetry, *Love Me Like You Mean It* (HerBooks). She teaches women's writing workshops called WRITE FROM THE HEART, workshops for women concerned about body image and eating called WHAT ARE YOU EATING/WHAT'S EATING YOU, and writing workshops for Jewish women, called GENERATING MEMORIES: REMEMBERING GENERATIONS.

CAROL ORLOCK is the author of the novel *The Goddess Letters*, which received the Pacific Northwest Bookseller's Award and the Washington State Governor's Award. Her work has also appeared in numerous national magazines and literary journals. She is a resident of Seattle where she teaches at the University of Washington and Shoreline Community College.

SHELLY RAFFERTY was born in 1956. She's a writer, poet, linguist and parent—a formerly battered woman, native New Yorker and young person's advocate. She contributes frequently to the gay press and works with the Rochester Lesbian Writers Group.

LOUISE RAFKIN is a fiction writer and journalist, as well as the editor of *Different Daughters: A Book by Mothers of Lesbians* and *Unholy Alliances: New Women's Fiction* (both published by Cleis Press). She lives with and loves Sparky and Dot (baby desert tortoises) who remind her constantly that the earth is a very old place.

JANE RULE was born in 1931 in New Jersey, moved to Canada in 1956, and now lives on Galiano Island, B.C. Her published work includes *Desert of the Heart, This Is Not For You, Against The Season, The Young In One Another's Arms, Outlander, Contract with the World, Inland Passage, A Hot-Eyed Moderate, Memory Board* (all published by Naiad Press), *Lesbian Images* (Crossing Press) and *Theme for Diverse Instruments*.

CANYON SAM has been involved in art and politics in the lesbian-feminist and Asian American communities in her hometown, San Francisco, since 1974. Following a year in Central Asia in 1987 she has been committed to working on behalf of the nation of Tibet and the Tibetan people. Her work has appeared in many journals and anthologies, including *Unholy Alliances* (edited by Louise Rafkin) and *New Lesbian Writing* (edited by Margaret Cruikshank).

ANN ALLEN SHOCKLEY is a novelist, short story writer, essayist and academic librarian. Her published work includes *Loving Her, Say Jesus and Come to Me* and *The Black and White of It* (all published by Naiad Press). She lives in Nashville, Tennessee with her dog, Bianca.

JUDITH STEIN has published poetry and short stories in *Sinister Wisdom, Common Lives/Lesbian Lives* and *Bad Attitude*. She was a contributor to *Hear The Silence: Stories of Myth, Magic and Renewal* (edited by Irene Zahava) and was a consultant for the latest edition of *Our Bodies, Ourselves*. She describes herself as a "fat working-class Jewish dyke who writes to integrate all of her identities."

Her writings about Jewish rituals are available through Bobbeh Meisehs Press.

KITTY TSUI is a writer, an actor, a competitive body builder and the author of *The Words of a Woman Who Breathes Fire* (Spinsters/Aunt Lute). Her work, both poetry and prose, has been widely anthologized, most recently in *Gay and Lesbian Poetry In Our Time* (edited by Carl Morse and Joan Larkin). She came out as a lesbian when she was twenty-one and is still one at thirty-six. "It wasn't a phase as my mother told me."

JESS WELLS is the author of two collections of short stories, *The Dress/The Sharda Stories* and *Two Willow Chairs* (both published by Library B Books). She is currently working on her first novel. She lives in San Francisco.

BARBARA WILSON is co-publisher of The Seal Press, which she helped found in 1976. Her published work includes *Cows and Horses* (Eighth Mountain Press), *Ambitious Women, Murder In The Collective, Sisters Of The Road,* and *Miss Venezuala* (all published by Seal Press). When she's not traveling, she lives in Seattle.

IRENE ZAHAVA (editor) has been the owner of a feminist bookstore in upstate New York since 1981. She is the editor of *Hear The Silence: Stories of Myth, Magic and Renewal; Love, Struggle and Change: Stories by Women; The WomanSleuth Anthology: Contemporary Mystery Stories by Women,* and *Through Other Eyes: Animal Stories by Women* (all published by Crossing Press).